*Books by* WILL BRYANT

Great American Guns and Frontier Fighters
Kit Carson and the Mountain Men (*juvenile*)
The Big Lonesome
Escape from Sonora

# Escape from Sonora

# Escape from Sonora

## BY WILL BRYANT

RANDOM HOUSE / NEW YORK

Library of Congress Cataloging in Publication Data

Bryant, Will.
Escape from Sonora.

I. Title.
PZ4.B9153Es [PS3552.R898] 813'.5'4 76-37031
ISBN 0-394-46995-X

*Wood engravings by the author*

For Dad
and Jack

PART ONE

# The Rambling Men March 1916

# (1)

John Perrell awoke slowly at daybreak under the railroad trestle near Gaviota, on the coast of California, hearing the cry of
gulls and the thunder of ocean surf.

He blinked his eyes and saw the gray water and puffs of
low cloud scudding past, brushing the white-frothed tops of
the waves. A flight of pelicans flew past in a long line, barely
off the water, winging and gliding. Then Perrell saw a man
walking down the beach toward him, perhaps a quarter of a
mile away. A shred of mist made it appear that the man was
somehow suspended over the sand, but then the mist tore free
and flew on past, and the man strode solidly on the sand again.

Perrell yawned and stood up stiffly, his blanket and tarp
draped around his shoulders like a shawl. He had skidded
down the bank under the railroad trestle in the dark and gone
to sleep half sitting up against a shelf of rock above the stream
bed. The seat of his pants was wet, but he had kept his blanket
dry and now the rain was gone.

He cast a glance at the sky. Up above the torn shreds of low
cloud it was clear, with a pale wash of rose light spraying into
it from where the sun was working up beyond the foot of the
mountains.

The rock ledge fanned out into the sand. Glimpsing some
dry sticks crammed in under an overhang, he gathered a few
and made a fire against the rock. Then he opened his canvas

war bag and pulled out a small chipped granite coffeepot and a cloth sack of coffee. There was water in the stream bed from last night's rain. He dipped some up in the pot, then spilled a little coffee into it and put it on some rocks at the edge of the fire. He dug into the bag again and found a can of beef and a can of corn. He shrugged, opened the can of corn with his jackknife and set it next to the fire. Then he sat back on his heels with his hands to the fire and watched the man on the beach.

A big man, heavy with bone. Gray blanket rolled into a bindle and slung from one shoulder. Closer now. Long in the leg, hat and gray suit crumpled ruins after the rain.

The man picked up a stone and threw it out over the water and watched it skip. At that moment the sun burst over the distant foot of mountain, and the fire of its light streamed along the beach, licking red at rocks and waves and sand. The man turned slowly to face it. He pulled his hat off and let his head rock back. A breaking wave thundered white on the sand and foamed around the man's ankles. And still he stood as the water hissed back to the sea.

The man put his hat back on and began to walk again, with strong slow steps, his head still rocked back to take the sun. He dug into a baggy coat pocket, and both hands went up to his face. A breaker crumped on the sand, but a moment later Perrell heard the windy wail of a mouth organ.

The coffee boiled and Perrell pulled it away from the fire. The man came to the bank of the stream, rip-rapped with slabs of stone to hold back the sands of the beach. He skipped down and jumped across to Perrell's side, then he began to play again. *Old Joe Clark, the preacher's son* . . . When he saw Perrell he stopped, forty feet away, close enough now for Perrell to see his face.

Gaunt and scarred and craggy, beaked nose broken and set adrift between high cheekbones, black eyes under jutting brows—a face ruined long ago, a face with hard luck written all over it.

Perrell waved a hand at the fire. "Coffee and a can of corn," he said. He was thinking: There stands the dismalest-looking happy man I have ever seen.

Later, when a freight train stopped at the water tank, they both climbed up the bank under the trestle, and when the freight began to roll they caught it. Perrell saw a half-open boxcar door, jumped for it and made it. But the big drifter swung onto grab irons at the front end of the car and the last Perrell saw of him, he was climbing up on top.

Perrell saw blue sky and rolling surf through the open door of the freight car and remembered how he had ridden in rain and fog all the way from Oakland to Pismo Beach. It had taken him two days and many freights to go that far because the railroad bulls and brakemen swept the trains clean of rambling men all along the line. San Jose, Salinas, King City, San Luis Obispo—to stay clear of the bulls, Perrell had walked through them all, then waited in the rain for the next south-running freight.

He suddenly thought of the foolishness which had put him under that railroad trestle. At Gaviota, which is just below Point Arguello, the train had stopped at a water tank. It was after midnight. Rain was gusting in over a thundering surf. A brakeman left the caboose with a lantern in his hand and walked along the train. All Perrell could see through the narrow opening of the door was a moving spray of light from the bobbing lantern, then the door rumbled back and the hot bright glare of the lantern was right in the car with him. He saw the brakeman's face below it, grinning at him.

"She's a leetle damp out tonight, boys," the brakeman said. There was one other man riding in the car with Perrell. "A body would jess purely hate to be afoot now, wouldn't he?"

The other man hesitated, waiting to see what Perrell would do. He was thin as a slat, his hollow cheeks pink and feverish. Perrell did not move.

"Yes, it's terrible raw," the brakeman prompted, picking at his red-veined nose.

The thin man reached into his pocket and pulled out a dirty dollar bill. "I won't even have coffee money," he said.

"You know it's worth my job to let trespassers ride," the brakeman said. The thin man handed the brakeman the dollar bill and the brakeman took it without appearing to notice that it had come into his hand. He stared at Perrell, who had sixty-five dollars in a money belt and who knew that what he was about to do was foolish, but he could not help himself.

"Not me," he said.

The brakeman frowned at him, then shrugged. "Oh, hell," he said, "I ain't unreasonable, if a feller is broke. Go ahead and ride."

"I'm not broke," Perrell said, "but I'll be damned if I'll pay." He knew he was being foolish because he had paid shakedown money to brakemen before, not once but many times, but something about the rain and the sound of the sea and the quivering, feverish bindle stiff in the car with him would not let him do it this time.

# (2)

At Ventura, the shining steel bears away from the ocean and follows the Santa Clara River inland through the tawny hills toward Santa Paula, Saugus and San Fernando Pass, and on into Los Angeles.

Perrell was stretched out next to the open door of the car on a comfortable couch made of hay bales. He had not seen a railroad bull or a brakeman since the rain stopped. That was always the way, he thought. The tawny hills rolled away behind the train. After a while the hills slid off along the horizon, and the train was rolling out into a broad valley with plowed fields stretching away into the distance. Then the chuffing of the engine slowed and the train rolled to a stop. Perrell merely glanced out the doorway. Farm town. Fair-sized town. He did not care if a yard dick came along or not. On a day like this, he thought, I would as soon walk to L.A.

The train jerked. Couplings clashed. Maybe they will

switch me onto a siding. Like that time in Sleepy Eye, Minnesota. He grinned to himself. A long time ago, that was. Just after McKinley was shot, so it was 1901, December, six days on a siding in a blizzard. Thirty below and the snow halfway up the side of the car.

The train jerked again, then rolled, trucks clicking over the rail joints, the town thinning out fast, then gone, the engine bearing away in a long curve, so that Perrell could keep the whole forward end of the train in sight without moving from his couch on the hay bales. The engine was four-by-six-by-oh, sixty feet six inches long—Perrell could spout engine specs with any steam man. She was a type built in Schenectady in the nineties, had two single expansion cylinders, boiler steam pressure one hundred and eighty pounds, weight on her drivers about seventy-five tons, and about thirty-five thousand pounds' tractive power. She could haul sixty-five thirty-ton freight cars at ten miles an hour over a mountain grade of one hundred and sixteen feet to the mile . . .

Suddenly a figure broke out of a clump of willows up ahead on the bank of the irrigation ditch that bordered the right of way. He was running hard because the train was already going too fast for him. Powdery ochre dust puffed out from under his shoes. His blanket was rolled up and held by a piece of rope over one shoulder, but there was something—it looked like a paper bag—in his left hand and he must suddenly have known that he was going to need both hands to make his grab.

It was a yellow car, sooty, and it was pulling away fast. He reached out for the rearmost set of grab irons, caught an iron with his right hand and hung on for five or six great, swooping bounds as the train pulled him along. But the paper bag was in his left hand—there was nothing to do but let go. He did. His body was twisted, pulled along by that one arm, and when he let go, his legs flailed, he stumbled and was lost to sight within the curve of the train. Thinking he had gone down between the cars, Perrell rolled off the hay bale and stuck his head through the doorway of the car, slitting his eyes against the coal smoke that whipped back into his face.

No, he was still on his feet, but he had slowed to a trot. He looked back to see how much of the train was left and saw the open door of Perrell's car bearing down on him. He started to run again, his blanket roll slapping and bouncing against his hip. Perrell saw that he was just a kid. Big, though. The doorway was right at the kid's shoulder. He still had the paper bag in his left hand, cradled there like a football. Whatever was in that bag, Perrell thought, could kill the kid. Perrell held up both hands, like a catcher. The kid saw him and threw the paper bag. Perrell caught it and at the same moment the kid made his jump, throwing his head and shoulders over the slotted iron of the threshold onto the splintery boards.

He hung there, clutching with elbows and fingers, his lean rump and long legs streaming back in the wind, the edge of the doorway jammed hard against his ribs. He kicked hard, but that doorway cutting into him held him fast. He looked up at Perrell, his mouth open and gasping, his face white—the doorway and the iron threshold had pounded the wind out of him.

Perrell leaned back against the hay bale and grinned at the kid. Then he took a tobacco sack and a book of papers from his shirt pocket. He thumbed out a brown paper, tugged the drawstring open with his teeth and sprinkled the little trough of paper full of tobacco grains, shielding it from the wind with his knees.

The kid's mouth was still open. The bill of his wool cap was unsnapped and pulled around over one ear, and hanks of sun-bleached hair shagged into his eyes. There was a big artery under the kid's jaw that stood out like a piece of rope.

Perrell rolled the smoke with the blunt thumb and fingers of his left hand. He licked the paper, slicked it down and twisted the end and put it between his lips, then felt along the band of his black hat for a wooden match tucked in there. The kid kicked again. He was getting his wind back and his face had turned red. Perrell struck the match with a thumbnail and lit his smoke. He thought the kid had slid back a little. He leaned forward and tossed the match out the doorway. He had to shout to make himself heard.

"Kid, I like your style. By God, I do." He winked and leaned back.

The kid kicked again, but he was starting to slide. His clawed fingers skidded on the planks of the floor. His eyes went wide—they were the color of cornflowers. Perrell blew out smoke and smiled warmly at the kid.

*"Gawdamighty, mister—help me!"* the kid gagged.

Perrell put his left hand on the frame of the doorway, reached over the kid's head, grabbed him by the seat of his britches and yanked him into the car. The kid rolled over once and sat up. He looked at Perrell and started to say something, but clamped his jaw down hard instead.

He has been taught respect for his elders, Perrell thought. And he is mad, but he doesn't know whether he is mad at me or mad at himself. He tossed the paper bag back to the kid.

"Why didn't you just tuck that thing inside your shirt?"

"There's a chicken in it. I didn't want to mash it."

The kid opened the paper bag and pulled out a fried chicken wrapped in butcher paper. He pulled back a corner of the paper and looked at it. He started to put it away, then plucked off a shred of golden skin and tasted it. He sighed. "I aimed to save it for supper." He broke off a leg and bit into the plump thigh. Then, with his mouth full, he held out the chicken to Perrell.

"Near forgot my manners," he mumbled.

Perrell smiled and nodded. He broke off the other leg and began to eat. "You would do better to pick a place closer to town to catch her. Time you tried it, she was going like sixty."

The kid grunted. "Wasn't time. I was workin on that farm yonder, where you see that silo. I milked thirty-three cows this mornin—at home I done forty. Gonnies, this chicken is good." He sucked the leg bone clean and tossed it through the doorway. He started to wrap up the chicken again, thought better of it and broke off a wing. He offered the chicken again. Perrell shook his head. The kid's wrist, where it stuck out of the cuff of his roll-collar button-front sweater, was as thick as a wagon tongue and his forearm swelled out behind it so that the knitted wool was stretched snug. His fingers were meaty with muscle. From milking all those cows, Perrell thought.

"I been there since a week ago Tuesday," the kid said, licking one of those meaty fingers. "The lady's husband is stoved up bad. I done the chores and milkin. I wanted to make a little stake, but she couldn't pay me but fifty cents a day. I could've went somewheres else and got a dollar a day, but she —I don't know . . ." The wing bone sailed out through the doorway. With a big square thumbnail, the kid sliced through the skin along the breastbone, then he slipped his thumb in alongside the bone and laid back the shell of white meat that covered the rib cage. He stripped off the meat and bit off a piece.

Beyond that doorway, the fields were flat as a pool table, stretching away for miles toward the distant hills, the furrows cut straight as rifle shots. Gray-green and leafy, the rows of the crop clicked past, hypnotic—like the spokes of a wheel, he thought, rotating around that hub out there where the rows converged at the base of the tawny hills, the hub slipping gently along the hill, though here, close up to the train, the rows rushed, snapping past far too fast to count. Then he imagined that the fields out there became an enormous turntable, its geared rim engaged to a worm gear spinning furiously beneath the plank floor of the car, the whole rig hanging out there in space and spinning against the blue sky, and with stunning clarity there flashed into his mind a meaning, whole and complete and geometrically perfect. With his eye fixed on that distant hub his mind glimpsed the perfection of it and he felt an absurd surge of joy.

In that instant there appeared on the canal bank the figures of a man and a dog, the man, black-haired and mustached with collarless shirt, one rubber-booted foot resting on the blade of a shovel, his hands resting on the handle beneath his chin, the black-and-white dog sitting tongue out and panting. Next to the man a floodgate in the canal was cranked up with brown water pouring through the chute into the field beyond and Perrell saw straight into the man's eyes. Then the man and the dog were whipped away, and the turntable was only a field again and the train was moving on—the marvelous, terrible logic Perrell had glimpsed for an instant was gone. He strained to grasp it again, but it was too late. He frowned. Up ahead, the steam whistle wailed again.

"She was mighty good to take me in, too," the kid said. "I looked turrible, but I said to her, I ain't a bum but I been hurt and if you'll let me stay a spell I'll work it out. And she said bless you boy, there is a sight of milkin to get done here."

Perrell could see the yellowish stain under the kid's eyes, a scabbed eyebrow and thickened lip, nose lumpy and out of line. "What happened to you?"

Having demolished the entire half of the chicken, the kid reluctantly rolled it up in the paper and stuffed the bundle back in the sack. He licked his fingers and wiped them on his pants.

"Well, see, there was a smoker at the Elks' Hall back there . . ." His chin jerked, back toward the town. "My manager, Cully—Chilkoot Cully he calls hisself on account of he claims he was up in Alaska in the gold rush—he wrote me a postcard in Salinas. I was workin in the slaughterhouse there. He said he matched me with a fighter name of Dempsey. I drawed my time at the slaughterhouse and bought a train ticket. Well, Cully, he come to the depot to meet me and we went straight to the Elks'. I never had no supper or nothin. I give Cully the six dollars I had left over from the slaughterhouse to hold for me.

"It turns out there is no Dempsey on the card. Cully has matched me with a hometown feller name of Marvin Hedgepeth, who is about two-ten. I am one eighty-nine and a half. Cully says the purse is only twenty dollars, but it will be good experience for me on account of I have only had six fights. Cully was only my manager from the fifth one—he seen me fight in Grants Pass. Before that I never had no manager.

"Anyways, this Marvin could as well have cut hisself a club. He hit me with everything else. I b'lieve there was something in his gloves. And someone had put some mustard plaster in my jock—pretty soon she heats up and I want to tell you I was on fire. Ever time I reach down, Marvin, he would hit me. And if I would go to clinch, he would butt me in the mouth—had a mean skull on him, Marvin did."

The kid was moving his shoulders and big meaty hands and grunting. "Then after he butts me in the mouth, he goes for the family jewels. I mean, a man don't wear his belt around his *knees*. And the referee, he don't see nothin—he is stompin on my foot, and he don't weight but about two sixty-five. By the third round, I'm a cripple. Well, now, Marvin, his gloves was tied with the laces wrapped around and big knots worked into the laces, you know?"

Perrell nodded. "Go on."

"First he butts me, then he rakes my eyes with them knots. The referee is standin on my foot, my crotch is on fire, I can't see nothing, and Marvin, he hits me. Only time I ever been down. So there I am with my head almost in the corner. I get one eye open just a teeny bit and there sets Cully, close enough to touch. Only Cully is lookin up at Marvin, and so help me, he is grinnin like a dog crappin a trace chain. I seen him *wink* at Marvin!"

Perrell pulled a bandanna from his pocket and snorted and honked into it, then mopped at his eyes. The kid's face was dismal with pain and outrage.

"So Cully, he has set me up for this hometown crowd. I am just near about burned up. Not just mad, but my crotch is still on fire, and that will pull a man off the floor. What I done is, I stuck my left into this Marvin's face and just held her there, then stepped in thisaway, you see, with a right uppercut, letting him see it, too, and he goes to block it and get that left out his face at the same time—but you see I stepped in *real* close and while he is blockin my glove, my elbow takes him directly in the solus plexer."

The kid rolled to a kneeling position and demonstrated—his elbow swung through like a wrecking ball, Perrell thought.

"Queensberry rules don't allow that," he said earnestly, "but by golly, they had near kilt me. It was ever man for his-self . . . Well, old Marvin, he was stiff as a fence post. The referee, he stretched out the count all he could, but it didn't matter none, he could have counted to a hundred. Without he tries it, a man don't know what a club his elbow can be. My Uncle Perce showed me that . . ."

"Good thing, too," Perrell said. "I can see from what's left on your face, Marvin must have hurt you pretty bad."

"No, Marvin near ruptured me, but he never marked my face none. You see, I didn't want to spring nothin on Cully until I got my share of the purse. He said go shower, kid, I'll collect our winnins and we'll go get some supper at the Chinaman's. Well, when I come out, he was gone. I went to the office and asked for him. Feller said he was just in, picked up his fifty and left. *Fifty!* I says—he told me twenty. They all laughed and the one feller says, well, rube, your manager knows rich livin is bad for fighters. I said rich livin?—I ain't even had supper.

"Well, I went on outside. I got as far as the alley. There was four fellers standin there waitin for me. Big fellers, all looked like Marvin—his brothers, I reckon. One says, well, rube, we want our sixty dollars. I says you won't get it from me, I ain't even got the price of a bait of beans and Cully, he has flew the coop. I said you are some bunch of farmers, to pay out cash money before the job is done. And right then something hit me across the back of the neck. I think it was a two-by-four . . ."

The kid shook his head and looked down at his big, meaty hands. "I couldn't hardly get my hands up . . . and right then when they had finished workin me over—I was stretched out flat on my back in the alley—I heard the train whistle blow and I thought, well, there goes Cully . . ."

He spread his hands slowly and grinned at Perrell. One of his front teeth was broken. "Sometimes Cully would talk about Tucson—said how the climate there done his sinus a world of good . . ."

# (3)

Perrell saw the big drifter again, sitting patient as stone on a stack of railroad ties in the Los Angeles yards. Well, he is pushing on through, then, Perrell thought—bound for somewhere. Perrell hid his bindle under a pile of scrap lumber and torn tar paper and walked out to a chili parlor he remembered near the old mission. It was fiery chili—it could take a man by the throat and shake him until his teeth rattled.

Perrell lingered over a second bowlful. If I go to that boarding house, he was thinking, it will start all over again. They broke us up pretty hard in Seattle. But a man can't back off from the movement because of a knob on his head or a few days in jail. Nobody sold me the IWW. It's my own doing. But dammit, a man likes to *work,* too, put in his time and make his wages. He opened and closed his square, blunt-fingered hands on the counter before him. That was another way the bosses had a grip on a man: if a man had a trade and was good at it, loved it, the way Perrell loved steel, the way it cut and filed and smelled and glistened under the oil rag—why, then he just naturally liked to work at it, so the bastards had him there, too.

He suddenly heard her voice again, Lucy's voice, soft in his ear and saw through the fluttering curtain at her window, down across the Embarcadero, seeing the blue waters of the Bay sparkling beyond, feeling her warmth next to him . . . *no, if you go back to the movement, don't come back to me. It means something to you, but I'm not made for it. And don't ask me to wait, either. Just go out the door and keep going* . . . and saying that, she turned to him and fiercely pulled him close, and he felt her hot tear run along his jaw.

A uniformed policeman came in. Perrell felt the back of his neck grow cold, but he grinned and nodded when the cop looked at him. He had to go back to the yards to get his bindle, but when he found it he couldn't bring himself to go to the boarding house. A freight was just rolling out of the yards. Perrell stood watching it, letting it go. He half turned away and at that moment he saw the kid again. The train was already beginning to work up speed. No yard dicks in sight. The rube will kill himself, he thought.

Perrell broke into a run, slanting from track to track, weaving between standing cars. Along the length of the moving train he could see a single boxcar with an open door. He waved and caught the kid's eye, then he pointed, first to himself, then to the kid, meaning *follow me.* The open-door car was bearing down on him. He ran a few steps with it, put his hands on the sill and jumped, twisting his body so that he landed sitting. A moment later the kid jumped, too. Perrell grabbed a fistful of sweater to anchor him.

"I was afraid you might try for the grab irons on the rear of the car again," Perrell said. "That's a good way to get yourself killed, because if you miss you can fall down between the cars, get it? Always go for the front irons if you can't go for the door."

The kid nodded. Perrell pulled up his legs and moved back out of the doorway and motioned for the kid to do the same. "If a brakie sees your legs hanging out there, he probably wouldn't stop the train but he would remember, and the next time she stops, that would be the end of the line for you. Besides, the doorway of a car is another good place to stay away from. Supposing the train slows down, slows down to a crawl, see? A man gets curious, sticks his head out to see what's going on, and *bang,* she runs up against a switch engine, stops dead. That door keeps going, takes him across the neck like a chicken on a chopping block." Perrell chopped the edge of his hand into the palm of his other hand. "See? That door could pretty near take a man's head off."

The kid nodded again. "A man told me this train was goin to Tucson. Reckon that's so?"

"Well, maybe. No way to tell for sure, but she's headed out that way, so it's a start. This is an old car and it's half empty. It could wind up on a siding someplace, or a rip track for repairs. Might take a couple of days to go a hundred miles. Never can tell. Or the brakeman could throw us off . . ."

The kid looked around the car with sudden interest. The forward end was taken up by stacked wooden crates and steel drums, then sacked grain made a low wall down the middle. He climbed to his feet and walked to the rear end and back, his legs spread and his body swaying to the springy bucking and lurching of the car. Then he reached out and grasped two of the sacks, each by an ear, one-handed, lifted and let them hang down. He turned slowly, holding the two hundred-pound sacks. The big artery thickened on his neck.

"I bet you never seen this done before," he shouted.

Perrell grinned and shook his head. The kid turned back and heaved one sack back into place. Then he put his right hand into the middle of the second sack and lifted it up to his shoulder, balancing its sagging weight.

"What do you reckon the world's record is for pitchin hundred-pound sacks? Well, I don't know neither. They ought to put it in the Olympics." He lifted the sack easily, held it overhead. "The only man I couldn't beat was my Uncle Perce. He done twenty-one foot. Then he got hisself a double hernia and couldn't throw no more." The kid eased the sack back onto his shoulder, then poised himself on his right foot with his left arm outstretched toward the far corner of the car. "But I've growed some since then," he shouted. "I b'lieve I could do twenty-one foot now." That right shoulder sagged down. Perrell saw muscles squirm and bulge in the kid's back and in that thick right thigh. His body started to uncoil—he was throwing . . .

"No, *don't!*" The scream came from that far corner of the car, behind the wall of sacked grain, and it caught the kid uncoiling. The sack thudded back down onto his shoulder, and a lurch of the car kept him from getting his foot back under him. The hundred pounds drove him heavily onto his back on the floor. The sack split and grain cascaded over him in a golden flood. Perrell rolled and came up kneeling.

He saw a youngster, dirty face gone wide-eyed with fear. Behind the youngster was an old man, pale-eyed, staring, silver-stubbled chin quivering. "Crazy son of a bitch!" he shouted, then paused, not satisfied, and in another burst of fury he flung out a clawed finger, pointing it at the kid and crying, "Shithead!"

The kid struggled up, red-faced, grain pouring down his body. "I never meant nothin," he blurted.

"You want to squarsh us?" cried the old man. He was fumbling at the wooden crates for support to pull himself up. "Crazy son of a bitch," he quavered.

The kid looked helplessly at Perrell, whose face was hidden in his bandanna. The old man quit trying to get up, let himself sag back down against the crate, where he glared fiercely at the kid. The old man and the youngster were dressed the same, in faded blue bib-overalls, the seams frayed to cottony tufts. But the old man wore an ancient round-skirted suit coat, while the youngster's skinny shoulders were covered with a limp and tattered denim jacket. The youngster looked to be thirteen or fourteen, Perrell thought, thin and awkward and grubby in the castoff overalls.

The kid, still red-faced with embarrassment, put out a hand in supplication toward the old man, who barked, "Bobby Joe, you git back here—keep away from that crazy son of a bitch!"

"Well, rube, you've got a real knack for making friends," Perrell said. The kid slumped down next to him and dug into the spilled grain with his fingers.

"Rube? Why does everbody have to call me rube?"

Perrell laughed. "All right, what's your name, then?"

"Buell Ashbaugh." The kid's voice was dejected. "Old Cully, he wanted me to call myself Kid Clancy—he said I couldn't amount to nothin in the fight game with a name like Buell Ashbaugh. He said I wouldn't be took serious. But that's it—Buell Ashbaugh, from Jump-Off Joe . . ." He half sang it, laughing. "Jump-Off Joe is the name of a crick that runs past our farm. My daddy always hollered for me that way—*Buell Ashbaugh from Jump-Off Joe*. It's in Oregon, near Grants Pass."

Perrell tried it. *"Buell Ashbaugh from Jump-Off Joe."*

Buell laughed. "That's it. *Jump-Off Joe.*" He looked over his shoulder and saw that the youngster, Bobby Joe, was watching him and laughing, too. Buell's big hands came up filled with grain—he put his head back and rolled his eyes, letting the grain spill down over his face and warbled, *"Buell Ashbaugh from Jump-Off Joe . . ."* Bobby Joe's scrawny shoulders shook. Perrell saw the old man's gnarled hand come up and pull Bobby Joe down.

"Crazy son of a bitches . . ." he heard.

Back in the Los Angeles yards, a railroad officer or yard dick named Folland had stood quietly between two empty boxcars and watched the eastbound freight roll away. When it was gone, he stopped at the telegrapher's office, a small room off the stationmaster's office. He whittled a point on a stub of pencil with his jackknife, licked the lead, then printed a message on a sheet of yellow paper. He waited for the telegrapher to finish tapping out a message, then he handed him the paper.

The telegrapher mumbled the words rapidly, frowning: "P. Costello Tucson Your man eastbound Yuma freight 1:30 pm today Folland L.A." He looked up. "Costello? We don't have no Costello in Tucson."

"Pinkerton man, Tom—you've seen him here now and then. It's railroad business, all right."

The train stopped, somewhere in the night. Cars jolted, squealed, were uncoupled, rolled away, coupled, steel clashing. Then silence wrapped around them.

"Could be Colton," Perrell said. "Big junction there."

But time passed. Each in turn slipped out of the car, to be gone into the darkness for a few minutes. The old man had to go, too. With Buell and Perrell helping him, he slipped down, then he hobbled alone into the darkness. Later they all sat looking out the doorway, drawn closer together in the dark. The old man seemed to have forgotten his anger.

"We set thisaway at Chattanooga once," he whispered. "Two, three days in railroad cars. They was a hell of a big battle after that, up on that damn mountain . . ."

Perrell thought again of the time in Sleepy Eye. "I sat six days on a siding once, and it was thirty below. Sleepy Eye, Minnesota, that was. A lot of fellows froze to death up along there. Then a guy showed me how to ride the mail trains. That is the way to stay warm, and hardly anybody knows to do it . . ."

"You mean passenger trains?" Buell said.

"Sure. You get up there on top of the dining car, see? Find yourself one of those smokestacks from the cookstoves. You sit down with your back to the wind and wrap yourself around that hot smokestack, you will stay warm in thirty below. Just wrap up your ears, is all . . . and say, doesn't it smell good! Bacon frying. Steaks, onions . . ."

"Well, I heard you just couldn't ride a passenger train any way atall," Buell said. "Where would you get on 'em?"

"There's a trick to it, all right. You have to be pretty quick on your feet. You catch the tender, up front, then you have to run back across the mail car and all the passenger cars to the diner. Most bo's will try riding the blinds at the head end there, between the tender and the mail car. That's the first place the yard dick looks. Now, say the dick is rousting bums off the train—no catwalk up on those cars, just the rounded top. Hardly any dick ever thinks to go on clear back to the diner. You get up around a place like Havre, Montana, in a blizzard in January, and that is a good thing to know."

The old man sniffed. "We wouldn't know nothin about it, ennaways—we ain't bums."

Perrell smiled in the dark. "No, I could tell that. Machinery is my game. Any kind of machinery. My dad was a blacksmith."

"No, by God. We ain't bums," the old man snarled. "We're farmers."

"You don't have to be a bum to ride the trains," Perrell said gently. "The way I see it, the railroads ought to belong to the *people.*"

"Any man calls me a bum is a son of a bitch," the old man said.

\*　　　　\*　　　　\*

The train began to roll again during the night. Perrell did not remember sleeping, but suddenly he found himself sitting up, cold and stiff, and it was daybreak. Buell was asleep on the spilled grain, his head pillowed on the broken sack, and Bobby Joe was curled up tight against his back, holding on to his sweater. The old man was sitting up, staring out the doorway, his chin wagging. He started, then looked around, and when he saw Bobby Joe in the gray light, he shook the youngster's shoulder. "Git up!" he barked. "You git away from him, Bobby Joe."

Perrell looked out the doorway. No farmland now. Just desert, open sand and scrub—greasewood, creosote and tumbleweed. Horned larks scattered in swooping flocks. It was a slow train, and a long one. On a curve, Perrell counted the cars. As near as he could tell, it was a full hundred-car train. The old man and Bobby Joe pulled apart from them and kept to themselves. The kid, Buell, finished his chicken. Perrell shook his head when Buell offered him some. If he really got hungry, he still had the can of corned beef. Until then, he thought, it was easier to go without than to eat just a little and stir up his hunger.

Later he looked out and saw the rippling shadow of the boxcar hurtling headlong, for the sun in its flight had skidded across the sky and was falling down into the west, behind them. As he watched the flicking shadow of the car, a blister of shadow lifted along the roof line, then swelled into a stirring hump. Because of the angle of the sun, the shadow was distorted, angular, but it was the shadow of a man, all right—a man trying to get comfortable up on that hard and splintery catwalk, sitting with his back hunched against the wind.

Perrell braced his foot against the door and peered out, taking the wind blast first on his face and then on the back of his neck to look the length of the train. No one else up on top that he could see. The shadow stirred again and Perrell wondered about him, that man up there alone in the March wind.

The train lost speed, then ground slowly to a halt with a steely groan of brakes and grinding clash of couplings. Perrell heard the shuddering hiss of escaping steam from the engine, then sudden quiet gushed over him. The train was stopped at a water tank. He saw the big nozzle swing down over the engine. A trainman swung down and walked along the cinders, bending and peering at the running gear.

The blister of shadow rose again on top of the car. Perrell leaned out the doorway and looked up. "Hullo on top. Come on in out of the wind, friend."

He waited. The shadow stirred a little. The voice, when it came, was raspy and curiously hollow, disembodied.

"I hear ye . . . hit don't bother me none . . ."

Perrell saw the shadow sink back into the roof line, then he remembered. The man on top was the big drifter he had first seen on the beach at Gaviota. But the trainman was there now, right at the car. Instinct told Perrell to duck back into the car, but stubbornness, unbidden, held him there, leaning easily against the doorframe. He felt the kid, Buell, standing just back of him and heard his muffled yawn.

The trainman raised his oil can, saluted with it, his walrus mustache shrouding a sociable smile. "Gents," he said. "She's a leetle warm out in the sun, but a fine day."

Perrell smiled and nodded. Buell said, "Well, how do."

The trainman was an old-timer. His overalls were clean and starched, faded pale blue; baggy and unbuttoned at the sides, they showed blue serge trousers underneath. He wore a clean white shirt with a paper collar and a bow tie of black oilcloth, and on his head was an old and dented brown derby hat.

"You're welcome to ride my train, boys," he said, putting the oil can on the floor next to Perrell's feet. He took off his derby and mopped the white skin of his bald head with a clean blue bandanna, then he held up a finger. "Only, dog it, don't use her for no privy. Why, dog it, you wouldn't *believe* what some of these fellers . . ." He was glaring at them.

"I already been," the kid blurted.

"That's the spirit, boy. Why, did you know, the bowels is the very heart of a man's constitution. You can tell by a man's disposition the shape his bowels is in. Yes sir. Ever day you must turn a trick . . ." The train was starting to move. The trainman stepped back, raised the oil can and sighted it at the kid like a pistol, glaring fiercely. "Yes, ever day—only not on my train, hear?"

A shudder rolled the length of the train as the couplings took up slack, the wheels thunked at the rail joints and the man dropped farther and farther back until, as the caboose overtook him, he put out a hand and foot, caught the ladder and swung aboard.

A lopsided moon skidded into the sky over the flinty mountains that erupted from the long slope of the desert floor. Perrell turned to the other door—in the warmth of the afternoon they had opened it, too, pushed it back—and saw the brush-stippled desert floor there suddenly mound softly into dunes, and the dunes rose rank on rank against the moon-bright sky, cresting like great pale waves in a sea of sand.

And staring at the dunes as they fled past, he suddenly saw a sandy swell rise, flow into the silken line of a vast naked hip and thigh—there it crested over bone, dipped down onto smooth belly, swelled again over the deep rib cage and curved onto soft-mounded breast . . . Perrell stirred and shivered, took a deep breath. He resolutely shook the splendid vision from his mind. The dunes melted back into sand.

A little later Buell suddenly sat up from where he was stretched out on the floor, half dozing. "I smell water." He rolled over and crawled to the door.

Perrell smelled it too, wet and strong and rank. Track rushed away beneath them, a mile or two, then they saw clustered lights and felt a wash of wet air from irrigated fields. The train slowed and the solid clacking of her trucks changed to the hollow rumble of a steel bridge, and darkness yawned beneath them, a broad ribbon of darkness pinpointed with stars. The river. "The Colorado," Perrell said.

"See, I told you I smelled water," Buell said. He reached out and clapped Bobby Joe on the shoulder. "Bobby Joe, we get near water, I want to see you wash the snot off your lip."

Bobby Joe flung off his arm and pulled away, crawled around on the other side of the old man. "Well," Buell said to Perrell, "it wasn't no more'n I'd tell my own brothers."

On the far bank a bluff, bone-pale, frowned down over the river and on it squatted a long, blocky, ground-hugging building. Memory tugged at Perrell. "That's the lockup. The old Yuma pen . . ."

The cars rumbled off the bridge onto solid ground. The boxcar lurched at a switch, then brakes squealed, steely and shrill. The engine gasped a long sigh. Died. Somewhere, dogs barked.

Lanterns swung and bobbed. Voices murmured, then Perrell saw the trainman's white shirt ghosting toward him out of the dark, above the lantern. When he saw Perrell, he grunted and set the lantern on the ground. Light pooled about their feet.

"We must pull her apart here, gents. Make up a new train. And there ain't another train out eastbound tonight." His voice lowered, almost to a whisper. "You want to watch your step here, boys. There is a couple of deppities lookin this train over."

Perrell slipped down out of the car. "Where would a man go if he didn't want to make their acquaintance?"

"Back yonder, down along the tracks and over toward the river—big willer thicket down there. You'll likely find a stewpot a-goin. That's where the boys jungle."

"We ain't doin nothin wrong," Buell said. "Besides, I ain't a bum."

Perrell laughed. "No, you are a citizen of the republic, right?"

"Hee hee," the trainman wheezed through his mustache. "You may take comfort—they will want to know all about that."

Behind them, Perrell thought he heard Bobby Joe and the old man slipping out the other side of the car. Then, up on the roof, shoe leather rasped on metal. A pair of legs descended into the pool of light. Heavy brogans, shapeless gray pants—above, a shape, no more, and a face that was a pale glimmer in the dark moon shadow. The man he saw on the beach at Gaviota. Without a word, the man turned away and began walking back fast, close to the cars.

"Now, he has the right idy," the trainman said. "If you boys will just foller him, I'll pick up my lantern and go to work."

"Much obliged, old-timer," Perrell said.

"Git, now."

Perrell took his bindle and started walking toward the river. The kid scuffed after him, a pace behind. "I ain't sure I want to let them deputies run me off," he said. "I ain't a bum."

"Good for you. I could tell you were a man with spirit."

A switch engine chuffed. Couplings clanked, then crashed, and the engine chuffed hard and fast—snapping her spine, Perrell thought, pulling her apart.

"No foolin—"

"Hush . . ." Perrell stopped and held up a hand. Footsteps crunched on crushed rock, close, very close. There, shoe leather whispered again, on the far side of the car from them. Perrell's fingers plucked at the kid's sweater steering him ahead, but the kid hung back. Perrell pushed and the kid blurted, "Doggone it."

A grunt sounded on the far side of the car, then the footsteps again, running on.

"See?" the kid said. "Only a couple of bums and we are the ones that scared 'em off."

"No, not us—get down in that patch of brush." Perrell's whisper was harsh. The kid balked and Perrell stiff-armed him. "Come on, rube—you're asking for a busted head."

They lurched down the grade embankment, skidding on cinders, and plunged into waist-high brush. Perrell ducked, but the kid stayed on his feet, sputtering.

"But doggone it, I tell you I ain't *done* anything!" He shook off Perrell's hand and turned to climb back up the bank. Perrell heard gravel crunch again up on top, footsteps—running, then stopping.

Behind the kid, a tall figure rose up out of the brush and pawed at the kid's shoulder, pulled him half around and chopped a right hand into the kid's midriff. He sagged back against Perrell. Up by the cars a breathless voice said, "Yonder, Walt. There goes two of 'em."

"Well, hell, let's have a look at the bastards," Walt said, and the footsteps moved on.

The kid's wind was gargling in his throat. Half holding him, Perrell had turned to face this man who had risen from the brush.

"Had to shut him up," the man growled. His voice was raspy, hollow.

"Will you give me a hand with him?"

The man grunted. He was taller, if anything, than Buell. Perrell was shorter. But each took an arm over his shoulders and set off along the foot of the grade embankment. They reached a sheet-iron shack set against the bank and stopped to rest. Buell was wheezing and gagging, trying to get his feet under him.

Lantern light sprayed over the lip of the bank above them, a wavering fan of light with dust boiling through it in clouds. Perrell and the drifter shrank against the iron shack. Up above, the voice was the same one they had heard before.

"That you, Isaac? Me and Walt's been down along there. Wasn't nobody but an old man and a kid."

Isaac's answer was lost in the chuff of the switch engine. The fan of lantern light rocked, then soared upward, fading against the night. In the instant of its passing, Perrell saw the drifter's face again, gaunt, scarred and craggy, the beaked nose adrift. The sound of footsteps above faded.

Perrell said, "You and I have had the pleasure—"

"I remember . . ." He hesitated. "Clint is my handle." The way he said it somehow told Perrell that merely saying his own name was a hard thing for the man to do. The kid was struggling under the big-knuckled hand that covered his mouth.

"I'm John Perrell, and this"—Perrell shook the kid—"this is Buell Ashbaugh from Jump-Off Joe."

"All right, I won't say nothin," the kid gasped. "Jesus, mister, that fetched me right in the solus plexer."

# (4)

A night breeze whispered through the rust-flaked girders of the old iron bridge. Down below, by the river's edge, it set cottonwood and willow leaves dancing. On it wisped the smells of night-cooled creosote and ironwood off the desert, and of alfalfa hay and citrus trees and cattle dung from farms and feed lots along the valley, and the muddy-wet smell of the mud-red river itself and its stagnant, green-slimed pools here and there among the willows of the hobo jungle.

Smoke drifted in eddies through the branches of trees and scrub. Perrell and Clint and the kid had smelled the cooking fires before they saw them—fires flickering here and there, five or six men to a fire, heads turning warily, looking them over when the firelight touched them, then the old man saying, "Take the load off, gents," the stubble on his chin glinting silver in the firelight, Bobby Joe, dirty-faced and scrawny, digging an onion out of a canvas war bag, peeling the onion, watching them. There were two other men there, ordinary bindle stiffs, a big one and a little one, hitching over to make room, no spoken welcome, but only the quiet acceptance of rambling men, one for another.

Perrell spooned up the last of the mulligan from his tin plate, then leaned forward and picked up the willow stick he had set aslant over the coals, with a twist of biscuit dough browning on the end of it. Ramrod bread, soldier bread. Hot, with feathers of steam curling from it. He blew on the bread, then pulled it off the stick and mopped his gravy with it.

Biscuit dough and stew, both, were the old man's doing. He was straddling a bleached cottonwood snag. He had rolled out and floured his dough on a square of oilcloth, then cut strips with a butcher knife and passed them to the men gathered at the fire. And each of them had given something for the stewpot. Perrell's bindle had yielded up that can of corned beef.

"Say, that was dandy bread, pop," one of the stiffs said.

"M'own flour, b'God. M'own wheat." The old man spit tobacco juice onto a coal at the edge of the fire, and a cloud of steam puffed up. He shook the corner of a flour sack that poked out of the canvas war bag. "The last of it, too. When that's gone, there ain't n'more. Homesteaded her in ninety-eight. Eighteen years I plowed the son of a bitch and now we've went off and left her, me and Bobby Joe. Eighteen years . . ." A tear trickled down alongside his nose. "A hundred and sixty acres . . ." He glared at them, his pale old eyes aglitter with tears.

"Say, kid, I seen you a-tryin to ketch the train—yonder in the valley, other side of L.A." It was the biggest of the two bindle stiffs talking. "You like to didn't make it."

"I made it all right," Buell said.

The big man elbowed his partner and grinned around stained teeth. "You was lucky. You shouldn't have went for it, goin that fast. A train is like a big fine-lookin woman, see? Takes a real man to rassle her down. Hi God and I never missed one I run for—train or woman, either one." He looked around, waiting for a little encouragement.

"Well, I see it's brag time," Perrell said.

Taking that as encouragement, the big man winked back. "I mean it, boys, and I mean I don't have to pay for it, neither."

"Are we talkin trains or talkin women?" Clint said.

The big bindle stiff's grin hardened to the grim frown of the dedicated truth-teller. He rapped his knee with grimy knuckles. "Just any town along the line. It don't take me long to find it when I want it—why, sometimes, hi God, when I ain't even lookin for it. Day 'fore yesterday, what town was that, Knobby?"

"Saugus." Knobby's chin rested glumly on one hand.

"That's it. Early of a mornin, it was, and that's the best time if you're itchin for a little piece—the old man is out the house, see, and she is maybe feelin a little frisky. It was a little place, with a lot of red geraniums along the sideyard. Well, sir, they wasn't nothin on my mind but a plate of bacon and eggs. 'Course I offers to cut a little wood. You do that later, says she, and she pushes the screen door open for me. Right then, I *knowed*—I seen her look me over through the screen. They can always tell . . ."

"Tell *what?*" the kid said. He was still sulky from the criticism.

"Tell? Tell, by God, if they've got a stud or not. They always know, and don't think they ain't a-thinkin about it, too, sonny. Same as I always know about them . . ." He let the words hang in the air, rich and heavy with mystery.

"Well, dammit, what happened?" the old man said. A tear still sparkled in a fold of his cheek.

"She sets me down at the kitchen table, says a man is no better than his breakfast. Four eggs, sausages and a plate of cakes is what she give me, and all the time messin around my chair, you know, *leanin* over me, callin me Ernie. And she is wearin one of them Injun-blanket robes, you know, so she stands at the stove and fans herself and says, 'My land, ain't it warm, Ernie,' then she opens that robe up to cool off, like . . ." The big man's voice trailed off and he hunched forward on the cottonwood log, both hands held up before him, quivering with the awesome vision they struggled to shape.

"Was she . . . was she *nekkid?*" the old man whispered.

The big man, Ernie, stared into the darkness beyond them. "Might as well have been—her nightie wasn't no more than a cobweb . . . she had . . . I could see . . ." He shook his head, desperate and helpless for words, staring down at his two hands as they gently lifted their splendid burdens.

She must have been a mighty lonely woman, Perrell thought, if indeed she existed beyond Ernie's fevered imagination. Yet, somehow, he thought, she *was* real—the geraniums, the Injun-blanket robe and all—but he wondered if truth didn't stop there at the kitchen table over the plate of eggs and cakes. He studied Ernie's square, bristly face, tufted ears, big sloping shoulders under the dirt-stiff denim jacket, the meaty thighs, thick as nail kegs. He was a bull, all right. Perrell saw the big fingers curving up under the splendid, imagined curve of soft flesh—and suddenly he saw her, himself, with the blanket robe falling back from her shoulders and he knew she was real. For an instant he suffered for her, the shuddering terror when she let the robe slip, the dark desperation of having to lure wandering studs like Ernie. Then he caught himself—oh, hell, he thought, maybe she just likes it.

"I mean, dammit, what *happened?*" the old man said. His voice was husky now with strain, his lips peeled back.

Suddenly Buell lurched to his feet. Perrell saw the big hands bunched into fists, and even in the firelight he could see the dark flush on the kid's cheeks. He glared across the fire at Ernie. "Can't you see there's a little kid here?"

Ernie started and his hands dropped. He looked at Bobby Joe, hunched next to the old man, head down, scuffing the dirt with the run-over heel of one ancient shoe. It angered Ernie to have his story broken, and to be called down that way.

"Well, *shit,* if he's a-travelin with men, it's time he heard man talk." He grinned ingratiatingly at Bobby Joe. "Ain't that so, bub? You're big enough to know what it's for, ain'tcha?"

Bobby Joe plucked at a frayed tuft of denim with thin fingers and shot a look at Ernie, then, pleadingly, at the old man, who stared into the fire, his jaw slack and wagging, his eyes swimming—seeing that woman in Saugus still, his ancient juices astir with yearning for her.

"Come on, bub," Ernie said, "pull it out here so's we kin have a look at it—we'll tell you if they's enough of it to git the job done. Come on, shake it out."

Perrell stirred. But Buell reached over and put a hand on Bobby Joe's shoulder. "Come on, Bobby Joe, me and you is goin to rustle some firewood." He pulled and the boy got up and came to him. In the firelight Perrell saw the dirty lip, streaked and smeared under the runny nose. Buell and Bobby Joe walked off into the darkness.

Ernie hitched himself to his feet. "By God, for two cents . . ." he said. His little partner looked up at him, his face glum.

"Oh, hell, Ernie. The kid's right."

Ernie grunted. "By God, nobody—" Then he looked at Perrell, who stared back at him. He turned to the hard-faced drifter, who stared back at him, too. His shoulders sagged and he shook his head. "Oh, dammit, I know it. I *know* it." He turned to the old man. "I never meant nothin, pop, with the kid, I mean."

The old man's fingers clutched, opening and closing. Suddenly his jaw snapped shut and his eyes swam into focus. He glared up at Ernie. "Well, Jesus, man—ain't you goin to tell what *happened?*"

Perrell smothered a laugh. Then he saw Clint and Ernie both stiffen. He flinched, deep in his belly, and the back of his neck prickled. Slowly, he turned.

"Now jess you folks set tight," the deputy said. A sawed-off shotgun with mule-ear hammers lay in the crook of his arm and his badge glittered against his dark vest above his watch chain. A chew was lumpy in his gaunt cheek. His gray hat was pinched into a sharp peak. "Me and Sheriff Edmon only want to acquaint you with a little town ordinance."

Another man stepped forward. He was older, heavier, with a thick, drooping mustache. His dark suit coat hung open and Perrell saw the plow-handle butt of an old Colt sticking out of his waistband. He unfolded a piece of paper and shook it out, then fished eyeglasses from his coat pocket and put them on, all slow and deliberate, Perrell noted, while he looked each one of them over in turn.

"This here is a notice." His voice was soft and pleasant. He held the paper to the firelight and read. "Says: 'Every idle man, hobo or mack found in Yuma twenty-four hours from this date will be locked up and put on the rock pile. Get out of town or take the consequences.' " He peered at them over the eyeglasses. "And, gents, she's a big rock pile."

"This town gits bums like a dog gits fleas," the deputy said.

The old man slapped the knees of his overalls with both hands and stuck his chin out. "By Jesus, I ain't a bum. I'm a farmer. A farmer and a war veteran."

"Had a kid with him," the deputy said. "How's come you got that pore little ol' kid out playin hooky? And where's he at, anyway?"

"Any man calls me a bum is a—" the old man started to say, then he blinked, startled, and peered around, shielding his eyes from the glare of the fire. "Bobby Joe? You here?"

Perrell saw panic taking hold. The old-timer can't remember, he thought—he was that far gone with the woman from Saugus, in her Injun-blanket robe.

"He just went after some firewood," Perrell said.

Less than forty feet away, Bobby Joe was being squeezed tight against the rough bark of a half-fallen cottonwood by Buell's straining body. He had one arm around Bobby Joe's shoulders and a hand pressed over Bobby Joe's mouth. They had scarcely stepped outside the ring of firelight when Buell stopped to see if Ernie would be coming after them, because if he was, Buell wanted to be set for him. In his mind he was seeing himself rip rights and lefts into Ernie's belly, and he grunted aloud as he swung the imagined blows. Bobby Joe pulled at his hand, gasping.

"Gimme some air." At that moment they both heard a strange voice back there saying, "Now jess you folks set tight."

"Hush, now," Buell breathed into Bobby Joe's ear—he could see the two thick barrels of the sawed-off shotgun the visitor was holding. Bobby Joe nodded, face buried in the thick wool of the kid's sweater, heavy with the smoke of their fire mingled with traces of sweat and biscuit dough and cow barn. They were smells Bobby Joe was used to and comfortable with, and the seeping warmth of Buell's big rangy body felt good. Away from the fire, the night air was sharp with chill.

"He'd ought to be in school," the sheriff was saying.

"He's my grandchile," the old man said. He shook his head and the voice cracked. "I ain't been well . . . I'm a-takin Bobby Joe back east to Tennessee. We've got kinfolk there yet, on the old farm. They will see Bobby Joe is took care of. Hell, s'posin I croak?"

"Couldn't you at least buy a coach ticket?" the sheriff said. "I mean, a kid like that . . . some of these bums get mighty randy notions."

The old man squirted tobacco juice into the fire. "There ain't a red cent betwixt us." He glared suddenly.

"No pension or nothin?" the sheriff said.

"Pension! What goddamn army you reckon I was in? Bragg. Ginral Braxton Bragg. I soldiered for him."

The sheriff shoved his hands into his pockets and teetered on his heels, blowing through his mustache. He looked at Perrell and Clint. "You boys travelin together?"

"No," Perrell said. Clint shook his head. His big hands were clasped tight together. The sheriff looked at Ernie and Knobby.

"Me and him is partners," Knobby said. The sheriff nodded.

"Sheriff, you don't meet all the trains to read that notice, do you?" Perrell asked.

The sheriff smiled. "Not atall I don't, but boys, we have been pestered with a gang of yeggs here. They have blowed three safes in this town and we are comin into an election year. It is my notion that they been jungled down here along the river while their gay cat scouts the merchants."

Perrell grinned. "I saw the date that's printed on your notice."

The sheriff held the paper out at arm's length. "December seven, nineteen oh five. Yes, well, I took it off the bulletin board at the office. It was under a lot of more recent stuff. Not current, maybe, but that don't mean it ain't still in effect, boys. She's signed by my predecessor in office and I hold with ever word of it." He jerked his chin at the deputy. "Come on, Isaac," he said and half turned away, then stopped.

He turned back to the old man. "My daddy was from Tennessee and he was with General Braxton Bragg, too. His two brothers was killed on Lookout Mountain, right before his eyes. Edmon, their names was . . ."

"Edmon . . ." the old man said slowly, then he shook his head. "It was a long time ago. Yes, we was whipped there, no good sayin we wasn't." He whacked his lean thigh with the flat of his hand. "But *oh God,* we was fighters!"

The sheriff stepped over to the old man and leaned down. "You bet you were." He pulled something from his pants pocket and stuffed it into the bib pocket of the old man's overalls. "You take care of that youngun, hear?" He turned back then and said again, "Isaac," and the two of them walked away —not toward one of the other cooking fires, but back toward the railroad yards and the town.

Perrell was thinking: They didn't come here to read that notice or to roust bums. Not the sheriff himself. They are looking for someone. Who? Yeggs, safe-crackers, the sheriff said. Maybe, but it's damn seldom any officer explains his business that way—punch a man in the kidney with a grub-hoe handle is more like it. They were looking for some escaped man, convict or . . . no, there was only the two of them, not a posse, and they didn't go on to any of the other cooking fires.

Well, hell, he thought, if they *quit* looking, that means they *found* him, whoever he was. He looked at the others around the fire. Ernie and Knobby. Maybe steal a chicken now and then, but they were just bindle stiffs.

How about me? I wouldn't want to see a badge in Seattle or Portland, no, nor San Francisco or L.A. There are warrants out for me in all those places, maybe more. John Perrell, age thirty-four, five feet ten, one hundred and seventy pounds, occupation: machinist, mechanic, welder—also malcontent, rabble-rouser, Wobbly. Yes, that is enough to land me in jail almost anywhere on the West Coast, but, hell, a man ought to be able to pass through Yuma, Arizona.

That leaves him, he thought. The drifter, Clint. Prison suit, it looks like. Prison haircut, growing out. And, Lord yes, he wouldn't ride inside the car—can't stand closed-in places. Claustrophobia they call that, or maybe too much solitary. But not an *escaped* con, or they would have picked him up. What then? Maybe they want to keep an eye on him. He could lead them to someone else. Maybe. I will do well to get shut of that gent's company, John Perrell thought, as the old man fished out of his bib pocket whatever it was that the sheriff had stuffed in there. Two one-dollar bills. The old man turned them over, held them to the light. "I'm a son of a bitch," he said. Then his shoulders shook and he cackled faintly. "B'God, I ain't seen this much cash money in . . . in . . . I don't know when. Now, why do you reckon he done that?"

"No John Law ever done as much for me," Ernie mumbled. "Kick over a feller's stewpot is more like it. The son of a bitches . . ."

"Last winter," Knobby said suddenly. "You 'member, Ernie . . . up yonder on the Santy Fee–Kingman it was . . . eighteen below zero and the snow a-flyin. We like to froze our butts off. Deppities rousted us off the train and taken us to jail. Thirty, forty men. Sheriff had a five-gallon can of coffee on the stove. You 'member, Ernie . . . He says, 'Boys, I'll turn you loose in the mornin, when she warms up.' What about him, Ernie?"

Ernie snarled under his breath. He was staring fixedly at the two one-dollar bills in the old man's hand.

"I mean, ever John Law don't have to be a son of a bitch," Knobby said.

"They're *law,* ain't they?" Ernie said. "Deppities, railroad bulls, shacks, yard dicks—it don't matter none, they're all the same."

"No," Clint said, his voice flat and raspy. "No, they ain't the same atall."

Ernie's jaw thrust out at him, but Clint went on with it. "Some is *worse.*"

"Well, by God, that's what I'm a-sayin," Ernie said.

Clint ignored him. "Maybe you boys have heard of Wala-pai Sam, railroad bull on the S.P. Used to work the division between Gila Bend and Tucson." The big drifter's eyes squinted. He was staring into the fire, elbows set on bony knees, the cuffs of his long underwear sticking out past his shirt cuffs as he thumped one big fist into the other palm, slowly, time after time. "You can't call a man like that a son of a bitch—it ain't fair to all the other *ordinary* sons of bitches, see? Walapai Sam, he liked to use a pick handle on a man. Or a forty-four. Feller could have his choice. That's ten years ago, maybe. I don't expect he's still there . . ."

"He's there," Perrell said. "I saw a man in Oakland last summer. Had all his fingers smashed. Awfulest-looking hands you ever saw. He couldn't even button his shirt. Said a bull pounded his fingers with a pick handle where he had a hold of a grab iron. I asked him where it happened and he said Gila Bend."

"That's him. Walapai Sam." It seemed to Perrell that something like pleasure warmed the drifter's face.

The old man stood up. The dollar bills were not in sight. "I b'lieve I will take me a leetle walk, gents." He stepped over his log. A vague smile bleared his face. "Boys, ye could tell my grandchile that Granddaddy won't be long . . ." They heard the whispered *slap-slap* of his overall legs, then he was gone.

# (5)

Sheriff Edmon's county car was parked next to the water tank in the railroad yards. A cone of light from an overhead lamp fell on it. The car was a 1910 Olds. It had enormous forty-two-inch wheels and two running boards, the better to mount to its lofty seat. The sheriff climbed up and settled himself, then he set the throttle and retarded the spark.

"Twist her tail, Isaac," he said. The engine caught on the first turn of the crank and the sheriff switched on the electric head lamps, which he had had installed in place of the original acetylene lamps. Isaac climbed in beside him, and with a gentle clash of gears, the sheriff swung the big Olds around toward town. Prison Hill loomed on his right, washed in moonlight. The car rocked serenely through a hazardous course of deep washouts cut by the recent flood of January twenty-third, when the Colorado had come close to washing Yuma off the map. He crossed Main Street, and less than a minute later he pulled up in front of his office. He turned then and stared hard at Isaac. "If you aim to grow old on the county payroll, you will forget you seen me get soft in the head on account of an old bum." Then he climbed down and entered his office. He put his Colt and his hat on his desk and ground the telephone crank, then took down the receiver.

"That you, Harriet? Sheriff Edmon. Get me Sheriff Newcomb in Tucson, hon. Try his house."

While he waited for his call to go through, he told Isaac to send out for a pot of coffee. Isaac went back to the drunk tank and unlocked the door.

"Come out of there, Laz'ro, and get us a pot of coffee. A little air will do you good." Isaac gave the prisoner, Lázaro Reyes, a dollar. "Pot of coffee and an apple pie, Laz'ro. Mind you get right back with all the change or I'll see you get twenty years—and don't spill nothin, hear?"

Sheriff Newcomb was on the line. "Yes, that you, Herb? You can tell Pat Costello that we seen the man he is lookin for . . . No, we never let on. Said we was lookin for some yeggs that done a safe job. I expect the man will pull out of here tomorrow sometime. We goosed him some, you know? . . . No, just tell Costello not to forget who spotted his man for him. And remember me to Mary Kate."

A few minutes later Lázaro Reyes came back across Main Street from the Gila Valley Café. He looked longingly down the half-block toward a steamy adobe cavern, a saloon known as La Luz de Mi Vida, or Light of My Life, but he knew that Isaac, the deputy, meant pretty much what he said when he promised him twenty years if he lingered along the way. Meant it near enough.

As he turned to go on back to the sheriff's office Lázaro saw an old man in faded overalls mount the high sidewalk under the arched portico. The old man was dragging one leg slightly as he entered La Luz de Mi Vida.

Buell and Bobby Joe found driftwood cast along the flood-line of the river. They each picked up an armload and started back.

"Shucks, I forgot somethin," Buell said. "I meant to take you down by the river and see to it you washed your face."

"Quit it," Bobby Joe said. "Leave me alone."

"I mean it. You're big enough to know better. Why do you want to go around with snot all over your lip?"

Bobby Joe halted. "You gonna leave me alone?"

Hearing the shrillness in Bobby Joe's voice, Buell sighed. "All right. But it's time you learned better. Come on now, don't get cranky with me. I think you need a good night's sleep."

"Any time you feel like it, you can quit tellin me what to do," Bobby Joe said.

"That's what I mean. You're cranky. At home, my mom would say you needed a good physic."

Bobby Joe stopped again. Buell said, "Oh, come on. Where you folks from, anyway?"

"We're from Oregon, too."

"Well, we're neighbors then."

"No, not neighbors. We come from the dry-lake country, way out past Wagontire."

"Never heard of it," Buell said. "How come you're on the road?"

"Granddaddy was sick all last year. Did you see how he is draggin a leg? He says he thinks it was a stroke. We just couldn't make a crop atall, so he's takin me back to Tennessee. He says he wants me to be near our own kin."

They approached the fire. Bobby Joe stopped suddenly. "Granddaddy ain't there."

"He's just likely went into the bushes," Buell said.

They went on, dumped the wood. "Your granddad said to say he wouldn't be long," Perrell said.

"He had two dollars on him," Ernie said.

"Yes, we had—visitors. One of them took a shine to your granddad and left him a couple of dollars." Perrell thought Bobby Joe suddenly looked stricken. The youngster's face was white under the dirt, with nostrils flaring. Bobby Joe turned away, caught at Buell's sleeve with plucking fingers. Buell followed the youngster back into the shadows.

"That money," Bobby Joe whispered. "Granddaddy has went after bob wire with it."

Buell laughed. "When my dad says bob wire, he means booze."

"That's what I mean, too—Granddaddy calls it that. If Granddaddy had two dollars, he ain't likely to git back for a week." Bobby Joe sniffed. "He don't know where we *live*, around here. He'll git lost."

Buell Ashbaugh's Uncle Perce was a drinking man, too, and in a moment of clear and instant recall, Buell could hear his dad, Tom Ashbaugh, say, "I don't care if he drowns in it, so long as he stays away from here when he's got a snootful." But Buell remembered how Tom Ashbaugh located Perce in jail in Coos Bay and brought him home to Jump-Off Joe to sober up—that time and many another time, too. Buell knew all he wanted to know about a drinking man, and he did not intend to get in the way of Bobby Joe's granddaddy's going on a two-dollar drunk. Bobby Joe pulled at his sweater.

"You got to help me find him."

"He'll get found, all right—you sit tight and he'll find you. Time you was in bed, anyway. You get your bedroll and I'll help you roll her out."

"*Please* help me find him."

Buell said, "Look, Bobby Joe—this is one thing I know somethin about and I'm tellin you I won't mess with your granddaddy if he's got his drinkin hat on. I mean it. You can do what you want, but if you've got any sense you will go to bed and leave Granddaddy to get back when he's ready."

Buell's voice was blunt, obdurate. Bobby Joe knew that even if the old man could be found, wherever he was, dragging him away without help was just not possible. Granddaddy had a temper like a stepped-on cat.

"All right," Bobby Joe said in a whisper, then pointed with eyes and chin across the fire to where Ernie sat in sulky silence on his log, "but I don't want to sleep near that bad-mouth bastard."

Buell laughed. "It'll be warmer by the fire. He's nothing but talk, anyway. And you don't want to give your granddaddy a fright, findin you gone when he gets back."

"I told you—he won't be back. Not tonight he won't."

Bobby Joe picked up a thin bedroll and quickly stepped away into the edge of darkness again, then turned and waited.

"Show me where you want to bed down," Buell said.

"Plumb away from here is where."

Clint had pulled out his mouth organ and was playing softly.

"Suit yourself," Buell said. "Sleep where you want."

Bobby Joe answered by not answering, but simply waiting.

Waiting. Until Buell, who was listening to Clint's mouth organ, noticed. "Now what? Ain't you gone yet? I bet you're scared. Is that it?"

"Yes," Bobby Joe whispered.

"Doggone it, you're a peck of trouble. I like it here by the fire and I like the music. I ain't ready for bed yet."

Bobby Joe waited, silent. Buell sighed and picked up his own bindle. Perrell glanced up at him. Buell said in a low voice, "If the old man gets back, me and the kid will be bedded down out there somewheres." He flicked a glance at Ernie, who was pointedly ignoring him. Perrell nodded.

Buell followed Bobby Joe through the willows toward the river, the wail of the mouth organ fading as they walked. They smelled wood smoke, saw dim figures, red coals glowing, and circled wide. Another campfire, like their own. Bobby Joe turned north, upriver. Behind them, girders of the railroad bridge strutted against a glow of light in the sky behind Prison Hill. The willows thinned. A big feathery tamarisk slanted across their path. Under it the ground was soft and spongy.

"What's wrong with this?" Buell said. He felt the ground. "These needles are soft as bed tickin. Feel."

Bobby Joe knelt beside him. Not five feet away, a hideous moan sounded—a snoring, gargling moan. Bobby Joe squealed in terror. Buell smelled the sour stink of cheap wine. He pulled Bobby Joe up and they went on.

Out from under the trees the lopsided moon, now high in the sky and no longer overpowered by the bright firelight, shone down on the river's pale banks as they—bounding the great dark stream of the Colorado—stretched away into the distance, reaching for the low mountains and tumbled badlands glinting on the horizon. Bobby Joe continued to walk. They left behind them the stink of the green pools and the hobo jungle. The air smelled of creosote bush and mesquite and the desert river.

"Just how far do you aim to go?" Buell said.

Bobby Joe pointed. "Yonder."

"You mean *wade?*"

Before them a narrower stream entered the Colorado, its

waters barely retained by low banks, its beaches feathery with reeds. In the mouth of the river, like a pale tongue, lay an island sand bar thirty or forty yards in length. The sands of the island clung to the roots of an old and twisted cottonwood tree and to the roots of reeds and brush grown up in its shelter. The island was separated from them by a channel of dark water only ten or twelve yards across.

Bobby Joe bent and picked up a white stone and tossed it out into the channel. It splashed into the water, slanted down and came to rest, a pale glow, barely visible.

"It ain't even a foot deep," Bobby Joe said and knelt down, picking at shoe laces, then scuffing out of the big shoes, rolling overall legs up above the pale shins and small knees. Holding bedroll and shoes, Bobby Joe waded out. "It's cold, but it ain't deep. Come on."

Buell pulled off his shoes and socks. He rolled up his pants legs. The little white rock glowed in the water near Bobby Joe. Buell had a feeling that he would not get so wet if he ran across that channel as hard as he could go. He took a crouching football start and ran. The water was icy.

*"Whoo-haw!"* he brayed. Just beyond the little white rock, there was *no bottom.* Buell plunged headlong. As he fell he hurled his bedroll across to the bank beyond. His clutching fingers hooked at Bobby Joe's overall strap, so they went under together, scrambling there for footing and clawing at each other until they crawled up onto the little island, spitting and coughing.

Buell, when he could get his breath, was surly-mad.

*" 'Tain't deep,"* he mocked. *" 'Tain't deep."*

The moonlight shone on Bobby Joe's face, against the sand.

"Well, at least it washed the snot off your lip," Buell said.

He heard a clicking sound. It was Bobby Joe's thin jaws chattering. "Come on," Buell said. "We'll build a fire and dry out." He slapped his pockets. "I forgot. My matches is all wet." Bobby Joe huddled in shaky misery.

Buell fished Bobby Joe's bedroll out of the reeds, untied the binding twine that held it together and shook it out. A single thin blanket was rolled in the frayed tarp. The tarp was wet and the blanket was half wet. He found his own bedroll, high and dry, where he had thrown it. He shook out the two dry and fleecy Oregon wool blankets. He looked at Bobby Joe cowering in the sand. Buell Ashbaugh had two younger brothers and a little sister—many a time he had warmed their scrawny bodies in his bedroll, deer-hunting time, or when they camped along the Rogue on fishing trips with his dad and his Uncle Perce. His own teeth were chattering now.

He made a bed on the sand under the old cottonwood—first, his own dry tarp, then one blanket, then another blanket, then Bobby Joe's half-wet blanket, with the wet tarp covering, the dryest side down.

"All right," he said, "shuck out of them wet clothes." His breath made fog on the chill air. There was no answer. He turned. "Bobby Joe?"

Bobby Joe was just coming back from the bushes at the end of the island, fingers twitching at iron buttons and overall straps. "Shuck, now," Buell said and peeled out of his own wet clothes. Stripped to his long underwear, Buell stepped away a few yards to the far side of the sandy eminence that supported the old cottonwood. He turned his back, and unlimbering with icy fingers, relieved himself.

"Say, what's your last name?" Buell called.

"Callaway. Why?"

"That's a long name. You couldn't do it, either."

"Do what?"

"Pee your name on the sand. Friend of mine named Jim Lillis, he could do it ever time—short name, see? What give him trouble was dotting the *i*'s. Say, my back teeth was afloat."

Under the bony limbs of the cottonwood, Buell skinned out of his long underwear. Naked, one hundred and eighty-nine and a half pounds, he launched into a jig, his heels slashing at the sand as he bellowed, *"Oh, have you seen my Cindy—she comes from way down south . . . she's so sweet, the honey bees just swarm around her mouth . . ."* He hurled himself onto the tarp and began brushing the sand off his feet.

"You ought to hear my daddy play that on the fiddle," he

said. "Hurry up, now, you'll freeze." He squirmed between the blankets. Bobby Joe was huddled in the blue work shirt, bare white legs a-shimmer in the moonlight. Buell reached up and slapped Bobby Joe's arm. The shirt was sodden, still. He saw the youngster's shoulders begin to shake.

"What's wrong? You ain't cryin, are you?"

Bobby Joe's head wagged and Buell heard the giggling laugh. "No, I was thinkin of what that feller wanted me to do, back there in camp . . ."

"I told you—he was all talk."

"Maybe so"—Bobby Joe gasped, peeling the wet shirt off, throwing it aside to hang on a clump of reeds—"but wouldn't he git a surprise?"

Buell stared up from the warmth of the blankets, seeing flashing roundness, curve of hip and haunch, as Bobby Joe threw the shirt and turned back to look down upon him, laughing, before slipping between the blankets. Buell would remember that instant for the rest of his life.

Bobby Joe was a girl.

# (6)

Buell Ashbaugh had risen in the dark of early morning to milk cows nearly every day of his life after the age of nine. Old habit startled him awake before four o'clock. The moon was hanging orange-red and huge over the far bank of the Colorado. He raised himself on one elbow and stared dumbly along the bright gold moon track on the water, then tipped his head back and looked up at the pale limbs of the old cottonwood coiled against the stars.

Breath flowed warmly against his arm. He suddenly felt the smooth dry warmth of skin next to him. He pulled the blankets away and the moonlight slanted across the cheek and bare shoulder of Bobby Joe.

Bobby Joe murmured, then stirred. A slim hand strayed, feeling for the blanket, then the head and shoulder turned, both sufficiently bony and boyish for Buell to shiver with uncertain memory. Then it flooded back and behind his eyelids he saw her again in that amazing instant, laughing down at him, her breasts quivering, quivering. And he, stunned, stricken, sapped, lay there with thudding heart and locked jaws, staring through the limbs of the cottonwood. Then he heard the whispered voice, *"It wasn't my doin to get us wet . . ."* And he, unable to answer, lying chilled and craven, for how long he had no idea, when she suddenly moved and came to rest against his arm, and through the roaring in his ears he heard, *". . . freezin,* just near about *freezin,"* and felt her warmth seeping along that one side, the rest of him still encased in icy, pimply chill, her fingers straying along his arm and finding his hand, then no more words at all as the sky wheeled and the warmth spread and time was the wheeling sky and murmur of the rivers mingling . . .

A bass jumped, lit *splat,* out on the dark water. Buell saw that her eyes had opened, were watching him, darkly gleaming. He pulled the blanket farther back and looked down on her. The moonlight was almost gone. For a moment it limned the fullness of her breast, but she was turning onto her back, pulling at the blankets, and the soft roundness flattened out.

"You're freezin me," she murmured.

"Where does it go when you lay back like that?"

"Where does what go?"

For a farm boy, there was really only one word for what Buell meant, and he did not want to say it. He gently rested his big hand on it, feeling the little mound in the center of it stir and nudge into his palm.

"You know . . ." he said.

"It ain't gone. It's there," she said.

"Not like it was. Where does it go?"

"It's still there, silly. You're just about freezin me."

"No, show me."

"I will if you put the cover back." Her hand pushed against his chest, then tugged at the tarp and darkened the stars over him. "There . . ." she said.

"It's too dark, now," he said. "I can't tell."

"Oh, *you* . . ." she whispered, then she moved again and he felt the blankets lift away from him and heard her breathing above him, then the softness was brushing his cheek and lips. "Is it there now?" she breathed.

Perrell awoke to see a mist hanging in the half-dark willows of the hobo jungle. Far away a dog was barking, and over in the yards the switch engine still chuffed and couplings clashed, steel on steel. He smelled smoke. Clint was feeding sticks to the fire. The drifter's melancholy gaze was fastened on the grim bulk of the old prison where it squatted toadlike on the bluff.

Perrell rolled out of his blanket and slipped on his shoes without speaking, then he picked up his coffeepot and walked to the river. Here and there in the gray light, the dim shapes of men stirred, shaking free of the earth, like locusts. He looked with distaste at the brown water lapping at the can-littered muddy bank, and turned and walked upstream. After a bit the willows thinned, then gave way to reeds and open, sandy beaches. He walked on until he came to an inlet. The banks were clean. He slipped down the bank, where he scooped a hole in the sand and watched it fill with clear water. After he filled his coffeepot he knelt and had a wash, then he squatted on his heels and let his face and hands dry in the cold air.

A great blue heron stretched its neck and sprang airborne with a slow flapping of wings. It banked away and flew upstream. Beyond it the flinty peaks of desert mountains were still purple-dark against the graying sky. The heron's serene flight broke into a sudden startled hacking of wings as it reached an old white cottonwood—the heron wheeled up and away, across the river.

Perrell saw movement under the tree; it was still some distance away from him, but he recognized the big kid, Buell

Ashbaugh, whose bare chest and shoulders were just visible over the tops of the rushes growing along the shore between them. Buell was flapping what appeared to be a shirt—night-damp, Perrell thought. Carrying his coffeepot, he walked along the water's edge, threading through clumps of growth until he rounded a shoulder of sandy bank and saw that the old tree was on a little island. Buell stopped flapping the shirt and felt of it. By then Perrell could see that it was a pair of overalls and not a shirt. Buell was wearing only his long drawers, while other articles of clothing hung here and there on the bushes and tree limbs. His voice drifted to Perrell's ears.

"They'll be dry, time we wade across. Put this on." He pulled a shirt off some reeds and held it out. Perrell heard Bobby Joe's muffled complaints. He climbed up the bank a little and through the pale-green branches of a palo verde tree he saw the bed of blankets in the sand. Buell was holding out the shirt and saying, "Come on . . ." The blankets flapped back and as Bobby Joe emerged from them, Buell draped the shirt around the youngster's shoulders and used it to pull Bobby Joe up, squealing and fighting the shirt, and Perrell saw then what Buell had learned last night, that Bobby Joe was not a boy. Buell dropped to his knees on the blankets, facing her, and she stopped fighting and lifted her arms and he slowly drew her body close until she was tight against him, her lips against his ear. His big hands slipped slowly down the length of her back, then he was pressing and lifting at the same time and she was turned over and stretched out again in the blankets with her hands linked around Buell's neck.

Perrell backed away from the palo verde tree, his astonishment giving way slowly to a delighted grin. He walked back the way he had come, stopping often to throw back his head and laugh. A flock of coots cruising on the river heard him and took wing, thrashing the water furiously.

When Perrell reached the cooking fire, Clint was hunkered down in the same place. The first red light of dawn was licking at the top of the prison blockhouse. The dog was still barking, somewhere not too far distant, and the switch engine was crunching freight cars together and coughing chuffs of steam. Perrell put the coffee pot on the coals.

"I thought you had fell in," Clint said.

Perrell began to laugh again. He saw Ernie sitting up in his blanket, sleepy and ugly. Perrell, laughing, said, "I saw a hell of a big bird, over there by the river . . ."

Ernie and Knobby were sharing a can of beans, passing it back and forth between them. Perrell poured coffee into Clint's cup, drank his own. His belly growled. "No grub," he said. "Now I'm wishing I had stopped for some groceries."

"A man gets a-rollin," Clint said, "he's on the move, rollin, ridin the trains . . . he don't like to stop once he's rollin."

"It's like, if he stops or turns aside, he might miss a train," Perrell said, "and that could be the train he waited all his life to catch, and once it's gone it will never run again for him. It's gone forever." Perrell suddenly found himself looking up at the sun-red hulk of the old prison and was unable to tell himself why he was there or where he was going. "That's the thing about trains. The going is what counts, not the getting there."

Clint shook his head. "No, it ain't *just* the goin. I been on the bum in my time, but right now, I *know* where I'm goin."

They heard footsteps and turned to see Buell and Bobby Joe. Buell was walking in the lead, looking mighty sober, Perrell thought. Merriment flooded up in him again. He tried to drown it in coffee and choked, and coughed, half strangled with coffee and laughter. Bobby Joe shuffled behind, the baggy overalls swinging free of the slim body, looking awkward and reedy and underfed, like a fuzz-cheeked fourteen-year-old, Perrell thought, instead of—what? Seventeen? Maybe nineteen . . .

Frowning, Bobby Joe peered around at them all. Ernie sniffed sulkily and turned his back. "Granddaddy ain't back," Bobby Joe said in a flat voice. She turned suddenly to Buell and hissed, "You said you'd help! We got to find him." She turned to Perrell. "Help us, mister?"

Perrell wanted to pull back, sensing that something was about to break the spell of his rambling, the numbness of it.

But then he suddenly found it hard to take his eyes off Bobby Joe, knowing what he did now.

Perrell turned to Clint. "Well, I was shy of grub, anyway. I could pick some up and look for the old-timer, too. What about you?"

Clint shook his head. "I'd sooner go hungry a day or two than run into them deputies. That freight is about made up and I expect I will be on her when she goes. But if the old gent gets back, I'll tell him not to stray."

Watching them, Knobby dug a finger into his ear and squirmed. Ernie was still hunched on the log with his back to them. "That freight," Knobby said, "me and Ernie—Ernie wants to git goin . . ." His voice trailed off. It was true about the freight. The switch engine was quiet at last. The dog still barked, beyond Prison Hill.

"Good riddance," Bobby Joe said tartly. Ernie stiffened, mumbled something into the ground.

"Watch your step, sis," Perrell said in a low voice. She swung sharply and stared hard at him, then at Buell, and her hand rose to cover her mouth, trembling. Perrell had not meant to say *sis*. He threw an arm around Bobby Joe's shoulder and turned her away. "Come on, kid," he said and pulled her along a few steps. Buell caught at his sleeve.

"Take your hands off h— Leave him alone," he finished lamely.

Perrell grinned. "That's what I mean—watch your step. Bobby Joe, if you let yourself get all female and bitchy around an ornery old stud like Ernie, he will go to paddle you and the jig will be up. Then he will want to give you something else and it won't be a paddling."

Buell fiercely pushed Bobby Joe to one side and grabbed Perrell's coat. "Just what do—I mean, how?" He was ready to throw that big right hand. Perrell stared at him, smiling still, but nettled, then he gently peeled Buell's fingers off his coat.

"I didn't find out the way you did," he laughed. "No, hold on, you don't want to hurt an old gent like me. Hell, I'm on your side. I'll dance at your wedding."

Bobby Joe put a hand on Buell's arm. "Don't say nothin,

mister," she said to Perrell, glancing back toward the men around their cooking fire. "It was all Granddaddy could think about, once he decided we had to make this trip—you know, what the bums would do to me. It was eatin him up. So I taken some sheep shears and cut my hair . . . pretty near cried my eyes out, too. I could sit on it. Then I put on some of his old overhalls and put a little dirt on my face, you know, like a snotty nose, and I went to show him. He tried to throw me off the place, said he didn't want no bums messin round. He come near to doin it, too, but our dog Jack knowed me and he bit Granddaddy. The day we was to leave, Granddaddy he dug a hole out back of the house, then he took Jack out there and shot him with his old cap-and-ball pistol, and then he throwed the pistol in on top of Jack and covered 'em both up. He said they was the only two things he had in the world that was worth anything and he would be double-damned if he would let anyone else have 'em. Afterwards, then, he forgot he done it. Now he thinks someone else shot Jack and stole his gun. You see, anymore, he is so forgetful . . ."

She was rambling on, half breathless. Perrell said, "You two hunt around the jungle here and up along the yards. I'll take a look over toward town."

Smell of mesquite smoke on the morning air. The long slope tailing away from Prison Hill, clumps of creosote and catclaw, scattered ochrous adobes half melted back into the soil, twisted posts under *ramadas* loose-thatched with river reeds, strings of red chiles hanging, chickens scratching the sand, that dog still barking—then the beginning of a dirt street, still gullied from the flood, and adobes squatting heavily.

How to backtrail the old gent? All right. Perrell let himself walk, let the slope and the street lead him, thinking: I'm an old-timer with a game leg and a hell of a thirst. Ahead of him, the main drag, the low morning sun streaming warm, two big-turbaned Yuma Indians sitting on the high sidewalk with their backs against a portico column, eyes closed to the sun. Across the street and half a block toward the river, he saw flaking blue and vermilion block letters across a mud-plastered portico—La Luz de Mi Vida—a Mexican boy sweeping out the doorway. Perrell crossed the street. Saloon stink, stale beer, the kid shaking his head when Perrell asked about the old man.

Perrell turned back to the street, thinking: Well, Granddaddy is either in the drunk tank or stretched out in the dirt somewhere—I won't go near the drunk tank unless I have to. So, I'm an old-timer with a load of booze in my belly and I can't remember where I came from. I hear that switch engine over yonder—maybe it tells me something.

He let himself go again, following the gentle slope of the street, drifted into the mouth of an alley, a board fence on one side enclosing an old livery barn. He saw it was crammed with defunct buggies, old furniture, a tipped-over anvil; then he saw the old man's hat, lying up-turned at the foot of the board fence. The alley opened into a warren of tiny adobe houses, clustered behind sagging fences of chicken wire and weathered pickets.

Then he saw the barking dog. It was a scrawny yellow cur with raised hackles, and it would bark four or five times, then lunge and snap at a man's leg protruding from behind a low adobe wall—a man's leg, a cracked work shoe, the denim overalls wet and tattered where the dog had worried it. Seeing Perrell, the dog backed off, snarling and barking.

The old man was lying on his side, his stubbly chin scummy with dribble. He had vomited where he lay and the crotch of his overalls was wet. Perrell swallowed against the gagging that caught in his throat, then set about getting the old man on his feet.

Bobby Joe mopped at the old man's face with a wet rag. Granddaddy grinned feebly, mumbled.

"You will have to decide," Perrell said. "We will help you get him on a train. He can sober up there as well as here, and you will be that much closer to where you're going."

"He looks sick," Bobby Joe said. They were alone by their cold fire, now. Clint, Ernie and Knobby, all were gone.

"Well, he *is* sick," Perrell said. "He probably poured close to a quart down his stack. Anybody would be sick."

The switch engine was chuffing again, over in the yards, piecing together another freight.

"He was bound we would get to Tennessee," Bobby Joe said. "Do you reckon he will be over it, time we get to—what's the next place?"

"Tucson is the next place that amounts to anything. He will still have a headache, but he ought to be through the worst of it by then," Perrell said.

"And I can help you," Buell blurted suddenly, then his face reddened. "That far, anyways."

She shot a look at him. He stumbled on. "I mean . . . I aimed to get off in Tucson."

Perrell saw hurt fall across her face, like a shadow. Now she's finding out how much it was worth, he thought. A hard little lump formed along the line of Bobby Joe's jaw. "If you will help me to get him on the train," she said to Perrell, "we'll go on." Her voice flared suddenly. "We don't need no more help than that!"

Buell touched her shoulder. "I never meant nothin," he said. She pulled away from him. He looked at Perrell in helpless misery. "I never said I would go to *Tennessee.*"

Perrell had to choke down a laugh. "Kid, why don't you go scout that train that's making up?" He jerked his chin toward the yards and winked at the kid. Buell stood up and looked down at her back, then he wrenched himself around and stalked off.

Hearing footsteps again a few minutes later, Perrell looked up and saw not Buell, but the scarred drifter, Clint, bindle slung over his shoulder, hands in pockets. He threw the bindle across a log and sat down. Perrell looked at him in surprise, glad to see him for some reason, though he had told himself he would do well to get clear of him.

"I thought you pulled out on that freight," he said.

Clint shrugged. "I found out it don't pull out till this afternoon." He nodded at the old man. "I see the old gent has had both front feet in the trough. He don't look too good."

"No, we're going to get him aboard the train, though. It won't profit him to stay here."

Clint nodded. After a moment he said, "There is a flatcar in this train they're makin up—there is a big thrashin machine on it, and some crates. She might be a good place to put the old man."

# (7)

The yard dick caught them at it when they went to lift the old man aboard the flatcar. When Perrell held out a five-dollar bill he said, "Hell, I can see the old gent is sick. Understand, though, this division ends at Healy." Like all railroad men, he said Healy, meaning Gila Bend. "You get to Healy and you're on your own. I can't do nothin for you there." He bit down hard on the match he was chewing and stared at Perrell. "My advice to you is to watch your step when you get there . . ." He pushed the five dollars away.

The train uncoiled from the yards, slithered north in a long curve to get around the red mountains, then it struck like a steel-spined sidewinder for the big bend of the Gila, a hundred miles to the east.

Perrell rode the windy splendor of the flatcar, stretched out under the great thrashing machine that sat like a steel-shelled insect, its plates and joints clicking and shivering. Next to him Buell Ashbaugh sat with his back against the iron wheel spokes, where he could look unhappily upon Bobby Joe's back as she knelt over the old man. He was stretched out in a space between tall wooden crates that were roped to ringbolts in the deck timbers. Clint dozed under the forequarters of the thrashing machine, his hat pulled down over his face. Ernie and Knobby were a couple of cars ahead. They had sneaked aboard while the yard dick was talking to Perrell.

The train was not yet clear of the red mountains. To the north, beyond wrinkled, salt-white desert, an immense dome heaved its bulk above the skyline. The light of the falling sun flared against the dome.

Perrell peered up into the guts of the great machine, tracing the linkages and the arrangement of belt drives. "See that tension wheel there?" he said to Buell. "Now, I call that a tacky arrangement. If it was me, I would use adjustable leverage that would work through a cam. See, right here you could weld on a bracket to take the lever arm. I would just tear that other thing right out of there . . ."

Buell touched his arm. "Somethin's gone wrong. Look at Bobby Joe."

She was staring down at the old man with one hand covering her mouth, her eyes wide with fear. Perrell and Buell scrambled aft. The kid got there first, then turned back to him in horror. "He's throwed up—it's—Jesus, what do you reckon he got into? It looks—I don't know—like coffee grounds."

"It's blood. All that booze has started him bleeding inside." Perrell kept his voice low in the kid's ear.

"Will it stop?"

"How the hell do I know?" Fury rose in Perrell now, for letting himself get into this mess. He remembered that moment when he could have just picked up his bindle and walked away to another fire—he was not bound to any of them—but he had let the moment go by. Why not now? He saw himself walking to the end of the car, grabbing those irons on the boxcar ahead and swinging up—hell, just climb over the top of the damn car and get lost—it's a seventy-car train, he thought.

". . . got to get him off this train," Bobby Joe was crying into the rush of wind.

"No, not now," he shouted back. "There's nothing to get him off for, understand? We'll just have to ride it out." He thought Bobby Joe had not heard him say anything about blood. She would find out soon enough. He tore a piece of rotted canvas off one of the crates and tried to clean up after the old man. The light was failing fast. He looked up and saw the top of that mighty dome glowing red as the last of the sunlight streamed against it.

Perrell went back to his place under the machine and lay back with his head on his bindle. Then the light drained away after the fallen sun and he was suddenly cold. He untied his bindle and shook out his blanket, then he lay back again and let himself go with the sway of the car and click of the trucks over rail joints, and watched the stars come out. He thought of that old man back there, thought of him, a young soldier lying under a Tennessee sky all those years ago, with his big old mule-ear Minnie rifle by his side, maybe knowing that when day came he would be plunged into the thick of one of those great battles—Lookout Mountain, it could have been—and feeling his heart thud through his body into the ground, and all of them the same, their hearts beating until the ground quivered. He thought of all the night skies and the years rushing away, and in his mind the wind of the train's passing was the wind of time in the void. He felt his belly suck flat with dread—that same heart was pumping out its burden tonight.

He saw Clint sit up. Then he felt it, too; the steady fast chuffing beat of the big Consolidated Hog engine was slacking off, the wind rush slowly dying. The car lurched and the great thrashing machine squealed and creaked, then the train was dead on the tracks.

A few yards ahead, lanterns bobbed alongside the train. "You don't suppose, do you," Perrell said, "that they are going to roust us off the train way out here?"

Clint crawled out from under the train and looked at the stars. "Way too soon for Healy," he said. "I b'lieve we're at the Mohawk grade. She's a long pull, see? They will either hitch on a helper engine, or cut us in two and take us up the grade in two sections . . ."

The lanterns had passed them. Stopped. Suddenly the engine chuffed and the train jerked into motion. "That's it," Clint said. "Two sections. We're in the front half."

The grade was almost imperceptible. At the end of it they

were shunted onto a siding and cut loose, then a minute later the engine went back in reverse to pick up the rest of the train. Silence settled over them, silence pocked by the distant coughing of the locomotive, then by a sudden metallic squeal. It swelled, then died to a groan. Perrell looked out and saw the dim bulk of a water tank standing against the sky, and next to it, the gaunt framework of a windmill. The night breeze stirred again. Perrell felt it on his cheek and heard the windmill squeal again in answer to it.

The old man was struggling to sit up. Bobby Joe tucked the blankets around his chin. "There is just no accountin," the old man said. His voice was like the whisper of two dry corn shucks rubbing together. "No accountin what a man's system will find congenial. A feller—don't have but a few sips of toddy —in the way of a tonic, is all. But them goddamn chile peppers in the free lunch, they would burn a man's guts out . . ."

Perrell heard the voice grow liquid, burbling. The old man's body jerked, coiled, and he toppled onto his side. The windmill shrieked and the pump rod clattered in the iron casing. Bobby Joe held on to the bony shoulders as the old man heaved and shuddered.

The locomotive was returning. When it passed, the bright flare of its headlight cut the darkness on the flatcar for an instant and Perrell saw where the old man had rolled over. He felt the sudden bump as cars were coupled, then lanterns bobbed past again, voices murmuring above them, and in the splash of light from the lanterns, he saw again. What the old man was giving up now was simply blood, red and liquid.

The train jerked and began to move. Looking up, Perrell saw the windmill and heard it squeal as they passed. Bobby Joe gasped and he heard the old man again and it seemed to Perrell that the shrieking windmill, with its clattering pump rod, and the coughing engine up ahead and the great drive wheels turning were all pumping together, pumping the old man dry of his life.

A Walapai Tiger, to old-time Arizonans, was an orange-winged, black-bodied wasp of legendary virulence, whose sting was so painful, it was said, that many a heart stopped beating from it, and once stung, no one ever fully recovered.

No one knew why Elmo Hollenbeck was called Sam. He came to work on the division in 1900, a big man, heavy-bodied, though light on his feet. But railroad men liked nicknames, and rare was the railroader who did not carry one to his death. A yardmaster in Tucson who saw Elmo Hollenbeck at work one of those first days on the line was heard to say, "I'd sooner mess with a Walapai Tiger than mess with him." So Elmo Hollenbeck was known from the first as Walapai Sam.

At dusk, the stationmaster in Gila Bend saw Sam Hollenbeck walk past his window on the way home to supper. The stationmaster, an old-timer known as Granny Honeycutt, fingered a piece of yellow paper on his desk on which was penciled the word *Sam*. It was a reminder to himself.

That morning the stationmaster had received a telephone call from the assistant division superintendent in Tucson. "Granny, that you?" the super had shouted. "The sheriff here has been in touch with us. But first, do you know if Sam Hollenbeck will be working Healy today, or somewhere on the line?"

"He don't tell me nothin," said Granny Honeycutt.

"The point is that the sheriff and Costello—you know him, don't you, the Pinkerton man?—have a line on a man who is bumming through on a freight. Now, it is no criticism of Sam, understand, but they would be obliged if Sam didn't hold this man up some way, you know?"

"I think so, only if you want me to tell him that, it ain't gonna do no good."

The line hummed, empty of voice, for some seconds. Then the super, whose name was Dennis, said, "Well, then, get Sam to call me here, soon as you can." And rang off.

So now Granny Honeycutt called "Sam!" through his open window. The big man stopped in mid-stride. Turned. He's a big one, Granny thought. Aloud he said, "Dennis called from Tucson. Asks for you to call back, soon as you can. That was this mornin."

Sam's eyes narrowed. He fished his gold railroad watch

from a vest pocket and looked at it. He said, "You should have told me sooner."

"I ain't seen you," Granny said.

Sam looked at his watch again. "Know what it's about?"

"Only that the sheriff and a Pinkerton man want you to—to not get in the way of some bum who is comin through."

Sam stared at him, unblinking. Pale-blue eyes under the hat brim, frosty and pale as a December sky. Yes, and the son of a bitch is boned like a buffalo, thought Granny Honeycutt, who had been skinner for a hide hunter on the Canadian River when he was nineteen, and knew how a buffalo was boned.

Sam shoved his watch back into the vest pocket with a thick thumb, turned on his heel without another word and walked away into the dusk.

Jaw on him like a cast-iron sink, thought Granny Honeycutt as he rolled down his desk top.

Sam Hollenbeck lived in a small frame house of the type erected by the S. P. for railroad personnel. It sat all by itself on a flat and gravelly plain of adobe next to a row of dusty-feathered tamarisk trees. His wife, Rosemary, seeing him through the kitchen window, tossed her cat out the back door—Sam was not partial to cats—then served out supper: canned spinach, cornbread, grits, ham gravy and biscuits, and stewed apples for dessert.

They ate silently. She, nervous and attentive. He, eyes fixed, but not seeing, on the salt and pepper shakers. Finished, he rose. She cleared the table, pumped water into the dishpan at the galvanized sink. Through the open door she saw him enter the parlor and turn up the green-glass-shaded coal-oil lamp. Wicker squealed as he settled himself in his chair. From the lamp table, he took a heavy book and placed it across his knees where it would catch the spill of yellow light from the lamp. Then he took a big square reading glass from the lamp table and bent over the open book, peering closely at it through the reading glass. Watching, she shivered.

She was a lean woman, with black hair pulled back and coiled so tightly behind her head that her eyes were stretched to slits. She dreaded to see him take that big book on his knees.

When she first knew Elmo Hollenbeck, they were both Sunday school teachers in El Paso. Elmo was also a young deputy in the town marshal's office. She remembered her father saying to her, "Yes, Elmo stands four-square for the Lord and the law, and he is sure God death on sin. If that is what it takes to make a good man, then he is a damn good man," and she had scolded him for his language. But all that was such a long time ago; she could scarcely remember the way Elmo had been in those days.

She and Elmo moved to Tucson when he went to work for the railroad, and lived in a little red brick house on South Third Street that had two chinaberry trees in the front yard and a chicken wire fence—not a *nice* neighborhood, railroad folks mostly, though. She used to like to get ice cream at that Chinaman's store on the corner, and she still taught Sunday school at the Methodist church on South Fourth Street. They could have lived on in Tucson. Elmo was a special agent for the railroad—she always hated to hear him called a railroad "bull," it was such a disgusting term—and it was his work to police the trains and yards in his division, so Tucson would have done as good as *Healy,* which was no town atall, just a divison point on the railroad, with a hotel for the layover train crews and a couple of saloons and scarce half a dozen *families.* But Elmo *would* move to *Healy.* He was deputized in the county because he was a railroad—*agent.* And because *Healy* was just a wide place, Elmo was the *only* law officer. He said no one interfered with him in *Healy.* That was true enough. But there was no talking to him about that any more, and precious little else.

Watching him bent over his book, she heard him suddenly hiss and catch his breath. He hunched closer to the open pages. She shivered again. Those books Elmo *studied,* all those—*bodies.* All with their works a-showin . . . It was like marriage—there was a side to it that a decent woman couldn't *talk* about, and those books were like that . . .

Elmo Hollenbeck did not drink or smoke or play cards for money or fun. His austere spirit fed on bitter fodder. As a young man he had only read the two Testaments or an occasional tract. But in 1902 he had discovered two books in the window of a second-hand bookstore on Congress Street in Tucson. The books were huge, their black buckram covers embossed with baroque funereal urns and drapes—one was *Paradise Lost,* the other Dante's *Inferno.* Then he had bought a big three-power reading glass, for it was not Milton's soaring verse that had captured him, or the florid translation of Dante's *terza rima,* but the awesome illustrations of Gustave Doré, page after page of naked figures writhing in vast lakes of fire, or coiling and squirming like hot snakes among the pinnacles of Hell, horny-winged celestial sinners abandoned and cast out by God, streaming down, down the boiling firmament—all rendered on the pages in wood engravings of brain-searing detail.

Elmo Hollenbeck, behind his three-power glass, could slip, as he was now doing, somehow *inside* the bounds of the page, there to roam like the melancholy, robed Dante, among the distraught, naked, fleshy shambles of condemned sinners, staring feverishly at the tossing bodies, the incredible clusters of breasts and naked thighs—so that his breath came hissing and clouded the glass.

Rosemary shuddered to see him set the book on the fumed oak table and climb to his feet, his eyes still fixed and staring at the hot-moist image shimmering on his retina.

Her first instinct was always the same—*always,* because it was a ritual, their parts fixed, inflexible, known, the way a recurring nightmare is known, recognized yet not evaded, played out as if forever happening for the first time, happening in the only way acceptable to each of them.

Fleeing into the bedroom and slamming the door behind her, she ran to the window, instinct telling her to darken the room, and there she pulled down the green-black roller shade and drew the thick mauve drapes over them and stood there with her arms up and clinging to them, the ball fringe dangling against her wrists as she listened through the pounding of her heart. His footsteps came to her ears like thunder.

The door was ripped open, hinges shrieking. He kicked

the door shut. Found her in the dark. She gasped, whimpered, as Elmo Hollenbeck, for his part, ended his tortured stroll through the anterooms of Hell by falling amongst the wriggling bodies of the condemned, brought down, toppled . . .

The wail of a distant steam whistle pierced the ball-fringed drapes. Elmo's breath came in hoarse, shuddering gasps. The whistle wailed again. The Yuma freight. A chair toppled with a crash. Elmo reached the door, flung it open and staggered into yellow light, pulling on vest, coat, his badge pinned inside (he liked it best when they did not see the badge). With the roll-brimmed hat set square, and the long-barreled .44 buckled on, he shouldered through the screen door; the cat, seeking to slip in between his feet, took a kick in the rib cage, squalled. He strode in the dark toward the tracks, two hundred yards away.

The headlight of the distant freight was a slender needle thickening, flaring as it bored head-on. He reached the tracks and stopped, hearing the faint song of the freight in the steel of the rails. He crossed the tracks and walked through a pool of light to the station shed. He stepped inside a door and reached up high to take down an instrument of his trade. Slick and heavy, bearing in one end a looped rawhide thong, it came to his hand. It was a pick handle.

The steam whistle sounded again. The adobe earth quivered under the feet of the railroad bull. The headlight beam from the approaching locomotive streamed down the shining steel. Walapai Sam, his pick handle in hand, straddled the black river of Hell and waited for the sinners.

# (8)

The moon had risen to throw its pale light slanting across the desert. The mighty Hog engine and its seventy-car train, free of the long grades at Mojave and Sentinel, rolled now on the night-chilled steel, into the moon's pale white eye.

Clint sat cross-legged on the flatcar, the great thrashing machine swaying and clicking over him, his shoulders slumped, his hands, thick and lumpy as oak roots, hanging over his knees. His whole body jounced easily to the springing of the car.

Perrell turned to look at Buell and Bobby Joe, huddled together over the blanket-wrapped form of the old man. Dread sagged within him and he was thankful for the night and the moon-shadowed darkness.

The train slowed. Leaning out into the smoky wind rush, Perrell saw the sprinkling of yellow lights ahead, the squat adobes darkly hugging the moon-flooded plain. He touched Clint's arm.

"Healy?" he shouted, half a question, knowing it was. Clint barely stirred. Yet his big hands knotted.

Steel on steel, rumbling, clicking, she grumbled to a stop. Groaned softly, hissed and sighed.

Clint did not move, yet Perrell sensed the tautness in him. Voices drifted and lanterns moved along the train. Off to the left where the lights were clustered, other lanterns moved out toward the train. The new crew, Perrell thought. Behind him, he heard rustling, then Bobby Joe's voice suddenly swelling.

". . . got to get Granddaddy off this train!"

"Not without there is a doctor here," Buell said.

"Let go!" Perrell heard her struggling, then a grunt of pain and surprise from Buell. Perrell saw her jump to her feet and faintly saw Buell's hand go to his cheek where she had clawed him. The old man sighed.

"Either you help me," she hissed, "or I'll pull him off by myself. We ain't goin another foot on this—" She bent suddenly and took the old man by his blanketed legs, pulling him out of the little bay between the packing cases. His head rolled and his hat fell off. Perrell came to his knees and caught her around the hips with one arm.

"Hold on, sis," he said. She twisted, her body taut under the loose skin of the baggy overalls. Her elbow drove hard into Perrell's face and she pulled away, protesting, "You cain't *do* this to us!"

Perrell, with his nose stinging and one eye blinded with a wash of tears, reached for her again. "Dammit, sis—there is no help for him here." Buell rose behind her. She ducked under his arm, scrambled under the great plated fantail of the thrashing machine, stood poised on the timbered edge of the flatcar. Buell crawled after her.

"Bobby Joe!"

*"No-o!"* She turned and leaped. Landed scrambling. Lurched hard into the massive knees of Walapai Sam. Startled, he grunted—the pick handle slipped from his grasp, hung by the leather thong. Sam pushed away the frenzied body with one meaty hand, swung open-handed with the other, a stunning blow on the side of Bobby Joe's head that popped like a blown bag. She was flung headlong, to fall skidding into a loose tangle of arms and legs, her brain struck numb, her moist mouth open and clotted with dirt.

Sam took a step toward her, his heavy boot set to swing. "Hey!" Buell cried from the flatcar. "You *hit a kid!"* He sprang down.

Walapai Sam jerked around, faced him. "Come and git it, bum," he said. "Come and draw your time."

Buell lunged for him. Perrell, crawling under the thrashing machine, saw the kid with his fists up, high and awkward. Sam speared the butt of the pick handle into the kid's belly, then in the same motion brought it around in a short arc aimed at Buell's jaw, but the kid was sagging down from the first blow; the second glanced off the top of his head, dropped him to his knees. Sam pivoted and stepped back, savoring the moment, but the kid swung around on his knees and drove hard out of his crouch, coming in under the pick handle, driving Sam's back against the flatcar. Sam, unable to swing, stabbed down at the kid's skull with the pick handle, butt first. Buell's head thundered with the blows; he tried to bury his head in the big man's belly. Sam reached down over the kid's shoulders and punched the pick handle into a kidney. The kid gasped and his grip loosened. Sam's heavy thigh snapped up into his face and the boy dropped at his feet.

Sam raised his pick handle. Perrell lunged, felt his jacket catch on a finger of metal under the machine and hung there in helpless fury. He saw a hand reach out from the flatcar a few feet away and grasp the end of the pick handle, snatching it down and under Sam's chin. It was Clint. He ground the head of the railroad bull against the flatcar with the pick handle. Sam's right hand tugged free of the thong and Perrell heard the flat slap of his hand on the walnut butt of the .44. The pistol swung up. Perrell's jacket tore free. He sprawled forward and caught the gun with both hands. He bent it back, twisting at the same time, and felt the hammer fall—the spiked fang of the firing pin bit into the heel of his left hand. He pulled, and the gun came away in his hand.

"Walapai Sam," Clint said softly. "You won't remember me, but you son of a bitch, I remember you."

Sam's hand clawed for his face, but Clint jerked the pick handle, crunching it against Sam's Adam's apple, and Sam grabbed it with both hands and hung on, chinning himself, his wind whistling. He suddenly lifted both feet clear of the ground, let his two hundred and forty pounds drop, trying to rip free, but Clint's elbows were planted on the car bed. He grinned and jerked the pick handle, but Sam straightened his legs and sprang back and up against Clint, whose body bucked off the car bed, and at the same time Sam reached back with one hand and caught the back of Clint's skull. Sam bent and pitched forward as he came down. Clint was ripped off the flatcar and hurled over his head. He landed rolling and came to his knees still holding the pick handle.

Perrell heard shoe leather on wood and metal, saw men on

top of the boxcar ahead, all bums, clustered around the brake wheel, drawn by the sounds of a fight. He recognized Ernie and Knobby among them in the moonlight. It flashed through his mind that all of them ought to be running like hell. Perrell saw no trainmen, no lanterns moving on this side of the train, away from the town—all this in the instant Clint rolled and came to his knees.

And Elmo Hollenbeck, startled by the loss of his pick handle and long-barreled Colt, stalked forward, bearlike, toward the crouching man. He stepped between the tumbled bodies, arms outstretched. The pick handle lanced into his belly. Sam shuddered and went on. Again the blunt lance thudded. Sam clutched at it, missed, and the polished ash speared at his face. When he threw up his hands to check it, Clint swung the other end around and clubbed it into Sam's ribs, and as the hands jerked down, he struck again at the side of Sam's skull. The big man dropped.

Perrell heard the hollow, chunking sound of the pick handle and was amazed to see the yard dick pull himself out of the dirt, wagging his head like a clubbed bull. Clint stepped back.

Elmo Hollenbeck dragged up his head. He saw the two sprawled bodies he had struck down. One—the big one—was, like himself, trying to get up. *"No!"* Sam growled. His foot lashed out and battered the man's ribs. The man toppled and rolled onto his back. But the third, the crouching one, prodded Sam again with the pick handle. Sam whirled and grabbed for it, and the man rapped him across the nose with it. Sam felt the bone give way, and agony flamed behind his eyes. As he lunged off his knees the pick handle caught him over the eye, where the bone itself was sharp as a grub-hoe blade. Something hung down over the eye. Sam brushed at and snorted through his mashed nose.

On his knees, Sam peered up past the prodding pick handle.

"I don't even *know* you," he said.

The man laughed. "You're gettin to know me fast. How does it taste, Sam?"

"You got no *call* . . ." Walapai Sam fumbled at his coat, pulled back the lapel. The badge glittered. "See there?"

The pick handle stabbed. Sam pulled back, swung his head. Around him reared the boxcars, looming dark, clustered souls up there, huddled on their pinnacled islands. A profound conviction shook him. He raised a hand to them.

"The way I done—was *different,*" he said reasonably, earnestly.

A voice floated softly down. *"Kill the son of a bitch,"* it said.

The pick handle chunked against his jaw. Sam snatched at it, clutched and caught a leg and one arm, hugged them close. He got a foot under him and lurched up, feeling the cramped, futile pick handle blows. He laughed and turned toward the flatcar, knowing he would now break the sinner's spine on its timbered rail, and turning, his foot caught against Bobby Joe's hip as she struggled to pull herself up. Sam, bearing the great weight of that lashing body, toppled backward.

Clint heard the strange sound as Sam's head chocked against the steel rail below the flatcar, felt the convulsive tremor that shuddered through the body. Fingertips fluttered against his leg. He pulled free. Sam's heels drummed on the hard earth.

Perrell leaped down. "For God's sake—he's had enough." The .44 was still in his hand. He slipped it into his waistband and pulled Bobby Joe to her feet, then slipped a shoulder under her middle and heaved her onto the flatcar. Buell was sitting up, feeling his head. Perrell prodded him roughly. "Come on, kid—on your feet. There's a lantern yonder, coming this way." He looked up. The tops of the boxcars were starkly bare against the stars. The bums had vanished. Buell got up and staggered against the car. Perrell said, "Hang on," bent down and put a shoulder under the kid's rump, lifted. "Get her out of sight."

Clint was still kneeling by the sprawled body of the railroad bull. He looked up at Perrell, his face hollow-eyed in the moonlight. "He's had enough, all right—he's dead."

Perrell knelt and felt the thick wrist. "Pull him under the

car, quick!" he said. They wrestled the heavy body across the rail and Clint dragged it back behind the wheel trucks. Looking around, Perrell saw Sam's pick handle and hat, and slipped them under the car.

Footsteps crunched on the gravel. Yellow lantern light lapped and surged along the train, like tidewater. The footsteps and the light halted on the other side of the wheel trucks. Perrell heard the man singing softly to himself, a snatch of a ragtime tune: *"Now I know that you are mar-ried, and you know I'm married, too-o . . ."* The man's hand slapped at the journal boxes covering the wheel bearings. *". . . but, sweetheart-t, if you talk in your sleep, don't mention my name . . ."* The footsteps moved on. *". . . sweetheart, if you talk in your sleep . . ."*

"He's dead, all right," Perrell said, his hand inside Elmo Hollenbeck's shirt on the matted chest. He glared furiously at Clint.

"I never aimed to kill the bastard," Clint said. "He come down awful hard on that rail."

"You realize where this puts us?"

"He was fixin to kill the kid—would have, too."

"Who would believe that? He's dead, that's what matters, and we've got to see that he isn't found until—hell, I don't know—a cop killed in the line of duty. It will just mean the rope, and no maybe about it."

A man's voice sang out, far down the train: *" 'Bo-o-oard!"*

"She's pulling out," Perrell said. "Look, there's a stack of ties on the other side. Come on." He put his head out around the wheel, looked both ways. No trainmen near. Lanterns swinging, fore and aft. They scrambled out, dragging the big man's limp body by the arms, twenty yards, thirty, and dropped him in close to the end of the low stack, then pulled the two-hundred-pound creosoted timbers over the body, rolling them down until Elmo Hollenbeck was bridged over, part of the stack. Perrell stuffed the pick handle and hat in with him. The steam whistle wailed. The engine chuffed and a jolt rippled down the long spine of the train as she rolled. Clint and Perrell ran, but Perrell suddenly wheeled. He pulled the yard dick's pistol from his waistband and tossed it in under the ties after the body, then he turned again and ran after the flatcar. He leaped and rolled in on his belly under the thrashing machine.

The train gained speed, the wind stiffening to its steady gale. Perrell saw that Buell had pulled the old man back into the sheltered bay. Bobby Joe was sitting up against a crate, her head lolling, and Buell was holding her, one hand under her chin. In the darkness of the moon shadow thrown over them by the car ahead, he could make out nothing more. It was too noisy on the open car to try to talk, and he was too winded and shaken and sick at heart to want to try.

He put his head back and looked up through the skeleton of the great machine and saw the curved, serpent's snout of the blower stack thrusting, nodding and quivering, up out of the darkness into the moonlight, blindly staring, gulping wind. Perrell's mind shuddered like the clicking and chattering machine that straddled him, and with an effort he pulled his thoughts together. Bitterly, he saw himself back in the S.P. yards in Los Angeles at the moment the kid, Buell, started running for the train—in that instant, Perrell realized, he had turned away from his crumbling devotion to the movement, letting the train take him, aimless and yielding, on its current. And now the current was— Oh, hell, he thought, stop it. A man is dead back there and you had a hand in it. There is a chance, more than a chance, that you will swing by the neck. You had better start thinking. Fiercely, he shut out the sounds of the wind and the train, and began in his mind to lay out his cards, like a hand of stud—seven-card stud, it would be. The old man and Bobby Joe, Buell, Clint and himself. Walapai Sam was one hole card—what was the other? He shuffled and played the cards, over and over, without seeing that other hole card. If he let his eyes stray from the cards, even for an instant, he saw again the moonlit, upturned face of the railroad bull, battered, mauled and uncomprehending, as he looked up at the gallery of bums on the freight cars in the last seconds of his life.

To Perrell's surprise, the train suddenly stopped. Then he saw Clint leaning back against the iron-spoked wheel, silently watching him.

"By God, he had it comin to him, but I never aimed to kill him," Clint said. "I never killed a man before, ever."

Perrell did not bother to answer that. "We're like fish in a rain barrel as long as we're on the railroad, but we've got to get on through to Tucson and get clear of the railroad before that body is found."

A jolt racked the train. "That's a helper engine," Clint said. "This is the grade from Bosque to Estrella—she's a long pull." He nodded toward the low mountains flanking the track ahead.

Perrell looked out along the train, which was on a siding. Bosque was nothing but a few shacks, with the desert tilting away toward the crumpled mountains. A lantern swung and the train jolted again, the two engines chuffing raggedly. They were not long out of Healy—fifteen or twenty minutes. Tucson was another hundred and twenty miles, about. He thought they ought to be there before dawn. The flat, scrub-stippled desert fell away behind them. The flinty hills were thick-grown now with tall saguaro and spidery ocotilla. Clumps of cholla glinted, frosty and pale under the moon. The engines kept laboring up the long grade.

Everything hung on how long the railroad bull's body stayed hidden, he thought, and that would not be long, in a place like Healy. Then even if they got clear of the railroad in Tucson, they were still anchored to the old man. Not Clint, of course—he was anchored to nothing. Being an old hand, he would disappear when it suited him. But the old man needed a doctor, and Perrell knew that Buell would not leave Bobby Joe to handle it alone.

And what about me? Perrell thought. He tried to picture himself slipping away from the train, putting them out of his mind. He could not do it. Stupid and self-destructive as it was, he knew that he could not do it—the thought filled him with a hollow dread. Any way they went about it, they were bound to be picked up, and both Buell and Bobby Joe were wearing the marks of a fight. There were plenty of witnesses, and the tough cops in a railroad town like Tucson would work those bums over until they got a story that suited them. Then they would question the two kids, who would talk and talk, and they would all be implicated then.

The low desert mountains were almost behind them. The train slowed again, about to shuck her helper engine. Perrell rolled to his knees and crawled toward the narrow bay between the packing crates.

Seeing him, Buell leaned close. "I guess I ain't cut out for the fight game," he said. "It looks like pretty near anybody who wants to can put me down."

"How is Bobby Joe?" Perrell said.

"Asleep, I think. She tried to talk to me back yonder, but she didn't make good sense. That feller hit her an awful lick." He saw that Perrell was looking at the old man, who was propped up, his head wagging to the rocking motion of the train. "He wanted to sit up, you know, after she pulled him down back there when the train stopped, so I fixed him that way. I expect he's feelin better."

Perrell thought he remembered somehow that wanting to sit up was not a good sign—something about shortness of breath. The thought skidded away from him. With moonlight falling across the old man's nodding head and one shoulder, it was easy to think he was just asleep. Perrell reached out, felt for the old man's hand. He had to pull the blanket aside to find it. It was bony, sharp and dry as sticks of kindling, and despite the blanket, it was cold. He moved his fingers to the old man's wrist.

Buell touched his shoulder. "Do I remember right—that I seen that man stretched out on the ground?" he asked, then without waiting for Perrell to answer, he said, "If I'm right about that, then I'm thinkin we could be in trouble. Are we?"

Perrell was shocked to think that the kid didn't know. His breath exploded in a short, cold laugh. "We sure as hell are!" The train was almost stopped, and in the sudden quiet he heard himself shouting. He lowered his voice. "The man is dead." Hearing himself say it, the words sounded meaningless—furiously, he said, *"Goddammit, the man is dead!"*

The kid stared back at him. Perrell placed his fingers again on the old man's stringy wrist. He was unable to feel a pulse. He reached for the old man's neck, felt gently with his thumb. There it was, thin and thready, like the merest flutter of a dying moth's wing.

"But that's *murder,*" the kid said at last. "Did I— Who done it?"

"After he clubbed you, Clint went after him—they fell and the bull hit his head on the rail. But, hell, we all had a hand in it."

"He was fixin to kill me . . ."

"You can tell that to the man when he puts the rope on you." He could see the kid was trying to put it all together. "Look, we put the bull—put his body—in a stack of railroad ties. If no one finds it for a while, maybe we can get on through Tucson."

"Tucson is where I'm *going,*" Buell said. "Why don't we just scatter?"

Perrell laughed again, bitterly. He nodded in Clint's direction. "He's liable to pull out any time, but how about the old-timer and Bobby Joe? He needs a—" Perrell stopped. The kid would have to see it for himself. Buell put his hand under Bobby Joe's chin, and tilted her head a little. Her eyes opened.

"I'll go call Jack," she said clearly. "It's his suppertime."

"No," Buell said. "I'll call him. You go back to sleep."

Up ahead the helper engine, unburdened, chuffed away with easy abandon. The train's Hog engine took up slack with a rippling jolt and a metallic groan shuddered from the bowels of the great thrashing machine. The old man suddenly slumped over. Perrell crawled back to hold him.

# (9)

Perrell was not certain when it happened. The thin tremors that racked the old man's body gradually grew more feeble. The fluttering moth that was the old man's life stopped struggling and the wind of the train swept it away.

He waited until the train was stopped on a siding to let a westbound mail train pass. It sped by them, clacking furiously, in a gale of whipping wind. Then he told them. He thought at first that Bobby Joe was still asleep, that she had not heard him, but she crumpled slowly away from Buell's arm and began fussing and plucking at the old man's blanket, her shoulders shaking silently. Buell knelt beside her. The instant his hand touched her shoulders, she whirled away from him. *"You!* You wouldn't go with me to find him! This happened 'cause we was . . . *messin round.* Yes, it did. God seen us and punished *him* for it. Messin round . . ."

Granny Honeycutt's dog, Sport, woke him from a sound sleep by barking furiously. Granny rolled over on squalling bedsprings, planted his feet on the sand-gritty board floor and levered himself to the window. The dog's barking faded to a whine.

"See who's out there, Dad," Mrs. Honeycutt said.

"God*dammit,* Mother," he said. It infuriated him to have her tell him to do something he was already doing. He saw the spotted dog wriggling and squirming before a dark figure in the deep moon shadow of the chinaberry tree. "Who's there?"

The dark figure floated into the moonlight, slender, streaming a shawl. The soft voice shook. "It's only me—Miz Hollenbeck—Mr. Honeycutt. Elmo, he ain't come home yet."

"Well, maybe he's went on the train, Miz Hollenbeck."

"He always tells me."

Granny held his clock to the moon. Twenty to five. Near

time to get up, anyway. "You wait right there, ma'am . . ." He found his hat in the dark, put it on first, like any old-timer who was used to sleeping on the ground, then he was hitching up his britches, stuffing in the tails of his nightshirt, stomping his feet into the familiar caverns of his high shoes. As his hand touched the doorknob his wife said, "Dad, you go help that pore soul."

"God*dammit,* Mother," he said.

He carried his lantern but left it unlighted; they could see farther in the moonlight without it. They walked the full length of the single street and back. Under the stuccoed, arched portico of the hotel where railroad men stayed over, they saw a sprawled figure.

"That ain't Elmo," she said. "I can smell the liquor from here. Elmo, he don't drink, you know, Mr. Honeycutt."

He looked, anyway. She was right. It was a Papago Indian named Ponciano who worked, when he was able, on a section gang. They turned toward the tracks, with Sport trotting in frisky circles around them, sniffing and looking for places to wet. They hunted all around the tracks and sheds. They were talking softly as they walked, of the winter vegetables leafing out in their gardens, when Sport went to lift his leg against a stack of railroad ties. He barked once, then backed off skittishly, growling. Granny bent over the ties.

"Take care, Mr. Honeycutt. There's a sight of rattlesnakes around. One crawled out of my closet and I—"

"Miz Hollenbeck, I b'lieve Sam—your husband—is under there." He held up a hat and heard the breath hiss through her teeth. "Account of my heart," he said, "I'll need help to move them ties."

"I'll help you, Mr. Honeycutt." They began rolling the timbers away.

"I've had dealings with the law," Perrell said, "and there is nothing in my experience that tells me we can expect tender treatment from the law. What we will get is a rope." He looked at the blanketed form of the old man. "So long as we could help him, I—but look . . ." His voice was raw and edgy in his own ears. "I won't let my life choke off on the end of a rope. We've got to get away, and that means—"

"You can just go," Bobby Joe said. She was listless and dazed after the one outburst of grief and rage. She was crouched on her knees, next to her grandfather's head. "We don't need no one."

It was hours after the old man's life had slipped away, but it was still dark. They were stopped next to a siding and a switch engine was pulling a car out of the train somewhere back behind them. Low, barren mountains sprawled back away from the tracks. The moon would soon be gone.

Perrell knew that she was having trouble understanding anything beyond the old man's death. He had tried to tell her that the man who had knocked her down was dead, but her mind would not hold on to it. She merely stared back at him.

Perrell turned to Buell, who shook his head. "I've made up my mind. I aim to stick with her—see she gets to Tennessee, or wherever she wants to go. She'll get over bein mad at me. We'll get her granddaddy buried, then we'll go."

"Then you'll go to a hanging. Now shut up and listen to me, dammit. I've thought about this all night and believe me, kid, I know how the law works. It's meant to do a job—like that thrashing machine—but you get crossways of it and it will tear the heart right out of you. That machine is made to do just one thing: it goes down a row of shocks and chews 'em up and spits out wheat. You could run a man through it, too, but it wouldn't know or care and it couldn't taste a mouthful of blood. The law is rigged the same way—it's rigged to find *guilt* and that's what it finds. There were plenty of witnesses back there—all those bums. They are all bottled up on this train with us and as soon as the law gets hold of them, they will pin this thing on us. The law will have what it wants."

Buell shook his head. "I ain't leavin Bobby Joe."

"I know it. We can't leave her to go it alone." Perrell could not tell the kid that the two of them, left alone, were certain to get caught, certain to talk, certain to implicate all of them. "The three of us have got to stick together. We can't leave the train away out here in the desert—there is no way to travel and no place to go. That means we stay with the train as far as Tucson, but we had better be off her before she reaches the yards. Then—"

"But what about her granddaddy?"

"The law will find him and take care of him—that's one thing the law is good for."

"It ain't Christian."

"We'll see that it's Christian. What he wanted was to get her to his family in Tennessee. You've got a choice now. You can either try to do what the old man wanted, or you can get yourself, and me, strung up. And, hell, I don't know what would happen to her. But they would sure as hell pin it on you, with all those marks on your face, and before they were through they would nail me, too."

"She won't leave her granddaddy. I know she won't."

"She will have to."

"But where can we *go?*"

"We ought to have a little time in Tucson before they find that yard dick in Healy. Now, it wouldn't take them long to find us in town, once they start looking, but there is a railroad branch line running south to the border. Mexico is only fifty or sixty miles . . ."

"But there is a *war* goin on in Mexico. The U.S. Army is down there."

"All that is a long way off. The law couldn't touch us if we got across the border. We would have time to work out something, see?"

"But *Mexico!*"

There was movement forward under the shadow of the thrashing machine. Moonlight touched the face. Clint. "You do what he tells you, kid."

"I thought you would be gone by now," Perrell said.

"Gone where?"

"This thing is your doing. And you've got nothing to hold you back. You don't figure to be with us, do you?"

"I never was with you. I never was with nobody. I'm tellin the kid you're right about the law—just get off the train, kid. Keep your head down and your butt down and keep movin . . ." And to Perrell: "A man is better off alone—there will be too many of you."

Perrell shrugged. He found a small notebook and a pencil stub in his coat pocket. He opened the notebook and turned so that the moonlight fell upon it. The train jerked and began to roll again. "What's Granddaddy's name?" he asked Buell.

"Callaway," the kid said miserably. "I don't know the rest."

"Henry Gillen Callaway," Bobby Joe recited in a small, schoolroom voice. "He was born in eighteen thirty-seven. They was Methodist people. He was not easy to do for. He had a turrible temper on him. One time, he . . ." Then her voice was lost to the clacking wheels.

A man was asleep in a room of the old Territorial Hotel in Tucson. Hearing a rap on the door panel, he woke instantly. "Who's there?" he said.

"*Teléfono,* Mr. Costello." The soft voice pronounced his name the Spanish way. "You can took it down the hall."

"*Momento,*" Costello said, letting his hand fall from the butt of the holstered .44 that hung from the bedpost by his head. He, too, found his derby hat in the dark and put it on, then slipped into his trousers. Galluses dangling, he padded down the hall to the telephone in his bare feet. "Costello."

"Sheriff Newcomb, Pat." The voice crackled over the wire like frying bacon. "I just heard from Dennis, the S.P. man. There's been a killin in Healy Bend."

"Another bum, hunh? You ain't tellin me it's my man, are you?"

"No. It's Sam Hollenbeck."

"I'll be damned. Walapai Sam. That noise you hear is me cryin my eyes out."

"The thing is, whoever done it, it pretty near has to be someone off the freight from Yuma."

"Could've been the westbound just as easy, couldn't it?"

"No, that run hours later. Granny Honeycutt told me the body was cold as a dead snake, time it come through. Anyway, the Yuma freight is near about due in. I've called every man

I've got to get down to the yards. We're going to shake that
train down."

"Well, goddamn, that will play hob with what I've got to
do."

"I know it and that's why I'm callin, but there ain't a thing
I can do about it. Your man will have to get picked up with the
rest. After it's over, you'll get another chance."

"Like hell. You know him—he's no greenhorn. What I'm
afraid of is he'll go on the dodge now, and it could take months
or years to put a finger on him again. Dammit, I understood
we had it fixed so Sam Hollenbeck would take a day off."

"I'm goin down to the S.P. yards in ten minutes, Pat."

Back in his room, Costello twisted the light switch, and the
single hanging bulb flared. He poured water into the stone-
ware washbowl, peeled his underwear top down over his waist
and had a quick wash. Costello was fifty years old and weighed
one hundred and thirty-eight pounds, counting one ounce of
lead. There were six bullet scars on his wiry body, actually the
work of only four bullets, but two had passed clear through.
The in-and-out pair of scars over his hip were put there by a
.30–.30 fired by Harry Tracy, the Oregon Mad Dog, back in 1902,
the year Tracy broke out of the Oregon pen.

Costello pulled on a clean blue flannel shirt with a soft
collar, a plain black knit tie, a .44 in a shoulder rig against his
ribs, and sitting on the edge of the bed, he pulled on clean
socks and size five handmade boots. Costello was a native of
Atascosa County, Texas, and for the first thirty-two years of his
life knew scarcely a thing of the world's works outside of cattle
and horses, so he had never learned to wear shoes. He squared
the derby on his head, slipped on his dark suit coat, brushed
his drooping gray-flecked mustache with his fingers and
turned to leave.

He stopped at the oak table and picked up a pocket-sized
card from among a scattering of letters and telegraph forms.
On one side of the card was a photograph, head and shoulders,
of a hard-looking, gaunt man, the face marked with what
might have been recent scars. On the other side, the top line
said P.N.D.A. (for Pinkerton National Detective Agency), with

*Denver* written in by hand. Below, also filled in by hand, the card carried such particulars as NAME: Ellred Clinton; ALIAS: none; NATIVITY: De Witt, Mo.; OCCUPATION: miner, powder man; CRIMINAL OCCUPATION: train robber. Farther down the card, following statistics of height, weight, color of eyes and hair, and so on, there was written: *Yuma Pen 1904 to 1909—transf to Ariz Pen at Florence 1909.*

And under the telegraph forms, Costello saw again the florid signature on a letter and the last couple of lines: ". . . any lengths necessary to recover the proceeds of that robbery which amounts, as you know, to some $60,000 and therefore put the matter to rest and close the file." At the top of the letterhead, ogling him stiffly from among the names of the officers and directors of the detective agency, was the celebrated Pinkerton eye, rendered in wood engraving and bearing beneath it the legend WE NEVER SLEEP.

Costello pocketed the card and left the room.

# (10)

*To Whom It May Concern:*
*You are asked to give these mortal remains the Christian care and respect due a Methodist veteran of the Confederacy. His name is Henry Gillen Callaway—b. 1837—Tennessee—please mark grave—friends & family will enquire*

Perrell folded the note and carefully put it in the old man's bib pocket where it would be seen. Bobby Joe was crying silently. He pushed her hands away and pulled the blanket neatly around the old man's body.

Day was breaking. In the first glimmer of gray light, he saw the blood on the planked decking of the car. Not wanting

Bobby Joe to see it, he tore what was left of the rotting canvas off the packing crate and covered the deck there as best he could. Then he turned back to Buell and Clint.

The train slowed, the Hog engine laboring. Lights were scattered ahead on both sides of the tracks. Tucson. Massive mountains, purple-black against graying sky.

Clint said, "There's a long slow grade as she gets near town, then she levels off into the yards. But she will be goin slow and that's the time to leave her, long before she gets to the yards."

"How do we get her to go with us?" Buell's voice in Perrell's ear was shaky. He indicated Bobby Joe with his thumb.

"We can either drag her or lie to her," Perrell said. "I would rather lie to her." He turned and knelt in front of Bobby Joe. He took her face in both his hands and leaned close, to make himself heard.

"Now, listen to me, sis. Granddaddy is past helping—you understand that? We've got to leave the train." He felt her shudder. "There's no way out of that. But we will see to it that the right people come to look after him. Understand?" Shivering, she nodded. "All right, then, you do just what I tell you to and don't make any noise or fuss about it, because we don't want the *wrong* people to get on to this. They would just come down hard on all of us, and Granddaddy would fail of getting Christian treatment . . ."

Perrell faltered, choking on the empty words. *"Promise?"* he said desperately, as he might have to a child.

The train was crawling—that would be the long, slow grade. The thrashing machine racked and squealed. Lights began sliding past—adobe houses near the tracks, sparse, scattered at first, then solid blocks of them as the train drew into town, more lights winking on as working people stirred from sleep. Perrell leaned out into the wind. Thirty cars ahead, the engine's head lamp bored down the dark track. The steam whistle wailed. Crossings. The engine coughing a slow *chuff —chuff—chuff.* A horse-drawn milk wagon moved slowly along the roadway, parallel to the tracks.

Up ahead, bright light suddenly speared against the train

from a side street—auto head lamps, he saw, as the lights swung with the train and moved on alongside it. Other cars were following then and turning, too, five or six right there at that cross street, and farther on, the side of the train flared brightly again, so there were more autos coming in, all along the way. Figures of running men scurried darkly against the streaming light, turned down the narrow dirt street that flanked the railroad right of way.

"They found him, dammit," Perrell said. He felt his belly coil with fear.

Just ahead, a big, blunt-nosed motor truck backed away from the row of squat buildings on the far side of the street, turning. Its rear end rocked up onto the railroad right of way.

"Right there—behind the truck," Perrell said. "Jump, kid." He saw Buell go over the side and run. He put his arm around Bobby Joe's shoulders and swung her to the edge of the flatcar.

"No-o," she moaned, and began to struggle. Unexpectedly, Clint was suddenly there, taking her other arm. "Now," he said, and together they swung her over and down. Buell caught her, stumbling, as Perrell and Clint jumped together. The truck's unmuffled exhaust blatted, mingled with the steely rumble of the train as, up on the flatcar, the great saurian hulk of the thrashing machine shivered and clicked and blindly fled.

A wailing cry emerged from Bobby Joe's throat. Perrell hugged her close, pressed her face against his jacket. "You promised, sis . . ." The truck was pulling away. "Come on now." She clung to him. Ahead, across the road, the kid and Clint ducked through a doorway. The kid turned and waved, his figure ghostly in the gloom. Half carrying Bobby Joe, Perrell went into the building.

He smelled cement, mortar, raw wood. The building was open to the sky. In the faint light, he saw stacked bags of cement, a pile of brick, and along one wall, stacked lumber. Ladders, buckets, mixing hoes, sawhorses cluttered the place. Holding Bobby Joe close, he sank onto the stacked lumber. The kid and Clint flattened themselves against the wall next to a front-window opening. A moment later the caboose trundled by and the grumble of the train faded. Light flared again and Perrell saw two big touring cars slowly trailing the train into the yards. They were both filled with men, many of them standing on the running boards.

"The place is swarmin with bulls," Clint said. "They'll strip that train down to the bone."

Perrell looked up past the roofless walls—the sky was pearling, tinged with rose. He was startled now to see the open room clearly. Bobby Joe's fingers clutched at his jacket and he saw dirt etched into the creases of her hand. "We've lost the dark . . ." His words sounded weak and inane in his ears.

The distant rumble of the train died. They heard shouts. Another auto sped by and the dust of its passing billowed through the open door. Clint and the kid both peered around the window frame after the auto.

"Oh-oh, Jesus," the kid said. "Look at that guy runnin." A moment later, he winced and turned away to sag against the wall.

"There's one poor bastard with a busted head," Clint said.

"Look, it won't be a rube cop running this," Perrell said. He was holding Bobby Joe's head gently against his shoulder. "He will pull some men out of the yards to comb back this way. We've got to get moving."

"You mean split up?" Buell said.

"No, wait." Perrell was concentrating fiercely. "They don't know anything about us yet, but an hour from now they'll begin to know what we look like. Hell, some of the bums who saw us in Healy are already trying to talk. Right?" He looked at the sky again, a long tail of cirrus clouds flaring red above them. A man in overalls with a lunch pail under his arm walked past the open door of the building and seeing them, nodded. "Mornin, gents," he mumbled behind his morning cigar.

Perrell stood suddenly. "Listen, it must be close to seven o'clock—it's *working* time. Kid, you make up a two-man load. Stack some lumber on that ladder—boards and stuff." He peeled Bobby Joe's fingers off his coat. She appeared dazed.

Her eyes were red and wet. Perrell said, "Don't move now, sis." He dug a double handful of cement from an open bag and began to dust it on her and slap it onto her overalls. He patted some on her cheeks. He slapped what was left onto his own dark suit. He put the wire bails of two battered, mortar-encrusted buckets into her hands.

"All you have to do is carry these buckets—will you do that?" She nodded, staring past him. He turned to Clint. "Do you know how to get to that branch line that goes to the border?"

"It comes out of the yards, then turns south, over yonder," the big man growled. "It's some piece to walk."

"Well, are you with us?" Perrell glared at him. "If you are, you can take one end of that ladder." It was a twelve-foot ladder, now covered with half a dozen long lengths of one-inch boards. Buell tossed Perrell's blanket roll and his own onto the ladderload, then threw a light, mortar-spattered canvas over them. Clint put his own bindle on the ladder and covered it.

Perrell picked up four or five long paper rolls of construction blueprints that were standing in an empty nail keg, and tucked them under his arm. "When you go out the door," he said, "walk toward them, not away from them, and walk like you had a long day's work ahead of you. And whatever you do, don't run. You can turn south at the first corner to get clear of the tracks. Right?"

Clint grunted.

"Let's go, then." Perrell stepped out onto the dirt sidewalk, pulling Bobby Joe by the sleeve of her denim jacket. Staring, she tottered after him, followed by Clint and Buell carrying the ladder.

Three men hurried toward them, almost running, one with a sawed-off shotgun, a chunky man. Their eyes roved excitedly. Perrell slapped his leg with a rolled blueprint and headed directly for the chunky one.

"Gangway, there, gents," he snarled. The chunky one with the shotgun had to break stride and go around him.

"Well, god*damn*," he said without looking at them, and hurried on.

Swaggering and slapping his leg with the blueprint, Perrell led them half a block past old adobe houses, some with tiny yards, some built right up against the sidewalk. At the corner, he turned right. A sign said COURT STREET. He looked back. Bobby Joe shambled after him, a single tear streaking the cement dust on her cheek. Two more deputies ran past them toward the tracks. Neither gave them a glance. Perrell let Clint and Buell come abreast of him.

"See? Nobody messes with a workingman—they're afraid it might cost some rich bastard two bits' worth of a man's sweat."

Narrow streets, hugged close by squat, shuttered adobes. Short blocks, a cross street—COUNCIL. A black Dodge touring car bore down on them. Perrell stepped into its path, casually flagging with a rolled-up blueprint. Brakes squealed and the driver furiously pounded the horn button—*ah-oogah,* the horn blared. He leaned out over the door. *"Move* it!" Perrell ignored him, stood fast and waved his crew across. The driver hit the horn again.

Inside the car, Sheriff Newcomb leaned forward in the back seat and tapped the deputy who was driving on the shoulder.

"What the hell, Sid," he said mildly, then he went on, "All right, go on down and follow the tracks a ways once more, then swing back on Pennington." And to Pat Costello, beside him, he said, "We'll stop at the jail—the boys will be bringin some of them in about now."

Costello's thoughts wandered restlessly, though his eyes were drawn to the foreman who had flagged down the car. "It won't matter none to me. You've spoilt my game."

"You can blame Sam Hollenbeck."

"Whoever done that deserves a medal and you know it. Now some bum will croak for it instead. Where is the justice in that?"

"Damned if I know," the sheriff said. The car turned obliquely onto Toole Street, parallel to the railroad tracks. Ahead, three deputies with shotguns were hustling some bums off a loading platform next to a warehouse siding. A big black police wagon waited below. One of the bums was staggering, holding his head. The sheriff said, "How come you to lose track of Clinton in the first place, if he done his time at Florence?"

"He fooled me," Costello said. "I looked for him to go directly to Bisbee, or maybe El Paso, then to go into Mexico, the way they done after they blowed the express car. But when he got out of the pen, he went the other way. Lost me. You see, he had a wife. It took me a while to trace her. She is married now to a section foreman on the S.P., Mexican feller—she was Mexican herself—and they live over on the coast. San Luis Obispo. I don't know what he done over there—maybe he just wanted to *see* her. Anyway, I put out word along the line to—"

"That's how come Bob Edmon called me from Yuma," the sheriff said. They cruised slowly down the length of the S.P. yards. The sky was aflame over the Rincon mountains in the east. The sheriff told the deputy to go on back toward the jail.

"I heard from a yard dick in L.A. about him, too," Costello said. "Then from Edmon. Reckon how the feller must have felt there in Yuma, sleepin in the hobo jungle—you know he done five years there in the old pen, up to nineteen and nine, when they shut the place down."

"He was a damn good man with dogs—he had charge of the hound kennel at Florence and he would go out with them on manhunts. He worked for me four or five times."

"Dynamite was his regular line of work. He was a powder man down at Helvetia," Costello said, "and then over at Tombstone. He was in Bisbee then and got into that strike in nineteen and four and busted a deputy in the jaw. He drawed six months for that . . . Hell, I wouldn't want to tell nobody about it, but I hit a deputy myself once, when I was about twenty-two or -three. Son of a bitch needed hittin awful bad, too, so I give him the best I had. Miles City, Montana, that was." Memory tinged his flat voice, like a thin film of old dust.

"Well, he was a damn good man with dogs," the sheriff said. The Dodge pulled up next to the jail. Costello could see the faces of curious prisoners pressed to the barred windows. Two or three cars had already arrived and deputies stood around a small group of prisoners. The police wagon pulled in behind the Dodge with its bell sounding *ding-ding-ding*. Another group of prisoners climbed down the steps at the rear of the wagon. A tall, skinny deputy saw the sheriff's Dodge and trotted over to it, grinning.

"You see the big guy there, Sheriff? He claims he seen it and he is anxious to talk. I think we're in luck."

"I see him. Public-spirited, is he? Let's just find out why he is so anxious to pin it on someone else."

The deputy frowned, intent on the sheriff's implication.

Costello saw the big prisoner suddenly try to lunge past the deputies who ringed him. In that moment it seemed to Costello that the big man was trying to get at a group of workmen who were just walking out into the street, led briskly by a foreman, but he never reached them. One of the deputies instantly swung his riot stick and rapped the prisoner smartly across the back of the head. The prisoner sagged into the dust with a choking cry. Another prisoner, a small man with sad eyes, bent over him. The workmen walked on, looking somehow vaguely familiar to Costello.

The foreman held up an oncoming car to let his men through. Suddenly Costello remembered and grinned, then his glance fell on the last of the passing workmen, a big man carrying one end of a ladder stacked with scaffolding.

"Did you see him try to bust loose?" the skinny deputy was saying. "Talk about a *confession*."

"I expect he'll have somethin to tell us," the sheriff said. "Are you comin, Pat?"

"No, I b'lieve I'll just take me a walk around—maybe my man will turn up somewheres in this mess."

# (11)

A stern-faced old lady in a long black dress and bonnet saw Bobby Joe carrying the two buckets.

"That chile ought to be in school!" she scolded Perrell.

He stopped and said to her behind a cupped hand, "Madam, please, the boy is simple—he is doing the best he knows how."

Abashed, the woman stood back. The crew of workmen walked briskly past. They had walked south through the narrow streets of the old town, emerging into a rundown neighborhood of old brick and adobe houses with wire fences and narrow dirt yards sparsely shaded by chinaberry trees. Two blocks after seeing the old lady, Clint directed them to turn left. "The branch line swings south out of the yards on up ahead there. If we keep on this way, we will come to the tracks." Adobe dust puffed beneath their shoes. The familiar *chuff* of a switch engine sounded off to their left where the main yards were. The bucket handles squeaked in Bobby Joe's hands. Patches of bullhead stickers crunched underfoot. Houses thinned ahead and there were the tracks, bearing in upon them from the left, beyond a barbed-wire fence. The street angled off to the right to follow the tracks, and swinging with it, they shortly came to a gate in the barbed-wire fence next to a loading ramp and some sheds painted the familiar sooty saffron-yellow of the S.P. Three or four boxcars were on a siding next to the loading ramp. A big dray wagon drawn by an eight-horse team was backed up to one side of the ramp; a crew of men was unloading the wagon and moving its contents into one of the boxcars.

A handsome Locomobile roadster was parked close to the loading ramp. A man and a young woman sat in the car—he intently watching the loading of the boxcar, she fidgeting distractedly. The man was nearing forty, a trifle inclined to flesh, but well-barbered and well-tailored in a whipcord driving suit. The girl's fingers strayed across the back of his neck.

He frowned. "Cut it out, Teddie," he said.

"You said we would take a *drive*, Ev." She was twenty-four or -five—pouting made her look younger—and she was wearing a pale-blue satin hobble skirt and matching jacket, with a big motoring hat that was trimmed with pink roses and a vast swath of netting.

"I said you would probably rather stay in bed, too."

"Alone?" She giggled.

"Cut it out—this is one thing I have to attend to. If this shipment doesn't go through, the damn mine can't operate."

"Do you call this *development* work?"

"I call it keeping fences mended." He sucked nervously on his cigarette. "That mine is presently the taproot for the whole setup—I've nursed it along all this time, hoping the damn Mexicans would get their revolution settled. Nothing went right until the day Pancho Villa raided Columbus, New Mexico." He grinned suddenly. "That son of a bitch is the best friend the Americans have got in Mexico, because he finally got the Congress of the United States to send American soldiers down there. Should have done it, hell, *years* ago. Why they didn't declare war I'll never know—get the job done right. American soldiers could clean up that mess in six weeks' time . . ."

He was talking to himself, because Teddie was not listening. Looking past Ev's shoulder, she watched a small group of workmen carry some stuff through the gate into the yards. Rough-looking men. The two carrying the trash and junk looked like they had been fighting and the boy looked like the village idiot, but the foreman carried himself in a compact and jaunty way that appealed to her. She saw them pass the dray horses, and she began to stare hard at the foreman, willing him to feel her presence. It was a game she liked to play with men and had been practicing since she was thirteen. There was something delicious and risqué about playing it here in broad daylight, and at the same time it was *safe* enough, up in the Locomobile with Ev sitting next to her. The workmen were passing the rear of the Locomobile when he looked at her.

Teddie swung around to watch him. It was almost a physical touch when their eyes caught and held, and in those seconds, without in the least changing expression beyond letting her tongue trace moistly along her parted lips, she poured her entire being into the look she gave him, letting him *see* her through that look, the way she truly was and the way she could have been for him that very instant. She saw understanding flicker in his eyes; his cheek twitched and she thought she felt a ragged tension in him, but he grinned at her all the same and suddenly, bitterly, she wished she did know him.

"Well, why in hell," Ev was saying, "do you ask questions and get me talking my fool head off and then not listen to a word I say?" He put his folded copy of the newspaper in her lap and tapped it with his finger. "You could just read this . . . Pershing will have Villa in the cooler in less than a month."

Her hand swept the paper off her lap. It fell over the car door and flopped to the ground. "Oh, Ev, let's get out of here," she said. Instead he climbed angrily out of the car and stalked up to the loading platform and began talking to one of the men there, handing him some money. Teddie felt a movement at her elbow—it was the man she had been looking at. He was holding up the paper to her, still smiling, but a muscle was twitching along his jaw.

"You dropped this, ma'am," he said and she knew that he had seen everything she had meant for him to see.

"No, you keep it." She pushed back the paper and for a moment she let her fingers touch his.

"Any other time . . ." he said softly, then he turned and walked after the others. In a moment, Ev came back and climbed up into the Locomobile.

"Let's pack a lunch and go up to Sabino Canyon," she said.

Perrell caught up with Clint and Buell and said, "Stop when you get around on the other side of that shed."

They turned the corner and he reached out and held

Bobby Joe's sleeve to keep her from walking on. She dropped the two buckets and sagged against a pile of crates. Clint and Buell put the ladder down, both tense and strained.

"This is what we want," Perrell said. "I heard the guy up on the ramp promise the other one that this car would be over the border by tonight."

"We're in for it now," Buell said suddenly, his voice sick. "I see some of them deputies comin this way from the yards."

A quarter of a mile back along the road, the Locomobile passed a wiry, sharp-jawed, mustached man in a derby hat who was loitering under a tamarisk tree. It was Costello. He merely gave the Locomobile a glance as he uneasily watched two men with shotguns hurrying along the railroad tracks toward the shed and loading ramps. He saw them look into and under three boxcars on the siding. They talked to a man on a big dray wagon, then one spoke briefly to the foreman of a repair crew whose men were setting up a ladder and some scaffolding against the side of the shed. The men with shotguns looked around uncertainly, then headed back toward town.

After a few minutes Costello crawled through the barbed-wire fence and bowlegged across two hundred yards of open ground to where a gang of Mexican laborers was loading tools onto a couple of handcars. In the atrocious Texas Spanish of his boyhood, he asked where to find the *jefe,* the foreman, and shortly, then, he was in a shack in the yards talking to another man, pointing down the tracks to the loading ramp and sheds where a big dray wagon was just pulling away. He came away from the shack knowing the numbers of the cars, and what time the train would be running south. He caught a ride part of the way back toward the center of town on one of the handcars, then walked the rest of the way to the sheriff's office.

"Well, did you get a confession out of that big guy?" Costello asked the sheriff, who was leaning back in his swivel chair with his feet on his desk and looking tired already.

"Dammit, Pat, you won't like to hear this, but it looks like Ellred Clinton is mixed up in this mess. The big guy claims he never done nothin himself, which I expect him to say, but there is six or seven more of them bums who all tell about the same yarn the big guy tells. I *know* all them bums ain't acquainted with one another. There is no way they could have cooked up the story between them." The sheriff ran a hand over his shiny head, then pulled his boots off the desk and let them thunder to the floor.

"What's more," he said, "we found a stiff on the train—an old gent, laid out all neat and tidy, but what a hell of a mess . . ."

"Well, what kind of a story did the bums give you?" Costello said.

"It don't agree in all particlars, but they say there was three or four guys on the flatcar where we found the stiff, and they say there was a hell of a fight with the railroad bull—that would be Sam Hollenbeck. The thing is, none of the bums we hauled in can put the finger on *anybody* we picked up. But they all say the big guy—Ernie, his name is—wasn't in on it." He sighed, then looked hard at Costello. "Your man never turned up, Pat. But from the descriptions we are beginnin to piece together, he could have been the—"

He was interrupted by a small elderly man with thick eyeglasses who shouldered past the deputy at the door and said to the sheriff, "I've got a baby to deliver over on East Ninth Street, so listen—I find that old party's death due to acute alcoholic—no, make it due to massive blood loss and shock caused by acute alcoholic gastritis. In other words, he got into some booze and bled to death. Gave up about a quart and a half of blood is my guess, and died two or three o'clock in the morning. No other marks on him. Someone"—the doctor pulled off his glasses and swabbed them with a food-spattered necktie—"someone tried his best to look after him. I hope someone cares enough to do as good a job for me when my time comes, but I'll likely be disappointed." With a wave of his hand he was gone.

Costello finished reading the note found on the old man's body and handed it back to the sheriff. "What do you aim to do with him?" He nodded at the note.

"Give him to the Confederate Vets," the sheriff said.

"They'll give him a hell of a send-off—drums and bugles and stars and bars. The whole works, by God. They're too old to start fights in the saloons any more, but they sure like a good funeral."

"So you're goin to try now to pin this on my man . . ."

"I never said that, but he is sure as hell a suspect now."

"It was a public service—if the word got out, he could get elected to *your* job, hands down."

"The way I feel, he could have the job—but, goddammit, Pat, Sam Hollenbeck was a *law officer*." The sheriff pushed back from his desk. "First thing to do is try to put these descriptions together so they make some kind of sense, then I've got to cork up both ends of the railroad again, and while I'm at it I'll send a couple of men down to the border."

Costello kept a poker face. "If it don't matter none to you, I could ride along with them, couldn't I?"

After the dray wagon and the crew of men left, Perrell walked out and looked over the boxcar they had seen being loaded. When he came back, his face was grim.

"The car is locked up tight." Bobby Joe put her face in her hands. He was not sure that she could handle much more of what they were going through. He heard the *chuff-chuff-chuff* of an approaching switch engine. "All right," he said, "that car is a real old-timer—it's got '88' stenciled on it. It's got six big old rods down under the frame to keep her stiff. We'll ride the rods."

"Won't they see us when they go to put the train together?" Buell said. Perrell saw that the whole side of the kid's face was stained a nasty yellow from the blow of the yard dick's knee, back in Healy. And Bobby Joe wore a purple-green patch running from her temple into her left eye.

"We'll run some of these boards across the rods," Perrell said, "as far up there between the trucks as we can get. That will give us something to stretch out on. And most men doing a job won't look much beyond their own hands and feet. Let's go now, before the switch engine gets too close." He bent to pick up some of the boards from the ladder.

# (12)

The road to Nogales followed the valley of the Santa Cruz
River south to Mexico, seventy miles distant, more or less, and
it was more or less the same road used by Padre Kino over two
hundred years earlier, a part of the legendary Camino Real,
but it had not improved appreciably over the years.

Alvin and Dave, the two deputies in the back seat of the
Dodge touring car, were violently, wretchedly and repeatedly
ill with motion sickness. Costello, sitting in front next to Sid,
was queasy and kept his breakfast down only by a determined
effort of will. The road snaked tortuously along the edges of
the hills bordering the bottomland and it swooped sickeningly
into and out of a multitude of dry watercourses, tributaries of
the Santa Cruz.

A stiff March wind blew up from the south, off the So-
noran desert, gusting head-on into the Dodge, stinging the passengers with driving sand. And fighting the wind, the engine
soon became overheated. Sid stopped to check the radiator; the
cap blew off and his left hand was severely scalded with
steam, then when the engine had cooled enough for them to
go on, Sid gave up the driving to Alvin, the skinny deputy, and
moved to the back seat, where he promptly became carsick
himself. Thereafter the car proceeded a mile or two at a time,
with stops to cool off, or throw up, depending. Within sight of
the ancient, crumbling Tumacacori mission, a horseshoe nail
caused the left front tire to go flat.

While the deputies changed the tire, Costello was pleased
to walk around, although his knees were watery and he dis-
tinctly felt the earth move under his feet.

At Potrero Creek, five miles north of the border, the left
rear tire blew with a loud bang. Since the spare was already
in use, the deputies squatted in the dust and argued about the
proper way to repair an inner tube. Patching it and pumping
it up again was hot work in the sun.

When the tire was hard, they climbed back into the Dodge, but the car refused to start. Sid said he could crank easily enough with his right hand. He wore himself out cranking. The skinny deputy said a vapor lock was to blame. He wrapped his bandanna around the fuel line next to the carburetor and poured water on it from the canvas water bag that hung on the front end of the car. When Sid tried to crank it through again, the crank kicked back and whirled around, striking him just above the wrist. He staggered away from the car with both injured arms between his knees, tears of pain and rage squirting from his eyes.

"Oh, God, I b'lieve she's broke!" he cried. Just then the sound of a locomotive floated to their ears and they saw the train—fifteen or twenty ancient and rickety soft-belly boxcars, pulled by a bell-stacked little locomotive that had come out of the works in Schenectady back in 1880, now sturdily chuffing out her pension years on the Nogales line.

"Well, *shee-it!* Yonder she goes!" Sid moaned. "We could as well have took the train ourselves."

"The idy of it," Alvin reminded him unnecessarily, "was to beat it down there, see, to meet the train."

"I'll tell you whur you can put your idy," Sid said.

Dave said, "Hell, I'll crank her over." He did so and the engine caught on the first twist of the crank. They all got into the car and drove away after the train.

Their orders were to stop at the office of the sheriff of Santa Cruz County, since they would be in his territory. As Alvin drove the Dodge into Nogales, they saw the train stopped on the Arizona side of the border, alongside the steep-roofed stone depot which was on their left as they approached. The sheriff's office was across the street from the depot. Fifty yards farther on, the border lay at right angles to the street and the railroad tracks. It was marked by a wire fence running down the center of a broad cleared strip of land which divided Nogales, Sonora, from Nogales, Arizona. The fence was open for a considerable distance to allow foot, road and rail traffic to pass back and forth across the border.

Alvin swung up to the curb in front of the sheriff's office. The sheriff, whose name was Stanton, listened to Alvin without taking his boots off his desk. "Dammit, why didn't you give me a ring? I could have had my boys shake the train down as she come into the station." He had to speak loudly to make himself heard over a noisy switch engine.

"Sheriff Newcomb told me to do that," Alvin said unhappily, "but the phones was tied up and I figgered we could get here in plenty of time to talk to you and meet the train. Trouble is, we had a couple of blowouts."

Stanton looked at Costello. They had met before. "Is this anything to do with that wire you sent me a while back?"

"It might be." Costello was finding himself in the peculiar position of hoping that Ellred Clinton would have time to get across the border. The interests of the local officers were running contrary to his own.

The sheriff noticed the Pima County deputy, Sid, who had slumped into a chair and was glumly holding both injured hands before him. "What happened to him?"

"He had his hand scalded by the radiator, and the crank kicked back on him too," Alvin said.

The sheriff had a hard time repressing a grin. "Well, Doc Elder is just around the corner. We'll head him that way and then go look the train over." Reluctantly, he pulled his feet off the desk. "Goddammit, you should have give me a ring."

They walked out the door of his office just in time to see the last four or five cars of the train rumble across the border into Mexico, its noise mingled with that of the switch engine.

The train rolled only a short distance into Mexico, then stopped again, its rear end less than a hundred feet inside the border, in plain sight of the Arizona side. The deputies stopped running and went to the portal for foot traffic, where they began talking to a uniformed Mexican. Mexican soldiers stood nearby leaning on their rifles, staring at the gringos. The Mexican officer shrugged and smiled, but made no move to step aside and let the Americans cross.

Costello felt that the man was enjoying himself. He was polite, but he was taking his time about cooperating. Over by the train, a Mexican freight agent in a white shirt and arm garters came out of a glass-windowed office shack built against the end of a loading shed. Carrying a clipboard, trailed by an assistant and two Mexican soldiers, he walked along the train to the last car. Costello could hear the switch engine at work. The train was making up for the run south, he thought, and he guessed that the man with the clipboard would be checking the contents of the cars from Arizona against his own manifests.

Costello took an envelope from his pocket and glanced at the number scrawled on it. The next-to-the-last car bore the same number. He saw that the Mexican agent had finished with the rear car and was now climbing into the next-to-the-last car. Costello waited anxiously, but nothing happened. He wondered where he had gone wrong.

The bell of the switch engine sounded, down past the loading sheds on the Mexican side. Several parallel sets of tracks ran through the yards in order to allow cars to be switched from one set to another in making up trains. The cars Costello watched were on the second set.

At the gate, Sheriff Stanton was growing red-faced. Then the Mexican officer smiled, and graciously, reasonably, allowed the Arizona deputies to walk across the line. Uneasily, Costello watched them hurry toward the freight cars. He walked through the gate and followed them slowly.

The Mexican freight agent jumped down from the car. He jerked his thumb at his assistant, who started to roll the door closed.

A deputy said, "Alvin, tell him we got to look in the car."

The Mexican agent said, "You don' hat to tol' me nothing. This car is don' got nobody."

"We got to look in her," Alvin said.

"By God, I'm tol' you," the agent said. "I been inside this sonabitch . . ." The switch engine chuffed, its bell sounding *ding-ding-ding,* and a freight car rumbled slowly back along the near set of tracks toward them. The agent put out his arm and herded the deputies back out of the freight car's way as it rumbled between them and the car they wanted to search.

A small boy carrying an ice cream cone ran suddenly

around the corner of the agent's shack. He tripped and skidded on his belly and his ice cream rolled out of the cone into the dirt. The boy sat up, weeping bitterly. The deputies stopped arguing and laughed. Costello knelt by the youngster and scooped the ice cream back into the cone, and as he did so, he looked beneath the moving freight car to the car behind and saw movement, figures rolling quickly out from under the car, then several pairs of legs climbing upward, out of his sight, but apparently through the open car door. The rolling car stopped, then reversed and went back the way it had come, the engine chuffing rapidly.

The small boy licked the ice cream, dirt and all. Seeing the deputies grinning at him, he jabbed at them with a middle finger as he climbed to his feet. They laughed. He clutched at his crotch and turned an imaginary stream of urine on them. Then he ran. Alvin spoke to the agent again. The man shook his head.

"I'm tol' you—look in those car." He pointed.

"What the hell, Alvin," Sheriff Stanton said. "He just looked in this one. Let's stay on the good side of him."

The Mexican agent motioned again. The door rumbled shut and the agent wired the locking handle and sealed it with lead. The deputies and the agent went on to the next car.

Costello wiped ice cream off his fingers with a bandanna. He was thinking about what the dispatcher in the Tucson yards had told him. "That car will be cut loose at a siding— place called El Tanque, about four hundred miles south. Not far, but hell, with all the battles and trains blowin up, it could take days—I mean, hell, if it *ever* gets there . . ."

PART TWO

Mexico

# (13)

Perrell was dreaming. He thought he was bogged in a shuddering quagmire, a great slide of mud, and he could feel it sloping off into the void. Then voices, laughing and shouting, penetrated the slow grumbling rumble of the avalanche. He awoke in darkness that was slashed by moving knife blades of light, panic fluttering beneath his ribs, not knowing where he was or if his dream had ended. Slowly, the rumble of the avalanche became the sound of the boxcar's wheels on steel rails.

He crawled stiffly over jiggling splintery wood, put his eye close to a sliver of light. He saw a low, sandy knoll with four or five scraggly trees on it which were thick with hanging bodies. Below the trees, soldiers in ragged khaki uniforms milled around, some laughing and shouting and waving at the train as it passed. Others merely stared sullenly—those, he saw suddenly, had their arms tied behind them and were wearing the same loose cottons as the hanging bodies. Clicking and rumbling, the train crept past.

Perrell sagged back on the packing crate that had been his bed. His mouth was dry and gummy with thirst. In the dim glow of light slivering through the cracks in the boxcar's weathered siding, he saw Buell sprawled in sleep, and beyond him on another level of crates lay Bobby Joe. She was covered with one of Buell's blankets, Perrell saw. He realized that they must all have collapsed into sleep; he could not remember when the train had started to roll.

He tried to swallow. His tongue rasped in his dry mouth, then he felt a touch on his shoulder and turned. It was Clint, holding out a can for him to take, the lid opened and laid back.

"Tomatoes," Clint said. "You cain't wash in 'em, but they will cut the dust."

Perrell drank greedily from the can, the juice dripping off his chin. He thought he had never tasted anything so good. When the juice was gone, he took his jackknife and began spearing the fruit into his mouth.

"There's aplenty of canned goods here," Clint said. "Boxes of it. And I found something else—crates of dried fruit. Apples and such. Well, I opened one. The apples was only a thin layer on top. And I found tools, tin kegs of carbide—this stuff is headed for a mine, somewheres. But why is the dynamite hid in fruit boxes?"

"They must have a lot of trouble shipping stuff through, on account of the revolution. Either it is too quick to get stolen, or the railroad doesn't want to carry it. Supposing the car is fired on—I wonder how safe that stuff is."

"What I seen was straight dynamite, forty.percent. Pretty safe. You could shoot into it, too, but I would as soon not try, especially if it sat around in the sun on a hot day. I mean, you can throw dynamite on a fire and it will just burn. Blasting caps would be something else, though—they'll go off if you look cross-eyed at 'em. There is likely some of them aboard, too."

Perrell frowned and spoke sharply. "How come you know—"

"Know about dynamite? I'm a powder man—blasting is my line of work."

"Is . . . or was? I'm beginning to get some ideas about your line of work."

Clint hesitated. "Is. I done a little of it in the pen, too, from time to time. Not as much as workin in the mines, but some. Things like blowin stumps, ditchin, breakin up rock."

It was the first time either of them had mentioned prison.

Perrell thought that being closed up in the dark made it somehow easier for the big man to talk.

"I wouldn't call that *indoor* work," Perrell said.

Clint laughed, a bitter sound. "No. I didn't spend much time indoors. They put me to workin with the mules right away; then an old-timer died and I worked with the dogs, too. Used to keep a dandy pack of hounds in Missouri when I was a kid. They was good dogs in the pen, too—bloodhounds mostly, but a few blue ticks and red bones, too. And when there was blastin to do, I done it. I'll tell you—I've had aplenty jobs on the outside that was worse. It ain't the *work* that eats a man up. It's . . ." He was a man raging softly, helplessly, against the outrage of time passing.

"I did ninety days once, in Seattle," Perrell said. "It seemed like half my life."

"Try ten years," Clint said. "I done the first four there in Yuma—that old pen up on the hill by the river where we camped. Nineteen and five to nineteen and nine. Then they shut her down. Jesus, them was *dungeons*. Hot? A man's eyeballs would fry in his head."

Perrell remembered their camp back in the hobo jungles in Yuma, awakening there at dawn to see Clint hunched on his log, his eyes fixed on the dark hulk of the old prison.

". . . so goin to the new pen and workin with the mules and dogs, that was pretty near as good as gettin out, except for the damn nights." He shook his head. "A man has plenty time to think, in there."

"Well, tell me this. That yard dick—was he one of the things you had time to think about?"

"There wasn't hardly a day went by, for ten years, that I didn't think about him."

"Do me a favor, then"—Perrell laughed harshly—"if there was anything else on your mind that way, you could let the rest of us know so we could get out of your way."

"I told you—I never aimed to kill him."

"Well, I was just taking a train ride myself. I didn't really count on being wanted for murder, or getting sealed up in a boxcar full of dynamite and shipped off down into Mexico."

He laughed again, his voice sounding a little wild in his own ears. "Did you see those bodies hanging from trees back there? Hell, we ought to start thinking what we can do to bust out of this car."

"That desert out there is no place to fetch up in afoot."

"I thought you didn't like being locked up."

"You can bet your whole damn roll on that, but I'm thinkin we're better off to stay with the car for a while."

Perrell considered. "We could whittle our way out with jackknives if we have to. But you could be right—it was an American who shipped this stuff. If it's going to a mine, there's a good chance that there will be some Americans there, and if the car is carrying goods like dynamite, all locked up this way, I'll bet some money has been paid to *somebody* to see it goes where it's supposed to go. The thing is, how far is it going?"

Perrell was thinking that the train ride was like life itself—no way to tell how long it would last until a man got to the end of it. And, also like life, a man could travel a certain path for no better reason than the nudgings of chance along the way.

". . . and I found one other thing that will help us," Clint was saying, "if we have to be on this car very long. Over yonder, in that corner, there's a place where some bums must have built a fire, way back—there's a hole burned in the floor there. It makes a tolerable backhouse."

Perrell discovered that he still had, folded up in his side pocket, the newspaper the girl in blue had dropped from the big Locomobile when she turned her smoky eyes on him. Remembering, he felt her presence, warm and breathing. He shivered, squirmed on the packing crate until a sliver of light fell on the folded newspaper. It was a Tucson *Citizen.* He began to read. The train stopped many times. Each time they would crawl behind crates and huddle there, fearful that now the car would be opened. They heard and felt the jolts and clashes that meant cars were being pulled out of the train, shunted onto sidings, or that other cars were being coupled on.

Now and then the train would stop in the desert for no reason they could see. It spent most of the first night and part of the next day standing in the yards of a town—red, flinty hills rising close by, the same squalid adobes. A little after daybreak, a long column of mounted men trotted past, following the tracks, and a little later they heard the crackle of distant rifle fire. Then the train started up again, going very slowly. After a few miles they caught up with the mounted column. The men had dismounted and were sitting or standing around in groups, their horses picketed. The train slowly rumbled through what was left of a barricade made of burning logs and brush. Perrell saw several dead horses lying here and there near the tracks. Then open desert again, flat and brushy, with salmon-colored low mountains studding the plain at intervals.

Though interrupted many times, Perrell read his newspaper through from end to end twice. Buell and Bobby Joe slept most of the time—day or night, it did not appear to matter. Like pups, Perrell thought. But the kid had stopped going near the girl. Clint roamed the car endlessly, moving crates here and there, prowling, or bringing out different kinds of canned food for them to try. Perrell saw that Bobby Joe was not eating—thereafter, whenever he saw her awakening, he would open a can and sit down by her and feed her. Then he would simply sit with her, wordlessly, until she went back to sleep.

When Perrell had finished reading the Tucson *Citizen* all the way through again, he moved over to where Clint and Buell were sitting, eating. Clint handed him an open can of sardines. Perrell tapped the newspaper with his finger, saying, "This tells how Pancho Villa's men pulled eighteen or twenty American mining men off a train, somewhere down there in Chihuahua. Lined 'em up and shot 'em."

"They'll likely do the same with us," Buell said morosely.

"There's talk of war with Mexico in Congress," Perrell said. "What they have done is to send a hell of a big army of horse soldiers down into Mexico. According to this, they expect to capture Pancho Villa in a couple of weeks."

Clint laughed. "They do, do they? By God, the man who

wrote that has never been to Chihuahua. Them people, on their own ground, will be slippery as a tub full of catfish."

"You see where that puts us," Perrell said. "We've got to figure there will be some Americans at the end of the line, wherever that is. Maybe a place where we can stay put for a while, out of the line of fire. I'm worried about her . . ." Perrell indicated Bobby Joe, a mere blanketed form in the gloom.

"There ain't anything more wrong with her, is there?" Buell said. His voice was anxious. "She won't say nothin to me—not a word."

"She sleeps most of the time, that's all."

"That's the best thing for her," Clint said. "There is times that's best slept through, and this is a time like that. Leave her sleep."

The train spent the third night near salt water. The adobe sheds near the tracks had a moldering, stained look and the smell of rotting fish seeped through the cracks in the car. Then it started again at daybreak. Perrell had concluded that it was simply too dangerous for the train to run at night.

For a while the train rumbled along very close to the blue waters of a tranquil sea. The three men sat with their eyes close to cracks in the siding and watched fishermen hand-lining from small boats, which were painted in dark greens and reds and had high, sweeping prows and sterns. Fish were breaking the water all around the boats; sea birds were wheeling overhead and plummeting into the water, and the sounds of their cries pierced the slow, steely grumble of the train's trucks. Then the tracks bore away from the water.

The train stopped again shortly after they saw the fishermen. They heard voices, shouted commands, then women, the voices of women. While the others huddled behind their crates, Perrell squinted out. He saw soldiers, raffish and tattered, with bandoliers of cartridges, rifles, machine guns knocked down to carry. The women were carrying canvas-wrapped packs, cooking kettles, trussed chickens, serapes, woven baskets full of goods, and, Perrell was stunned to see, *babies* and small children. They all began to climb up onto the tops of the cars, shrieking, laughing, arguing, singing.

Voices were suddenly close. A burst of rapid Spanish sounded at the door of the car and someone was jerking at the handle of the dogging irons. Perrell shrank back; his belly sucked in tight with alarm and his heart thudded. Then he heard a man's voice shouting.

"Someone is givin 'em hell," Clint whispered. "Says to leave the door alone or he will feed their babies to the buzzards."

Footsteps rasped on the corrugated-iron roof of the car. Dust sifted down inside. The voices were right above them. Bobby Joe awoke suddenly and sat up. Perrell saw the whites of her eyes in the gloom, saw her mouth open to scream. He caught her quickly in the curve of his arm and pressed her face against his shirt front, whispering to her, "Just a lot of women and kids riding up on top, sis. Now listen, hear that baby cry?"

The train started to roll again, the voices up on top cheering and laughing, then starting to sing, one or two at first, then more joining in: *"Adelita, Adelita, mi novia . . ."* Sad and lilting.

The train stopped at several villages, always with much laughing and shouting. Late in the afternoon it stopped again. Perrell saw a siding—no village, really, just a few scattered adobes with brush fences. He heard a sharp burst of shouted orders. The roof of the car began to creak under moving bodies. Protests, complaints, a child waking up and wailing. More shouts. Perrell heard a metallic clank from the forward end of the car. A moment later the distant *chuff-chuff* of the locomotive sounded, the car lurched suddenly, then was motionless.

Yet the steely rumble of the train continued—the chattering voices fading, fading, until at last all sounds of the train had gone. The boxcar was left alone on the siding.

# (14)

Perrell heard the sudden roar of an unmuffled engine starting up. Squinting out, he saw a truck backing toward the door of the boxcar. Three men wearing big straw hats were riding up on the truck bed. A second truck was parked nearby. Beyond, the ground broke away from the track in gentle swells, blanketed with thick brush and cactus. Distant, hazy mountains were red with the light of the falling sun.

Perrell said, "Bobby Joe, get down now—there are three men, another driving. I . . . let them see me first." His mouth was dry and he heard a pulse thudding in his ears, yet his mind was curiously detached.

The truck's engine died. Hands fumbled at the door, then the dogging irons squealed. A voice, laughing, said, *"Ábralo, hombre."* The door rumbled back and light flooded the car.

The Mexican, still laughing, stepped from the truck into the car; seeing Perrell, the laugh died on his dark Indian face. *"Por Dios!"* he breathed, then he stepped backward, back onto the truck.

"Don Treci!" he called over his shoulder.

Nearly blinded, his eyes running tears in the sudden glare of light, Perrell saw a man turn from the steering wheel of the truck, a gringo wearing a peak-crowned gray hat, his eyes lost and staring behind round glasses, his jaw blurred by a stubble of reddish beard. In his hands, swinging up, Perrell saw the twin barrels of a shotgun.

*"Amigos—"* Perrell blurted, the word tasting foolish on his tongue. He put his hands up, the palms showing empty. "Take it easy, mister."

"Friends are you? By God, get out here where I can see you—who's back in there?"

"We're U.S." He felt Clint move up next to him. "Us two and a couple of youngsters inside. We're not armed."

"Well, goddammit, get 'em out here, only make it careful—I'm just pretty damn nervous. This car was supposed to be *sealed.*" He made it sound like a betrayal.

Bobby Joe and Buell stepped out into the light.

"Get your hands up!" the man snapped. Buell raised his hands, but Bobby Joe, her chin quivering, suddenly buried her face in her hands instead and sagged against Perrell.

"Oh, hell," the man said and lowered the shotgun. He climbed over the back of the seat onto the bed of the truck, the gun cradled in the crook of his arm. He appeared to be about forty-five. He was wearing a stained and wrinkled corduroy Norfolk jacket, a gray flannel shirt with a black string tie, and scuffed leather puttees over whipcord breeches. "I mean, it was supposed to be locked up at the border. I suppose you wouldn't want to tell me what the hell you are doing in it."

"It was sealed, all right," Perrell said. "We got ourselves locked up in it."

"Trying to hijack the stuff, I expect," the man said. Absurdly, Perrell wondered if the man ever cleaned his glasses—flecked and smeared, they caught the sun's dying glow, gave him the open-eyed stare of a fish.

Perrell tried to laugh. "No, just trying to get across the border without . . . without a fuss. You're out some canned goods, that's all. Nothing more."

"Nothing more you could get away with, you mean."

"I told you. We got ourselves locked in."

"How can you expect me to believe that? No Americans are coming over the border these days—my God, an American in Mexico has got one foot in hell."

"Look, mister, I'm trying to come clean with you. We just got locked up in it. We could have busted out of the car—it's just a crate—but we saw a hell of a lot of people hanging from trees back yonder. That was day before yesterday, somewhere north of here. And we decided we would do better to stay with the car, then, because we figured we might run into Americans that way."

The man scratched his stubbly chin. His blind-eyed stare gave him a curious, intent look—intent, but flawed. "Dammit, we're wasting time. I've waited for this train since yesterday afternoon. We ought to be loaded and gone."

"We'll help you. Let us—"

The man shook his head irritably. "Just come out of the car so my boys can get started. *Ahora,* Rafael, *ándale*—get going now."

The three Mexicans sidled uneasily around the four gringos, their huaraches whispering on the planks of the truck bed. They were short, sturdy, in rough-spun white cottons with frayed seams. The older man had a fine, thick black mustache.

Perrell said again, "Let us help you, mister. We . . . we don't even know where we are."

The man was looking distractedly at Bobby Joe. "Can't you get him to stop that? I'm not going to eat him."

"That's just it. She . . . she's a girl."

The man bent forward and stared myopically at Bobby Joe. Disbelief pulled at his face like a tic. He muttered something in Spanish.

"She's had about all she can take," Perrell said. "She needs a place to rest and get a grip on herself again."

The man stared now at Perrell. "You talk as if you expect me— Look, I'm in the *mining* business." He wagged his head.

Perrell said, "At least let her sit down—you can keep an eye on her and we'll help your men load the trucks. Hell, it'll be dark before they can get the job done now." Without waiting for an answer, he pushed Bobby Joe forward on the truck bed. She leaned against the back of the seat, staring down, with the fingers of one hand pressed over her mouth. "Go on, sis, climb over and sit down," Perrell told her; then, still looking at the man, he said to Clint and Buell, "Let's pitch in, boys."

The man glared at Perrell. "By God, you watch your step—you can go ahead and help load. I mean to see if anything is missing from the shipment." The Mexican with the big mustache turned his dark Indian face to the man, questioning, as Clint and Buell stepped back into the boxcar.

*"Bueno, bueno,"* the man said. He waved his hand distractedly.

The truck was a big old Hewitt with chain drive and a

stake body. The other truck was a Reo, newer, but battered too. Both had seen hard service.

"Well, then," Perrell said, "let's move the other truck up here so we can sort the stuff as it comes out."

He jumped down and walked to the Reo and cranked it. It caught with a roar, but ran roughly. He climbed up on the seat and backed the truck in close to the Hewitt. Perrell winced at the blatting sound of the engine.

"What's the matter?" the man said. He had put the shotgun aside and sat with his feet propped up on the cowling next to the steering post. Bobby Joe sat next to him half turned around, her head cushioned on her arms over the back of the seat.

"I just hope it is downhill all the way," Perrell said. "This thing barely runs."

"What you're saying is, you don't know how we got along before you showed up."

Perrell grinned and said, "That's right." He turned to Clint and Buell, who stepped out onto the bed of the Reo carrying a heavy wooden crate between them. "Let's show this man how working stiffs can move the goods."

The man shrugged, then he reached down on the floor beside the seat and found a bottle. He blew dust out of a chipped enamel cup, poured a splash into it, then held the cup toward Perrell, as if to toast him. "Go to it, boys." He took a drink from the cup.

"We had best keep the dynamite all together," Clint said. "It will likely get unloaded at a powder magazine separate from the other goods."

"You know about the dynamite, do you?" the man said.

"We was in the car for three days," Clint said. "Anyway, I'm a powder man. I can smell the stuff."

The man's eyebrows lifted, but he said nothing. He took another sip from the enamel cup. He had a clipboard in his lap and from time to time he checked it, making tick marks with a pencil. Then he put the clipboard aside and began reading a book. When the truck was nearly loaded, he stopped Perrell. "You said you're a working stiff—do you follow a trade?"

"Machinery," Perrell said. "Just about any kind of machinery is my game. Welding, too. Or shoeing horses, if it comes to that." He grinned.

"That other fellow—is he really a powder man?"

"He says he is. I wouldn't want to say he isn't."

"He looks like a hard case."

"Well, we have all seen some wear and tear lately—you could put it down to that."

"What about the kid? Can he do anything?"

Buell came out of the doorway of the boxcar carrying a wooden crate with a stenciled legend: IDEAL PUMP WORKS, NEW HAVEN, CONN., and under that: NET WT. 240 LBS. He set it down gently, kneed it into place.

"He can throw a hundred-pound sack of grain over twenty feet," Perrell said.

"My God, I believe you," the man said. He poured himself another drink.

Perrell straddled stacked crates up on the Reo, taking bundled twenty-foot lengths of half-inch galvanized pipe as Clint passed them to him. The Mexicans were passing crates of canned goods out of the car from one to another, tossing them with an easy rhythm, singing and laughing, talking softly. They stopped to admire the way Buell Ashbaugh carried the crated pump, and a little later, hundred-pound boxes of pipe fittings, two boxes at a time. *"Qué hombre,"* the youngest said. The one with the thick mustache shrugged elaborately and said, *"Es un niño, no más, pobrecito"*—"he's just a baby, poor little thing." They all laughed.

As they laughed, Perrell, with apparent carelessness, allowed the end of a length of pipe to swing across the seat of the Reo. He probed at the coil box hanging on the dash until he felt the pipe catch against the ground wire that tailed off the box. The Mexicans were pitching crates. Perrell jabbed, felt the wire tear loose, then put the pipe in the stack with the rest. The gray-hatted man turned a page.

Perrell roped down the cargo on the Reo. Clint and Buell helped the Mexicans finish loading the Hewitt. When it was done and the load secured, the man snapped his book shut. He climbed back over the Hewitt's cargo and looked into the empty boxcar. Then he said, *"Bueno—vamos, muchachos."* He motioned to the older Mexican and pointed to the Reo. "Chalo, Carlitos, *p'alla, en el Reo.* Rafael, *conmigo."*

"He's tellin them two to go on in the one we loaded," Clint said. "The other one is to come with him."

"What's he fixin to do with us?" Buell said softly.

The man made a cranking motion. "Rafael, *da le vuelta, con el* crank."

Rafael went to the front of the Reo and cranked it. Cranked again and again. *"Otra vez,"* Chalo said, motioning for him to crank some more. Rafael collapsed against the radiator and rolled his eyes. The others laughed.

The gray-hatted man sighed. He was chewing his lip. The sunlight, glowing red, struck fire from his smeared glasses. "I'll be damned," he said. He turned and looked at Perrell, who had climbed down to the ground. "Is that anything you can fix?"

"I might," Perrell said. He walked stiffly to the Reo, put a foot on the hard tire and swung up. Standing on the tire, he looked down into the engine compartment. He touched each of the plug wires in turn, feeling sudden embarrassment at his shoddy deception. He swung around and stared bitterly back at the blindly glaring eyeglasses.

"There's nothing wrong with it—just a wire I broke myself a few minutes ago." He reached in under the dash, found the broken wires. Taking out his jackknife, he quickly skinned the broken ends of wire, then twisted them together. He nodded to Rafael, who pushed his big hat back so that it hung down between his shoulders; then, muttering under his breath, he cranked ferociously. The engine fired and Rafael leaned against the jiggling radiator, laughing.

Perrell listened to the engine, then adjusted the carburetor mixture until the engine beat lost its loping sound. He climbed down and faced the man again, feeling certain somehow that the man had seen him break the wire, had let him flounder through his charade. Yet, the blurred face and the staring eyeglasses told him nothing. Buell and Clint stood silently in the door of the boxcar and Bobby Joe was still hunched on the seat of the truck, plucking at the frayed seams of her overalls.

Perrell was not certain that they understood what he had tried to do. He clamped his jaw, feeling stubbornness and fury both. Then he almost laughed, remembering how his stubbornness had made him refuse to pay the brakeman a couple of dollars shakedown money on that rainy night when the train stopped by the ocean at Gaviota. So he had slept under the trestle in the rain and the next morning he had seen the solitary drifter walking along the beach—everything that had happened since started there. He was still playing out the string. He laughed aloud, shaking his head.

"What's funny?" the man said. "You've put me in a hell of a fix. Do you understand that?"

"Yes. I understand."

The man shook his head suddenly. "Sixty miles," he said, as if each mile were part of a burden, a conspiracy against him. "*You* drive, dammit."

# (15)

The twisting, narrow road was like a pale scar winding through the deep-matted pelt of brush and cactus. Rising hills showed blue-dark ahead, to the east, then a bend in the road put the coastal lowlands where the train had run in sight to Perrell's left and for a moment he saw a dark band of red still glowing along the distant horizon.

He stopped then and lighted the acetylene head lamps, hearing the hiss of the gas as he adjusted the water flow and the muffled *pop* as each one ignited. Then he climbed back behind the wheel. The truck rocked ahead, lurching on hard tires. Ahead, in the hot glare of light, rose clustered arms of cactus.

"*Pit'haya* is the name for those skinny ones," the man said over the noise of the engine, pointing at a clump of the cactus. "The big heavy ones we call *hecho* around here." A lurch of the truck threw him against Perrell's shoulder. The road doubled back on itself, then hairpinned back the other way to make the grade.

"I'm Tracy Hazard," the man said, "and I'm the engineer at Dos Cabezas. I'm forced to admire your composure. It's beginning to dawn on me what it must have been like to be locked up in a boxcar for three days. I should have warned you. This road leads . . . to the tail end of the world."

Perrell fought the steering wheel around another hairpin curve. A branch tore at his sleeve, whipped away. "We've used up all of our choices," he said. "The tail end of the world will suit me just fine."

Tracy Hazard laughed. "Wait until you see Baroyeca."

"If President Wilson has ordered all Americans to leave Mexico, how come you are still here?"

"Most of us have left—that includes our superintendent and the two men who were doing my mechanical work. I'm the only *yanqui* left—working, that is. The wife of our super has stayed on, for reasons of her own. I don't mean to imply that her husband has abandoned her—he is expected back. After all, he is the super."

"His name wouldn't be Ev, would it, by any chance?"

He felt Tracy Hazard twist on the seat, trying to get a better look at him in the flickering, reflected glow of the head lamps. "Everett Sibley. How did you know?"

"I saw him for about thirty seconds at the time the freight car was being loaded, in the Tucson yards. I saw him, but not to speak to, understand . . ."

Perrell shifted down again to meet the next grade. The heavy roar of the burdened engine caused them to fall silent. The truck bucked and lurched in the gullied road. Tracy Hazard put an arm around Bobby Joe's shoulders to steady them both. Even with her head rocking against the man's corduroy-jacketed shoulder, she seemed somehow to have lapsed again into a kind of doze. Perrell thought that Clint was right—some times were best slept through. He remembered her back in the hobo jungle in Yuma, fierce and tough-minded, if you could say that about a little country girl. She has let her mind go underground, he thought, like a ground squirrel when the big freeze is on. And putting it that way made him think that she might weather what was happening better than any of them.

Sixty miles. Most of the time, a man walking could have kept up with the lurching, swaying trucks.

Darkly brooding, enormous, the Sierra Madre loomed against the rose-pale dawn sky. The road, swinging through rounded foothills, came abruptly upon a deep arroyo coursing down along the flank of the mountain.

"Arroyo Guajaray," Tracy Hazard said suddenly, pointing with his chin into the cañon. They were the first words he had spoken for hours and his lips seemed stiff as leather. "It runs on south and west into Río Mayo and from there west to the Gulf. But the sun will be coming up out of Chihuahua. Pancho Villa country. Of course, we are separated from him by the Sierra Madre"—his hand swept out in an expansive gesture at the vastness of the mountain range—"and a good thing, too— Pancho Villa would make short work of us gringos. I expect you heard about the American mining men his people shot over there at Santa Ysabel?"

Perrell nodded. The road sloped along the cañon wall to- ward a timbered bridge that spanned the dry and rocky water- course, perhaps a mile away. And across the arroyo, the far wall rose steeply, clifflike in places as it merged with the larger bulk of mountain, and from the bridge the road slanted back up to the right in a long grade. Following it by eye, he saw a cluster of buildings on an open bench far above the arroyo, almost directly across from where he now drove the truck.

"That's the village," Hazard said. "Baroyeca. Now look back along the edge of the arroyo to your left. Under those two rocky peaks, you'll see a kind of cup—a white house is perched there over the cliff. That's where we're going." He pointed. "Dos Cabezas . . ."

Perrell saw the distant house, and high above it, the two craggy heads of stone. On the lower of the two, a jaw of stone hung aslant. "Up there are the Dos Cabezas, the two heads. The one with her jaw wagging there, the people call La Vieja, the old woman—because of the way she is nattering at him, I expect. This road goes first to the village, then back along that cliff to the mine, a half mile or so."

Both the village and the distant white house disappeared from view as the truck dropped lower into the arroyo. Perrell wrenched the wheel and cornered hard at the bridge, timbers thundering under the hard-tired truck, then right again along the arroyo wall after the bridge, higher and higher. Great clusters of the monstrous *hecho* loomed from the bank over him, arms upthrust like giants throwing boulders down the mountain. Off to his right, across and beyond the arroyo, the foothills rolled away toward the gulf, still purple-dark and hazy in the dawn. Turkey buzzards—four, five, six of them— lumbered into the air from a lime-spattered shoulder of rock and glided across in front of the truck, their flight feathers splayed like thin black fingers.

The truck's engine snarled and throbbed in low gear. At the end of the long grade, the road bore off abruptly to the left on the bench of ground he had seen from across the cañon. Suddenly he was driving the truck along a narrow village street, bumping onto an ancient cobbled surface—smooth river stones, he thought, set in patterns. The wheels of the truck set up a tooth-chattering rumble.

Adobe buildings crowded close. Brick showed under cracked and fallen mud plaster. Tall shuttered windows wore grills of ancient ironwork. Double doors, deep-paneled, filled the doorways—one pair, weathered and cracked, sagged awry and Perrell saw with a start that the roof had fallen in and chickens were scratching and pecking under broken beams.

"That was the home of the colonel of the garrison back when the States were still colonies—Baroyeca was a provincial capital then."

Ahead of the truck, two boys in tattered serapes drove five or six burros along the street. The burros were bundled high with wood. The blatting engine caused the burros to break into a jouncy trot. An alley opened to the right and the burros turned into it, their ears laid back and their eyes showing white—the boys chased after them, laughing and whacking with their switches. Perrell smelled wood smoke, sharp and biting on the chill morning air.

The street opened into a narrow, dusty plaza, overhung with enormous old jacaranda trees that were aflame with flowers. A circular fountain, far gone in decay, caught the fallen blossoms. The open arcade of a marketplace lay beyond the plaza. Other streets branched away from it at odd angles. Perrell glimpsed dusty green trees through a narrow, cobbled alley and a tiered church tower of pale stone, rising.

"Swing on around the fountain to the left. The road goes back out of the village and along the edge of the arroyo to the mine." Hazard nodded toward the church tower rising beyond low adobes. "That tower was once covered with sheets of solid silver—this was Nueva España, man, *think* of it . . ."

Moments later the road turned up along the very lip of the cañon, and the dry bed of the arroyo lay hundreds of feet below. Far away to his left, Perrell saw the western sky still tinged with the dusk of night. The truck pitched and rocked, her drive chains chattering. A ridge of mountain lay between the village and the mine. The road swung in a long curve to round the lower end of the ridge. Abruptly, a gallows of heavy timbers appeared ahead, straddling the road, carrying over it an inclined wooden chute. Above the chute, a timbered head-frame shielded a tunneled opening into the mountain. Perrell saw a shed, a thatched *ramada,* between the upper end of the wooden chute and the mine opening, with people moving about under it.

"Go on under the loading chute," Hazard said. "That's *la boca de mina* up above it—the mouth of the mine. Those men are *tanateros,* ore bearers—see, they have baskets on their backs. One man can carry eight *arrobas*—that's about two hundred pounds, so he moves about four tons of ore a shift. It goes into that pile under the *ramada* there, where the women hand-sort it."

"Women?"

"Sure. They are better at it than the men—they don't stop all the time to smoke cigarillos and they don't steal much, either. One woman will sort over a ton a day."

Perrell frowned. Tracy Hazard grinned crookedly back at him. "This is Mexico. It's no different than the women working in the fields or the mills in the States." He shrugged. "Anyway, the good stuff goes into the chute. It holds one truckload. The other half of the chute is open—it's for the waste, to carry it over the road there. Neat, right? From here, a loaded truck has a level run on around the mountain to where we mill it. I opened this tunnel myself—the old *boca de mina* was right close to the mill and the men packed the ore to it on their backs. You know, there is a hell of a lot of ore in the ground that is no good to anybody because it is just too damn hard to get out. It would be like that here, too, if we tried to ship ore. Only the pure stuff leaves here. Bullion, that is. Bar silver. And damn little of that any more."

The truck rumbled between the straddled legs of the chute. Just beyond it, a low building of timbers hunkered on the edge of the cliff, followed by a low platform carrying steel drums—a powder house and fuel dump, Perrell thought. Ahead now, a couple of hundred yards distant, lay the white adobe house he had seen from across the arroyo. It clung to a terraced shoulder of rock, with the mountain rising behind it to the massive, blindly staring Dos Cabezas. Bougainvillaea spilled over a stone garden wall and hung down the cliff like a frozen fall of wine-dark water. He saw that the road turned right at the house, and swung into an open area of more or less level ground held in the mountain's rocky embrace. This would be the bottom of the cup Hazard had mentioned; of course, the arroyo side of the cup was broken away. Out in the center of the compound he saw an adobe building, other buildings beyond, stables, corrals, a tall chimney off to the right . . .

"Stop there." Hazard pointed to the far end of the long brick-pillared veranda fronting the house, where yellow lamplight still glowed through a window. Perrell stopped the truck and switched off the engine. The sudden stillness was like cool water.

Tracy Hazard disengaged himself gently from Bobby Joe, who was stirring awkwardly on the seat, a puzzled look on her smudged face. The Reo roared up alongside and Hazard waved it on.

"Amanda," Hazard called softly, "are you awake?"

A woman's voice answered. Perrell could not make out quite what she said, but he saw Hazard wince. "Mrs. Sibley," he said to Perrell in a half whisper. Then there was movement behind the window and the voice said clearly, "I couldn't very well sleep in the midst of bedlam, now, could I?"

"I didn't mean to wake you," Hazard said, "but I saw the light . . ."

She leaned out and looked down, pulling a light shawl around her shoulders. A long coil of dark hair swung against her arm. Her eyes were very large and dark against the pale oval of her face. "Oh, never mind, Tracy," she said tiredly. "I wasn't asleep, anyway. I haven't been to bed, as a matter of fact. Did you . . . ?"

"Yes. We had to wait twenty-four hours for the train, you know, or I would have been here."

"It doesn't matter," she said. "Have one of the boys put it on the veranda . . ." Her voice trailed off. She appeared for the first time to notice the strange faces on the truck. Her eyes brushed Perrell, went on.

"Yes," Hazard said. "But I have to ask a favor of you. I was able to hire some men to replace the ones who left with Ev, and—well, the problem is, they have a girl with them."

Amanda Sibley looked questioningly from one to the other of the truck's passengers. "I don't see—well, what does it matter? Send her over to the Domínguez place. I'm sure they will look after her."

"I would do that, Amanda, except that . . . the girl is from the States."

The woman laughed—a harsh sound. "She may as well get a start on learning the language."

"She's from the States," he said again, "and she has had

a bad time of it. She needs—I would be deeply appreciative, Amanda . . ."

"Really, Tracy." The woman had turned away from the window. Perrell saw her shadow suddenly, huge in profile, flickering against the ceiling inside as she leaned close to a lamp chimney for a light. Then she returned to the window, a frown line between her dark eyes. She had a black cigarillo between her fingers and regarded them now through a curling wisp of smoke. "You might have asked me before doing . . ." She blew a thin plume of smoke and looked away angrily toward the spray of sunlight that flared across the sky through the gap in the mountain. When she looked down again, her gaze fell on Perrell. He stared back at her. For a moment their eyes held one another. I have known women like you, he was thinking. In the old days you would have had a man beheaded for looking at you. He waited until she looked away, and he thought she hated that moment.

"Very well. I will have Lupe see to her."

She started to leave the window, then hesitated.

"But I really should *see* her first, shouldn't I?"

Hazard put his hand awkwardly on Bobby Joe's shoulder. "Her name is Bobby Joe Callaway."

The woman stared. "My God, Tracy—what is this?" She braced both hands on the window sill, causing her shawl to slip. She was wearing a loose eyelet chemise and its ribbon tie was unfastened, stringing down casually so that both of her shoulders were bare, and the chemise was saved from falling only by the fullness of her blue-veined bosom which now quivered with agitation.

"She is just a youngster, Amanda, and she's dressed this way because she has seen some hard traveling." Hazard paused awkwardly, trying to fill in his story. "There's fighting up north along the railroad, you know. I have to put these men in the bunkhouse and I can't very well put her in with them. It would not be—"

"Oh, God, Tracy, never mind telling me that. Have her come in. This is a temporary thing, of course." When she saw that her shawl had slipped, she caught the ends and pulled it back around her, yet something about the gesture was as care-less as if she had left herself uncovered. Her eyes left Bobby Joe and fell once more on Perrell's face. He remembered sud-denly the girl in the Locomobile, and the secret knowledge it gave him of the woman at the window made him uneasy. Then she turned away into the room.

Perrell climbed stiffly down from the Hewitt's seat and walked around the front of the truck. He saw Buell lean down from his place upon the crates to touch Bobby Joe's shoulder. "Bobby Joe," he whispered.

She pulled away. "You git away from me," she said.

Perrell reached up to help her. She stepped onto the tire and jumped down beside him and for a moment she stood with her hand on his arm, looking up at him. He tried to grin, feeling the gritty skin of his cheeks crinkle beneath the growth of beard. Her cheeks were stained with the dried tracks of tears, and the bruise left by the hand of the railroad bull had turned a patchy purple, but the dazed look was gone from her eyes.

"You never meant to go back for Granddaddy," she said in a small, quiet, but fierce voice. "If I could have got away from you then, I would have, only I . . . It hit me awful hard, his goin like that . . . It needn't have happened, except that I didn't look after him. It *needn't* have happened."

"You could say that about being born," Perrell said, "—about pretty near anything that happens."

"Maybe so, but . . . Anyway, I could tell we wasn't goin back for him when that big ugly Ernie seen us there by the jail." She sighed and her nostrils flared. "Granddaddy was as mean as sin most of the time, but I should have looked out for him, no matter what you or anybody else said."

"Hindsight is no help," Perrell said. "We did what we could. The law would have given you no comfort, I'll tell you that."

"Come on," Tracy Hazard said. "Mrs. Sibley is waiting."

As they turned and walked back along the front of the veranda she left her hand on his arm, a very feminine gesture that he found oddly touching. They mounted the broad flight of stairs leading to the veranda. Perrell saw that a long guttered ramp also sloped up to the veranda, next to the stairs. Tracy Hazard directed Rafael and Buell past them to the doorway, each carrying a couple of wooden cases with the stenciled lable COURVOISIER—NAPOLEON. A soft-voiced Mexican woman led them inside.

Buell came back out through the door and stopped next to them. "Señorita?" the Mexican woman said. Bobby Joe stood on her toes and took Perrell's face in her two hands and kissed him on the mouth, then she turned and swept past Buell—as if, Perrell thought, a lace train fifteen feet long trailed from her overalls.

Perrell felt the kid take him by the arm. "Now, what was *that* for?" Buell said.

Perrell pulled the big hand loose. "Dammit, kid, that was because she's a female—it was nothing to do with me."

Buell turned away and walked down the stairs, his shoulders hunched stiffly. He stalked to the truck and climbed up on it with jerky, furious movements.

"What's eating him?" Tracy Hazard said.

"He's sweet on Bobby Joe," Perrell said. Looking down, he noticed that the gutter that ran down the ramp along the veranda's edge actually emerged from the house, beneath the double doors, crossing the veranda, then to the ramp. Puzzled, he said, "Is that some kind of drain?"

Tracy Hazard laughed. "You could say that. A stream of silver drained through here, flowing from the mines of Dos Cabezas to the treasuries of Spain. That gutter was worn there by the hoofs of mules, over generations of time."

"You mean to say they brought the mules right in the house?"

"Sure. When the silver was smelted, the bars of bullion were loaded onto mules and packed up this ramp, right through the center of the house to the silver room. The house is called the Ibarra house, after the old gent who built it a couple of hundred years ago. Mrs. Sibley uses the silver room now to store . . . her brandy." His mouth twisted wryly. "Come on, let's get this stuff unloaded."

# (16)

Perrell started up the truck and drove it to a barnlike iron-roofed adobe building near the center of the open compound, almost a quarter of a mile from where the Ibarra house brooded on the cañon's brow. A big pair of roll-back barn doors were open in the side, and the Mexicans were already unloading crates from the Reo and carrying them inside.

Wire coops and pens were built against the end of the storehouse, where lanky chickens strutted in and out, squawking if the men stepped too close. A Mexican boy of thirteen or fourteen emerged, with chickens running after him, and began to scatter grain from a coffee can. Hazard led Perrell into the building. Inside, it was lofty and dim, with a row of dirty windows along the end to his left admitting a wash of light onto workbenches. Perrell smelled the forge even before he saw it—the acrid, scorched, raw iron smell of it, mingled with the other smells, of grease and kerosene and wood and dust. He saw the anvil, bedded on a thick stump next to a cooling tub half full of oily-black water. Tongs, hammers, files and scraps of iron cluttered the blackened bench, and beyond the anvil was the low brick hearth cradling a bed of dead ashes. Perrell's memory stirred and carried him for an instant back to his father's blacksmith shop on the Peninsula, south of San Francisco, and he remembered with a sudden pang how bold and strong he felt—five years old, he was—when his dad let him heat horseshoe nails in the coals and pound them out flat on the anvil, and the sharp buzz of sound when he tonged the hot iron into the cooling tub . . .

"The chickens are mine," Hazard was saying. He waved a hand—some of the gawky birds had elected to run after him instead of the boy with the grain. "One of my distractions, or maybe I should say aberrations. I'm a curious man, Perrell, and my curiosities turn into monsters. Like the damn chickens—" He waved again and the birds sprinted before his hand, thinking they were being fed. "I began to raise chickens according to a . . . to what I thought was an ingenious plan. The principal result is that now everything is covered with chicken crap."

Perrell laughed. His eyes were becoming accustomed to the dark. Not until that moment did he see the towering shape of the huge-bodied touring car hulking before him in the gloom.

"A *Flyer,*" he said, hearing the wonder in his own voice. "A Thomas Flyer . . ."

His eye caught the dull gleam of brass from the stark snouts of the enormous acetylene head lamps that cannoned out before the radiator, then traced along the arrogant line of the flaring fender to the sweeping curve of the cowling, and from there followed the rake of the steering post to the high seats—the back seat, with the down-folded bows of the canvas top sweeping back around it, rising from the great hull like the high poop of an ancient galleon. Then he saw that the tufted cushions were limed white with chicken dung, and that the hood was off, with wires sprouting from the gutted engine like weeds growing through a rotting corpse.

"A derelict," Hazard said impatiently, "like everything else around here. Age . . . decay . . . I should have pushed it out of here a long time ago, but it belongs to Mrs. Sibley, so there it sits, dammit."

"Why not just fix it?" Perrell said.

"Fix it! Everything was wrong with it. It's been five or six years, I guess, since it was running. After the revolution started, it got to be almost impossible to get anything shipped in here. We had one man who could do mechanical work, but it took all his time to handle the machinery around the mine and keep the trucks going. He left when Ev Sibley left, months ago." He grinned crookedly. "You don't think, do you, that you are here because I'm tender-hearted? After you get the truck unloaded, we'll put a plate of beans in front of you, and then we'll see if you are working stiffs or charity cases."

*          *          *

Costello tasted blown grit on his teeth. It was a warm day in Tucson for March and the sky was tinged with yellow. Sand skittered along the streets and sucked through the cracks under doors in tiny windrows. Costello felt it crunch under his boots on the floor tiles as he entered the lobby of the Cosmo House. He looked again at the crumpled envelope he carried in his pocket; the freight agent in the yards had penciled the destination of the freight car across the back of it: *Dos Cabezas Mining Co. Baroyeca, Sonora, Mex. Shipped by Ev Sibley— Cosmo House.* The desk clerk sent him upstairs.

Sibley answered his knock. He was in his shirt sleeves, his dark hair damp and freshly combed. His eyes widened when Costello identified himself. Involuntarily he glanced across the room toward an open door. Costello saw that it was a suite of rooms, handsomely furnished mission-style in fumed oak.

"I only have a minute," Sibley said, "but come in. Drink?"

Costello shook his head and took the seat offered him, an oak-framed Morris chair with leather cushions and a button to push on the arm if you wanted the chair back to recline. "You sent a shipment of goods into Mexico a few days ago," he said, "to a place called El Tanque. Now, I think there's a chance that a man has got hisself locked up in the car. I want to know what kind of a place El Tanque is and where a man could get to from there."

Sibley frowned. "Goddammit, that car was supposed to be sealed."

"Would the car be left there, or would the train wait while it was unloaded?"

"The train would just uncouple the car and go on; there's a siding there and the train would be met by my people from the mine. We have to truck the stuff on to Baroyeca—that's about sixty miles east of the railroad, up in the Sierra. The next stop that amounts to anything would be Navajoa, but if the man stayed with the car, there is not much of any place he could get to, near El Tanque."

"What about El Tanque itself?"

"Oh, hell, it's just a siding—some corrals and loading chutes for cattle, a couple of houses. There's water there, a big dirt tank. The Acuña family there is connected with the Murillo ranch, a hell of a big cattle outfit. Look here, is there a chance that shipment is messed up? My God, if you knew—"

Costello shook his head. "I don't think so."

"Well, is he a jailbird, a killer, or what?"

Costello started to say no, but realized that he would be wrong on both counts. Instead he said, "He is more apt to want a place to stay. He ain't lookin for trouble. Say a man left the train there—could he get a horse?"

"Felizardo Acuña has horses for working the cattle, but you know there has been fighting along the railroad. That is the main reason why this shipment is absolutely vital. Look, if you go there, you can use my name. And here is the name of my engineer . . ." He scrawled a note and handed it to Costello. Beyond the open door, Costello heard a woman's voice, humming. Looking uncomfortable, Sibley leaned forward.

"Look here, my wife is at the mine. I had to come north on business a while back. She stayed, but now she ought to get out of there. All hell is breaking loose in Sonora with that butchering idiot, Rodrigo Vega, running wild. He's worse than Fierro, or Villa." The woman's voice sounded again, merrily. Sibley flushed but went on lamely, doggedly. "Pershing's army is somewhere around Colonia Dublán, but that is over on the Chihuahua side of the mountains . . . things are deteriorating fast. I may not be able—I mean, you're apt to get there before I do. Will you tell her for me that I want her to come back north?"

"I'll tell her if I see her," Costello said. He got up and walked to the door. "Say a man gets to Baroyeca—is there any way he could cross the mountains over to Chihuahua from there?"

"No. Wait, though. You mean *any* way? There was a road in the old days across the Sierra from Baroyeca to Chihuahua, a silver road. Camino de Plata, they called it. The old-timers used to transport the silver from the mines in big two-wheel *carretas*, drawn by mules. But hell, that hasn't been used for thirty years or more. It was closed down in the Indian troubles. The part I've seen is no kind of road any more. I suppose a man could make it on horseback, though. Will you let me know if you learn anything about that shipment? I thought it was finally all set."

A telegram was waiting for Costello at his hotel. He tore it open and leaned close under the leaded stained-glass lamp-shade that hung over the desk. It was from the Denver office, directing him to proceed as he saw necessary. URGE REPORT EARLIEST, it said. Costello did not doubt that in Denver they were remembering back to 1909 again, when he had dropped completely out of sight in the Argentine for over half a year.

In his room he took his valise, bedroll and a pair of saddle-bags from the closet and laid them out on the bed. He put everything he would need into the bags; box of .44 cartridges, ivory-handled razor, piece of soap, stockings, underclothes, shirts, a change of each. He rolled an old pair of Levis into the bedroll and wrapped that in his slicker. The bedroll was two blankets and a tarp. Everything else, and that was not much, went back into the valise, which he checked at the desk when he paid his bill.

With the saddlebags over his shoulder and the bedroll under his arm, he walked across Congress Street, turned a corner and walked into the sheriff's office. Sheriff Newcomb saw the saddlebags and bedroll and put down his newspaper.

"I don't have much to go on," Costello said, "—your boys was right there with me—but I think my man got across the line."

The sheriff frowned. "Goddammit, Pat, you know more than you're tellin me and I'm pretty near burned up about it."

"I didn't say I seen anything directly," Costello said mildly. "And if I had, it was across the line, anyway—your boys was just too late."

"You know we could have maybe struck a bargain with the Mexicans to get him back. Hell, I was willin to work along with you to keep an eye on him, but this is a murder charge we're talkin about now." He put up a hand. "And don't say nothin to me about self-defense, or that Sam Hollenbeck has been asking for it all these years. You've put me in a hell of a fix."

"How's that?"

"It looks like if I ever want to see Ellred Clinton again, I'll have to play along with you—and what I'd like to do is throw you out of here and put me up a big sign that says 'Pinkerton dicks keep out.'"

Costello grinned. "What have you got on him, in the way of evidence?"

"Testimony, is all. But everything I can piece together puts him there at the scene of the fight with them three other people and the old gent who passed away." The sheriff glowered. "I 'spect you've got an idea of your own where he's headed."

"I always figured that he would head for Chihuahua when his time was up, but I think this manhunt drove him over the border here at Nogales. Now he is somewhere down in Sonora, with the Sierra Madre mountain range between him and Chihuahua."

Costello studied a big yellowed wall map that was half buried under "Wanted" posters. It showed southern Arizona and New Mexico and the adjoining states of Sonora and Chihuahua in northern Mexico. The date on the map was 1885 and it bore many notations in faded ink or pencil. A number of red lines had been drawn on it, from mountain peak to mountain peak.

"That map was used by General Miles' staff when they was running down Geronimo's bunch," Sheriff Newcomb said. "The red lines show the heliograph stations they set up for sendin messages—that was what whipped old Geronimo, see? The sun was one thing he couldn't outsmart and couldn't outrun."

Costello nodded. He was tracing the line of the railroad south from Nogales. He saw that in 1885 the railroad had ended at Guaymas. El Tanque, the name he was looking for, was not on the map. It would be somewhere south of Guaymas. He saw a few names that meant nothing to him—Esperanza, Batacosa, La Estrella. There it was—Baroyeca, on the edge of the Sierra Madre. He let his finger trace eastward. There were no roads, no villages up in there, the mountains only vaguely indicated by cartographer's symbols. Then, well over into Chihuahua, he saw the outposts on that side, end-of-the-road places like Ocampo, Tecanachic—Costello caught his breath —and Cusichic. Looking back, he saw that Cusichic was less than a hundred miles from Baroyeca. Yet they were separated by the vastness of the Sierra Madre. The map, he thought, could fool a man if he let it. The Sierra Madre up in there was called *Sierra oscura*, unknown country—*la tierra incognita.*

Costello moved his head slightly and noticed a faint smudged pencil line sketched across the Sierra, an almost illegible notation—*Gerónimo/Nana silver train '81*—and a small penciled X. He traced back to Cusichic and tapped the paper. "Right here is where I caught up with 'em. Nineteen and five, that was. Wiley Haines and Ben Avery, Hole-in-the-Wall bunch. What they wanted was a stake. I heard later they aimed to use it to get to South America, the way Cassidy and Sundance done. And Ellred Clinton. He wasn't nothin but a powder man and all he ever done was hit the deputy during the strike I told you about and drawed six months for it. Some jailbird put him in touch with Wiley and Ben and they talked him into blowin the mail car on the El Paso and Southwestern at Bisbee."

"I remember," Newcomb said. "I was a deputy here then."

"Prettiest job a man ever set eyes on, too. I was in El Paso, and the Denver office put me right onto it. They crossed into Old Mexico. I followed them down along the Bavispe—bad country, some of that. *'Muy desolado,'* the Mexicans said. They aimed to get to the railroad, but the horses played out . . . To keep going, they stole some horses. *Federales* caught up with them at Cusichic and there was a hell of a fight. I got there just at daybreak and you could still smell gunsmoke. It was a kind of an inn yard, see? A low adobe wall around it and a fountain in the middle. Wiley and Ben was dead. No sign of the mail-car money—and of course I didn't want to ask about that because all the soldiers knowed was that the gringos was horse thieves.

"So then I asked about the other gringo, the third one. The officer—the *capitán*—said he was dead, out yonder by the corral. So we went to look, and by golly, he was gone. We tracked him. It wasn't hard—he was shot full of holes. We pulled him out of a little hole in the rocks, way yonder in the mountains—he was passed out, almost gone. The *capitán* pulled a gun—fixin to shoot him right there, see? I give the *capitán* a ten-dollar gold piece and said he could shoot him if that was what he had to do, but first I wanted to ask him some questions."

"How did you get him out of Mexico?"

"We packed him back to Cusichic. Put him in a back room at the inn. I come to an understanding with the *mayordomo*—that was another ten-dollar gold piece. Me and the *capitán* shared a meal then and in a few minutes the *mayordomo* rushed out and said the gringo was dead. We went in there and the señora had Ellred covered up and candles burnin around him. The *capitán* didn't care—he had his ten dollars. So the soldiers went away with the stolen horses. A few days later I hired a wagon and hauled Ellred to the railroad in Guerrero and got him on a train. I said he was a sick mining man, which he was. But Ellred showed no appreciation for the way I looked after him. Never a word did I get from him, then or later. He drawed ten years. Served it too, ever damn minute of it, but he never said a word about the mail-car money. So it could be any place. And without Ellred Clinton puts a finger on it, it's gone forever."

The sheriff slapped the table, his face morose. "Well, what the hell—you've waited a long time for him, but it still leaves me lookin like a rube cop."

Costello put his saddlebags across his shoulder again. "I've got a train to catch."

The sheriff tapped his newspaper. "A train was ambushed down there two, three days ago. It was Rodrigo Vega and his Gringo Legion. The train turned out to be full of soldiers, so the Legion was hurt pretty bad, but they are still around, what's left of them. You better be damn careful."

"A big party of Carranza's politicos is goin south today so the train will carry plenty of soldiers."

"The thing is, we're holdin old warrants on about half of those gringos, so you want to watch the company you keep."

"Sure. If you could go through that outfit and take the men you wanted, you could clean out the Pinkerton files with a pitchfork, but I've only got business with one man in Mexico."

"Maybe so, but there is just aplenty of men in Mexico who would jump at the chance to shoot you."

Costello rode in an ornate but ancient and battered coach. The wine-colored plush on the seats had faded to a muddy brown and the worn pile was thickly sown with soot. He was the only gringo aboard. For a time he sat under the smoldering stares of a squad of soldiers, but his indifference outlasted their efforts to concentrate.

Near Hermosillo he saw a knoll with several scraggly trees on it which bore strange and ghastly fruit. *Zopilotes,* buzzards, accustomed to trains, were not disturbed at their work. In among their glossy black bodies and red naked pates, Costello saw a head of hair the color of straw.

The Gringo Legion, Costello thought. Rodrigo Vega's bunch. Turning in his seat as the train rolled past, he looked back, watching until the knoll was out of sight. The Legion— it was a pet cavalry outfit of Pancho Villa's, back in the early days of the revolution. Helped take Juárez in 1911. Costello remembered bullets thudding into his hotel on the U.S. side of the line while that battle was going on. The Legion then was made up mostly of cowpunchers looking for excitement and of professional fighting men who had run out of wars to fight, besides outlaws—what was left of the Wild Bunch. And there were so many deserters from other armies that the Legion had as many Krauts and Frenchmen and Turks and whatnot as real gringos. And Mex soldiers, too—bad *hombres* from other outfits that wouldn't put up with them. Then after the battle of Agua Prieta, when President Wilson betrayed Pancho Villa, Villa's army was broken up and the Legion was on its own, outlaws of the revolution—*renegados.* A good outfit in the beginning, Costello reflected, but now it was the manure pile of the Mexican revolution.

# (17)

At Dos Cabezas, the morning was half over by the time the trucks were unloaded.

"You say machinery is your game," Tracy Hazard said to Perrell. "Before I get you men settled in the bunkhouse, I'll show you what I want you to do." They followed him out of the shop as he walked briskly across the open compound toward a knoll overlooking the arroyo road between the loading chute and the Ibarra house, where Mrs. Sibley lived. A windmill and a big wooden water tank sat up on the knoll. Waving to them to follow, Hazard climbed a twisting path through thick clumps of prickly pear.

On top, the windmill sat on a squat wooden derrick. It caught a gust of breeze and squealed lustily. Hazard looked up at it. "The windmill is about played out," he said. "I want to put in an electric generator. Would have done it a long time ago, except for the revolution. Anyway, the same engine can drive both the new pump and the generator. Can you install the whole layout?"

"Sure," Perrell said. "If it's that reciprocating pump we unloaded down there, then I think I would bed it on concrete. The engine, too—it's the water-head job with the big flywheel, right? I don't expect you get much frost here—we can scratch out a few inches of dirt and build a form and pour the slab right here near the casing."

"All right. The kid can be your helper. Maybe after he gets over the miseries, I will be able to get a day's work out of him." Hazard laughed. Buell flushed and kicked at the ground.

"When you get done with that, I want you to set up the new steel cyaniding tanks to replace those three big wooden ones over there—the kid can tear those down when he's not busy with you. The boards in the tanks have soaked up a lot of silver, maybe a thousand ounces, so I'll show you how to burn the boards so we can recover the silver."

"How could wood soak up silver?" Buell said.

"The silver is separated from the crushed ore in the cyaniding tanks, where it is in the form of a kind of slush—slime, we call it. And a lot of it soaks into the boards. You can see the whole layout from here . . ." He waved a hand.

Perrell saw again how the level ground of the compound lay cupped against the mountain in a kind of bowl. The mine buildings were strung in a rough arc around the bottom of the bowl, where the compound faded into the slope of mountain behind. From the Ibarra house there were no buildings at all for almost a quarter of the arc, then a series of ancient adobe houses were strung in a loose cluster along the lower slope.

"Those houses were all filled with miners and their families in the old days," Hazard said. "There are only a few living here now. Most of our people walk up the road from Baroyeca. To the right of the houses there are the stables and corrals, then the *arrastre,* where the ore is crushed. You can see the mules there now—they're hitched to the rotating beam, which drags grinding rocks around and around the pit, crushing the ore. Primitive, but that's Mexico for you. To the right of the *arrastre,* on the hillside there, is the old smelter."

Perrell saw the great stone-buttressed terraces of the ancient structure, a tall chimney rising among the ruins, a long black slag heap extending out along the hillside, a lumpy, glinting shelf, barren and weedless.

"In the old days," Hazard said, "the smelter was fired with charcoal, and it took a hell of a mess of mules and men cutting and hauling wood and burning charcoal, just to keep the fires going."

Next to the smelter were the cyaniding tanks Hazard had pointed out, with smaller tanks stepped down the hill below them. "The crushed ore goes into the cyaniding tanks," Hazard said. "The mud you get at the end of the cyaniding run is almost pure silver—after it's dried, we melt it into bars at the forge. We don't use the old smelter any more; it's too big and inefficient. It's all a lot more complicated than I'm telling you now, of course."

He turned to leave the knoll, then swung around suddenly, stiffly, to face them. "Look, I don't know what kind of a jam you boys are in. Probably best if I don't know. But you will have to leave it all behind you if you want to stay at Dos Cabezas, understand? I need help or I would not have taken a chance on you, but you give me nine hours' work a day with no head-aches and we've got a deal. Is there anything you want to say?"

"Before I do any blastin," Clint said, "I want to go over everything in the powder house to see if any of it's went bad. If it has, I want to burn it. The rest I'll stack again so as to put the fresh stuff in back."

Hazard nodded. "You do that and I'll get you started in the stope. How about you, kid?"

Buell cleared his throat. "At the slaughterhouse in Sali-nas, I was makin a dollar a day. What about—"

"I'll give you four bits a day. But there's nothing to spend it on, so it will go a lot farther than that dollar did. See, I'm one of the *yanqui* capitalists who are drinking the life blood of Mexico, and you'll get rich if you stay with me . . ." He grinned sourly. "All right, you don't have to hit it too heavy today. You were up all night."

"We'll quit when the others quit," Perrell said.

The bunkhouse was at the lower end of the cluster of adobe houses strung along the edge of the compound. Of its three rooms, two were already occupied by Mexican miners. These rooms were heated by squat iron stoves—more desir-able in winter, no doubt, than the small adobe fireplace in the room the gringos were to have. There were three bunks in the room, framed of heavy timbers, rope-strung, ticks stuffed with corn shucks to serve as mattresses. The floor was paved with heavy, coarse tiles. The window openings were wood-framed, without glass. The ceilings were high, carried on beams of the dark amapa wood. Scurfy whitewash flaked from the ancient plaster, and the scent of adobe dust was everywhere.

"You can wash up in the trough out back," Hazard said, "and there's a privy yonder behind that thicket of pit'haya. The house farthest from this one belongs to old 'Nacio Domínguez, who is my foreman. The one nearest it is where I live. 'Nacio has four daughters—one of them looks after my place"—Perrell thought he saw Hazard flush slightly—"the others set a dinner table out there in the open under that *ramada* this time of year, for the men bunking here who don't have families. But grub is the only thing they put out, get me?" He glared at them.

They walked out the door. Broken tile steps crumbled away from a narrow veranda. Down by the shop building, the boy was looking after the chickens. "That's the Domínguez boy, Encarnación," Hazard said. "He's my bird handler. They're fighting chickens, see?" He peered at them to see how they took that. "Very special birds. Great fighters. You'll see— there'll be a cockfight in the village Saturday night. One of my birds is going into the ring."

Perrell and Buell hauled lumber, tools, a sack of cement and nails to the pump house on the knoll. Perrell found some wire screen in the shop and put Buell to work screening sand while he knocked together a form for the concrete slab. "I'll send up some grub as soon as it's ready," Hazard had promised. Then he had taken Clint on to the mine.

From the knoll Perrell could look out over the great arroyo and the brush-stippled hills rolling away to the west. On his left, he could just see the *boca de mina* and the thatched *ramada* where the women were sorting ore, and he could hear the ore rumble into the loading chute that straddled the road below. After a while he saw Clint emerge from the mine entrance and go down a set of rickety wooden steps and cross the road to the powder house, which was built on a shelf of rock jutting out over the arroyo. A safe place to have it, Perrell thought. It was about ten feet square, built of timbers. The roof was boxed and filled with sand, probably eight or ten inches deep, Perrell thought, to insulate the interior and to protect against—what? Stray bullets, or whatever.

He heard the muffled clop of horse's hoofs and looked up to see the Domínguez boy jump down off a gray horse in front of the Ibarra house. Mrs. Sibley came out of the house and tied a boxlike affair with folding legs behind the saddle. She mounted smoothly and cantered toward the village. Looking down from the knoll, Perrell saw Clint standing back in the shadowed interior of the powder house with a case of dynamite in his hands, watching her as she rode by. Perrell saw the white of her face under her hat brim as she looked up, then she was past the loading chute and on the cliff road, out of his sight. Clint stood in the doorway looking after her, and the intensity of his stare made Perrell think of the way the big man had turned his face to the flaring sun that morning on the beach at Gaviota.

Buell looked at the sun. "It's way past dinnertime and I could eat a raw skunk. When do you reckon—"

"Maybe now," Perrell said. The Domínguez boy came up the hill with a small basket. He offered it to them with a shy whisper, *"Señores . . . su lonche."* In the basket wrapped in cloth were half a dozen big white-flour tortillas rolled and filled with fried beans. The boy was slender, with fine dark eyes. He wore frayed white cottons and was barefoot.

"Hey, pal, tell me about them chickens," Buell said.

*"No inglés, señor."*

"Chickens . . ." Buell flapped his arms and crowed. "Are they really fighters?" He shadow-boxed, throwing sharp rights and lefts, snorting through his nose. The boy's expression became fierce. *"Sí. Muy fuerte, señor—muy batallosa."* Buell laughed.

By late afternoon the concrete was setting up in the form with some half-inch bolts embedded in it, ready for the pump and motor. Perrell felt a *crump* beneath his feet. The ground quivered and dust blew out of the *boca de mina.* Buell flinched. "Hey! What's that?"

"Dynamite. Clint is back at his old trade."

The sun was hanging huge and red, and the western horizon was lost in haze beyond the distant rolling foothills. They cleaned up the tools, then walked down to the shop.

Chickens clucked at them. The great hulk of the Thomas

Flyer was huge in the gloom. Half a dozen chickens were already roosting on it, on lights, fenders and seatbacks. One was on the big steering wheel, its yellow horny knuckles clenched around the brass throttle quadrant.

Buell climbed up on the running board. Chickens squawked and flew noisily from their perches. "They ought to run this thing off a cliff," he said. His face was pale and slack with fatigue.

"It was a Flyer that won the New York-to-Paris race eight or ten years ago," Perrell said. "Nineteen-oh-eight I think it was. That was a four. This is the big one, the six-seventy—she was a great machine."

"She's a sure-'nough mess now." Buell leaned over the engine and saw the tangle of loose wires, the open cobwebbed holes yawning in the top of the engine. Her great springs squeaked under his weight; the Flyer rocked gently and a shower of dust spilled down a fender.

Perrell wiped the dirt from a spot on the fender and saw the dark glow of red lacquer, the finely lined gold striping. He brushed the cloth over a huge head lamp. Brass gleamed dully. He leaned over and peered into the ravaged engine. "Seventy-two horses she puts out. That's a Marion-type engine, a T-head with open tappets—see them on the side down there? You can pull the valves out through the valve ports without taking the cylinder heads off, and that's what somebody has done. The valves are gone, see?" Perrell stuck a finger through the cobwebbed hole, feeling the cool dry steel. "They're probably lost. But there's no rust. Dry climate. I guess she had some burned valves."

Buell kicked at one of the tires, then walked around the car. All four tires were flat and the huge wood-spoked wheels were sunk to the rims in dirt.

"They should have put her up on blocks," Perrell said.

"Run her off a cliff is what I say," Buell said.

They washed up at the trough in back of the bunkhouse. The other men were already there. "I seen the workin face at the head of the tunnel," Clint said. "She looks pretty good. It's a new stope—what he done, he cross-cut away from an old drift about thirty feet and hit the vein, so we're stopin it."

"You mean you seen the silver?" Buell said.

"The face of ore. It sparkles some, is all. It has to be milled, see? The first batch of ore from this stope is the stuff that's in the zinc boxes over on the hill now. He will know how good it is in a few days when he melts her down and assays it."

Supper was tough beef shredded onto coarse plates of fired clay, covered with chile gravy thickened with cornmeal, and there was a big clay pot of beans set in the center of the table with platters of steaming tortillas alongside. The Mexicans used rolled tortillas to eat, deftly dipping and swabbing. Two daughters of 'Nacio Domínguez stood next to an adobe char-coal hearth, gravely and with dignity watching to see that the plates of the men stayed full. They were called Eufemita and Rufinita and they were fifteen or sixteen years old.

Buell's eyelids drooped forlornly through the meal. He finally put his fork aside with a clatter, mumbled something and stumbled toward the bunkhouse. Perrell saw that Clint had turned half around on the bench and was leaning there on an elbow while the Mexicans rolled themselves corn-shuck cigarettes, speaking softly in answer to his questions. From their gestures Perrell understood that they were describing the layout of the mine and the surrounding country.

The sky in the west was washed now with a strangely luminous, opalescent light. Warmth seeped through him, unaccountable for a moment, then he realized that it was simply contentment. He watched a vermilion flycatcher dart out from a branch of mesquite, dip back. Dart out and dip back. Contentment. After days of being on the run, either from himself or from the law, he had come to rest. Like the birds now as evening wore on. He said *"Gracias"* to the girls, nodded to the old man and left the table. Beyond the foot of the cobbled roadway lay the open *terreno* and the shop building.

He set out walking. As he came abreast of the shop he stopped, felt in his pockets for the makings and started to build himself a smoke. Then he noticed that the door to the shop was slid back. He was certain he had closed it. Perrell walked to the door and looked in.

It was almost dark in there, the gloom washed by a weak seep of light from a sky nearly drained of its light. She was sitting up in the high driver's seat of the Flyer, gripping the steering wheel with both hands, her head back as if flung there by a fierce rushing wind stream, and she was staring straight ahead through the open door, her gaze set, intent and burning, on the brushy flank of the mountain rising toward the still-glowing Dos Cabezas. Chickens, bereft of their roost, strutted restlessly, clucking, scolding her.

"Fifty . . . sixty," Mrs. Sibley said. "Oh, how she could fly." Her fierce gaze broke. Her hands relaxed, slid down the curve of the wheel. She looked at Perrell. He saw the faint gleam of wetness on her cheek. Her voice was husky and soft, not petulant. "I would be obliged if you would fix one of those for me," she said, nodding at the half-made cigarette in his fingers. "I am altogether out of anything to smoke."

"Yes, ma'am," he said. "My pleasure." He rolled it, started to lick it, hesitated and held it out. "Don't you want to . . ."

She laughed. "No, you go ahead and lick it—I would just spill it all." She leaned forward and took a glass from the curving cowl in front of the steering wheel, sipped from it. He finished the cigarette, twisted the end and stepped over to hand it to her. She let him light it, lightly touching his hand to steady the match, then nodded her thanks through the smoke. He saw that she was wearing boots and a leather riding skirt that ended just above the ankles, an embroidered blouse with a ruffled bosom, and a light leather jacket trimmed with braid. A felt hat, hanging from her arm by a strap, was trimmed with braid and silver cord.

"You are one of the new men, I expect," she said.

He touched his hat. "John Perrell."

She laughed shakily. "That sounds like—danger. Or trouble. John Trouble, is that it?"

Perrell smiled. "I am no stranger to trouble." The fading light of evening allowed her face to glow softly, yet did not hide the smudged circles under her eyes. Her brows were thick and dark, arched, her nose short, her mouth a trifle wide and her jaw a trifle square, and there were tiny lines webbing out from the corners of her eyes. About thirty-four or -five, Perrell thought, a handsome woman—with a glass in her hand and a tear damp on her cheek. He made himself another smoke and lighted it, then said, "I've been looking over your machine."

She lifted her glass and saw that it was empty. "It was a wedding present from my father." She had twisted around and was feeling along the back of the seat, searching for something. "Where is that . . . aha!" A leather case was fastened there, the top of it thickly encrusted with chicken dung. She raised the lid gingerly and pulled a silver flask from the case, the silver black with age and neglect. She held the flask close to her ear and shook it. Perrell heard a faint sloshing. She laughed. "Can you believe it? Five . . . let's see . . . six years. *Six* years."

She unscrewed the silver cap. It telescoped out to become a small drinking cup. She sniffed at the neck of the flask, held it out to Perrell. "You don't suppose it could go bad, do you? Brandy?"

He sniffed. "No, I wouldn't think so."

She poured some of it into the little cup and handed it to him. "Well, then, John Trouble, join me, won't you?" She filled her own glass, reached out and touched the edge of the glass to his cup. She sipped, tasting, shrugged and drank half of it off. She looked about her, at the car, turning head and shoulders to look into the back and along the folded bows of the top that lay racked astern. One of the chickens had flapped up onto the top bows and perched there, clucking, watching them sideways through one eye, and as it watched, it dropped a squirt of excrement onto the dusty canvas. Mrs. Sibley winced.

"He told me that I could have either the auto or a trip to Europe. I had already been to Europe, so I chose the Flyer. Ev and I—he's my husband—motored way out on Long Island, to the very tip. Montauk Point. It was glorious."

"How did it get here?"

"The next year Ev and my father formed the syndicate that took over the mine here. We shipped it to Tucson. We packed it with tents and camping things and *drove* it to Baroyeca." Her eyes gleamed. "I think it was the first auto to go over that road, but that same year a Flyer just like this one

won the New York-to-Paris race. She could go *anywhere . . ."*
She poured the last of the brandy into her glass, upending the
flask to make sure it was empty, then drank it in a swallow and
handed the flask to him to cap for her and replace in the case.
It was almost dark in the shop. "Sometimes," she said, "I like
to just come and sit awhile in her." She lifted her hands, let
them fall helplessly, then slipped from behind the wheel and
stood up, rocking a little. As she stepped over the long brake
and gear levers thrusting up from their quadrant above the
running board, he gave her his hand. They went outside into
the dusk. Behind them he heard the chickens flutter noisily
back up onto their roosts. He started to walk back with her.
She said, "No, don't bother. I've been here before."

# (18)

Perrell did not sleep well. He squirmed on his corn-shuck
mattress, fragmentary pictures racing endlessly through his
mind. He saw the face of his jailer in Seattle, the man picking
his nose and stupidly mouthing obscenities at him, and this
gave way to the beach that morning near Gaviota, the long-
boned drifter stalking across the sand through the torn shreds
of mist. Then Mrs. Sibley—the hollow bitterness of her laugh
sounding again and again in aural memory, her face bruised,
distorted with the effort of trying to speak to him, her mouth
soundlessly open as he heard the crowing of roosters and
thought vagrantly: *After I'm gone from here I'll remember
that in Mexico the roosters crow all night.* He was grateful for
the dawn when it came.

Buell helped him lift the engine and the pump onto their
new mounts and bolt them down. Then there was pipe work.
Perrell set up the pipe vise on its spindly legs out in the sun.

He liked the heat of it on his back as he worked. He liked the feel of a wrench in his hand again, and the smell of oiled steel in the pipe-threading dies and in the new pump and the smell of fresh concrete, and the damp wood in the big wooden water tank that squatted rotundly a few feet away, sweating bright beads of water.

"What do you reckon she's *doin* down there?" Buell said. He sat on the timber, tossing pebbles down the slope.

Perrell swung around and looked. By leaning a little, he could also see the Ibarra house. "What do you mean? There's no one in sight."

"I mean, where is she at?"

"It's my guess that she has slept most of the time."

"Slept! That's all she done on the train."

"That was different. On the train she just let her mind go, see?" Perrell was fitting a length of pipe to the pump. He took up on the fitting with his wrench, feeling the bite of the threads. "She'll come around now. The way she treated you was part of it, too. She needed someone to help her carry the blame and you were right there handy, so you were elected."

It was hard to say anything that would really ease the kid's mind or give him comfort, Perrell thought. Bobby Joe was taking his love and using it to make him crawl—some women could not help doing that to a man. Good women, too, some of them, except for that. Perrell thought it had something to do with sin. Not real sin, but a certain idea of it. So a couple of youngsters would yield to nature, then the girl would get to feeling guilty about it and wind up using it to punish the poor fool.

"It wasn't fair." Buell tossed a pebble at a big strutting grackle and it flew, vaning the air with its boat-shaped tail.

"No, maybe not. Hardly anything is *fair*. But it was human, or female, anyway."

Buell grunted, tossed another pebble. "I s'pose you're tryin to tell me something."

"The only thing I know is that it will just work out, one way or another, and then it will be in the past. And whatever happens to you between here and there is likely to be the farthest thing in the world from anything you planned or expected."

"A man would be better off to stay in bed, then."

"No, you do what's in your nature to do, like this old wind pumper." Perrell slapped the dangling pump rod and heard it clatter up under the gearbox where it was pin-linked to the wind-driven crankshaft. "Sometimes the wind blows for you and sometimes it doesn't. There isn't a damn thing you can do about that part, but when it does blow, you swing around and face into it and pump like hell."

They heard the clatter of an engine and saw Hazard driving an open Model T Ford with a truck bed built on behind the seat. He pulled up at the foot of the knoll, left the Ford and walked up the hill. He looked the job over. "Good. When you get it pumping, you can start putting the tanks together. The kid can start dismantling the old ones now—it's a good time for it because this run of ore has gone through and we're ready to clean out the zinc boxes."

"That's the stuff you melt down?" Perrell asked.

"After it's dried. One run yields half a ton of concentrate and that melts down into five hundred-odd pounds of bullion."

Buell whistled. "What's it worth?"

Hazard shrugged. "In dollars, six or seven thousand, I guess, depending on how much gold runs with it. It varies. In the old days Dos Cabezas was a good gold producer. I figure there's still some in there, if you could only tap into it. That's why I keep on doing exploratory work." He pointed across to the hillside that ran behind the smelter. "You see that row of prospect pits? I put down those prospect holes and traced the structure, tapped into it from the side. My idea is that there could be another vein structure in the system, parallel to this one."

"The powder man said you were into something new," Perrell said.

"Can't tell if it's really something new, or if it's just a piece of the vein tailing off there from the original system. Can't tell how big it is yet, either. If you can carry the whole ore body away in a washtub, then it's a damn expensive hole in the ground—that's what Sibley claims, anyway."

"You claim otherwise?"

"Sure. He is against my doing exploratory work, but my job is to find metal, and to do it you have to keep hunting." Perrell heard subdued excitement in his voice, and frustration, too. "That's what mining is all about, as far as I'm concerned, or any mining man."

"But not Sibley?"

Hazard pushed his hat back and ran fingers through his sandy, graying hair. "No. He's not a mining man. His game is making deals. He could as well be in cotton, or ladies' underwear." He laughed. "By God, that's a good one—I'll have to remember that. Well, this is nothing to do with you guys. Kid, you come with me and I'll show you what to do with the tanks."

A little later Perrell saw Mrs. Sibley ride out the arroyo road toward the village again. She saw him and raised a gloved hand. He waved back. By then he was ready to test the engine and pump. He put the new leather drive belt in place and cranked the engine through. It started on the second pull, firing in the irregular fashion of its kind, driving the piston arm of the pump with a steady, grunting sound. He adjusted the fuel mixture slightly, then walked back away from the tank and looked up. A bright stream of water spouted from the pipe and splashed downward into the open-topped tank. The little Ford was parked by the shop, out in the center of the open compound. Perrell gathered up his tools and started down the slope. He saw movement on one of the terraced levels over behind the Ibarra house. From that distance he could make out Bobby Joe's small blond head. She was wearing a skirt, probably something of Mrs. Sibley's. He smiled to himself and went on down.

Hazard was standing next to one of the chicken coops at the end of the shop building with Encarnación. He put something in the palm of his hand and held it next to the wire. Perrell saw with a start that it was a piece of raw meat. A big, long-legged red rooster with a cropped-off comb lunged for the meat and pecked it away, its neck feathers glinting green lights. "This is my *muchacho,*" Hazard said, "the one we are getting ready for the pit. Look at the build on him, will you?

I saw Fitzsimmons fight Corbett in Carson City in 'ninety-seven, and Fitz was built just like this bird. Looked like him, too. My first mining job, that was. Do you know anything about fighting cocks?"

"Not much."

"I used to like football," Hazard said, "baseball, too. We're a long way from anything like that, here. A man has to do *something*. For a while, I made booze. I had a terrific idea, I thought at the time. Made it out of *lechuguilla*, which is what they use for the local product—only I improved on it, or so I thought." He shuddered. "Nearly poisoned myself." They walked on into the shop. "I heard you running the engine. She'll move a lot more water than the old windmill."

"Maybe so, but I wouldn't tear the windmill down."

"No? It's a wreck and it screams like a banshee."

"A little grease is all it needed. Supposing the new engine quits on you? I just disconnected the pump rod and locked the tail vane over. To tell the truth, I would hate to see it torn down, anyway."

"I thought you liked machinery. The new pump rig is a beauty."

"No, I just mean that a machine doesn't have to be complicated—it just has to do a job the best way there is. If a machine will do that, it's being honest with you. That's all you would ask of a man."

Hazard smiled. "You win. But let's use the new pump, anyway. It's taken me almost four years to get it. You going to start on the new tanks now?"

"Yes. I'll set up the little portable horseshoe forge and rivet the tanks right there in place . . ." He hesitated, then nodded in the direction of the Thomas Flyer. "What would you say if I was to get that car running?"

"I would call it a waste of time."

"I thought if I could get her running, we could get it out of here, maybe into the shed over behind Mrs. Sibley's house."

Hazard frowned. "She'd like that all right, if she could drive it again, but it's pretty far gone." He opened a rear door on the car and took out a heavy piece of shaft, with a toothed sprocket on one end. The other end was broken. "Look at this chain-drive shaft. Can you fix that? It looks hopeless to me."

"I might. What are the chances of finding some tires for it, say in Navajoa?"

"Nonexistent, I would say. I mean, nothing is moving now. Everything is frozen up tight, banks included. I couldn't even get payroll money. It's not just the revolution now. It's Pershing's army cutting through Chihuahua and it's Obregón screaming that he will invade the States and take San Antonio. And there are bandits, too—renegades like Rodrigo Vega and the Gringo Legion. No one knows where that bastard will turn next."

"The newspapers in the States call Villa a bandit, too."

"That's the official line, now that Wilson has dumped him. Look here, the revolution is pure poison to American interests; the rebels want to run us out of the country, and just between the two of us, I don't blame them. We have taken a lot out of the country and left precious little behind, mostly bribes, squeeze . . . *mordida*. Who are the bandits in that picture?" He pounded on the fender of the Flyer. A startled chicken squawked and ran. "I'm getting long-winded. It makes Sibley sore as hell; he says I'm talking like a goddamn Wobbly."

Perrell stiffened. He felt himself flush. Carefully he said, "No, you're not. I understood you to say there are no tires for this machine."

Hazard moved his glasses on his nose and looked closely at Perrell. "Oh-oh. Stepped on some toes, have I? I wondered why a top-notch mechanic was on the bum—would it be something to do with that? Well, no offense, my friend, but you are a long way from pie in the sky here. Remember, you asked me to take you on. It wasn't my idea."

Hazard was silent for a moment, then he turned and studied the decrepit Flyer. "Too bad about this old wreck. She was driving it when I first came here, and let me tell you, the two of them, that woman and this snorting red monster, they were something to look at." He kicked at one of the tires and shook his head, like a man who has walked into some cobwebs, Perrell thought.

"My impression was that you were not friends," Perrell said.

"Things change—our interests diverged. That is to say, mine and her husband's. And we changed, no doubt. Mrs. Sibley has been too much alone. I would have been a friend to her . . ."

Buell leaned back and allowed Eufemita to put another sizzling slice of beef on his plate and yet another serving of the fried beans. He winked and rolled his eyes at her to make her giggle again, avoiding her father's fierce glare. Tearing at a mouthful of beef, he frowned then, his brow furrowed under damply combed pale hair. "He had me burn them boards on a big piece of sheet iron, then wash the ashes into a tub. Then he put me to cleanin black slop out of them boxes. Now, you can't tell me there is silver in a mess of ashes, nor in that black mud, either. I would as soon clean dung out of the cow barn —at least there a man knows what he's workin with . . ."

After supper Buell mumbled something about taking a walk. Perrell saw him heading for the Ibarra house and grinned to himself. Clint and the Mexican boys sat at the table talking and drinking coffee. Perrell wandered idly back to the shop. Inside, he shooed the chickens off the Flyer and looked down on the big engine. It carried two complete sets of spark plugs, he saw, so it had two complete and independent ignition systems. A handy thing in Mexico.

Dirty, spattered with chicken droppings, the holes and ports yawning darkly, the thick exhaust headers clenched like arthritic knuckles—nothing in life, he thought, appeared more despondent than a neglected piece of machinery. He thought of Mrs. Sibley and amended his idea—nothing in life except maybe a woman similarly neglected. He picked up a cloth and began to wipe away the crust of congealed dirt and oil. When he had the worst of the grit off, he filled a can with kerosene from a drum and washed the metal down with it, then he polished it with a dry cloth until it gleamed softly. Chickens clucked behind him.

"John Trouble, whatever are you doing to my lovely Flyer?"

He turned to see Mrs. Sibley; he had not heard her footsteps. She was wearing a full, long skirt of cotton, black, with colored flowers embroidered on it, and a white blouse with lace along the neckline, and she carried a light shawl. For a moment she looked very young, then she stepped closer and he saw again the dark smudges around her eyes. Her hair was pinned up in coils, held with a carved shell comb.

"Nothing yet," he grinned. "I just cleaned her up a little."

"I thought—for just a moment, I thought you might be fixing her. She does look better, though. Not so broken down, you know."

"Just dismantled, instead of falling apart—is that what you mean?"

"Yes." She looked curiously into the engine, then her eyes were drawn back along the car's great body, grimed and dung-streaked. She frowned. "I suppose it was too much to hope for, really—to see her run again." Her voice was a trifle blurred with huskiness, and faintly, through the kerosene, he caught the odor of brandy.

"Impractical, maybe—without tires, I mean." He smiled. "But I expect she would *run*, all right. It would take some work, but it's fine machinery—that hasn't changed. I see some burned valves and a broken drive shaft, otherwise it's probably mostly just dirty and run down. Of course that still leaves the tires."

"It would be grand just to *hear* her again." He caught the carefully subdued hope in her voice and regretted for a moment having suggested that the engine could be made to run. He shook his head.

"I would have to see if there is anything else actually broken, like that drive shaft."

"She never ran again after that happened. Ev—my husband—was driving. There was a stone in the way of that wheel —it slid down onto the road just as we were passing. He hit full throttle and let the clutch pedal right out. The car just leaped and there was a terrible noise when the shaft broke. He was *furious*. We got her back here with a lot of grinding noise underneath, but she never ran again. Ev was always going to get her fixed, but it seemed that more and more needed doing

—valves and things. By then the revolution had started. We sent away to the Thomas Company in Buffalo for parts—that shaft thing for the chain—but the only thing that came through was a set of tires and they were the wrong size." She laughed bitterly. "So my lovely Flyer is just . . . rotting away."

"Not really," Perrell said. "She's a machine, not flesh and blood." He had an uncomfortable feeling that the woman's concern for the car ran deeper than mere regret.

"You're shaking your head," she said. "Why?"

Hastily he said, "I was just trying to figure this thing out." He pointed to a small pump mounted on the dash, the brass handle protruding toward the driver's position.

"That's a gas starter. It's supposed to start the car with acetylene gas so you needn't crank it, you see."

"Supposed to? Doesn't it work?"

"Well, I don't know. As soon as we heard about it, we ordered it—that was the only thing I didn't like about her, the cranking—but it came along too late. I never had a chance to try it. There was that shaft thing, and the burned valves to fix, too. One of the men installed it, but since the new shaft didn't come, my husband and Tracy put him to work on something else. She's been like this ever since."

"Most of the companies are going to an electric starter now," Perrell said, "but I think I saw a gas setup like this on a Stevens-Duryea. Let's see, it takes acetylene from the tank on the running board." He traced copper tubing to the pump on the engine side of the dash. "You would turn the valve on, then pump a few strokes—gas is injected directly into the cylinders through those bronze fittings, then you would flip a switch to get a spark and she would kick over and start firing. That would draw gasoline through the carburetor and you would be on your way, without hand cranking, right?"

She laughed. "I suppose so."

He pointed to one of the bronze fittings. "This would have a check valve in it. The gas could come this way into the cylinder under pump pressure, but the check valve would prevent anything going back through the other way, otherwise the power of the engine would escape."

"That seems perfectly clear. My husband would never explain it to me."

"Part of the masculine conspiracy." He grinned. "Men like to keep their women weak and ignorant, lest they rebel. Like the power conspiracy that keeps the populace weak and ignorant."

She frowned. "That sounds like—who? Upton Sinclair?"

"Some, maybe. Eugene Debs, Jack London, even Walt Whitman. Karl Marx, too."

"You would have my husband ranting. Are you one of those bearded men who go about with bombs?"

"No, I'm not an anarchist. Just"—he hesitated—"a workingman."

"A radical, then. A rabble-rouser?" She was teasing, but he felt himself bristle.

"A little of each, I expect."

"Well, you see what that line of thought has brought to Mexico."

"Long overdue, according to Tracy Hazard."

"Oh, *him* . . ." She waved a hand. "I mean, there is nothing that justifies all the killing."

"Oppression is the slow murder of a people's spirit. In the end they will lash out, to save themselves—that is what revolution is. There may or may not be killing—I would say that is up to the oppressors. It certainly was in Mexico. And it was in France. The people knew too well what a guillotine was for—it was for cutting off heads."

"I see." Her smile had faded as he talked. She was silent for a moment, then she said, "Well, John Trouble, I can see that an argument with you could become a very prickly thing. I will know not to look for polite agreement from you, won't I?—respectful submission, that sort of thing . . ."

She started to turn away as if to leave, then stopped. "I wonder—what will you think about this?" She touched the Flyer and laughed nervously. "A broken toy—and a woman, let's say a spoiled woman, complaining about it. How would it go in your jargon—pampered parasites—something like that?"

"I don't trust jargon myself. Anyway, what I said was a general thing—nothing personal about it. Besides, I wholly agree with you about the Flyer. There she is and she ought to be running. Something like the Flyer is reason enough, by herself."

She slowly smiled again. "You can be kind, I see, but I'm relieved to hear you say that. One feels . . . vulnerable, sometimes, especially after a long time alone. Perhaps you should know, John Trouble, that to a woman, hardly anything is *general* and almost everything is personal."

"I'll try to remember that." He saw that it had grown too dark to see the engine. They walked out the door together. He said, "I saw Bobby Joe over there by your house, looking like a girl again."

"Yes. I gather she went through something dreadful, is that right?"

"She was . . . traveling with her grandfather. And he died."

She frowned. "That's brief, but all right. I resented her at first, I'm sorry to say. Then I was curious. She was like someone stunned. But she's a sturdy little thing. She saw our garden on that terrace yonder and wanted to work—she said that was something she knew about. That big young man—Buell is it?—came over this evening and she gave him a shovel and set him to digging."

Perrell laughed. "That's what the kid did all day."

"Well, he's still doing it." Walking away, she looked back once and smiled.

# (19)

The locomotive ground to a stop. The conductor anxiously beckoned to Costello. It was better for the train to keep moving. *"P'alla, señor—*El Tanque." Through the dust-bleared window, Costello saw some corrals and a cattle-loading chute near the tracks. Farther back, a couple of hundred yards away, an adobe house, its yard fenced with spidery-stalked ocotillo branches closely bound together. More corrals. He saw movement in one of the corrals. Horses. Good. The conductor beckoned again, gold watch chain dancing across his round belly.

Costello shouldered his saddlebags, took up his bedroll, walked to the end of the car and swung down. Thick chalky dust puffed under his boots. Barely stopping, the train was immediately chuffing away. Looking after it, Costello saw flags fluttering from staffs on the front of the engine. The tops of several of the cars bristled with soldiers. One grinned at him and swung his arm up in a familiar obscenity. *"Toma, gringo,"* he shouted. *"Toma."* Other soldiers heard him and laughed. Costello grinned back at him and waved, then began walking through the thick dust toward the adobe house. Beyond, there were impenetrable thickets of cactus and brush and scrub trees, and towering over the scrub were immense, heavy-bodied cactus like saguaros grown obese and clumped together.

Costello passed the corrals and saw the horses—gaunt, sore-backed, brush-scarred, some indeed with open wounds, hoofs splintered. He felt a flicker of apprehension, but the train, of course, was already gone. He walked on toward the ocotillo fence.

An eye placed close to the ocotillo fence could see through between the spiked stalks and tiny leaves, although the viewer himself could not be seen from the other side if he did not move. As the train chuffed into the distance, half a dozen men knelt or squatted silently behind the fence and watched a slight, bow-legged man in a dark suit walk toward the house.

The fencing on the side of the yard away from the railroad was torn down along part of its length, and the garden inside was trampled, hoof-marked. Flies were crawling on the face of the vaquero, Felizardo Acuña, who lay where he had fallen, a few feet from his house. His son, also a vaquero, was sprawled close by, the great-roweled spurs on his heels now struck futilely into the powdery earth.

Colonel Rodrigo Vega sat at his ease in a rawhide-bottomed chair in the shade of the *ramada,* undisturbed by the bodies. He was eating a plate of beef and beans, part of the last meal prepared by the elder Acuña.

One of the men at the fence suddenly grunted. "I'll be damned," he said softly. "I know him—he's a Pinkerton dick named Costello."

Rodrigo Vega nodded. He was twenty-nine years old. A silky black mustache drooped at the corners of full lips. His face was pale and narrow, with slightly slanted eyes that were hooded by bluish, oddly translucent eyelids. His gray suit was cut in the French fashion, shoulders narrow, waist nipped in and skirts flaring. He wore silver-buckled leggings of soft black leather and a low-crowned, uncreased Stetson of the type Mexicans called a *tejano.*

He was curious about the Pinkerton man, but the train itself had been a disappointment—it was bristling with soldiers and plainly impossible to attack. Several days earlier, Rodrigo Vega had attacked a train near Hermosillo, only to learn that the train was a rolling ambush—most of the cars had been filled with soldiers. Rodrigo Vega had lost half his remaining men and horses, already sadly reduced at the battle of Agua Prieta. More, and worse from Vega's point of view, a packhorse had disappeared during the fight. A certain packhorse which carried his own baggage, and under the baggage, his personal treasury of gold coins. Later his men had seen him put his head in his hands and weep—battle-scarred, they thought his tears were for their dead *compañeros* and they were touched.

They did not know that his intention had been to ride with them only as far as the port town of Mazatlán, where he was certain, he thought, of getting passage to Lima or Santiago de Chile. Now, with that packhorse gone, none of that was possible. He no longer had enough men to ride into a town even the size of nearby Navajoa. The banks were there, but so were the soldiers, the hated Yaquis of General Alvaro Obregón, the man who, more than any other, had broken Pancho Villa. And Obregón, hating Villa, loathed his Gringo Legion.

Vega and his men found themselves not merely defeated soldiers but fugitives. Vega needed a place to hole up and rest and he needed money and time to restore his tattered fortunes.

The Murillo ranch, too, had been a disappointment. It was already stripped, and yielded almost no horses or supplies. Under persuasion, a vaquero had blurted out that most of the Murillo horses were at El Tanque, where cattle were being loaded. It was a lie, for which the man had paid in advance with his life. There were only four horses at El Tanque—and two vaqueros, upon whom the flies now crawled.

Costello lifted a wire loop that held the gate closed, opened it and walked through, then stopped short, his jaw hanging open, his flinty composure cracked. Instinctively, his hand moved toward the Colt under his coat.

Vega shook his head and said, "Don't do that, Mr. Costello." A ragged giggle escaped him. Costello stood very still then. A red-haired man with buckteeth and a frayed sombrero hanging down his back reached under Costello's coat and took the Colt from its holster, then the wallet and sheaf of papers from the breast pocket.

"I told him your name, Pat," the red-haired man said. He handed the papers to Vega. "I vouched for you, see?"

"Yes, I see, Red," Costello said, looking at Red Durkin, and turning a little, at Charlie Slotter. "Well, you boys have the advantage of me."

He half turned, sensing movement behind him, and saw that with the train now gone, Vega's men had silently drifted out of the clumped thickets of pitahaya and cholla. In the one quick glance Costello saw tattered clothing, half-empty cartridge belts, bare feet and a flutter of filthy bandages. Costello turned again. He saw that Charlie Slotter's cheeks were hollow, his milky eyes feverishly bright. There were stains and rips in Vega's splendid gray suit. One of his boots was split. Vega set his plate aside and dabbed at his mustache.

Leafing through the papers from Costello's pocket, Vega paused over the wire from the Denver office. "Ellred Clinton is the lucky man, is he? I don't think I know him . . ."

Costello saw Red Durkin stiffen at the mention of Clinton's name as Vega went on. Yet Durkin said nothing. And Vega, who was looking at the line about a $60,000 mail-car robbery, read it silently, his lips moving. Then he turned to other papers from the wallet and read on. " 'Dos Cabezas Mining Company, Baroyeca.' Where is Baroyeca, Mr. Costello?"

"I've never set foot there, but it's somewhere yonder in the mountains. Not much of a place, I expect." Behind him, Costello heard the harsh rattle of breath in a man's lungs. Rodrigo Vega opened a folded map on his knee. He squirmed and giggled again, looking at the map. Costello's skin felt cold—hysteria hung in the air, like a smell.

"A mine," Vega mused. "Silver, no doubt. And mines have payrolls. Food. Horses, no doubt, or mules. That train—it was filled with those shit-eating Yaqui soldiers of General Obregón. We have seen too much of them for now." He looked from one to another of the men, as if, Costello thought, measuring their capacity to endure. The strange giggle hovered in his voice. "With a hundred men, I would have gone on—Navajoa, Mazatlán. Last week we were more than a hundred, Mr. Costello. The Legion . . ." The giggle burbled through his voice. He waved a hand jerkily. The men were beginning to fidget.

"Let's shoot the son of a bitch and get out of here," Slotter said. He took hold of Costello's shoulder.

"Did you find any meat?" Vega said, apparently irrelevantly.

Startled, Slotter said, "They was near half a beef hangin out back."

"Good. We won't butcher a horse then. That means that you will ride along with us for a while, Mr. Costello. I am curious to hear more about Ellred Clinton. And Baroyeca. It appears to be about sixty miles. A two-day ride." He folded the map. Men were saddling horses, silently, without banter. Costello thought he had never seen a sorrier outfit. He heard the chunk of an ax as the half of beef was cut up, then the ax stopped chunking and the pieces were wrapped in canvas and tied behind saddles.

Rodrigo Vega moved slowly about. Costello saw a tic twitch at his cheek, like a worm under the skin. He looked like a man who was about to scream.

Charlie Slotter grunted orders to a tattered *renegado,* who went away and returned leading a horse for Costello. Slotter's eyes were opaque. He kicked at a saddle that was thrown down against the ocotillo fence. Costello saddled the horse. It was a stumbling rack of bones with shrunken withers and a spine like a butcher knife.

Mounted then, they rode slowly away from the adobe houses and the sprawled bodies. Costello counted—*forty, make it forty-odd.* The Gringo Legion. Five or six looked like Mexicans, but that was hard to tell. He thought he heard two or three languages among them, other than English and Spanish. Vega's hooded eyes flicked at him, and Costello felt a tremor run through his bowels. According to the map, Baroyeca was a two-day ride. Costello thought he would be afoot by then, if he lived. The horse lurched on.

At Dos Cabezas, when the men went to wash up in the morning, they broke ice in the trough and their breaths hung frosty in the clear air. After breakfast Ignacio Domínguez, the *mulero,* and his son, Encarnación, came to the cyaniding plant with a span of mules and some logging chain. The steel tank sections had been off-loaded from the truck at the foot of the hill. Domínguez and the boy hitched up the mules and began skidding bundled steel plates up the hill to the job.

Perrell set up the little cast-iron forge on its pipe legs. He lighted his charcoal fire in the bowl and cranked the blower to get it hot, then put in a ring of rivets to heat. He showed Buell where to build a fire off to one side on the level ground of the old slag heap, and told him to put a tub of pitch on to heat. "That will be for the seams. Later we'll caulk them with oakum, then we'll give the whole inside a coat of pitch. I'll tong the rivets into the holes and you hold the bucking hammer up snug on 'em, then I'll head 'em."

Seeing Buell's glum expression, Perrell joshed him. "I'm just grateful you had a nice restful visit with Bobby Joe—I expect you'll be a tiger for work today."

*"Shew,"* Buell said.

"Well, what did you talk about with her?"

"Onions and squarsh. I dug up half a acre of ground. You'd of thought she aimed to farm the place."

"You see now, you give a woman a taste of playing house and love flies out the window."

"She is worse than Simon McGee, I'll tell you that."

Hazard came by in the Model T. He left it at the foot of the hill and walked up to the broad terrace in front of the old smelter where silver concentrate was spread out to dry on big sheet metal trays. He poked at the silver with a rake and knelt down to look closely at it. Then he walked out along the slag heap to where Perrell and Buell were working. He looked over what they were doing and nodded, then he said to Buell, "Kid, I want you to spend a few minutes every hour or so raking the stuff in those drying trays." As he was getting back into the Ford, he looked up at them and called out, "Don't step in the trays or your shoes will be worth a month's pay."

"Do you believe that?" Buell said.

Perrell laughed.

Mrs. Sibley did not appear that day at all.

Once in the night, Perrell woke suddenly. He got up and went to the window. A light glowed yellow in the Ibarra house. Perrell looked up and saw that the Dipper had rocked far down in the sky. It was almost dawn and her light was still burning. He thought of what Hazard had said: "Mrs. Sibley has been too much alone . . ."

In the afternoon of the next day, standing at the little forge, Perrell saw Mrs. Sibley ride out again on the gray horse, carrying the box contraption behind her saddle.

Hazard came again to inspect the concentrate. Finding it dry, he put Buell and one of the Mexican boys to work cleaning the trays and putting the powdery concentrate into metal drums. They trundled the drums to the shop in a wheelbarrow and stored them inside. Hazard stopped several times to fuss around the chicken pens.

At quitting time Perrell found himself with a number of red-hot rivets still glowing in the coals of the small forge. He wanted to finish the seam. The ground crumped underfoot— the last blast of the day, underground. A few minutes later he saw the powder man and the Mexican miners heading for the bunkhouse. Buell came out of the shop and started toward him. Perrell waved him on toward the bunkhouse. He tonged a rivet into the hole, feeling the heat of it on his cheek. His hammer peened and the red-hot iron mashed out like cheese. Work was a luxury now, he was thinking, after what he had been through lately. It let him put off serious consideration of what he was going to have to do with himself. Reluctantly he headed the last rivet, then walked down and put his tools away in the shop.

Iron clanged, calling the men to supper. Perrell filled a bucket with water from the faucet and had a quick wash. Hoofbeats sounded over by the Ibarra house as he walked out the door. He watched Mrs. Sibley dismount and hand the bridle reins to the Domínguez boy, then walk up onto the veranda carrying the box, which, because of the folding legs, Perrell took to be a paint box. She saw Perrell and stopped. For a long moment they stood looking at each other across the broad and open ground, yet the distance was great and Perrell sensed nothing but the directness of her gaze. She turned and entered the house. She had a predicament on her hands too, Perrell thought, as serious in its way as his own. And like himself, she appeared to be doing nothing about it.

Perrell found a seat at the rough-hewn table next to Clint. He was still eating when Tracy Hazard stopped at the table and spoke to them.

"Boys, in case you have lost track, this is Saturday. Tonight my bird goes into the pit. You ought not to miss that, because we contend that he is the first of a long and noble line of champions." He looked at 'Nacio Domínguez and grinned, a little uneasily, Perrell thought.

"*Sí,*" Domínguez said gravely. "*Un campeón.*"

Buell mumbled something then and slipped away from the table. He walked rapidly down the old cobbled roadway that fronted the adobe houses.

"His mind is not on fighting chickens," Perrell said. "He wants to see Bobby Joe."

"How about you fellows?" Hazard said. "I'll stand you a drink at Molina's place."

"I've got to clean up first," Perrell said. "I'll walk on down a little later."

"If you get lost," Hazard said, "ask for the *pelea de gallos.*"

Clint and Hazard left Perrell to finish eating and walked down past the crumbled adobes and the bunkhouse to the shop, where the Ford sat next to the chicken coops at the end of the building. Hazard leaned down and peered through wire at the long-legged red rooster. Clint saw that his hands were shaking. The rooster stood on one foot and looked at them sidewise with one yellow eye. "Do it, boy," Hazard said. To Clint he said, "I'll stand you that drink now. It will help settle my stomach." He turned and climbed into the Ford.

"Ain't you takin the chicken with us?" Clint said.

Hazard grimaced. "No. The Domínguez kid is my bird handler." He looked slightly embarrassed. "To be honest about it, I'm too squeamish for this game." He set spark and throttle. "You want to drive?"

"I don't know how," Clint said. Hazard shot him a startled look. He pushed the left foot pedal halfway down and let off the hand brake. The Ford rolled away very slowly, down the gentle slope toward the Ibarra house, gravel whispering under the narrow tires. Clint saw Buell talking to Bobby Joe—the kid's shoulders were hunched and his chin was down. She was giving him a bad time. Suddenly Buell made a chopping gesture with his hand, turned and walked away from the girl. Hazard switched on the ignition and pushed the pedal to the floor. The car backfired and jerked forward. Clint grabbed the edge of the seat with both hands.

"It beats cranking," Hazard said, over the clatter of the engine. Hearing the engine, Buell looked up then, waved and ran to meet them.

"The kid wants to come, after all," Clint said. Hazard stomped on the brake pedal and Clint was thrown forward. Buell jumped onto the truck bed back of the seat. His face was flushed and angry. Clint grinned to himself. The Ford jounced away again. Hazard hunched over the wheel now, intent on the narrow arroyo road. "Nothing to it," he shouted.

To Clint, the Ford seemed to lunge and stagger in the chalky ruts. Far below, he saw the white slash of the road and the wooden bridge. The sun hung red and bloated over the hazy, distant plain. Closer, a dust cloud boiled up from the rolling foothills. Someone pushing a herd of cows, he thought. The fire of the sunset was flaring high, reaching out across the sky overhead.

Clinging to the seat of the Ford, Clint said, "I never had nothin to do with autos. My first ride was comin up here in that wagon."

"Truck," Hazard said. They wheeled onto a narrow street. High adobe walls. Barred windows. The Ford turned around the big circular fountain—Clint remembered it from the truck ride—and swung into a long, narrow plaza. Great jacaranda trees streamed their feathers down the center of the plaza. Hazard braked the Ford. It lurched against the high curb on the right, rocked, died.

"Molina's place," Hazard said. "Good man."

Double doors stood open, sagging at mortised joints, the ancient mahogany panels weathered and cracked. Inside, Clint saw white-plastered walls, several men standing at an ornate mahogany bar along the wall at his left, and beyond, through another doorway, a patio enclosed by a covered portico, with pillars of kiln-fired adobe. An ancient bougainvillaea glowed coolly under the fiery sky. A black goat stood next to a pile of unshucked corn, chewing. The goat fixed its ice-white square-eyed gaze on Clint.

Hilario Molina turned from lighting coal-oil lamps behind the bar, a plump man in a white shirt with arm garters and string tie, a man with an exceedingly fine head, hair parted high and dressed in two sweeping wings over his brow, with the sides combed forward at the temples. Hazard spoke warmly to him, then introduced the Americans in Spanish. The other men at the bar nodded in grave courtesy. Molina set out glasses, salt, *limón*—lime.

"No hard stuff for me," Buell said.

"Give him *leche de cabra,*" Hazard said, nodding at the black goat, "goat's milk, to make him grow." To Clint he said, "Drink up, man. *Salud.*"

The powder man took a sip. When he sucked the lime, its tartness tamed the sour bite of the tequila on the back of his tongue. He shivered. A drink was something he had not had in a long time. But he was not a drinking man—a drink was not what he had missed in prison. At that moment a young Mexican girl of fifteen or sixteen appeared in the patio and fluttered her apron to shoo the goat away from the corn. Her brown shoulders were bare and her breasts bobbed against the thin cotton of her blouse. A pang struck him beneath his ribs. *She looks the way Elena did,* he thought—but Elena belonged back there, a long time ago. When he went to see her after getting out of the pen, he had stood across the street waiting for a glimpse of her and when he saw her he was stricken like a man clubbed. *I wouldn't have knowed her . . .*

Feeling his eyes upon her, the girl laughed shyly. The laugh faded to an uncertain smile under the big man's brooding stare, then the girl turned quickly away.

Clint blinked. He thought of how she had looked a moment earlier, shooing the goat with her apron. He ground his teeth together and took a deep breath. First, he thought, I've got to find me a way to get across the damn mountains to Chihuahua. To Cusichic.

He saw that his glass had been filled, then heard the voices of the men at the bar. Cockfight talk.

Molina leaned over the bar and said to Tracy Hazard, "Tell me, *amigo,* this eagle of yours—what class of bird is he?"

Bobby Joe watched Buell as he ran and caught up with the Ford. She wished that she had not snapped so sharply at him—not that what she said wasn't every bit true. But she had not aimed for him to leave her alone. She turned away from the heavy mahogany doors and her sandals rasped loudly on the tile. The house suddenly seemed vast, dark and empty. She was furious with Buell for leaving her alone. To get away from the darkness, she walked out into the patio, past the fountain and down the tile steps onto the swept earthen floor of the terrace. She stayed back from the stone wall—it made her giddy to look down that terrible steep cliff. The sun lay like a huge coal in its ashy bed of haze beyond the brushy hills. Its red light glowed pearly on her skin. A cloud of dust drifted in hanging shreds, like distant rain. A big mess of cows yonder, she thought.

The breeze was turning chilly. She wanted to get back into the house and get some lamps lighted before dark. Inside, she found a lamp on a great carved table and lighted it with shaky fingers, then she scurried from room to room lighting other lamps until she had pushed back the darkness. In the kitchen she found that Lupe had gone off and left a pile of dampened laundry. Bobby Joe stirred up the fire in the stove. There were four irons on the back of the stove. She opened the damper and moved the irons forward. She shook out a piece of laundry, a white petticoat of Mrs. Sibley's. A tear trickled down Bobby Joe's cheek.

Granddaddy had always been ornery and mean as sin, but he was *company*. As far back as she could remember, she had never been alone. She licked her finger and tried the iron, and hot metal popped to her touch. She began to iron the petticoat, fiercely stabbing and thrusting with the hot iron. That dratted, mule-headed Buell—he had to go and get his back up, when if he had knowed it, he could have just give her a little kiss instead. That was all she wanted, but he made it so blamed hard to tell him so. Tears splattered the petticoat and hissed under the iron.

Everyone was gone from the bunkhouse. Perrell went out back and shaved, then he stripped and had himself a stand-up bath next to the trough. His dark suit was a ruin. He had been working in old clothes left behind by former occupants of the bunkhouse. He put on Levis, clean but ancient, faded pale blue, a flannel shirt with the elbow out, and then his suit coat after he slapped the dust from it.

He walked toward the arroyo road. The red sun hung in haze over the horizon. Passing the shop, he saw that the door was open again and there was movement above the gleam of the Flyer's head lamps, a stroke of white in the gloom. He walked closer. The white was the ruffled front of Mrs. Sibley's shirt and she was sitting at the wheel of the Flyer. She was wearing her leather riding skirt and jacket. Next to her on the seat was a dark woolen poncho, called a *cobija*, with her braid-trimmed hat on it. Standing on the brim of the hat was the Flyer's silver flask, now clean and lustrous and no doubt at least partly full—the telescoping cup was in her hand.

"I see you're traveling, ma'am."

"Yes, traveling, Mr. Perrell ... old roads, old voyages." She sipped from the cup.

"I saw you ride out again today. Where do you go?"

"Here and there—lately out to the old silver road. I go to paint. I'll have you know I went to art school in Philadelphia, something like a century ago. It used to be a serious thing with me."

"Used to be?"

She shrugged. "It's a way of . . . exploring. But it's a two-edged sword. It cuts both ways. The limits of girlish enthusiasm are soon explored. It can be depressing."

"I don't quite see . . ."

"All right, say you have an idea—a glimpse beforehand into . . . whatever it is. Like another country. Then you see what works out under the hand. Never, never the same. That's what I mean." She poured into the cup and handed it to him. "Would you know about that?"

"I'm just a working stiff, Mrs. Sibley. But it may surprise you that I know exactly what you mean." He handed back the empty cup. She laughed suddenly.

"It may surprise you, Mr. Perrell, but I *knew* that you would know." She poured again into the cup. "You're going down to the village?"

"Yes, I understand there's going to be a cockfight."

"A cockfight," she said. "Splendid. I do loathe these disgusting chickens that Tracy Hazard keeps, but a cockfight—that's something else again." She sipped, considering. "John Trouble, I would like it very much if you would allow me to go along with you to that cockfight. Watching a couple of chickens peck one another to death would suit my present mood precisely."

He hesitated. "I may as well be honest with you, Mrs. Sibley. I may sound like trouble, but I don't willingly seek trouble."

"My husband has been gone from here for six months. It is sometimes necessary for me to go here or there. Certainly no one expects me to go about alone." She passed the cup again.

Still he hesitated. She said, "In Baroyeca, women are not seen at the cockfights, ordinarily. I would simply feel better going with someone. Childish, no doubt, but what do you say, John Trouble? Will you humor me?"

"Taken in that light, Mrs. Sibley, I will be happy to humor you." He was not happy, precisely. He was uneasy. But he found himself not wanting to leave her, for reasons which were obscure to him. He drank the brandy and handed the cup to her. She replaced it on the flask and slipped the flask into the large pocket of her leather skirt. He reached to help her and she jumped down, half turned against him, looked up, her eyes suddenly wide, startled, as he was suddenly to find himself kissing her—awkwardly kissing for uneasy seconds, their arms stiff and bodies misaligned, noses bumping. Then with a gasp, her mouth opened and she squirmed hard against him, her hands, mouth and body moving, the unease and the bad awkward angles melting as Perrell strained and sought with her in sudden hunger.

She pulled her head away, gasping for air, and sank against the fender. When he moved to touch her, she put a hand on his chest and shook her head. After a moment she turned and picked up her hat and the poncho, then she walked past him to the door. He thought the incident—whatever it had started out to be—was over and done, but she turned and said in a shaky whisper, "The chickens won't wait for us, will they? Come on."

They walked past her house and on under the timbers of the loading chute and onto the narrow arroyo road without exchanging a word. The sun was gone and the hazy distant plain was a molten red sea. Closer, over the foothills, a purpling dust cloud hovered. On the twisting shelf of road, with the cliff falling away into the arroyo, they were very much alone. She stumbled once or twice, then stepped too close to the edge of the road and he pulled at her sleeve. Smiling, she took his arm and walked on. Near where the road turned toward the village, she stopped and put the silver flask in his hand. While he pulled off the cap and filled it, she looked musingly at the dust cloud, frowning a little. They shared the cup, passing it back and forth. He started to put it away and she said, "No good trying to walk on one leg," so he filled it again. The flask was light in his hand. She said, "Forgive me for not talking. I didn't want to hear myself say something stupid." He bent and kissed her again, quickly.

"Don't then. Come on."

# (20)

Entry to the cockpit was up a long cobbled ramp, through an archway of stone into which was set a pair of two-inch-thick oak doors, studded, bound and hinged with iron.

The building was one of the very oldest in Baroyeca, older even than the church, having been built as a storehouse for ingots of silver. The cobbled ramp was deeply trenched from the hoofs of countless mules that had entered or left bearing untold thousands of pounds of silver. Inside, the cockpit was twenty-one feet in diameter, and four rows of plank seats rose above it.

When Perrell and Mrs. Sibley came to the old storehouse, it was dark. He saw a ramp ahead, with yellow light spilling out over it from inside. Tracy Hazard, tottering a little, was just walking up the ramp with Clint, Buell and a number of Mexicans. Mrs. Sibley strode confidently ahead and joined the stream of people. In a moment Perrell, too, was caught, her elbow was against his ribs and he let the press of warm bodies move him toward the lighted archway.

He tilted his head back, saw errant beams of light escaping through broken tiles in the roof, curling wisps of tobacco smoke caught in the funnels of light. Then they were inside, taking seats. He saw Hazard and Clint and Buell across a corner of the cockpit. Mrs. Sibley sat beside him with her chin on her fist, staring. Two bird handlers entered the cockpit with roosters under their arms. Perrell turned to watch them.

Tracy Hazard felt the tequila working inside him. Shuffling figures swam in an ochre blur—among them he saw Amanda Sibley and the new man, Perrell, as he wrenched his eyes into focus for a moment, then felt them skid away. Next to him, Hilario said something about the first fight. It made him want to gag. He swallowed hard, thinking of his bird.

He heard an explosive *spawk!* and shook his head to bring the pit into focus again. Three feet off the earthen floor, a puff of feathers swirled and drifted. Beneath the feathers, a tan cock lay on his breast—thank God it wasn't his bird!—its wings awkwardly half spread, the bright-yellow legs stretched straight out beneath it. A drop of blood formed on its beak. The bird's head swung once in a slow arc, then the head toppled, beak first, and the drop of blood rolled free in the dust. The cock's wings and toes stiffened in a shudder. Tracy Hazard heard Hilario shout, close to his ear, *"Hombre,* one big shot, that's all."

A little smile took shape on Mrs. Sibley's moist lips. Losers moved around to pay off. Handlers moved into the ring again and Hazard's stomach churned for a moment, and then he saw that his own bird was not to be in the fight. His mind wandered. The birds were pitted—a white bird flecked with black against a wiry black rooster with a metallic green ruff and tail. Time blurred.

"That cockroach betrayed me!" Hilario exclaimed. Hazard was startled to see that the fight was over. Then Hilario nudged him. "Your chicken, *amigo*—now he fights."

Hazard's stomach heaved. For a moment he had almost forgotten. The boy, Encarnación Domínguez, stepped into the ring with the Baroyeca chicken under his arm, his face arrogant with pride. Up in the tiers of seats, bets were being made. Around Hazard, a cluster of men rose noisily to stand for the Baroyeca bird. Hazard fumbled out a handful of bills and coins and gave them to Hilario to bet for him.

Seeing him do that, Mrs. Sibley rose and called out, "Fifty dollars, Tracy—fifty dollars gold against your smelly chicken." Looking down at Perrell, she laughed and said, "He'll pay dearly now, John Trouble—did you *see* what those nasty things did all over my lovely Flyer? He'll pay now." She swayed, then sat down. Across the corner of the pit, Tracy was nodding grimly at her, his glasses askew.

The referee, a village ancient named Gregorio Alarcón, shuffled forward with a peculiar hitching gait and motioned the bird handlers into the ring. He held out his hands, palms up, and turned his head in a slow, sweeping movement, his white-bristled chin thrust out fiercely. The babble died away. The old man grunted and brought his two forefingers together in front of his face, *pico a pico,* beak to beak. The bird handlers held the roosters out at arm's length. Thus suddenly confronting each other, the birds struggled convulsively to free themselves, eyes fixed, glittering like agate, their beaks poised like lances while fury stirred and pumped through their bodies. The old man's hands clapped together sharply. The handlers released the birds and stepped back out of the ring of amber light.

Wings slightly spread, neck feathers ruffed, the cocks crouched; at first almost perfectly still, then probing tentatively with their outthrust beaks, they started to circle. Abruptly the Baroyeca bird began to bob its head in a series of rhythmic feints, then without any visible signal the cocks leaped high, wings flapping furiously, their legs a blur of raking gaffs. Standing on their tails in the air, they rose for an instant, then their legs tangled and caught and they fell in a puff of dust. On signal, the handlers smoothly separated the cocks, gently disengaging their feet. A bright stain of red showed on the Baroyeca bird's thigh.

Pitted again, the birds circled once more. Again the flurry and beat of wings fanning the smoky blue air above the birds—the smoke boiled. They flurried again and Hazard saw that his red bird was clearly slower. Its left wing hung low, and it lurched when the black-and-white bird drove it to circle. The black-and-white speared for the Baroyeca bird's cropped comb—its beak caught there on a shred of flesh and it swung under with gaffs slashing. The red Baroyeca bird toppled onto his side and lay there, blood now marking the shuddering breast. The black-and-white lanced with his beak for the fallen bird's eye, missed, but drew blood on the head. Hazard's heart sank into his bowels. Then the black-and-white stood back and crowed.

Gregorio Alarcón snapped his fingers and motioned the handlers in. They scooped up the birds. Encarnación was white-faced. He dabbed a cloth in a can of water and bathed the rooster's ruff, blowing on the bird and talking to it in frantic whispers.

The referee pitted the birds again. Immediately the Baroyeca bird staggered and toppled onto his side. Alarcón began his count, chopping out the cadence with his hand. Laughing aficionados picked up the count and chanted it, and Hazard saw a blurry Amanda Sibley laughing and clapping, chanting with the count: *"Cinco, SEIS, SIETE, O-OCHO . . ."* Hazard turned away and held his head in his hands—the room was spinning for him.

*"NUEV—"* The crowd's chanting broke into a gasp. Hilario's hand was pounding his shoulder. Hazard's head felt very loose on his shoulders. He gagged, trying desperately not to be sick.

*"Mire, hombre—mírelo.* Look." Hilario had taken hold of his chin and was pulling his head around.

*"Cuidado,* man, with my head," Hazard moaned. The gasp of the crowd had turned to a chattering din. His eyes

opened. The room shuddered to a precarious stop, rocking a little.

The Baroyeca bird, incredibly, was on its feet, staggering, its wings dragging. The black-and-white cock was on its back, its feet in the air. It was stone dead.

Someone had hold of Hazard's hand, was turning it over and cramming coins into it, saying, *"Qué bueno, qué bravo!"* Encarnación scooped up the Baroyeca bird as it sagged down, cradled it in the crook of his arm. Tears streamed down the boy's face. Hilario helped Hazard with the coins, stuffing his pockets.

"The black-and-white—that crazy chicken," he was saying, "he stopped to crow, and our bird, *por Dios!*, our eagle got up and cut him down!" Hilario smote his chest savagely. Silver coins spilled from his fist and rolled on the planks of the bench. "He came up out of the dirt and cut the bastard down, and I thought he was dead!"

Mrs. Sibley turned unsteadily and thrust her face close to Perrell's, her eyes blinking. He felt the warm softness of her bosom against his forearm. "Oh, John Trouble," she said very carefully and earnestly, "that nasty, *stinking* thing!" Her eyes wandered. He realized that the heat of the room and the excitement had stirred up the fumes of the brandy and that she was quite drunk.

Perrell was trying not to grin. He thought he heard a kind of rumbling sound, but the aficionados were all on their feet, standing on the plank seats. Even so, he thought he heard it again, a drumming in the earth. He thought of coal spilling down a long chute. No, like cattle on a wooden bridge, rumbling.

A shot sounded outside, in the night. Instantly the room fell hushed, people staring, one to another. Another shot sounded, then four or five in a string, very loud, the echoes racketing among the buildings, followed by a long, terrible scream.

The boy, Encarnación, clutched the sabered body of the dying rooster to his shirt front and moved with the others under the guns of red-eyed bearded men in tall-crowned sombreros, crossed cartridge belts, and filthy scraps and tatters of uniform. He saw mounted horsemen ringing the people as they streamed down the ramp into the street, then felt his father's hand against his shoulder. The boy pressed the limp form of the rooster into the hands of the *patrón,* Don Treci, then his father's hand swept him behind the massive, studded door. He felt the hard blunt thumb stab at his spine. *"Ándale, muchacho,"* his father breathed and was gone, shuffling with the others.

Outside, Rodrigo Vega sat on his horse in the narrow plaza as the people were herded before him. The darkness was cut by a spray of dim yellow light from the doorway of the old silver house. His eyes quickly found the small cluster of Americans, one a woman who was partly supported by the man next to her. He raised a hand and waited while the babble slowly died.

Costello sat in the ring of horsemen behind Vega. His hands were lashed to his saddle horn, and his halter rope was secured to the saddle horn of the rider on his left. He, too, saw the Americans, including a big man with a familiar scarred face. Because of the dim light, Costello could not tell if he himself was seen by the Americans.

When Rodrigo Vega spoke, his voice was almost gentle. *"Ahora,* now we will speak to the *alcalde,* the mayor."

An aged cabinet maker named Alberto Torres, called *jefe* by the people, politely removed his straw hat and shuffled forward, looking up at the young man with the strangely hooded almond eyes.

"Señor?" Alberto Torres said.

A worm wriggled under the skin of the young man's cheek. He raised a pearl-handled Smith & Wesson and shot Alberto Torres in the chest—for Torres, the sound of the shot was lost in the noiseless thunder of the bullet crashing into his breastbone, and the shocked cries of the people were the roaring that filled his ears as he was hurled back into the arms of Hilario Molina.

Shocked, hot tears of fury streamed from Molina's eyes as

he lowered his friend to the cobbles. He shook his fist and cried out, choking, *"Asesinos!"* Instantly, Vega fired again, the gunshot concussing like a cannon in the narrow plaza, echoing distantly, raggedly, off the hills. Hilario Molina fell on his side. Tracy Hazard sank to one knee next to him, still clutching the wounded bird. Molina tried to speak to him, then his eyes roved away and froze into a stare.

Bit chains chinked and saddle leather squealed. A horse blew. Softly, in the hush, Vega said in Spanish, "This is merely to say that the revolution has come to Baroyeca. We will expect immediate obedience to the discipline of the revolution."

The faint sound of weeping scratched the silence as Vega scanned the stunned faces.

"Now it is our intention to be taken to Dos Cabezas, and we will be accompanied by the gringos who are stealing Mexican silver from the people."

He waited a moment, then his lips peeled back and the worm wriggled. He pointed the pistol at one of the gringos, a sandy-haired man with eyeglasses who held a chicken in his arms. *"Por Dios,"* Vega said, then he lapsed into English. "It is easy to make death."

Tracy Hazard's mouth hung open. Drunk or dazed, he did not answer, and Perrell saw a tremor shake the hand that held the pistol. Still holding Mrs. Sibley, he shouldered past Hazard and looked up into the hooded eyes.

"We'll take you to Dos Cabezas."

Vega smiled. Reasonably. Companionably. *"Bueno.* All of you," he said. "We want all of you gringos." He frowned slightly, looking at the faces before him. "This man Clinton—is he here?"

Perplexed, Perrell hesitated. The man's cheek squirmed. "He's here," Perrell said. "With us."

"Splendid," Vega murmured.

Through the crack at the doorjamb, Encarnación saw the deaths of the *jefe* and Hilario Molina and heard the *asesino,* the murderer, say that he was going to Dos Cabezas. He saw Don Treci and the other Americans herded at gunpoint onto the Ford. With armed *renegados* on the running boards, the car was started. The boy slipped from behind the door and fled down the ramp, then darted into a narrow alleyway that cut between the crumbling adobes to the edge of the village and the old footpath that snaked over the hill to *la mina de las Dos Cabezas,* where at this hour there would be found Encarnación's mother and sisters and the women and children of a few other families and all of the animals. It was a steep and flinty trail, but much faster than the arroyo road if one had the wind and the heart for it.

Bobby Joe carried a stack of folded ironing into Mrs. Sibley's room. With her free hand, she held a lamp before her. Yellow light washed across the plastered walls, glowed from spiral-carved posts of a vast baroque bed, gleamed back at her from the three tall mirrors over the dressing table. She put the lamp down and opened the paneled doors of the great mahogany *armario*—and gasped, for she had never seen such a glorious treasure. Gowns and robes hung in rich folds of velvet and silk, frothy with lace and plumes of ostrich and bird of paradise.

Her fingers fumbled at her blouse and skirt. They slipped to the floor. She saw herself in the mirrors, standing in her plain long cotton drawers. She wrinkled her nose and wriggled out of them, at the same time reaching out to take a champagne-colored lace gown off the rack.

A long time later, Bobby Joe stood before the mirrors in a wine-colored velvet gown. On her head was an enormous ostrich-plumed hat that matched the velvet gown. She shrugged and then let the gown slip off her shoulders. It slid down and caught at her hips, the soft drapes clinging, wine-red. Seeing her own bare shoulders and breasts, she was aware of her nakedness for the first time since she had opened the *armario.* She had never seen her whole body reflected in a mirror, much less a three-paneled mirror that revealed her to herself not only from the front, but from the sides and other angles as well. She turned slightly, fascinated with the naked stranger staring so intently off to one side. An ostrich plume curling off the brim of the big hat tickled her breast. She giggled. The velvet folds slipped off her hips and dropped around her ankles. She stood wearing nothing but the big hat, feeling wicked and abandoned, hearing but not noticing the muffled clop of horses' hoofs and the slow clatter of the Ford's engine out on the arroyo road.

Until the Ford backfired. She heard the crunch of its tires as it swung around before the veranda and halted. Her own room was at the other end of the house, by the kitchen. She stepped out of the velvet folds and darted into the hall. The big hat flopped over her eyes and she pulled it off, aware now of the sound of men laughing, the sound of booted feet on the tiled steps. Holding the hat, she ran down the long tunnel of the hallway, hearing, as she passed, the massive click of the door latch.

The doors swung open. Charlie Slotter and Red Durkin, drawn weapons in their hands, stepped inside followed by the slender figure of Rodrigo Vega.

"The place is all lit up," Slotter said. He cocked his Colt revolver, then jerked his chin at Durkin. Together, they began to walk down the hall.

# (21)

Perrell sat with his hands on the steering wheel of the silenced Ford. Mrs. Sibley slumped against him wrapped in her poncho, her head lolling. The other three men sat behind on the truck bed. Hazard, with glasses askew on his nose, still held the wounded rooster. Horsemen surrounded them.

Lanterns winked and flared as some of Vega's men rode out across the compound toward the houses strung along the slope. The houses were all dark. A cow bawled somewhere in the hills nearby.

Shadows moved along the lighted windows of the Ibarra house. Then, inside the house, a squealing screech sounded. And a man's voice, furious.

Buell jerked to his knees on the truck. A rail-thin, bearded *renegado* snarled at him in a strange language and prodded him sharply with a short-barreled Mauser rifle. Buell thumped a meaty fist against the back of the seat.

"Them dirty son of a bitches," he whispered to Perrell. "I let her get me mad, see? Now them bastards have got her."

In the thin wash of light from the windows, Buell's face was white, the old bruises like stains. They heard the man swearing, another laughing as Bobby Joe screeched. The latch rattled and the door swung open.

"You keep your stinkin paws off me," Bobby Joe snarled.

Charlie Slotter pushed her through the door onto the veranda. She was wearing her old frayed overalls again, unbuttoned and flopping at the sides, one shoulder strap unhooked, the stained blue shirt buttoned all wrong and the tails flying. Slotter's booted foot thunked solidly against her rump and drove her sprawling down the steps. "By God, I ought to tan your ass with a cinch strap," he said. Behind him, Red Durkin leaned against the door, laughing. Slotter glared down at Perrell. "It's time somebody learned this little shit some manners. I can't stand a snotty kid, dammit. Never could."

Bobby Joe clutched at the seat of her overalls and scuttled over next to Perrell. Durkin laughed again. "Shut up, Red," Charlie Slotter said.

"Get up on the truck, Bobby Joe," Perrell said. She climbed up behind him. He turned to look back at her and saw Clint staring fixedly at one of the riders clustered near the truck, a small man, mustached, with a derby hat. The man's hands were tied to his saddle horn. Beyond him a lantern bobbed— one of the renegades coming back from looking over the compound. The man rode his horse close to the veranda and spoke to Durkin. "Yonder is the best place to keep 'em, Red." The rider pointed toward the shop building. "It's out in the open and there's bars on the windows."

Vega appeared in the doorway. He spoke inaudibly to Durkin. Orders, Perrell thought. Vega's hand flicked toward the prisoners, then he went back into the house. Durkin looked down at Perrell. "Start up the auto, friend." Buell climbed down and cranked the Ford, and Perrell drove it slowly to the shop with riders herding close around the car. They swung around in front of the big roll-back door and Perrell switched off the engine. Durkin and Slotter went into the shop. Lanterns were lighted. The two men moved around inside, looking at the banks of storage shelves and bins and the loft above.

At the doorway Durkin said, "It will do."

"There's a hell of a lot of junk in here," Slotter said. "They could get into mischief."

"There ain't anything like dynamite. The rest is trash and I'm too wore out to sort through it. Tell you what—" He turned to Perrell. "You people come on in here. Keep two lamps burnin all the time. There will be men outside watchin you, don't forget that."

Perrell helped Mrs. Sibley down. She slumped against him, her head against his chest. Her shoulders were loose under his arm as he walked her into the shop. He opened the rear door of the Flyer and eased her up into the seat. A chicken clucked and pecked at his hand.

"Him too, Red," Slotter was saying.

"That's right—you too, Pat." Durkin grinned mockingly and jerked his thumb at the man wearing the derby. Someone cut the cords that bound his hands to the saddle horn. The man swung down and entered the shop behind Buell and Bobby Joe. Clint turned away from the others and faced Durkin stiffly.

"You don't aim to keep me locked up in here now, do you, Red?" the powder man said.

Instantly Charlie Slotter drew a gun and jammed it into Clint's ribs. "You git on in there, by God . . ."

"Hold on, Charlie," Red Durkin said. "Me and him"—he nodded at Clint—"we was like, you could say school chums. We done time together at Yuma."

"How about it, Red?" Clint said.

Durkin rubbed his bristly jaw with a dirty thumb. "You're a powder man, chum. I bet you know where the keys are."

"The key to the powder house is hangin on that board yonder above the bench," Clint said. "Nothin else is locked."

Slotter went and got the key. A bunch of lousy cons sticking together, Perrell thought furiously.

"All right, Red," Clint said. "I mean, god damn, how about it now?"

"C'mere, chum." Durkin's big hat bobbed as he jerked his chin for Clint to follow. He walked away several yards, and standing between two banks of shelves, the men spoke in low voices, Clint insistent, Durkin grinning still and affable, shrugging his shoulders under crossed cartridge belts. Perrell could not hear what was said, except that he thought Durkin said something about Chihuahua, wagging his head under the straw hat, then the powder man's shoulders stiffened and his fists knotted up as Durkin talked on. After a couple of minutes they came back and Durkin was saying, ". . . it don't pay to mess with Vega. I can't do nothin without he tells me to do it." Durkin was still grinning, but the powder man was scowling darkly.

Durkin looked out at his men and said, "Simmons, you and—make it Sarky—you two can build you a little fire yonder 'mongst that mess of timbers. A little guard duty, see? Trade off walkin around."

Simmons was a scrawny young gunman with straw-colored hair whose face also decorated a Pinkerton card. "Jesus, Red, I'm just wore out for sleep. I ain't—"

Durkin's bucktooth grin vanished. "You son of a bitch—do what I tell you." He turned back to the prisoners, mockingly affable again. "See there, now?—we have been on the go for a long time and our tempers is running short. We'll iron all this out in the mornin. See you keep them lamps lit, hear?"

Soft yellow light from the oil lamps sprayed out from the workbench along the end wall, past the hooded brick hearth of the forge, and touched the Flyer here and there on brass or lacquer. The rear door of the Flyer was open and Mrs. Sibley was asleep inside, her head pillowed on one arm, the hand outflung and dangling. Her mouth was open and she was snoring gently.

Through the dirty window at the end of the workbench, Perrell saw the small fire set by the two men guarding them. Lights glowed in the windows of miners' houses where the renegades had billeted themselves. He swung away from the window and walked stiffly around the great dead hull of the Flyer. He slapped at the horn of the anvil, gripped it hard—down the flume again, he thought. Bobby Joe had climbed up on the workbench. She sat with her knees drawn up, shivering. Buell found a piece of sacking and put it over her shoulders, holding it there with his hands. His voice was shaky. "Are you all right?"

She twisted away from his hands. "You! You had to git mad and leave me there alone." She looked at Perrell and tears hung in her lashes. "When they come in, I was—there wasn't hardly time . . ." She fingered the strap of her overalls. "I told them you was my dad."

"If I was, I'd have paddled you long before this," Perrell said, trying to tease away the tears. They splashed, anyway, and quickly he said, "No, you did just right, sis."

The wiry stranger who had come with the renegades blinked. "Sis, is it? Well, I'll be damned." He sat quietly on a nail keg out at the edge of the lamplight by the Flyer, his hands knotted around one knee.

"How come you to be with that outfit?" Perrell said.

The man chewed on a kitchen match. Reflected lamplight gleamed from shadowy eyes beneath a derby hat. "They picked me up when I got off the train at a siding. I expect they wanted to stop the train, but it was full of soldiers."

"Well, all right, but what were you *doing* there?"

The man hesitated. Clint laughed. A sharp bark.

"Go ahead and tell him," he said. "It's been a long time, but you didn't think I would forget, did you?"

Costello bit off a piece of the match and spat it out, then said wryly, "I didn't aim for you to see me just yet."

Clint said, "How come they didn't put another man on it?"

"There wasn't nobody who could have took the same personal interest in it—I asked for it. I wanted to close the file on you myself."

"The file *is* closed. I done my time, every damn minute of it."

The man didn't answer. Clint glared fixedly. A sputtering laugh exploded from Perrell. Both men looked at him, surprised. He bent over the anvil, shaking his head. He caught his breath. "So you're a John Law. By God, that's rich—the fox and the chicken locked up together. Tell me that ain't funny." He laughed again. "Trouble is, the rest of us chickens are locked up with you, too. Are you railroad law, or what?"

"His name is Costello," Clint said. "He's a Pinkerton man."

"Pinkerton!" Disgust was in Perrell's voice. "Well, sure—any other law would have stopped at the border. Look, mister, you were with those people. What are they really after? I mean, hell, a place like this."

"They're on the run," Costello said. "They've took a couple of bad lickins. Some of them are hurt or sick. They need a place to hole up where them Yaqui soldiers won't find them. They need money and fresh horses. Vega will want to keep the money for himself. He lost a few thousand in gold coin at Hermosillo."

"What money?" Perrell said.

"Whatever he gets here—from the mine. It's a silver mine, right? They're talkin silver, or a payroll, maybe."

Tracy Hazard sat rocking on a crate near the forge, the chicken limp on his knees. "No money here, no silver, no payroll. Everything . . . Navajoa."

"You'll never convince Vega of that," Costello said. "He'll tear this place apart."

"No silver."

Costello frowned. "He'll make short work of us, then."

Mildly spoken, the words were almost meaningless. Incredulous, Bobby Joe said, "You mean he would *shoot* us?"

"Not right away, I expect," Costello said. "He'll figure we're coverin up, so he'll want to make us talk, make us tell where the stuff is hid."

"You don't know that for sure, mister," Buell said.

Costello turned his hands up. "No."

"All right, let's see where that leads us," Perrell said. "Supposing there *was* some money here? Could we buy our way out?"

Costello thought for a moment, then shook his head. "You've seen Vega. Killin don't mean anything to him. He'll take whatever he can get out of us, then step on us."

"I say we can strike a . . . strike a bargain," Hazard said. "You know—ransom. Company money."

"But that would take time," Costello said. "It would mean bringin someone else into it, and there would be the danger of soldiers gettin wind of it."

"Sure," Hazard said. "This Vega, he wants money. Long as he thinks we can get it for him, he'll treat us okay, see? We're no good to him dead."

"No, Vega won't wait. If you think you can stall him or sweet-talk him—by God, mister, you've *seen* him kill."

"We can't take a chance on him," Perrell said.

"No?" Hazard smiled indulgently, his eyes wandering a little behind the cocked lenses. "How do you propose to *not* take a chance on him?"

"We've got to bust out of here," Perrell said flatly.

"Not a chance," Hazard said. "Where would you go?"

Clint's head snapped up. "I could be out of this barn in two minutes."

"Okay, but what then? Sixty miles to the railroad. On the road they'd run you down. All brush and cactus if you get off the road. Man on foot would be torn to pieces."

"He might make it," Perrell said. "I mean, they might let him get away with it. If he had a good start, one man wouldn't be worth following. But they would come down hard on the rest of us. Whatever we do"—he turned and faced the powder man—"we have to do together."

"Let them bastards knock us all off together, is what you mean? Not me." Clint's voice was splintery.

"No. Bust out together." Perrell stared hard at him. "I mean it, Clint. No one is going to leave here alone."

"No?" The powder man rose to his feet. Yellow lamplight threw cavernous shadows on the scarred face. "S'pose I'm fixin to skin out of here tonight? I want to know what you would do about it."

"Do you, by God!" Perrell flared, sudden fury thick in his throat. "You scatter trouble wherever you go, dammit—it's on account of you we're here in the first place."

Clint lumbered toward him, crowding him close to the workbench. "That wasn't none of my selection and I won't be hobbled by it."

"I'm telling you—if you skin out and leave us to hack it alone, I will holler for Vega's outfit—"

In his fury and because of the dim light, Perrell did not see the big fist coming. It took him in the ribs a little below the heart and bounced him off the workbench, and the left hand hit him high on his skull. Going down, he felt Clint's forearm club him like a chunk of wood. Dazed, he landed on his knees, knowing the boot was coming. He drove into the sharp shin, clutching at the thick legs. Clint leaned over his back and chopped at his kidney. Hot spike of pain—Perrell gasped and loosened his grip. The knee slammed into his cheekbone and tore him loose, hurled him up and back in a spinning blur of white faces, the lamp's low flame slashing a sabered arc in the dusk. He struck hard on his back, heard his own sharp thudding grunt, tried then to rise, astonished that his own hands, arms, fingers would not answer, and he felt himself gagging on his tongue as the big man towered out of the blur.

Hands clawing at the front of his coat snatched him from the dirt, and he was slung against the side of the Flyer. He slid against the horn bulb and heard the bray of the horn and Mrs. Sibley's small sharp cry in his ears. He thought if he could just find his hands he could hit the bastard, but the flung hands were lost to him and regret was like a deep pang of sadness. Heavy fists pounded his body. The man was snorting like a hog in a trough of slops. The two sprawled over the curve of fender onto the engine. Clint's head was a bobbing patch of grunting dark, then the heavy thumb slid under his jaw and his ears were roaring—Perrell was on a train and the train was in a long dark tunnel.

The thumb skidded away and Clint's face blurred down and the crushing weight was gone. The train was out of the tunnel. Far away, down across his shirt front and the distant promontories of his knees, he saw Clint sitting on the floor with his head wagging.

"Didn't think I hit 'im," Perrell mumbled. His tongue was huge. Then he saw Costello. He had forgotten Costello.

The detective held up a pick handle, slick and yellow-new, and shook his head. "You didn't." He put down the pick handle and looked at Clint. "You all quiet now, Ellred?" Clint nodded slowly. Costello leaned over the fender to help Perrell.

"No, wait," Perrell said. He did not want to move his arms and legs until he had located them and was sure they were still on straight. He was almost comfortable, looking at Costello now through a shock of spark-plug wires.

Costello drew back his hand and frowned. "Are you hurt?"

"No, I'm thinking." Perrell raised a hand and watched it flop back against the softly gleaming brass carburetor.

Costello grunted. "Well, you tell me when you get done thinkin." The others had come close and stood at what appeared to be curious angles—Mrs. Sibley almost upside down to him, white face and dark eyes framed among brass spokes of the wooden steering wheel.

"What I'm thinking," Perrell said, trying hard to talk around the great coil of his tongue, "is how we're going . . . bust out . . . here. What we do, see—" He fluttered his fingers at the engine under him. "What we do is we get the Flyer running. Big, see? Take us all. Get her running . . . bust out."

"Try to suck in some wind," Costello said. "You'll come around in a minute. Damn good thing ol' Ellred don't know how to hit—he had you where he could have hurt you."

Perrell blinked at him, struggled to pull himself up. Buell and Costello took his arms and eased him to his feet. He sagged against the fender and slid down to sit on the running board. "No, I mean it. Look at her."

"Yes. Oh, yes," Mrs. Sibley said above him. She slipped behind the walnut wheel and gripped it gently. Her hair had fallen from its coils and her face was puffy, but when she gripped the wheel a smile tugged at her mouth. She stared into the darkness beyond the lamplight. "Oh, yes. My lovely Flyer."

Costello stepped back. He saw the long, high body,

streaked and spattered, the gutted, dead engine, the down-folded bows and tattered canvas of the top with their burden of chicken droppings, the wheels sunk into flat tires and buried to the rims in dirt. Costello did not understand or trust machinery, except possibly railroad trains. The giant automobile looked to him like the wolf-gnawed carcass of a fallen bull.

Tracy Hazard snorted. "Damn machine is a pile of junk. We've got to *deal* with the man!"

"What have we got to deal with?" Costello said. "Promises? What we know about Vega is that killin don't mean a thing to him. He likes it." Uncertainty crept into his voice. "That machine, will she really go?"

Perrell hugged his aching ribs and took a deep breath. "It will take some work. I looked her over. Everything is there except for some valves, and they must be around here, someplace."

"That chain-drive shaft, it's *broken,* goddammit, *broken!*" Hazard's voice was strident. "And what are you going to use for tires?" He strained to speak clearly.

"I haven't got that far yet," Perrell said. "Look, I know the shaft is broke, but we've got a forge . . . tools."

"How would you fix the shaft?" Hazard demanded.

"You could do it a couple of ways. I thought I would make a sleeve out of a piece of pipe, or if I had to I could forge a sleeve right on the shaft, then drill it and pin it."

"But you'd need to fire up the forge for that, right? And you'd have to use a hammer on it, too. So you're hammering on the goddam anvil, and s'pose you do have to start it up . . . noise like locomotive. What in hell will *they* think about all that?" Hazard stabbed a pointing finger toward the Ibarra house. His face was patchy with fury and exasperation.

"We'll have to cover it some way. I mean, we've got to *think.* It won't cost anything to give it a try, but it won't get done by itself, either."

Clint swallowed noisily. His fingers were probing at the back of his head. "Say it runs—where would you go in it?"

They looked at one another. Costello said, "The railroad?"

"It will have to be the railroad," Perrell said. "Not too far. Downhill most of the way. I mean, I think she'll run, but I don't know how far she'll hold together."

"If we got a good start out of here we could hoof it," Buell said.

"You'd better forget that, kid," Perrell said. "They are certain to come after us. We've got to get a good start on them, all right, but if it comes to walking we're finished—we need plenty of miles. At least as far as the railroad. Maybe more. Suppose the trains aren't running? We *need* the Flyer."

Costello nodded. "The railroad it is then, for a start. You with us now on this, Ellred?"

"Will she really run?"

Perrell stared at the great decrepit monster. "Yes, by God, she'll run."

"Don't think you can get me to go clear back to the border with you," Clint said, looking at Costello.

Costello shook his head. "I don't have no paper on you, nor any way to keep you from goin wherever you want. I'll tell you this—there's a warrant out for you in Tucson. Suspicion of murder, on account of what happened in Healy. Fact is"—his glance took in the others—"you would all be pulled in on it. It's an open warrant, see? Only it's none of my job to serve it. I had the number of that boxcar soon enough, only it didn't serve the company's interest to work too close with the Tucson officers. You understand that, Ellred?"

"Near enough. Don't keep callin me Ellred. My mother was the only one ever called me that."

"We've got worse trouble than that warrant, right here," Perrell said. "If you're with us, you can help. You talked about breaking out of here—maybe you could get at the dynamite, rig something to keep them from getting right after us."

"It's all locked up in the powder house," Clint said. A flush darkened his face. "Some damn fool handed them the key . . . there's caps and fuse here, though."

"All right, the gasoline drums, then. *Something.* We'll need gasoline for the Flyer, too. There is just part of a five-gallon can here—enough to try her out, is all. It would be easy enough to cut through this adobe wall. You could sneak out there in the dark before we bust out, couldn't you?—and fill three or four of these five-gallon cans and wait for us over there by the loading chute."

"Ten minutes ago," Hazard mumbled, "he was going to take off and leave us. You trust him now to do all that?"

"He says he's with us," Perrell said. "We've got to start someplace." He looked at Clint again. "Maybe you could even fuse the gasoline so it would go off after we go—it would make a hell of a fire. Anything to hold them back, see?"

Clint nodded. His jaw was set and he was frowning at Hazard, who got unsteadily to his feet and staggered a few steps past the end of the forge to a long, plank crate that served as a seat next to the workbench, where he slumped down again, still holding the injured bird. He was shaking his head and mumbling disgustedly to himself.

"How much time are you going to need for all this?" Costello said.

Perrell shook his head. "Hard to say. Don't even know all there is to do yet. The exhaust valves are out of her, so they are probably bad. First, we have to find them. So there's the engine, the drive shaft, the tires . . ." He ticked them off on his fingers. "And gasoline. We'll have to fix all that and figure some way to cover up the noise—especially if I have to use the forge. He's right about that, but we'll have to do it some way." Perrell nodded at Hazard and saw that he had slumped over on his bench. His eyes were closed, but he was still mumbling to himself. "All right," Perrell said, "let him sleep it off. He's no good to us this way. Maybe he can think of a way to swindle some time for us."

"Time—maybe there won't be enough time at all," Mrs. Sibley said.

"That's a chance," Costello said. "I take it you are Mrs. Sibley, ma'am." She nodded. A faint smile disturbed Costello's flinty jaw. "I saw your husband in Tucson. He asked me to say, if I was to see you, that he wants you to leave this place. It could get dangerous."

Her eyes crinkled at the corners in the ghost of an answering smile. "He was . . . well?"

"Yes," Costello said. She looked directly, searchingly, at him. Costello, remembering a girl's merry voice in the Cosmo House, looked away. Slowly, a hot flush suffused her face. She stared ahead.

"All right," Costello said hastily, "we know we can't take too long. Vega won't sit still for us. But I expect you'll need what's left of tonight and all day, at least, so Vega will have to be stalled that long, anyway. What do you figure to be the soonest we can break out?"

Perrell wanted, unreasonably, to laugh. His belly knotted with apprehension. "Sometime tomorrow night. Just before dawn, say. Catch most of them sleeping, see?"

"If they let us live that long," Costello said.

Perrell did not answer. He was looking at the drums of silver concentrate clustered inside the door where Buell had put them. He looked at Hazard, who was now sleeping soundly. Perrell shook his head distractedly.

"We'll have to take it as it comes. Let's get started."

# (22)

They hunted for the lost valves, creeping about below the level of the windows so as not to be seen from outside. After almost half an hour, their first eagerness had turned to dejection, then Buell said "Shew!" and held up a rusty coffee can that held the lost valves and springs. It had apparently been knocked from a shelf long ago and fallen into an old nail keg full of horseshoes and scrap iron.

"They're burned," Perrell said. "Not much metal left on most of them—we'll have to grind new faces. We're lucky most of it will be downhill."

"What do we do about the tires?" Buell said.

"The tubes are bad," Perrell said. "Even if we patched them we couldn't trust them, and once we get started, a blow-out would finish us. What we have to do is fill the tires with something besides air."

Buell's face was troubled, then he grinned. "My Uncle Perce, he drove his Ford from Jump-Off Joe out to the lava beds. Huntin, he was, and tires all blowed out. He come home near froze to death cause he stuffed his bedroll in the tires."

"That's the idea!" Perrell said. "Now climb up in the loft and haul down that bunch of tires."

Buell handed down the bundled tires. "I told you," Mrs. Sibley said, "they're much too small."

"They're too narrow, all right," Perrell said, looking at them. "Three by thirty-six. But they're the same rim size."

The men jacked up the Flyer's rear end, then Perrell got down on his knees by the Flyer's great wood-spoked artillery-style wheel and began to unbolt the clamps holding the split rims. When they were loose, he levered the rim off. Metal squealed. Bobby Joe, on the bench next to the window, shaded the glass and looked out at the guards. She shook her head.

"What we'll do," Perrell said, pulling the tire off, "is stuff the little tire into the big one."

Buell clamped an arm over the smaller tire and broke it down like a struggling calf. It snapped free of his hands and filled the empty void in the larger tire. He squeezed it.

"That's hard. She's like an iron wagon tire now."

Perrell shook his head. "Not hard enough—they'll have to carry close to a ton apiece. The rubber is old and brittle. If it flexes much on the road surface, it'll break up. She needs more stuffing—" He looked up suddenly. "Something like a big hawser. I remember a guy in San Francisco who worked on the docks—he swiped some hawser and made a tire out of it. Wired it to the wheel."

"There's some steel cable in the loft," Buell said.

"That ought to do it—it's stiff and springy. Coil it in there till it won't take any more, then clamp down on it with the split rims." He got stiffly to his feet. His ribs hurt when he breathed and he was sore in a dozen other places. "What time is it? Anybody know?"

Costello fished a gold watch from his vest pocket. "Half after one. It was about ten when we broke up the cockfights."

"About five hours to daylight then. We had better be through with the engine and the tires by then, or they'll catch us for sure. It's got to look just the way it did before—to them."

Perrell secured a valve stem in the chuck of the old hand-crank blacksmith drill. He had an oilstone clamped to the working bed of the drill, blocked up to meet the beveled face of the valve at the proper angle. He put a few drops of oil on the stone and began to crank. There was a chirring sound as the whirling valve face met the stone, something hypnotic too, about the sound and the whirling, the bright metal glittering. A soft mantle of fatigue thickened about him. Doggedly he cranked. A hand touched his arm. Mrs. Sibley.

He tried to smile, the muscles in his face sore, stiff as rawhide. After a moment she put her hand on his own right hand, the hand cranking the drill. "Here now, let me turn it." He let her have it and rubbed his aching shoulder.

*"Hist!"* Bobby Joe said. "One of them guys is comin." Chickens clucked sullenly from the roosts outside. Perrell saw Buell and Costello stretch out where they were. He put his own head down on folded arms. Mrs. Sibley had quit cranking and toppled over on the bench, her face only a few inches from his own. He felt the warmth of her breath on his hand. Outside, gravel crunched, steps moved slowly along the wall. A chicken squawked suddenly and a man's startled voice spat a sharp alien word. The sound of steps receded then. Perrell turned his head on his arms and opened his eyes—a few inches away, Mrs. Sibley's large eyes regarded him darkly through tumbled hair. He hated to move.

Clint tried to help Buell and Costello remove the rims and tires, but he was awkward with the tools. Over and over in his mind, he saw himself giving the keys to the powder house to Red Durkin. He thought about that lock. Hazard was extra touchy about handling dynamite—it was a big lock, hard steel, set in a massive forged hasp. He left Buell and Costello and began to prowl around among the banks of shelves and the boxes, crates, kegs and cans stored there. But the lamplight did not reach back there.

Clint found a box of small brass Justrite miner's lamps. He opened a drum of carbide and filled the two chambers of a lamp with carbide and water, then he turned the little brass tongue that allowed water to drip onto the carbide and generate the acetylene gas. Hearing the gas hiss from the tiny nozzle, he spun the little toothed wheel on the flint igniter; the lamp popped alight, burning with a bright jet of blue-tipped flame.

His mind was occupied with finding a means, other than the dynamite he had so foolishly put out of reach, of stirring up mischief for Red Durkin and Vega and the whole damn rannygade outfit. The pop of the lamp exploding into light caused him to pause now and stare at the lamp. Frowning, he contemplated it for some seconds, as if he had never before studied the phenomenon of a carbide lamp, but his head still hurt from the rap with the pick handle. He decided that he would get his dynamite caps and fuse, anyway.

Holding the lamp, he went back among the shelves and pawed down a wooden box. As he stood back, his elbow struck another box on the shelf behind him and knocked it to the floor, spilling its contents. He kicked, and something skidded into the white light of his lamp. A rattrap. Clint picked it up, studied it. His craggy face crumpled in a slow smile. The box contained two dozen Nevermiss rattraps.

Perrell finished refacing the valves at ten minutes past four in the morning. "Can you put her together now?" Mrs. Sibley said.

He shook his head. "Got to grind them into their seats. Make each one fit. The gas explodes on the power stroke, see? That valve has to be closed, perfectly seated, or the force of the explosion blows out around it and the power is lost." He squinted at her, his eyes feeling as though they were full of sand. "Is that something a lady would care about?"

She turned the valve in her fingers. "I've begun to care

very much. It comes down to caring about a lot more than this, doesn't it?"

"The two back tires is done," Buell said, "but that was the last of the cable. How about rope?"

"Too soft, I'm afraid. Wire. Try the coil of electric wire."

"There ain't enough of it left."

"What else is up in the loft?"

"Cement, tar paper, chicken wire, feed sacks, stovepipe . . ."

"We can rig a silencer for the engine with some of that stuff, so leave the tires for now. Pull down the chicken wire and feed sack. We'll need a couple of drums, too."

"There's a whole stack of them old carbide cans, like the ones I put the silver stuff in, from the tanks."

"Good. What we have to do is unroll the chicken wire and spread the sacking over it. Wet it down good, and roll it up tight, then pack each one of the drums with the chicken wire and sacking. Then we run a piece of pipe from the engine's exhaust into the first drum, then more pipe to the second drum, then punch a little hole in the adobe and run the last piece of pipe on out the wall. When we fire up the engine, it will run the noise and fumes into the cans of chicken wire and gunny sack—what I'm hoping is that nothing will come out the other side of the wall but a little hot air. She will be choked down to a whisper."

"How we goin to carry this whole rig?"

"We don't. When we go out that door, we just pull away and leave it. From then on, the noise won't matter. But make sure the joints are tight, or she'll leak noise."

"We could smear some pitch on 'em—the stuff we used on the tanks."

"No. It would get hot and start to smoke and stink. Maybe burn. Hold on . . . *pitch!* There are your front tires, kid. We'll stuff a lot of chicken wire into those tires and pour hot pitch in on it. Heat the stuff when I get the forge going . . ."

Perrell needed abrasive for grinding in the valves. There was no emery to be found. Finally he scraped the oilstone with a chisel, collecting the black powder in an old snuff tin. He

mixed a few drops of oil with the powder, smeared the mixture onto a valve face, then seated the valve. The head of the
valve was slotted—he put a screwdriver blade in the slot and
began twirling the handle between his palms. After all the
work he had already done, this only took a few minutes. He
cleaned away the abrasive and put the valves and springs in
place. Daylight was seeping into the gloom when he finished.

Outside the shop window, a rooster flapped its wings and
crowed. Inside, the wounded fighting cock tried to respond and
flopped weakly against Hazard's arm, where he lay on the
planks of the crate, his legs trailing off awkwardly. Hazard
awoke and sat up with a groan, suddenly shocked to see the
blood-spattered, half-dead bird there next to him.

Through slitted, grainy eyelids he saw Amanda Sibley.
She was sitting on the running board of the red car next to—
yes, Perrell, who was rubbing his eyes with the back of a dirty
hand. And the small man with the black mustache—he and
the kid were doing something with some pipe and a couple of
drums behind the car. Hazard's head ached frightfully. He
strained to pull his fragmented thoughts together. He was the
possessor of a gigantic hangover—a *crudo,* Molina would say.
Memory images flashed by, and for a heartbreaking moment
Hazard was on his knees looking down into the glazed eyes of
his friend Hilario Molina.

Hazard shuddered and pressed his palms against his temples—a fight, he remembered something about a fight. And
Amanda's old car. Covertly he examined the car. It was the
same. Derelict.

The chicken flopped against his hip. He pushed at it. Then
he saw that Perrell's eyes, red-rimmed and squinting, were on
him.

"The engine is ready to run any time we want to start her
up," Perrell said. "But I'm going to need the forge to fix the
drive shaft. Do you understand what that means?"

"But . . . you said you could fix it with a piece of pipe."

"Can't—I've looked everywhere and there's no steel pipe
here. Only cast iron. It's too brittle, see, it would crumble.
So I have to do it the hard way—roll a piece of flat stock

around the shaft to make the sleeve, then forge-weld the joint."

Hazard tottered two steps to the cooling tub, splashed water on his face and wiped his glasses on his shirttail. When he slipped them on, he saw that Perrell had one of the drums of silver concentrate next to his knee.

"It means," Perrell said, "that we need an excuse to fire up the forge—something Vega will swallow."

Hazard sat down again, memory rushing back. "What are you getting at?"

Perrell nudged the drum of silver concentrate. "Mrs. Sibley has been telling me that you cook this stuff up right here at the forge"—he gestured toward the workbench behind Hazard, at cast-iron molds below on a shelf, and at the crucible— "and that you pour the bars here."

"Yes, but what—"

"Okay, you thought we could *deal* with him. Now we can—we've got something to deal with. Only, what we are buying is time. And a fire in the forge."

Hazard thought he was going to be ill. He resented Perrell's telling him what to do, the more so when it was so absurdly beyond reason. He shook his head. "No. I mean, this run of stuff is only worth four or five thousand, maybe less. That isn't enough to—"

"Dammit, then *lie* to him!" Perrell angrily walked over to Hazard and grabbed him by the shoulders. "You're the only one who will know what the stuff is worth. He'll have to believe you."

They heard the sudden familiar clatter of the Ford's engine starting up, over by the Ibarra house.

Hazard stared blankly. Perrell shook him.

"Will you do it?"

Early morning sun streamed through a notch in the Sierra Madre and sprayed out across purple-dark cañons above the *terreno* of Dos Cabezas. Wood smoke from cooking fires curled up, wisping blue against the bright sky as Red Durkin started up the Ford and drove it in a sweeping circle before the Ibarra house, where he stopped close to the veranda. Durkin swept off his battered vaquero hat with a flourish as Rodrigo Vega emerged from the house.

Vega was refreshed by sleep, a bath and a glass of coffee mixed half-and-half with Mrs. Sibley's brandy. His suit had been sponged and pressed by a renegade named Tranquilino, once a pimp and thief in Havana who was also known as El Leñador, the woodcutter, for having murdered one of his charges with an ax. Vega yielded to Durkin's invitation and boarded the wretched auto, masking his uneasiness behind an austere smile.

With Charlie Slotter and a couple of others on the running boards, Durkin drove the Ford up along the *terreno* onto the tooth-chattering cobbled roadway with its row of adobe houses, all waving as *soldados* of the Legion came out to watch. Then Durkin responded to a gesture of Vega's gloved hand, drove on around and pulled up before the storehouse where the gringos were housed. He switched off the engine, and the Ford's jiggling ceased. The guard, Youssuf Sarkisian, stood at the corner of the building. He had just captured a chicken from the pens, and the bird hung head down from his fingers.

"Open up, Sarky," Durkin said. The door rumbled back.

Standing with both hands on the windshield frame, Rodrigo Vega looked in at his prisoners. He had slept in Mrs. Sibley's huge baroque Spanish bed. He had seen the *armario* filled with beautiful gowns. Everything about the ancient and splendid house persuaded him that he would regain a significant part of his lost *tresoro* here at Dos Cabezas. Vega was impatient now to determine precisely how much and what form it would take. If silver, there would be the problem of transporting it and of arranging transactions later on to convert it to gold.

Yet the prisoners were not impressive. The woman's face was puffy and smudged with dirt, and her snarled hair hung down in dark clots over her poncho. The others were equally unkempt. They must have spent a sleepless night—not, he thought, without reason. His contempt for them was something sour in his mouth.

His words, spoken in the florid Spanish he had found effective, came easily, for he had said them often. Perrell, not understanding the Spanish, thought he heard a tremor in the voice, a thready, shrill current, like a muffled shriek. ". . . but you would rather hear English. We are all gringo, yes?" Laughter bubbled in his voice. "I too, yes. I was born in New Orleans—an accident, one might say, but my poor parents left Havana very much in a hurry." He laughed again, and Perrell, trying to concentrate on Vega's words through his own exhaustion, lost the meaning in a droning blur of sound. He forced himself to listen. ". . . and you are to understand that the revolution extends to you now a privilege. You are to be allowed to return to Mexico some of the flesh you have stripped from her bones"—a slight movement of Vega's hands took in the mine and the mountain, then he proceeded to make his demands in his archaic, mannered speech— "since this is, after all, a silver mine, is it not?"

Sudden quiet as he waited. It was unreal and out of focus to Perrell. Then Tracy Hazard was answering, and Perrell was dismayed to hear the man actually trying to bargain.

"A silver mine, yes, but the silver was shipped to Navajoa a week ago and the banks there would not release cash, so we failed to make the payroll here. But the company expects to have a draft clear. By now, there will be funds. One of us . . . someone . . . could arrange—"

A faint tremor shook Vega's slight body. The hooded eyelids dropped. What Hazard was saying, Perrell thought, could only appear evasive, treacherous, to Vega. Beside him, Amanda Sibley breathed, "Tracy . . . *stop!*" Perrell's eyes fastened on the Smith & Wesson and he *knew* that Vega's hand was already moving toward it when he heard his own thick tongue mumbling, *"You crazy bastard."* He was appalled that Hazard could fail to comprehend the deadliness so apparent to them all. He thought of Hazard lying in the dirt with mud in his mouth like Hilario Molina—if Hazard was gone, they were all gone.

"No . . ." It was his own voice.

The hooded eyelids lifted.

Perrell took a dragging step forward, hearing the voice, his own, doggedly run on, telling the man about the drums of black powder; he saw himself as if from a distance, pointing to the metal containers. He picked up a handful, let it spill back through his fingers.

". . . but the stuff has to be melted down into bars, see? And he is the only one who knows how to do that." Perrell nodded at Tracy Hazard. Vega blinked.

"And the worth of these bars?"

"Don't know exactly, but this will run over five hundred pounds, in bars. Good gold content, see? It could go thirty thousand dollars, maybe more." He heard Tracy Hazard's shocked grunt and saw Amanda Sibley restraining him, her hand on his arm as she hissed fiercely into the man's ear. The Ford's springs squealed as Vega stepped down. He walked through the doorway, and frowning, looked from the drums to the forge to the cast-iron molds and the crucible. Durkin and Sarkisian stood with him.

"This would be done here?" The voice, musing, still had its thin saw edge. Perrell nodded.

"And the time—how much time would it require?"

"Two days—say, today and most of tomorrow. Yes, that long at least," Perrell lied. He was not sure if it would take more than a few hours. Hazard opened his mouth fretfully. Vega looked at him. After a long moment Hazard nodded.

"But it won't go thirty thousand," he said. Mrs. Sibley's hand tightened on his arm. "I . . . I would have to assay it. You can't tell just by looking at it."

Vega tilted his head back, as if the better to peer at Hazard beneath the hooded lids. "Do it then," he breathed. He suddenly reached out his left hand and took the captured chicken from the startled Sarkisian. Holding the bird by the legs, he took its head in the gloved fingers of his right hand and with a quick twist pulled the head off. He held the decapitated, shuddering bird straight out toward Hazard's face, the wings beating, blood jetting. Mrs. Sibley cried out and turned away as Vega released the bird. When its frenzied wings drove the stump of its neck into Hazard's chest, he pawed it away in horror. The bird fell thrashing. Vega smiled, tossed the severed head into the dust at Hazard's feet. With a slow look at the others, he turned and walked back to the Ford. Sarkisian gathered up the chicken with a black-toothed grin, then rolled the door closed with his shoulder.

*"Damn you,"* Hazard whispered at Perrell. His face and glasses were splattered with blood, and his shirt was wet with it.

"You were as good as dead," Perrell said.

"He's right, Tracy," Mrs. Sibley said.

"That man don't want promises," Costello said. "He wants the hard stuff, and we better make him think he's goin to get it."

"But . . . *thirty* thousand!"

"Who cares?" Perrell snapped. "All we can buy with it is a few hours' time and a chance to fire up the forge. It had to be worth it to him."

Hazard looked down at the blood on his shirt. His hands were shaking violently. He sighed. "All right. Let's build a fire."

# (23)

Fire burned in the hearth. Hazard packed charcoal around the crucible, and flames nibbled at it. Amanda Sibley pumped the long bellows handle, and a small fierce gale of wind *hawed* up through the hearth. Ashes swirled. Perrell placed the ends of the drive shaft in the coals behind the crucible. Heat licked at his belly and face, and the old sharp hot iron smell was in his nostrils. On a back corner of the fire bed under the iron hood, pitch slowly warmed in a small tub. There, Buell and Costello waited with one of the front tires, which was stuffed with wadded chicken wire. A piece of canvas was thrown across the Flyer's fender to hide the naked wheel.

On the bricked-over working surface of the forge, Hazard laid out his two cast-iron molds, each with its three loaf-shaped, tapered cavities, along with his ladle and chemical fluxing agents. He put the molds next to the coals to warm, then mixed a thin mud of iron oxide. When the molds were warm, he painted the cavities with the mud, which would keep the silver from sticking when it was poured. It dried quickly. "Any moisture at all is bad business near molten metal," he said. "The stuff would fly around like bullets." The surface of the concentrate in the crucible quivered in the heat. He waited.

Perrell removed the shaft ends from the coals. Seeing the question in Hazard's eyes, he said, "I'm taking the temper out of them so I can drill them for the pins."

In the crucible, the concentrate sank in upon itself and slowly began to puddle.

Drilling pin holes in the shaft ends and the plate of mild steel that was to be shaped into a sleeve took almost an hour on the old hand-crank blacksmith's drill. By then Hazard had already poured a mold, making three bricks, and more concentrate was melting down in the crucible. Perrell cut pins from rod stock, then pinned the plate to the shaft with light taps of the hammer. He heated the steel. When it glowed cherry-red, he turned to the anvil and began to strike, light ringing blows of the hammer. Glancing up, he saw the faces turned toward him. The fear.

"My god, Perrell—the *noise!*" Hazard's face was white, the freckles splotchy.

"You could hear that a mile off," Buell said.

"I know." Perrell's hammer rang. "If anybody moves a whisker out there, sis, we want to know about it." The red metal curled slowly under the hammer, darkening.

Bobby Joe was at the window. She was lookout. "They hear

you now—them two guys is comin," she hissed. "The redhead and the nasty one."

Perrell dropped the shaft hissing into the cooling tub and snatched up Hazard's ladle. The door rumbled back.

"What the hell is goin on?" Slotter said.

Perrell held the long handle of the ladle over the anvil and struck it with the hammer. Frowning intently, he said between hammer blows, "You have to keep the fluxing iron straight. The heat warps it." He sighted along the handle.

Slotter approached the forge. "By God, I never heard of nothin like a fluxin iron."

Perrell, who had never heard of one either, wet the ladle in the cooling tub, then quickly dipped up some of the concentrate with the wet ladle. As Slotter bent forward to peer into the crucible, Perrell dumped the moistened ladleful into the molten metal. The crucible coughed a gushing splatter of liquid droplets and white roiling steam. Slotter yelped and jumped back.

"Look out!" Perrell scolded. "It could explode."

Slotter swore and slapped at his neck and at the smoldering black holes in his shirt and pants. "Damn you! You done that on purpose!"

"No," Perrell said earnestly. "You got to flux the nitrates or she'll blow up." He dumped in the rest of the ladleful, and the crucible huffed another cloud of steam and zinging droplets. Slotter flinched.

"The nitrates are building up!" Hazard shouted. "Give it more flux." Slotter scrambled for the door. Red Durkin leaned there, laughing.

"You ain't cut out for honest work, Charlie."

"Shut up, dammit." Slotter pointed to the tub of pitch heating on the back of the fire bed. "What the hell is that stuff?"

"That's the flux," Perrell said. He put the ladle across the anvil and struck it again. "She's warping bad . . ." The door rumbled closed.

Bobby Joe held the wounded fighting cock against the bib of her overalls and stroked it as she stared out the window. She was hungry, her eyes were grainy from staring, her throat was hot and raw from the heat of the forge, but she was not dispirited. Perrell said the Flyer would carry them and she believed him, though not simply because she trusted him. A buckboard, or hay wagon, or Granddaddy's dreadful old buggy was all she had ever known. The Flyer, decrepit as it was, was still to her a marvelous grand machine.

Most of the men within sight through the window—she was not inclined to think of them as *soldiers*—sat around in the sun and loafed, ate, played cards or slept. Some of them heated water in a tub near the bunkhouse and did some washing. "I bet there's aplenty of graybacks drownded in that tub," Bobby Joe said firmly.

She glanced at Buell and Mr. Costello, the bow-legged man with the hard hat. They were pouring tar stuff into the tires, a little at a time. Buell looked up and saw her. He rolled his eyes and crossed them, letting his tongue hang out, and she laughed in spite of herself.

Later, when Perrell was almost finished beating on the iron thing out of the car, she saw that Vega's men were beginning to rustle themselves something to eat again. Twice, bunches of them came to the chicken pens next to the shop and ran down some of Mr. Hazard's lanky hens. Small loss, she thought, except that she was so hungry that she would have eaten one raw herself. But Mr. Hazard took it hard. She could hear him mumbling and talking to himself while he melted down the black stuff in the pot on the forge. For that reason she herself had begun to fuss over the wounded bird that he called Ruby Robert, after some prize fighter, giving it drops of water from time to time, when she really would as lief have seen it put out of its misery, especially when she was so *hungry*.

Then she remembered something Gram had shown her once when she had a pet dove. She ran back to the bin where the chicken feed was kept. She scooped up a canful and went back to her window, where she put some of it in her mouth. The chicken feed was mostly corn and made mighty hard chewing, but instead of swallowing, she held Ruby Robert up to her face and placed his beak between her lips. He was so weak that his poor skinned head fell over, but once he tasted the chewed grain, he took strength from somewhere and she felt his beak chattering away, sucking it up. It was soon gone. The lingering taste of the corn left her hungrier than ever. She picked up a hammer and began to crunch the grain in the can. When it was ground to a coarse meal, she stirred in a little water to make a kind of mush out of it, then she began to eat.

The little man with the mustache and the hard hat left off what he was doing and came bowlegging over to her. "I didn't hear the dinner bell, sis—what's on the bill of fare?" Her mouth full, she nodded at the can and the spilled grains. He laughed. "Chicken feed! I declare. You know, there's many a time I've eat what my old horse left in the nose bag and been glad to get it." He scooped up a little with his finger and tasted it. "*Pinole* this is, and just about all that a lot of these folks in Mexico ever eat, especially Indians. Now, you cook this and you've got a johnnycake. It don't put tallow on you, but a man can work on it and I'm thinkin it will taste awful good before we get this old girl to market." He nodded at the Flyer. "But what you want is something better to mash it with, like a rollin pin . . ." He moved off along the bench, peering and poking through the ancient litter beneath it.

Bobby Joe was thinking that chicken feed by itself was mighty slim pickins, even for Indians, when Costello came back carrying a heavy piece of iron. Shaped like a rolling pin, maybe, but with a big bore drilled in the end. "It looks like a cannon," she said. He examined it then, frowning. He looked up and caught Ellred Clinton's eye, beckoned with a jerk of his chin. Clinton put down a tin can and came over.

"Ellred, what do you make of this?" Costello said.

It was about sixteen inches long and four inches through. Shafting steel, probably. Clinton pushed a hammer handle down the bore—it measured about twelve inches deep. There was a little hole drilled in the side, even with the bottom of the bore.

"Two things it could be—a rivet buster or a stack gun. Either way, it's a gun. Say you've got a hell of a big smokestack

and the stack is all sooted up—maybe one like that one, yonder." Clinton nodded toward the ancient stone smelter stack
on the hillside. "Then you fuse her and load her with powder
and a little wadding, nothin else, see? You put her in the bottom of the stack, pointed up. Touch her off and the blast
shakes the soot loose. It all falls to the bottom and you just
shovel her out."

"Wouldn't it blow the chimley down?"

"You don't blow nothin up there but air and powder
smoke. It's the blast that does it."

"What do you charge her with?"

"Black powder—Kentucky Rifle or Double-F G . . ." Clinton's voice trailed off. "I've got a part of a can of Triple-F back
there that wouldn't do too bad. Old stuff, but dry. What are you
thinkin?"

"I'm thinkin that if we get out of here at all, we'll have
them rannygades all strang out after us like a pack of dogs. It
wouldn't hurt to have a discourager with us . . ." Costello saw
that Buell was ready to pour the pitch again and needed his
help. He hurried away.

Bobby Joe found a piece of iron plate under the bench. She
lifted it up, cleaned it off, and began to roll out more chicken
feed with the stack gun. She watched Perrell and Mr. Hazard
lift the little round pot with a long kind of handlebar and pour
the glittering stuff into the molds. She had always helped
Granddaddy mold bullets for his old cap-and-ball Colt, and so
far as she could tell, this was no different, except that the
molds were bigger and shaped like little loaves of bread.

Perrell was strangely light-headed. He felt strength in his
hands and shoulders, yet his legs seemed remote. His strength
was fire-fed, he thought. So long as the bellows sighed and the
stream of wind flowed up into the coals, he would go on. If the
stream stopped, he would fall on his face. The wind sighed.

Pumping the bellows handle, Amanda Sibley stared at the
vast bulk of the derelict Flyer. She thought of the great machine thundering along the beach road past the Hamptons,
toward Montauk. She tried to remember his face, Ev's face the

way it was then, laughing, the dark hair curling out under his motoring cap, but what came to her now was the sulky set of his lips and the way his eyes would skid away.

She pulled the handle. The wind sighed, faded. There were beads of moisture on her lip. She looked into the red-rimmed eyes of the rough-stubbled face next to her, thinking, I know you better this minute than I know him after nine years.

Over by the Ibarra house, an engine coughed and chattered. The Ford. Then a deeper, blatting roar. "That's the Hewitt," Perrell said, looking up. Someone whooped. Gears clashed. The Reo truck started up. Through the window in the rear of the shop, they saw the machines lumber out in a wide circle around the compound. Men ran to catch up with them, clambering aboard until the trucks were filled with *renegados,* their sombreros clustered like yellow blossoms among the black spikes of the rifles.

"The party starts now," Costello said, watching from another window. "I 'spect they will run the damn town up a tree."

"Who is left here?" Perrell said.

"Half a dozen in sight, probably sick or wounded, and one man guarding us, the big-nosed gent."

"Let's keep at it, then." Perrell staggered to the cooling tub and rinsed his face. His ribs still hurt and his knees were shaking. He saw the tumbled pile of bright metal bars. "You'd better go slower—string it out," he said to Hazard. "Let's use one mold from now on."

The morning wore away. The sleeve was welded, the shaft aligned. Perrell tapped heads onto the pins. Then he heated the sleeved section of the shaft again, watching it closely for color, cooled it at just the right moment, to lock the temper into the fibers of the metal. Buell and Costello were pouring the second tire. Perrell crawled under the Flyer, fitted the shaft into the differential case and secured the sprocket end in its housing on the frame. He left the old oil in the differential case—this is not Indianapolis, he thought. He put on the drive chain and took up the slack with the adjuster.

Then he went back over the engine. He added a couple of

quarts of oil to the crankcase. Must take plenty of oil with us, he thought. She probably drinks the stuff. He stowed the can in the cargo rack. The flat leather fan belt was dry and cracked, needed oiling, patching. Harness leather hung from a nail. He found thread, needle and an awl.

"Now, that is somethin I can do," the powder man said. He began stitching and patching the leather. The radiator hoses were brittle. Perrell wrapped them with black friction tape. The radiator . . . He started to fill it with water, then suddenly remembered the ice in the wash trough yesterday morning. "She'll freeze up on us," he said.

Hazard pointed along the back wall beyond the Flyer, at wooden kegs, glinting copper vessels. "Alcohol? Booze—the mescal I made?" Perrell drew off some, tasted it and shuddered. "It's double-distilled," Hazard said, "about a hundred and twenty proof." Perrell filled the radiator with mescal.

Gasoline. He found the five-gallon can he had drawn off for the new pump engine. It felt light. He poured it into the Flyer's tank. "Three gallons or so. Not much. She will drink it fast, loaded down with all of us—she might get about eight miles to the gallon. We ought to leave here with a full tank, or close to it, which means"—he looked at Clint—"you will have to steal three of these cans full, and be waiting for us there when we come through . . ."

He stared through the window, across the open *terreno* to the long timbered platform holding all the drums of gasoline. At that moment they heard the nasal clatter of the Ford, returning along the arroyo road. It came into sight and pulled up at the Ibarra house. Durkin was driving. Vega climbed out of the car and went into the house. Then Charlie Slotter moved into the driver's seat. Durkin sat next to him. Three *renegados* sat on the truck bed, behind. Something flashed. A bottle. The Ford lunged away from the house, stopped, backfired, took off again in a wide circle along the edge of the *terreno,* got two wheels rumbling on the cobbles in front of the bunkhouses, broke clear, backfiring, and swung past the shop, the *renegados* screeching and whooping. Perrell saw Slotter frantically working spark and throttle levers—he missed the footbrake, hit the "back" pedal and the Ford instantly changed directions, then he hit the "go" pedal and it charged away again, backfiring. "Drunk as skunks," Costello said.

Perrell jumped to the Flyer. Standing alongside, he set spark and throttle, then shoved the stout brass gear selector lever into the neutral cross slot. "Quick, while they're making all that racket—let's fire up the Flyer!" He swung Amanda Sibley up to the driver's seat and waved to Buell to get on the crank. "Twist it, kid—wind her up." He threw the lever that relieved compression in the cylinders. Buell's shoulders heaved. The great machine rocked on her springs, dust dribbled along the fenders, streamed to the floor. Perrell heard the suck and plop of big five-and-a-half-inch pistons driving, pulling. He sniffed at the carburetor and cupped his hand over the intake as the Flyer jounced and squeaked. "A long time dead—dead and cold . . ." He was talking to it, coaxing. It fired, died, then fired again. He let air through his fingers to keep it going while Amanda Sibley eased the spark lever down, the gas up. The car was quivering, rocking. It was alive, yet strangely silent because of the improvised muffler. The block was growing warm under his hands.

He motioned to Amanda Sibley to put it in gear. The wheels were still blocked up. Timidly she engaged the clutch, and the chains clicked taut. The huge wheels began to turn. She leaned out and looked back at the spinning wheel. Tears stung her eyes.

From the direction of the arroyo, there sounded suddenly the mingled booming snarl of the two trucks. The Ford backfired again. War whoops from the trucks. "They are loaded for bear," Costello said as the trucks lumbered into sight. "My God, they're racing!" Perrell went to the window. He saw the Reo pulling up on the left side of the Hewitt— *renegados* screeching wildly. The driver of the Hewitt forced the Reo hard over. There was a thunderous rumble as the Reo crashed down the length of the fuel-dump platform, fifty-five-gallon steel drums rolling and bounding before it. Gasoline sloshed along the ground.

Red Durkin stood clutching the windshield of the Ford

with one hand, waving the other and bellowing, "You crazy son of a bitches!" at the hapless drivers. He jerked the wheel of the Ford and shouted instructions at Slotter, who was full of tequila and was also driving a car for the first time in his life. The Ford swerved toward the trucks. Slotter pulled everything in sight trying to stop, finally hit the "back" pedal and Durkin was thrown forward onto the hood.

*"Kill the goddamn engine!"* he screamed.

Throttle open, Slotter switched off, then on. A tremendous backfire ripped from the Ford—a two-foot tongue of flame lanced from her rear end. Gasoline ignited with a dull, booming *hoosh-sh-sh* as flame and black smoke roiled beneath the trucks. Slotter's feet stomped pedals. The Ford seesawed back and forth as *renegados* screamed and sprinted through the flames. The Ford lurched forward, backfiring like a Gatling gun, igniting a fresh patch of ground with every explosion. Slotter's despairing wail rose above the din. The Ford cleared the flames, traveled out onto the open *terreno.* There, unaccountably, it stopped.

Flames roared fifty feet high. Black smoke boiled into the sky. The driver of the Hewitt had managed to follow the Ford out of the flames. He stopped on open ground and jumped down, slapping his clothing, peering anxiously underneath the smoking truck. Uncertainly he retreated. Durkin was waiting for him. The man backed into him, turned, and Durkin knocked him out from under his big yellow hat.

"If the fire gets to the powder house," Clint said, "there won't be nothing left of us but a streak of spit."

# (24)

Very slowly, the flames subsided. The Reo continued to burn, black smoke billowing from her tires, a heavy *crump* when her fuel tank went.

"Oh, Jesus, we're finished now," Buell groaned. "Every drop of gas is burnt up."

The last of the drums was wreathed in flames. It suddenly burst and a pool of flame roiled on the ground. Perrell was looking at the Ford and the Hewitt, both stopped out on the *terreno* only thirty or forty yards from the shop.

"Listen, there ought to be some gas left in the Ford and in the Hewitt," he said. "But, my God, it will be hard to steal it now."

"Durkin is comin!" Costello said.

Perrell heard a faint clicking. He turned. The Flyer still quivered gently.

"I forget to turn it off!" Amanda said. "It's been running all this time."

The big door was grinding back. She leaped for the Flyer's ignition switch and hit it just as Durkin appeared, rocking unsteadily in the dust-filled stream of light. His crooked, buck-toothed grin was still there, but his eyebrows were patchy smudges of soot and his clothes were scorched.

"The Ford, she run out of gasarene. Half a minute sooner and we would have been fried chicken."

Metal snapped and popped. The Flyer was cooling. Durkin's eyes strayed to the big machine. Perrell felt his belly knot up—steam was wisping up from the engine silencer they had made. Glossy streaks of pitch streaked the front tire. His heart pounded. Durkin stepped forward, staggering, reached out to steady himself on the hot radiator, but just as his hand was about to touch it, steam gushed from the crucible on the forge and hot metal *popped* under Hazard's ladle. Durkin flinched. He left the Flyer and walked toward the forge.

"Nitrates, hunh?" he said with the confidence of experience. "Got to flux 'em, right?" He reached out to the tumbled
pile of silver bars and touched one, but jerked his hand back.
It was still hot. He felt among them for a cool one and lifted
it. A small bar, two inches by three inches by six inches. He
whistled at the weight of it.

"About sixteen and a half pounds," Hazard said.

"You say there's thirty thousand here?"

Hazard sniffed. "I can't tell until I run an assay." He
glared at Perrell. Durkin stroked the bar.

"How long will it take for you to do that?"

Hazard chewed his lip. "An hour or two, I guess."

"Well, go ahead and run it then."

"All this will take longer if I stop to do that." Hazard
waved at the crucible.

Durkin rubbed his jaw. Whiskers powdered away under
his hand. "Mister, if I was you, I would just drag all this out
as long as I could. S'pose you run the assay . . ." He grinned,
but his eyes strayed back to the silver. He frowned around the
thought that struggled to surface in his mind. "I got to get
some gasarene for the Ford. Don't tell me that was all there
is."

"That's exactly what I'm telling you," Perrell said. "Your
boys burned it up, every drop."

Durkin's face was bleak. Then he grinned suddenly. "I'll
dreen it out of that other truck. There's bound to be some. How
far will that Ford go on, say, a tankful?"

"About a hundred and fifty miles. Depends on your load,
see?"

Durkin's eyes returned to the silver. "Say you had a load
of five, six hundred pounds," he said evenly. "Would she carry
it?"

"Is that with the driver?"

"Say you had the load and . . . two people."

"Her springs would be pretty flat. She might do it if you
took it real slow."

The grin flickered, then faded under the burden of figuring. "Run the assay, then—you don't have to say nothin about
this to the colonel, see? I'll tell him myself." He looked again

at the silver. "Put that stuff into boxes and throw somethin over it. And you can find me a piece of hose to suck up the gasarene with."

There was a piece of rubber hose connected to the cooling tank on Hazard's still. Perrell unfastened it and handed it to Durkin, who suddenly said, "I'll put the damn Ford right under my window—that will keep them bastards from messin with it." Turning toward the door, his glance fell on the Flyer. He shook his head and said peevishly, "How come you keep that old junk heap here?" Still wagging his head, he left. Sarkisian pushed the door closed and the hook rattled.

Despair tainted the air. The prisoners stared at one another. "We'll never get the gas now," Hazard whispered.

"Durkin has his own plans for it," Costello said.

"How much gas is left in the Flyer?" Amanda asked.

"I burned some, running her," Perrell answered, "but I'm guessing that we could go fifteen, maybe twenty miles on what's left."

"They'll run us down easy." Hazard gingerly touched the dried blood on his shirt front, as if he had just discovered it.

Amanda Sibley leaned her forehead against the high padded armrest of the Flyer's driving seat. She stroked the leather with her hand. "A pity. A pity," she said softly. "But let's run her, anyway, John Trouble—run her as far as she will go." A shiver, like a sudden fright, racked her shoulders.

"We could scatter then," Buell said. "Some of us would make it." He put out his hand and touched Bobby Joe. In sudden anguish, she caught the hand and held it to her cheek.

Perrell turned away frowning, his eyes narrowed and squinting. He walked to the wooden kegs of mescal racked against the wall. He turned a spigot, and clear liquid flowed into his palm. He walked back to the forge and poured the alcohol from his cupped hand onto the coals, which blackened, then *whooshed* into flame. "That's all gasoline does—it burns . . ." His voice was rapt, distant.

"Are you thinking of burning *alcohol?*" Hazard's voice shrilled. "Not that stuff!"

"Engines will run on alcohol," Perrell said.

"Pure alcohol, yes. That stuff is half water."

"Sure, but it could be distilled again." Perrell raised his hand. "I know—there isn't time. Not to make fuel out of booze, anyway. What I mean is that gasoline is not the only thing that will burn in an engine." He stared fiercely into the glowing coals. "Look, anything that is gaseous or vaporized and will ignite to a spark will do it. Plain old coal gas, right out of the cooking stove will do it, maybe better than gasoline."

"We're a long way from a gas main."

To Perrell, Hazard's voice was infuriatingly smug. He slammed his fist down on the bricks. "All I'm asking you to do is think! Those bastards will have us hung up like sides of beef!"

Hazard flinched as if stung and blinked. Perrell waved a hand at the lofty gloom, the choked clutter of the shop. "This place is stuffed with junk—now, somewhere in here, there ought to be *something* . . ."

"Charcoal," Hazard said. He took a piece from the hearth and held it up. "The gas given off by burning charcoal will run an engine—it's been done. They're doing it in Paris! You need a cooker, some kind of a fire bed, and a big tank to trap the gas—"

"A steel drum would do it," Perrell said. "You could hang it on the cargo rack, behind the car." With his hands he shaped the imagined charcoal burner, then he turned to the big racked kerosene drum. "A drum like this . . ." But he was already shaking his head. "It could take *days,* cutting and fitting." He rapped on it with his knuckles. A deep, full note sounded. A drop of fluid hung from the tap. Perrell took the drop on his finger, sniffed it. He held it up. *"Kerosene.* Plain old coal oil."

"No." Hazard's voice was flat. "It won't vaporize. Not cold, it won't."

"Supposing you heated it? Piped it in good and hot. The draft in the carburetor would vaporize it then."

"No," Hazard insisted. "I remember my schoolwork very precisely on this—coal oil would have to be heated several times as high as gasoline before it would vaporize sufficiently to combust. In an engine, on the order of four hundred and fifty degrees."

"The temperature is more than that inside the Flyer's cylinder. What it comes down to is that coal oil *will* work in a hot engine and will *not* work in a cold engine."

"Well, there you are," Hazard said.

Hearing them argue, Amanda Sibley thought that Perrell, hunched over the Flyer's engine with his fists knotted, looked predatory. She had lost the thread of the argument, though. Perrell was saying something about getting the engine hot: "We'll start it on the gasoline, let it heat up and then switch to the coal oil."

Hazard was shaking his head. "Not hot enough, not for sure."

"All right, a coil then. Run it through a coil around the exhaust manifold. That will preheat it."

"The worm from the still," Hazard said. He scuttled around the forge and bellows and pulled copper tanks from the shelves, lifted out a coil of half-inch copper tubing.

"I'll make a tank out of that old gear-oil drum," Perrell said. "Mount it here on the left side up high, gravity feed. We'll run the tubing to the manifold, then bring it in to the gas line here, with an on-off valve. I'll need the forge to make the rack. You had better go ahead and make the assay. How much have you melted down?"

"About half. Eighteen bars so far. It won't be worth any thirty thousand dollars, though."

"Red Durkin is fixin to pull out," Costello said, "and he means to take the silver with him. If you fake the assay figures up high, he won't want to burn up his gasoline chasin after us."

"Kill as much time as you can, making the assay," Perrell said. "It'll keep you from finishing the melting too soon. By tomorrow we'll be gone, anyway, and it won't matter how much is left undone."

Hazard was startled to find himself deferring to Perrell's initiative. A Debs man, my God, a Wobbly, he thought, a *radi-*

*cal.* Something for nothing. Hazard opened the cupboard where he kept his assay materials, found the eighth-inch drill bit and fitted it into the chuck of the bench drill. He put a bar of silver onto a piece of clean paper and set to work, the shavings curling up from the sharp steel until the bit was buried. He ran the drill back up, flicked it clean of the curled crumbs of bright metal and collected them on the paper. Then he weighed them on his assayer's balance scale and funneled them into his small assay crucible. He added a wafer of lead for malleability, put the crucible on the fire and huffed the coals aglow with the bellows.

*Pie in the sky.* Hazard, a mining man in Mexico, did not grasp pie in the sky. His life was devoted to an equation, and the factors of the equation were expressed in tons of ore per man-shift, daily yield of miners and muckers, and of the swinging beam of the mule-drawn *arrastre* that crushed the ore to feed it into the cyanide tanks and the zinc boxes and bring it at last to the assay crucible. The crumbs of silver shimmered and he pumped the bellows arm again. The crumbs shuddered into a bright button. He lifted the crucible off the coals and the button jelled. He tweezed the button onto the anvil and pounded it into a flat strip—the *hojuela*, "tiny leaf of metal" the Mexicans called it. He measured nitric acid into a beaker, plunked the *hojuela* into it and leaned back, waiting for the ravenous bite of the acid to eat away the silver and the impurities. What was left would be pure gold. Its weight, compared with the weight of the original drill shavings from the bar, would tell him the proportion of gold to silver in the bar, therefore the value. A very slight difference in the amount of gold would alter the value sharply.

Every run of ore was different, of course, but at Dos Cabezas he was accustomed to bars that assayed about 90 percent silver and 1 percent gold. The other 9 percent represented copper and zinc, a little lead and impurities. One run at that rate was worth about $4,000 U.S. A run in which the gold content went up to 2 to 3 percent, as occasionally happened, would double in value, because gold was more than thirty times as valuable as silver. However, Hazard, like most mining men, thought of the stuff in assay terms, the number of ounces of metal per ton of ore, rather than its dollar value. So in his mind it was product, not money. The banks, the Ev Sibleys, worked it all out in dollars later. Today was different.

He fidgeted, waiting. His nerves were on fire. He tried to focus his mind on this insane plan to escape, and his stomach churned with dread. It was more than just physical fear. He would be leaving his work, the mine, everything that mattered to him, the life he had carved out for himself in Mexico—and not a damn thing to show for it, he thought.

Hazard looked at the *hojuela,* the wafer of metal, and saw that it was porous and spongy from the hunger of the acid. He plucked it out with tweezers, washed it and quickly remelted it into a tiny gold button, then returned it to the scales. He dropped slivered weights into the balance tray until it equaled the weight of the button and bobbed down. Counting up the weights, he blinked in surprise and felt a stir of excitement touch his heart.

Moments later he stared incredulously at his scrawled figures. He quickly turned back to the scales and weighed the button again, his lips moving as he forced himself calmly to add up the weights and work out the simple problem in proportion. Then he sat back again, shaking his head. It checked out. His assay was crude and hasty, of course, but certainly accurate within a few percentage points.

The assay told him that the new stope he had opened was yielding bars running 32 percent gold. Hazard was stunned. No, no good figuring it all again. He remembered his words a few days earlier when he first showed the powder man, Clint, the working face in the stope. "Damn good-looking rock," he had said. "Not the best, but damn good-looking."

There was nothing fantastic about it, of course—Dos Cabezas had been a good gold producer in the old days. Such a gold content was certainly high for a silver district, but not remarkable for small stopes. It would run $100 to $150 a ton of ore—he remembered a stope in the old North Lilly in Utah that ran $35,000 a ton. Small stope or not, his mining instincts had been right.

He thought of the fights he had endured with Sibley—the bleak line of prospect pits running down the mountain—blind, probing stab wounds seeking out the parallel vein structure that Hazard's instincts told him existed. There was the difference between himself and Sibley. Every *mining* man, no matter how barren the yield of his rock, responds to the mystery of the hidden structures mischievously puddled into the deep crust of the earth, seeing pools of the precious metals secreted from him by perhaps only a few feet of rock. Sibley saw nothing.

He scribbled again on the pad. When the run was through, there would be thirty-odd bars of metal, say, something over five hundred pounds. They would actually be worth close to $40,000.

Perrell was tightening a brass fitting on his fuel line. He looked up and saw Hazard, white-faced, holding a piece of paper in a shaking hand. "Look at this . . ." Hazard said, but Perrell shrugged and shook his head.

"It doesn't matter now," Perrell said, turning the wrench, too exhausted to go into it. "As long as they think it's worth more to them than chasing after us."

"I'll finish the run then," Hazard mumbled. His face wore a stricken look. He pulled the bellows arm, and coals glowed under the crucible.

At the forge, Amanda Sibley and Bobby Joe made cakes out of *pinole;* they were scorched on the outside, wet in the middle, but to hungry people, they were fragrant and savory.

Clinton and Costello had been the first to eat. Then they slipped out through a hole chopped in the adobe wall, in back of the huge bellows that pumped air into the forge. They took with them a number of cans, and the powder man's pockets were lumpy with Nevermiss rattraps and coils of fuse. After they left, the hole was covered over with sacking.

Eating, Perrell walked slowly around the loaded Flyer, checking her cargo with Buell. Tools, of course. Water bags and canteen. Rope, canvas, tire chains, a coil of baling wire, shovel, ax. "It's sixty miles to the railroad, and anything can happen. Suppose the trains aren't running and we have to live out of her for a while?" Perrell said.

The new fuel tank sat high on the left side of the Flyer next to the rear seat, supported on a rack of strap iron. The copper fuel line ran forward to the exhaust manifold on the left side of the engine, then back up to the dashboard, where it met the gas line in a simple selector valve.

A strange assortment of cans hung from the Flyer's cargo racks, or were jammed in among other gear, all cans prepared and stowed by Ellred Clinton. Whether they had once held paint, tar, oil, or whatever, each of the cans now carried an ordinary old kitchen-style Nevermiss rattrap wired to the underside of its lid. The striker bar of each trap rode cushioned on a small chunk of wood which kept the bar from touching a dynamite cap taped to the wooden body of the trap beneath it, where the bar was to strike. Each can held a handful or more of a dry, granular chemical, the same carbide used for the Flyer's head lamps and for the little brass Justrite lamps of the miners.

Perrell threw canvas and pieces of sacking over the Flyer to hide her cargo. He was staggering and his face felt numb. "There is no need to watch any more," he told Bobby Joe.

"What do we do now?" Buell said.

"She's all ready to turn over. We just wait. Sleep a little." Amanda Sibley handed him another steaming cake of *pinole* from the piece of sheet iron on the forge. "We want to go through that door just at daybreak . . . that gives us almost four hours."

Amanda Sibley looked at Perrell's bristly face, the pallor and staring eyes. She left the forge and walked back among the banks of shelves beyond the Flyer. She found a bundle of dirty canvas on one of the shelves, an old tent. She pulled it down and spread the musty folds on the dirt floor. She went back to Perrell, and touching his arm, she said in a low voice, "Sleep for you now." He followed her obediently, and when he saw the canvas he dropped to his knees on it and toppled over.

"Go on—go to sleep," she said, and dimly in the gloom she saw an answering movement of his hand, heard him whisper something. She knelt down beside him.

"I said . . . the food is good and I don't mind the work, but the hours are terrible."

"Go to sleep," she said again, lightly touching his hand. Standing, she could see beyond the Flyer, to the forge and the workbench where Tracy Hazard sat on his high stool, hunched close to the oil lamp, mumbling to himself. Twenty feet away Bobby Joe was stretched out on the bench with the wounded bird in the crook of her arm, and Buell had made himself a bed of sacking among the old dynamite boxes. Until now, helping Perrell with the work on the Flyer, she had kept her mind from wandering beyond the narrow circle of light from the oil lamps, because when she thought of the obscenely sleek and twitching Colonel Vega, she was filled with utterly helpless terror and revulsion. But now, away from the light and the warmth of the forge, fear moved in close to her, like something heavy-bodied, crouching—the way it moved in night after night and squatted at the edge of darkness when she was alone in the Ibarra house. She felt her breathing grow ragged.

Her fear was nothing as silly as being afraid of the dark, though it came to her in the dark, when she was alone. It was time, the rush of time and emptiness, that haunted her. She had seen the powder man looking at her several times in the past few days, the eyes intense in the scarred face, and she thought she saw in them the same despair she herself felt. It had come upon her slowly, after Ev began making his trips longer and longer. For a long time she had kept it away by turning up the lamps and feverishly working herself to exhaustion with brush, knife and paint. But in the daylight she was appalled at the barrenness of what she had done, appalled and filled with panic because she had nothing more within herself and the years were rushing away. After a time she knew that she was using the precious hours of daylight merely to gain strength to hold another night at bay. Then she had discovered that time could be measured in inches of brandy. And blurred.

She shivered. Her heel touched crackling canvas. She turned, suddenly past caring, let herself down next to the sleeping man. It was very cold. She pulled some sacking and a flap of the old tent over the two of them, squirming close to him. The stiff old canvas slowly caught their seeping warmth. She smelled raw iron and motor oil, adobe dust and sweat. But she was not alone.

Thirty yards away, Youssuf Sarkisian squirmed on his saddle blanket and leaned back against a baulk of timber, letting the wood dig into the flesh where his kidneys ached. His head ached also and his bowels rumbled like a summer thunder storm. He contemplated getting up and walking a circuit of the building. Make rounds every quarter-hour or oftener, Durkin, the *yanqui,* had told him. How to tell such a man about the prodding ache of the back, how it penetrated, like a sharp stick, or complain to him that twice now, on two successive nights, he, Sarkisian, had drawn the guard duty? Durkin knew, but he thought it was funny to give the Armenian every lousy detail that came up.

A rustling, scratching sound came to his ears. The chickens on their roosts, he decided. He listened again, but a snore covered the sound. He looked at his partner, Simmons. The straw-haired, pimple-faced *yanqui* son of a pig was sleeping soundly with his mouth wide open. Durkin had let him go to the village with the others and he had come back with a bellyful of mescal, mouthing endless lies, too tired to stand his share of the watch. "You watch em, Sarky," was what he had said, "they ain't goin nowheres . . . I got to catch me some shut-eye. Jesus, did I have me a time." Sarkisian thought of how he would like to fill that open mouth . . .

Ellred Clinton and Costello walked very slowly, feeling for the ground ahead every step before putting a foot down. Clinton remembered how the moonlight had flooded down, near bright as day, on the hobo jungle and the old pen at Yuma— dark of the moon now, though, and a damn good thing. The canteen slapped against his chest and he felt the weight of the small sack of carbide hanging from his belt. Between them, he and Costello carried eight of the cans he had prepared, one in each hand, one under each arm.

They stayed well clear of the pile of timbers where the two guards had settled down. Then the ground sloped up gently underfoot. Presently he heard the soft blowing and stomping of horses in the corral, guiding upon them until he came to the fence itself. He made a faint hissing sound to warn Costello, then he knelt and carefully put his four cans down in a row so that he would be able to find them by feel.

During the day he had seen that the forty-odd saddles of the renegades were either racked on the corral fence or set down on the ground on their sides nearby and covered with their saddle blankets. He turned to the fence. He could not precisely *see*—it was that dark—yet something, dark against dark, came to his eyes.

He felt a saddle under his hands. It was a Chihuahua saddle, with a rawhide-wrapped horn six inches across, the tree itself naked of leather. He lifted the lid of a can, very gently rocked back the striker bar and set it, all by touch, the way he had practiced, removed the little wedge of wood next to the cap, then splashed water from the canteen onto the carbide. Instantly, he heard the foaming hiss and smelled the sharp stink of the acetylene. He closed the lid and pressed it down. He heard gas hiss faintly through the holes punched for the wire that held the trap inside. Then he hung the can from the rail under the saddle with a short piece of wire. He felt for the little coil of harness thread taped to the lid of the can. One end of the thread ran through a hole and was tied inside to the trigger of the Nevermiss rattrap. He loosened the coil and tied the free end to the cinch ring of the saddle.

They mined five saddles with the acetylene bombs, then they slipped away from the corral, crossing the pavement of cobbles to the crumbling *galería* of the bunkhouse. Clinton put a can next to the doorway and tied the trigger string to the latch. Snores sounded within, rising and falling in sawing discord.

With Costello again, he set out toward the Ibarra house, holding close to the brush on his right. An arm of pitahaya clawed at his sleeve, and he stepped around it, feeling the skin of his face prickle at the nearness of the thorns.

They mined the front and side doors of the Ibarra house. There were at least two more doors, but they had no more cans. Then they followed the arroyo road along the cliff, past the charred fuel dock and the powder house. The overhead loading chute was a black smudge against the stars. "That chute is near full of ore," Clinton said, "and there's a trap door under it."

"What makes it open?"

"A big handle yonder, like a brake handle on a wagon. There's a rope on the handle. After our auto comes through, we'll tie that rope across the road."

"What's the little building back there at the edge?"

"That's the powder house."

"There ought to be some way to get into it."

"She's locked up tight, a good lock, too. She's got a hell of a thick door, ten inches of sand on top, and the walls are timbers, hard as rock."

"Nothin you could rat-trap her with?"

"The cans we used are likely too little. A drum, though— a drum might could do it. A feller could bunker it up with timber and rocks on this side so she would blow into the door . . . and there's half a drum of carbide up at the mine portal, stuff kept there for the miners' lamps."

Near the burned hulk of the Reo, they found one fifty-five-gallon steel drum. It was empty, dented, but sound. They lifted and carried it back to the powder house and set it up in front of the door. They climbed the rough wooden stairway up to the *boca de mina*. Clinton refilled the cloth sack with carbide. A stack of heavy mine timbers sat close by. Laboriously but very gently, they began skidding timbers down the slope, manhandling them one at a time across the road to the powder house. There they slowly laid up a low wall, closing in the drum against the powder-house door.

Stars wheeled in the moonless sky. Coyotes spoke to one another in the distance toward the Sea of Cortez. The two men carried rock from the dump and piled it against the timbers. They moved slowly and it took a long time. Costello quit when he could no longer stand straight.

"It will blow or it won't blow," he gasped. "One more rock won't help it."

"You've forgot what honest work is like."

"I never did know, Ellred. It takes an ignorant and backward-minded man to make a cowhand . . . a cowhand don't know he's workin, see. He's got to think it's fun, even when his ass is froze to the saddle, or there wouldn't be nobody to do it."

"No, I mean, you are a long time quit of the cow business. How come you to go with the Pinkertons?"

"I busted a leg in three places. Ogallala, Nebraska, that was. I turned my horse into an alley, see? The wind was blowin and a lady had hung out some wash in a yard there. A sheet flapped in the wind, the blamed horse snorted like a cannon and sunfished. He come down all tangled in the wire fence, with me underneath him. A few weeks later, there I was settin around in front of the hotel all day, whittlin. My leg was tied up in splints and my roll was pretty near played out. A man sits down next to me and he starts a-whittlin too. He has whiskers down to his watch chain and eyes like bullets—what you would call a severe look. He says to me, 'I understand you are acquainted with the Hole-in-the-Wall country. If so I will make you a proposition'—"

"*Son of a*—you mean to tell me that's the only reason you are in the manhunt game, chasing poor dumb bastards like me?"

"Let me tell you the rest of the story."

"By God, I don't want to hear nothin more about it."

Tracy Hazard was unable to sleep. He sat on the high stool with his chin in his hands. Bright metal gleamed from beneath a flap of sacking. He had cast, finally, thirty-five bars. His hand closed over one of the small slick loaves of metal. Precious metal. How many tons of the stuff had he torn from the earth's guts and never coveted an ounce for what it could buy? Blind, stupid idiot, he thought, to be down here drawing a stinking wage while Ev Sibley chased skirts in Tucson and scattered double eagles by the handful, like chicken feed.

*          *          *

Youssuf Sarkisian's head lolled. He came awake with a start. The fire had burned down to ashes and he was very cold. For a moment he was a boy again, tending his father's sheep in the flinty Armenian hills. The stars told him that dawn was very close. He yearned for the warm sun on his back. He stretched convulsively, and groaned aloud with the pain that knifed through his kidneys and back.

Simmons stirred, mumbling in his sleep. Sarkisian saw a glint of star shine at his elbow. A bottle? He took a hesitant step, the pain quickening. Yes. He tipped the bottle up. It was empty. Pig, he thought. *Pig.* He was suddenly furious. His nose burned and tears came to his eyes. One drink was all he wanted. For the pain. *The bunkhouse!* he thought. Those swine all had bottles. He started to hobble away. No. He checked himself. That German sergeant would skin him alive if he caught him off his post.

A horse whickered softly in the corral. Sarkisian hugged his arms against his aching body and turned that way in the darkness. Vega, he thought. There was always a silver flask in Vega's saddlebag. The only man in the Legion who could leave a bottle untended on his saddle and know it would go untouched.

But not this time. Sarkisian hurried. He bumped into the corral rail and grunted, caught himself. Which was Vega's saddle? He started along the rail, feeling each saddle as he came to it . . .

# (25)

The blast flowered white-hot. Windows shattered in the shop. The iron roof thundered under a rain of dirt and blown rubble.

Perrell clawed up through folds of crackling canvas. He was on his knees in the dark under still-thundering iron, and he didn't know where he was. Fingers bit into his arm. He heard a voice shrill with terror. Bobby Joe. Yellow light glowed along the floor, splaying barred shadows through the Flyer's wheel spokes. The Flyer! The fingers pulled at his arm. Amanda Sibley. He snatched at her hand and ran.

Buell was brushing a thick frost of shattered glass off Bobby Joe. Both of her hands were over her ears, and her mouth was open in soundless terror. Tracy Hazard was leaning against the bench with his glasses hanging from one ear and blood trickling from a tiny cut on his cheek.

"They blowed it too soon!" Buell cried. "It's *dark.*"

"Crank her—we're going!" Perrell shouted. He shoved Amanda up onto the front seat and shouted to Hazard. "Climb in!" Buell pulled Bobby Joe off the bench and heaved her onto the rear seat. She cried out, pointing, and Buell snatched up the wounded chicken and thrust it into her hands. Light, Perrell thought, we need light. He reached down and turned on the acetylene generator; then, fishing a match from his pocket, he ran to the front of the car and flipped open the heavy glass head-lamp cover. Gas hissed at him. He raked the match along the seat of his pants and thrust it flaring into the lamp. A tongue of flame *popped* at his hand, steadied into a bright jet.

Buell was cranking next to him, grunting, his big shoulders heaving. Perrell heard the pistons *suck* and *plop,* then fire. He opened and lighted the second lamp as the engine coughed, then fired again, raggedly, the sound muffled in the two big drums. Perrell slapped the kid's shoulder. "Go on." He followed, scrambling up over the two big brass levers to the driver's seat. He fed it more throttle, waiting for it to even out. *"Go, man!"* Hazard shouted. Perrell shook his head, fed more throttle. The Flyer throbbed under them, the engine's sound a muttering rumble. He cocked his head and listened. A hand pounded his shoulder. He shook it off. Out of the corner of his eye he saw Amanda Sibley's face like a cameo cut against the darkness.

The engine smoothed—he sensed the heat flooding through the great turning shaft and the plunging pistons. Go now. The door was twelve feet away. *Go now.*

He eased in the clutch, feeding throttle as drive chains clicked taut, then suddenly he struck the throttle lever all the way down. The Flyer seemed to hang motionless for an instant, the engine sound a distant, muffled murmur, then she lunged, tore away from her silencer with a roar and burst through the plank door, broken wings of wood flailing and twin streams of light boring into the dark toward the stables. The Flyer pounded through the ashes of Sarkisian's fire, shearing past the stack of timbers.

Ahead, his lamps reached out and touched the running figures of men, the corral rails. An explosion tore the darkness. In the flare of light, fence rails and dark objects spun brokenly, and the Flyer thunked solidly into concussion. Dirt showered down as Perrell fought the great wheel around. The Flyer's rear end broke loose in a wheel-spinning skid. Perrell eased back on the throttle to give her traction, felt drive wheels biting, spitting a rain of gravel.

Two more explosions burst among the *renegados* back at the corral, flashing white against the night-black mountain. The Flyer thundered toward the Ibarra house. At that moment Vega's man, Tranquilino, ran out through the side door, and in the glare of the head lamps, he was swallowed in a gush of flame and powdered adobe. The Flyer pounded through the appalling, concussive wall of blown dirt and noise.

At the corral, another saddle blew. *Renegados,* seeing one of their mates with a brass saddle horn driven between his ribs, milled in indecisive terror. No man would touch a saddle. Horses bolted over the shattered rails.

The Flyer skittered along the cliff's edge, past the burned Reo, past the powder house. Perrell glimpsed Clinton and Costello crouched by the legs of the loading chute. He passed on through, braked to a shuddering stop, the engine's roar softened to a throaty rumble. In their wake, back beyond the shoulder of the hill, they heard shouts and rip-saw whinnies of terrified horses. Perrell squirmed away from the steering wheel to stand and look back. He saw Costello stringing a rope across the road directly beneath the chute, tying it off, his shirt and face pale blurs against the dark. There was a faint gray wash of light behind Dos Cabezas. Costello climbed over the side-mounted tank and dropped onto the car's rear seat.

"Where the hell is the powder man?" Hazard fumed.

"He's fixin to blow the dynamite," Costello gasped.

"No!" Hazard shouted. He started to climb out of the car. "The mine! You'll blow in the whole—" Buell held the struggling man. At the powder house, a match flared in cupped hands. Sparks showered. Seconds later, Clinton was aboard. The Flyer's wheels spun and gravel spewed. Her head lamps cut a scything arc in the gloom as Perrell swung her down the curves of the arroyo road. The car felt massive, heavy under his hands, the steering stiff and unyielding. He fought the wheel, forced the Flyer's great snout into the turn that carried them down into the village itself, down the narrow cobbled street, her engine thundering between ancient adobe walls.

Then she was into the *plaza mercado* and an old man leaped stiffly into a doorway before them. The Flyer slewed broadside past the circular fountain at the end of the plaza. Perrell swore and cut back on the throttle lever, barely staying with the cobbles as the Flyer clawed for traction. Then he swung right again, and she was out of the village and heading down the lower arroyo road toward the bridge, far below Dos Cabezas.

At Dos Cabezas, Red Durkin and Charlie Slotter had both been knocked down in the corridor of the Ibarra house by the blast set off when Tranquilino ran out the door. They struggled to their feet as Rodrigo Vega burst from Mrs. Sibley's room at the far end of the corridor. He, too, was barefoot and in his underwear. He carried the Smith & Wesson.

"Obregón? Yes, by God, it's Obregón!" he snarled.

"The son of a bitches are shooting artillery at us," Slotter gasped.

"No," Durkin said. "I seen them when the blast went off —it's them people we locked up. They was in that old auto."

"That *wreck?*" Slotter almost screamed.

"They must have got into the powder house," Durkin said.

*"Mierda.* Get after them!"

Durkin caught Slotter's arm. "Jesus, not out that way, Charlie. That door is probably—"

At that moment a frightened *renegado,* bearing word of the disaster at the corral, ran up the steps outside, snatched at the door and his world exploded in a blue-white fireball.

Coughing and choking from blown dust, their ears pealing from the blast, Durkin, Slotter and Vega crawled to their feet. "Go out the damn window!" Durkin shouted. He pushed the sash back and tumbled out onto the *galería* as a man galloped up bareback and fought the terrified horse to a plunging stop. Other horses, riderless, ran aimlessly. The man shouted, "Someone has set dynamite under the saddles!"

The roar of an engine swelled up nearby. "Yonder they go!" Slotter screamed, pointing down the arroyo road.

"Round up some of these loose horses!" Durkin shouted.

The sound of the Flyer's engine was fading toward Baroyeca. Durkin, Slotter and Vega ran back inside the house to get their clothes. Other riders appeared, some bareback, a few with saddles safely snatched up in the first rush to the corral. Durkin stumbled back out onto the *galería,* struggling to pull his pants on.

"Every man who can get a horse under him, get on after them!" he yelled. In the faint gray light, he could see a dozen or more men mounted.

*"Vámanos, hombres!"* shouted a sergeant named Muller, once a noncom in a Silesian regiment of the Kaiser's army. Riding bareback, he neck-reined his horse around with a halter rope and raced down the road, his slung carbine slapping

his thigh. Screeching their *gritos* and war whoops, the others followed. Muller was three lengths ahead when his horse passed under the loading chute and struck the stretched rope. The tripped horse somersaulted and Muller was thrown clear. Behind him, tightly bunched horsemen rode into solid tons of ore raining down from the chute. Men and horses were engulfed, and others, unable to stop, piled into them from behind. Six or eight men milled their horses in the dust that boiled around the mound of half-buried kicking horses and struggling men. One man's horse wheeled with him and the man saw a spitting shower of sparks in the low dark mass of the powder house, a few yards away. A single word escaped him as he tried to turn his horse—an ancient Hungarian plea for salvation.

The Flyer thundered down the narrow arroyo road toward the bridge. She bucked on the gullied road, hit bottom and soared. Amanda Sibley caught at the seat and hung on. The light from the head lamps had paled. Perrell saw great many-armed *hecho* cactus and, dimly, the graying arroyo wall outside the light beams. Far above, he glimpsed Dos Cabezas, the two great heads of stone against purpling sky, and the Flyer's mad run filled him with a surge of ecstasy.

Flame erupted from the shoulder of the mountainside above—an enormous red-brown deadly flower, silent for an incredible frozen eternity before brain-splitting thunder and concussion pounded against them. It appeared to Perrell that the whole shoulder of the mountain shivered beneath the blast like a wet dog, then began to slide downward, a monstrous avalanche. On its surface, like a thrown chip, he saw the timbered loading chute turning end over end as it broke up. For a long moment the Reo truck appeared to hang in the air, then it too fell tumbling.

He hit the brakes and the Flyer screeched. The road ahead disappeared under the dark cascade. A single great boulder rolled ponderously down toward the Flyer, pulped giant clumped arms of cactus. Then it was gone, bounding over the car, turning over and over until it crashed among the rocks below with a noise like scattered artillery.

Dribbling sand, then. Dust billowing. The Flyer's front wheels half sunk in dry dirt. Muttered swearing from the seat behind. Perrell turned to see Costello, the curled brim of his derby filled with dirt. The others were shivering, coughing, slapping away the blown earth.

The road was gone. Buried. Erased.

"Idiots! *Idiots!*" Hazard blurted. *"I tried to tell you."*

"I never aimed to blow the road, too," Clint said. "I—"

"By God, you've *trapped* us, do you understand that?"

The big man caught Hazard's coat in his fist. "Mister, don't give me no more mouth."

"Shut up, dammit!" Perrell snapped. He threw the gear lever into the reverse notch on the quadrant, eased throttle and clutch. The Flyer pulled back, streaming dirt and gravel.

Tracy Hazard pounded on the seat. *"You can't go back!* They'll run us down in the streets."

"It's time to split up," Clinton growled. "The farther we get into the hills, the better chance there is."

Buell Ashbaugh rose and put his leg over the side, then leaned back and took hold of Bobby Joe's arms. He had a wild, scared look on his face. "Me and Bobby Joe is leavin—they can't foller us all." He started to lift her over the side of the Flyer, but she cried out and grabbed Perrell's shoulder.

Perrell tasted panic, sharp and sour. Their escape, so close, was shattered. He caught Buell's wrist. "Hold on, kid. They would see you for miles, down there. The whole cañon is wide open." He started the car backing again. The folded top bows were too high to see over. He leaned out over the side, looking back along the arroyo wall. Brush slapped at his face. He fed throttle to her, fought the infernally stiff steering. The Flyer rumbled backward. He backed her around on a tiny pull-out and headed her back up the road toward Baroyeca. Slow, painfully, grindingly slow in first gear.

"Where do you think you're going?" Hazard shouted in his ear.

Perrell turned to Amanda Sibley. "I want you to show me the silver road."

She shook her head, her eyes large with fright. "It's all ruined."

"It's either that or drive her off the cliff!"

Costello's voice broke in. "Horses, son—I see horses on the road from the mine. They got past where the powder house blowed up."

The Flyer crawled on the steep grade. "She can't make it," Perrell said. "She's breaking her back. Help her, dammit! Get out and push!"

Buell and Clinton climbed from their seats and leaped. The Flyer was faltering. Perrell glanced back and saw Costello jump, coattails winging, with Hazard after him. The lightened Flyer picked up speed, her hard tires grumbling. The grade eased, swung left. Broken cobbles ahead, houses. Baroyeca. Faster she rolled. Faster. "Climb on!" he yelled. And they were clutching handholds, scrambling.

The Flyer thundered on the cobbles, the wheel chattering under his hands. "Beyond the fountain, go right!" Amanda Sibley cried, pointing. High curbs, the narrow plaza, the jacaranda trees, her hand waving him on—then horsemen streamed in on his left, around the fountain. He saw the winking light of gunfire. But horseback gunfire, he thought. Wild. He hit the spark lever and blipped the ignition. Explosions ripped from the Flyer. Backfiring, she staggered, skidded madly. Perrell saw horses bucking, then he was into them, broadsiding through; a horse was down kicking. *"Oh, hell, I missed the turn!"* and he let her go, clear on around the fountain, backfiring all the way, horses squealing like pigs under the knife. Then he swung her away from the fountain; she leaped the curb onto the grassy plaza and sped roaring among the tables under the jacaranda trees.

"The alley at the end of the plaza!" Amanda cried.

The Flyer hurtled into the narrow cobbled alley, backfiring an ear-splitting cannonade, then she burst out into the big Plaza de Armas, a palm-bordered square of ancient gardens embraced by decaying town houses, the church beyond. He skidded her around the square, not backfiring now, straightened, a long *galería* on his right, massive round columns. Amanda waved him past the crumbling church onto a long grade. They glimpsed frightened faces at the windows, shutters slamming, then the houses were falling away behind them. Branches of alamo trees slashed at them, whipped away, and clouds of birds exploded into flight.

"They must have turned back," Costello shouted. "They never came through the alley."

The road narrowed. Pale hills, dark-studded with clumped oak and cedar, shouldered up on the left, rising steeply toward the enormous dark spine of the Sierra Madre. The road, rutted and gullied, swung around the long curve of the hillside. The sky brightened overhead, yet the Flyer appeared to be nosing into darkness. Then Perrell saw that the darkness was the gloom of a vast barranca opening before them, a cañon that was like a gash in the flank of the mountain. The road turned out of the tawny hills onto the steep sloping wall of the barranca. The bottom, far below, was thick with trees and brush. The road twisted sharply, following the ragged wall, and ahead it was like a broken thread, appearing and reappearing through the brush until a turn of the cañon obscured it completely. Beyond, and high above the turns of the barranca, the red light of dawn streamed through a deep notch in the mountain.

Perrell braked the Flyer to a sudden stop. Four or five oak trees had grown up in the middle of the gullied road. Buell climbed over the side, lifted an ax from the cargo rack and jogged to the trees. He began to swing, the ax chocking solidly. Clinton trotted after him with the other ax.

Perrell reached down over the dash and turned the handle of the brass fuel valve, to shut off the flow of gasoline and switch to kerosene. He advanced the throttle a little. The engine missed and faltered. Fear stirred in his belly. He retarded the spark a trifle. The Flyer smoothed and held, rocking to the shivering beat, the exhaust suddenly smoky.

"From now on she drinks coal oil," Perrell said. "I didn't dare switch tanks back there—that means there won't be much gas left now. Enough to heat her up once more maybe."

Costello had climbed down and walked back along the road. He cocked his head, listening, then said, "We're still clear of them. They must figure we can't go far, though. They will want to see what Vega means to do, and get some saddles and grub. Then I 'spect they'll be after us."

A sturdy little oak toppled under Buell's ax.

"Why would he follow us at all?" Amanda Sibley said. "You said he wanted to get to the coast."

"That's right. It won't profit him none to chase after us, except he will naturally want to pump us full of holes."

"What he *really* wants," Perrell said, "is that silver. He would be crazy to go off and leave it, just to run us down."

"That's the nut of the matter right there," Costello said. "He's crazy, all right, but we don't know *how* crazy."

Another tree thrashed down and Clinton rolled it over the side into the cañon. Amanda gestured helplessly at the trees. "From here on the road is hardly more than a footpath. The woodcutters use it, or Indians." She shook her head, looking down at the quivering Flyer beneath her.

"But you say it goes to Chihuahua?" Perrell stared intently toward the distant notched gap in the vast mountain.

"That's the pass," Amanda said. "Chihuahua is on the other side, but you surely don't think—"

"Yes," Perrell said. "We'll keep going."

Behind him, Hazard made a strange noise in his throat. Perrell turned. Hazard stared at him, his lips compressed into a thin, tense line. He nodded jerkily. "If we get up into the cañon as far as we can go, say a couple of hours, we can run the car off the road and hide it. Our own people from Dos Cabezas will be in the hills to the north. We can find them."

Perrell shook his head. "I mean keep going. This road goes to Chihuahua."

"No machine—nothing on wheels—can cross the Sierra Madre. Not here, on this road."

"We're taking the Flyer as far as she'll go. Then, by God, we can walk. There's an American army over there on the Chihuahua side someplace."

"Preposterous! I tell you, it's impossible."

"Maybe so," Costello said, "but he's right. We've got to try. We can't go any way but east. Walk, swim or fly . . ." He held up a hand as Hazard spluttered, trying to find words to protest. "No, Vega is all washed up in Chihuahua. He is sure to quit when he sees we are really going over the mountains. There is nothing in it for him, see?"

Hazard's face wore a chilled, pale look and the fiber was gone from his voice. "It's seventy miles, maybe more, across the Sierra to any kind of village."

In his mind, Costello thought *Cusichic.*

"Look, stay if you want," Perrell said. "We're overloaded, anyway."

Hazard sank back in the seat. "I . . . I'll stay with the car."

Buell and Clint heaved trees off the road and waved the Flyer on. Perrell climbed up behind the wheel. A moment later the Flyer was rocking slowly, straddling the stumps, then passing on, her exhaust smoking darkly.

PART THREE

# The Sierra

# (26)

When Muller's horsemen galloped away from the Ibarra house after the fugitives, Vega screamed at Durkin to start the Ford. With Charlie Slotter, they ran around the corner of the house to where the Ford was parked. Then the powder house blew up. They were sheltered from the explosion by a corner of the house, but even so they were knocked down, dazed, battered by the enormous blast. Still groggy, Vega shouted hysterically at Durkin to start the car. Durkin staggered around and cranked the Ford. Dirt was still sifting out of the sky and the air stank of dynamite fumes. A string of spit was hanging from Vega's lip.

"Get on with it, *hombre!*" he shouted.

"Hold on, Colonel," Durkin said. "We've got what we want right here. No, listen"—Vega was turning on him, wild-eyed—"listen. We could go after them, but we would burn up all the gasarene. The machine is full now. She can carry us, and the silver, to the coast, understand?"

Vega climbed into the Ford with stiff, jerky movements, staring straight ahead with the whites of his eyes showing all around the iris. Durkin stomped the pedal and drove the Ford to the fuming chasm where the powder house had stood. Dim gray light revealed the carnage in men and horses from the ore chute and the explosion. A narrow ledge of rubble-strewn road remained where the ore chute had stood. Durkin peered through roiling dust and dynamite fumes—none of the riders had gotten through. He climbed out of the Ford and looked over into the dark arroyo. Far below, the beams of the Flyer's head lamps moved slowly backward, away from the avalanche. He saw that the avalanche had not touched the bridge. He felt movement next to him. It was Vega.

"The road is destroyed," Vega hissed. "We will corner them in the village."

"Let the men run 'em down," Durkin said quickly. "There's no place they can go now." He turned to Slotter. "Charlie, get them bastards movin, before somethin else goes haywire." He pointed, stabbing a finger fiercely toward the confusion of men and horses in the compound, and Slotter trotted away. Durkin's mind was racing as he tried to put his plans back together. "Colonel, we've got the silver and we've got the Ford. The bridge is still there. We can round up people from the village—they can move enough dirt from the slide to let us get through to the bridge. S'pose it does take a couple of days. When we pull out with the silver, the only way we can get away from *them*"—his hand gestured at their own men, a number of whom were mounted now and approaching at the gallop as Slotter shouted at them to hurry—"the *onliest* way, is in this Ford."

Horsemen reined in before them, milling, their horses shying away from bloody debris. There were eight or ten men and more coming, most of them bareback and still in their long underwear, but armed. Vega stepped forward and flung up his hand to wave them on. He cried out in Spanish, "You will apprehend them in the village! *Adelante, amigos!*"

Slotter was back, breathing hard. "Reminds me of Agua Prieta," he mumbled. "We follered the son of a bitch and they murdered us."

"We'll get out of this," Durkin said, "and we'll dump that crazy bastard on the way."

The horsemen fought their blood-shy horses past the smoking devastation and galloped toward Baroyeca, whooping. In the arroyo, the Flyer's head lamps smeared a bright streak in the dusk, the light now probing toward the village as well.

Vega climbed back into the Ford. Durkin beckoned to Slotter; they too got into the car and drove to the shop without speaking. Durkin was uneasily aware of Vega's fixed stare and the tremor under his calm. They left the Ford outside the shop and walked in over the splintered wreckage of the door, looking curiously at the somehow naked spot where the Thomas Flyer had sat. Beyond the cold forge, several dynamite boxes sat on the bench, covered with sacking, next to assay scales and scattered sheets of paper. Vega threw back the sacking.

*"Merde!"* he shrieked. Durkin's belly squirmed with shock. The dynamite boxes were empty. The silver was gone.

Vega hurled the sacking into the ashes of the forge, swept the boxes to the floor and kicked them to splinters. Suddenly he stopped and stood quivering, a ropy pulse surging in his throat, saliva stringing down. *"Porquería,* anus of a pig!" he enunciated softly. Durkin flinched—there was no way of knowing how far Vega would go in one of his rages.

Charlie Slotter held up a piece of paper. "What do you make of this?"

Gunfire spattered faintly in the distance. Grateful for the interruption, Durkin took the paper and studied the scrawled figures. "Must be the assay. 'A-U-three-two percent,' it says. Hell of a mess of numbers . . ." He mumbled along, trying to follow the figures. "There's five hundred and seventy somethin pounds of the stuff, and here it says forty thousand. Big numbers. Must be what it's worth." His mouth was dry with excitement. He whispered hoarsely, "Forty thousand dollars U.S."

"Almost six hundred pounds," Slotter said. "That's one hell of a load for that old junk pile, with all them people."

"They can't get far, anyway, by God," Durkin said, "because there is no way they could have got the gasarene."

Riders galloped up outside, back from Baroyeca. Rodrigo Vega was pulling on his gloves. "I will see them strung up in their own guts," he whispered. Durkin wished he would wipe his mouth. Shouts, outside. He went out to listen to what they would have to say; he was perfectly certain that the big old automobile was bottled up in the village, probably shot full of holes, and the damn people hogtied. What he heard staggered him.

Thirty minutes later the Ford was creaking through the rubble left by the blast, then clattering noisily down the arroyo road toward Baroyeca. It carried beef and canned goods wrapped in canvas and tied on behind. With the Ford rode twenty-four *soldados,* the remnant of the Gringo Legion. Each man carried a sack of corn for his horse and a bottle or two of mescal for himself. They led half a dozen extra horses, which were fed and rested, though now shy of sudden loud noises. Getting them past the hideous mess at the scene of the blast called for whip and spur. Several men, wounded or injured and absolutely unable to ride, were left behind. There was no doubt of what would happen to them when the people returned.

The Legion clattered through Baroyeca in noisy but orderly, almost military fashion. Wood smoke drifted blue and wispy against the dawn, yet not a villager's head showed, nor child, nor goat, dog or chicken.

Durkin gave the Ford throttle and pulled out ahead of the riders. He was certain that he would see the touring car ahead any moment, stalled or wrecked. He wanted time to transfer the silver to the Ford—the less the men of the Legion saw of it, the better. But when he reached the place where the trees had been cut, he stopped the Ford, appalled at the vastness of the barranca that opened before them.

*"Shee-it!"* Charlie Slotter exclaimed. "I thought you said they couldn't go far."

"Dammit, I know what I said. I still say it. Maybe they had a little gasarene rat-holed, but it couldn't carry 'em far. Anyway, the damn road is certain to peter out before long."

Vega remained silent. He stared beneath the hooded lids of his eyes into the barranca, the worm wriggling under the skin of his cheek, plucking the corner of his mouth into a cadaverous smile. His calm was almost cataleptic.

Hoofs clashed on stone behind them. Durkin pulled the throttle lever down, let off the hand brake and stepped on the "go" pedal. Lank and spidery, the machine lurched onto the time-blurred road.

The Flyer looked like a galleon thrown wallowing onto a steep shore and abandoned there by the tide. She was tilted far over, her tires rasping at the crumbling incline. Any more and she would roll. Above her, Ellred Clinton, Buell Ashbaugh and Costello all heaved back on ropes run across her and tied off on her low side to keep her from rolling, or skidding down sideways. Bobby Joe and Amanda Sibley clung to the high side to help hold her down, as Perrell gently gave her throttle and clutch.

She was crawling out across the face of a great yellow scar, where an avalanche a quarter of a mile wide had sheared down the wall of the barranca and carried the road with it. What was left was a footpath, cut again since the avalanche by burros, wild cattle, deer and the less abrasive feet of the *serranos,* the people of the Sierra. A thousand feet below the Flyer, water glinted through green fronds of scrubby palm trees, like a glistening twist of silk.

Perrell cut back the throttle. The trail was blocked by boulders of red volcanic stone and a sprawled, dark-tufted pine tree. Looking up, he could see where the tree had broken out of the lip of the cliff and come skidding down. He climbed gingerly out of the tilted Flyer. He caught the gummy, upper end of the pine, and with Hazard helping, swung it aside. Hazard put his shoulder against a huge rock and heaved. It rolled and bounded crashing down the mountain. "Volcanic, see? It's full of air bubbles." He laughed. Together they cleared away the other rocks, which were astonishingly light.

"There's one hitch in all this," Costello said above them. "We're gettin through all right, so far, but whoever comes along behind us will find the road cleared."

Perrell straightened, panting. "You still think they are following?"

"We would do well to figure they are." He squinted at the sun. "It's near noon. They've had time to pull themselves together and get after us again. With horses, they can move faster than we can. Or with the Ford, too, now that we've cleared the trail."

Perrell shook his head irritably. "It doesn't make sense. What the hell, they've got the silver. Durkin won't burn up gas coming after us."

Costello shrugged. "It is a wise outlaw who keeps an eye on his back trail." He grinned at Clinton, who glared back at him. "Look at it this way," he said then to Perrell, to them all. "That Colonel Vega, he's a white-eyed man. If a horse shows you that much white to his eye, you're just damn sure he'll try to kick you in the belly or clamp his teeth in your butt. Begging your pardon, ladies."

Perrell was back in the seat, gear lever in its slot in the brass quadrant, coaxing the Flyer past the tree. Above him, the three men dug in their heels and leaned back on their ropes, moving along with the Flyer as she rolled. Hazard went on ahead, rolling rocks aside and kicking small stuff into holes. They were nearly across the broad, rubbled face of the avalanche. The Flyer shuddered up the last few yards toward the broken lip of the old road.

Costello was arm-weary from taking his turn with the ax, and his hands were blistered. When he leaned back on the rope, the hard-twist manila bit into the blisters—time was, he thought, when you couldn't blister his hands with a blowtorch. A flicker of movement caught the corner of his eye. He looked back across the avalanche.

Dust puffed from the sloping face of rock above him, then a shrill whine. And an instant later, the shot.

"Hey!" Buell said.

"Four or five riders," Costello barked, "and the damn Ford is there, too." Another bullet spanged.

Perrell opened the throttle and the Flyer's tires skittered. She shuddered on rubble, skidded down a foot and caught there. Her two high-side wheels rocked up as she tilted, and both women cried out. Perrell saw Tracy Hazard's face in that instant, turning back toward him, white with apprehension, the eyeglasses flashing, a hand lifted.

Above the Flyer, Buell felt the pull on his rope and set

himself, but he was out on bare stone and the rope pulled him, skidding, slipping. Clinton, ahead of him and higher, caught at the twisted butt of a manzanita coiling from a cleft in the rock. He pulled a loop of rope around it and took a hitch, and the manila thrummed taut. Slowly the Flyer rocked back.

On all fours, Buell scuttled like a crab along the face of tawny stone. Ducking under Clinton's taut rope, he went on to a knob of rock and whipped a turn of rope around it. The Flyer was moving, a plume of blue smoke gushing from her exhaust.

Clinton released his rope and let it pull free. He bounded down to the Flyer and ripped loose a can wired to her cargo rack. Then he was sloshing water into the can from a canteen and running—back toward the fallen tree. Costello skidded down and ran with him. They reached the tree and together heaved at it, hauling and lunging, until they had swung the tree back across the trail. Ducking down behind it then, Costello pulled at the rubble to make a hole. Clinton took a deep breath and willed his hands steady, then armed the Nevermiss rattrap.

Beyond them, across the rock fall, the Ford edged out onto the rubble, bucking and clattering. Horsemen overtook it and galloped past to stumble awkwardly, slowed on the loose stone.

The Flyer was half up onto the road, its tires sawing, spitting plumes of red dirt. Perrell shouted for help. Buell skidded down to the car, got his shoulder against the rear end and heaved, heaved until his ears roared, aware that Hazard and the two girls were pushing too. The Flyer lurched, then rolled up onto the shelving road, picking up speed. Over the staccato blast of her exhaust, Buell heard ragged gunfire. The Flyer rounded a shoulder of rock and Perrell braked her there in its shelter.

"Where in hell is Clint?" he shouted. With the engine idling, it seemed suddenly quiet. He slapped his fingers against his thighs. They were like claws from gripping the wheel. Then he saw that Costello was missing too.

Buell looked around the rock. "They're coming!" he called. He saw Clint loping over the rubble toward them, Costello scampering behind, his coattails flying, both men crouched low. The tree was about sixty yards away and beyond it he saw the Ford. It was out on the rocky incline, heeled far over with dust billowing beneath it, close enough so that he clearly heard frantic shouts from it. Horsemen out ahead stopped their mounts uncertainly and turned back—riders back by the Ford were already shaking out loops in their rawhide *reatas.* In a moment the Ford was caught in a web of rope, strung to the four horses aligned on the slope above. She was struggling spiritedly, creeping along the trail.

Buell turned and ran as Clint and Costello passed him. They hurled their weight against the Flyer again. Ahead, the road angled back into clear view of the avalanche for a few yards before it turned away out of sight beyond the rock wall into another long bend of the barranca. Slowly she rolled. Driving hard and coughing from the dark exhaust, Buell turned so that his back was against the Flyer. He could see the avalanche again. One of the horses was straining back on its haunches, ahead and a little above the Ford, the rider intent on his rope. The horse backed into the downed pine tree.

His name was Wilbur Rawlins and he was from a sod-shanty homestead in the Red River country near Frederick, Oklahoma. Years of stealing cattle had helped to make him, as he liked to put it, a crackerjack roper. Neat as heeling a steer, he had dropped his loop across the Ford and caught the bar sticking out there to support the framework of the folding top. He had taken two dallies around the saddle horn and was playing the rawhide lariat with artistry and subtle skill when his horse backed into the tree and triggered a Nevermiss rat-trap.

The old tar bucket, well covered with rocks, exploded directly under the horse's tail. The animal hurtled as if cata-pulted, turning slowly—or so it seemed to Wilbur Rawlins—in midair with him, so that the rope slacked for an instant, then snapped tight on the downside, jerking the Ford loose from its tenuous hold on the steep slope of the rock fall.

Red Durkin leaped clear—Vega and Charlie Slotter had

preceded him. Two of the other horses were jerked down, kicking, and the last bolted back the way they had come. Durkin rolled to get away from the kicking, screaming horses. On his hands and knees, through the drifting dust of the explosion, he watched the Ford turning over and over, shedding fenders, wheels, parts and cargo in its long passage to the bottom of the barranca.

# (27)

Perrell had to stop the engine. The radiator rumbled, boiling. The road ahead was thready and indistinct against the rearing dark mass of the Sierra, but he saw where the pale scar of the road switched back and forth above them, seeking to climb out of the barranca. Sunlight slanted low through fast-scudding clouds, and brushed dark-ruffed patches of timber and brush with bursts of fire. He got a wrench from the dynamite box full of tools on the floor and climbed down.

Birds scolded. He saw them, pale gray against an encino —dark crested heads and long tails scissoring down.

"Magpie jays," Amanda Sibley said. " 'Nacio Domínguez says they tell the weather."

"Granddaddy always claimed the same thing about sage chickens," Bobby Joe said.

"How?" Buell asked. "What do they do?"

"He never said. He just said they knew."

"Well, *shew,*" Buell said.

"Oh, my God, *stop* it!" Hazard exclaimed, glaring. To Perrell he said, "What's wrong?"

"She's boiling—I'm afraid she'll bust a hose. And she's missing, cutting out." He held up a blackened spark plug. "Plugs are fouling up, see? Missing that way, you get chain lash—the drive chain snapping tight at the sprocket—and it could shear the pins where I sleeved the drive shaft."

"Yes," Amanda Sibley said. "That was what broke it in the first place. Chain lash."

"There's something haywire in the ignition, too. I didn't get to run it long enough to check it through." Perrell passed the spark plugs to Amanda and Hazard to clean.

In the back seat, Bobby Joe was cooing to the rooster as she rustled in the grain sack. She chewed a mouthful of grain, then held up the wounded chicken, supporting his scabby head with one hand, and put his beak to her lips. He strained to eat. Buell watched intently, nibbling at blistered skin on his big hand.

"Gonnies, I'm near about *starved* and there you set feedin that chicken—when you goin to do that for me, Bobby Joe?"

She glared at him over the rooster's head.

"I ain't had nothin to eat but blisters," he went on. "I could eat that bird raw this very minute."

"Oh, *you,*" she said.

Clint took up an ax. "Come on, kid."

"Bobby Joe is fixin my supper," Buell clowned.

"It'll keep. Bring the shovel and water and one of the cans." Buell and Costello followed the powder man back along the road. An icy wind funneled along the barranca and whipped powdery dust away beneath their feet. Clint pointed with the ax. "We want to drop that pine right across here."

"They're on to that, now," Costello said. "Horseback, they will just ride up around it, where it stumps out by the prickly pear. That's what I would do."

"Sure," Clint said. He turned to Buell. "So, kid, you dig us a hole right under the prickly pear and that's where we'll set our can." Buell's shovel rang on the hard ground. Clint looked up toward the head of the barranca. "See how the road cuts back and forth up there. From here on they'll make better time than we can, so we've got to make 'em work for every foot. We can't bomb everything, but a couple of rattraps in just the right places will make 'em *nervous.* The son of a bitches will pee down their legs ever time a grasshopper jumps."

"Until dark," Costello said. "Once the light is gone—by God, they won't dare go another step. We can light the lamps and keep goin. What plagues me is why they haven't quit. Can you tell me that, Ellred? It has cost them too much, if all they want is to shoot us."

Buell stepped back from the hole. Clint poured water into the can. The carbide frothed. He set the trap and closed the lid. Holding the can very carefully in both hands, he bent to lower it into the hole. He grunted and flinched when his elbow brushed a needled lobe of prickly pear. A sharp *snap* sounded within the can. He froze, then sagged, his face suddenly white. He pried the lid open and turned it over. The trap was sprung. The striker bar was sunk into the piece of wood he had slipped under the tape to keep the bar from riding on the cap.

"I forgot to take the stick out," he whispered. "It's near bit through." He took the wood out and reset the trap. When he had finished covering up the can, he ran the thread around an arm of the prickly pear and back to the pine stump. From a few feet away, it was invisible.

They walked back along the road toward the Flyer. "A jumpy powder man is a friend to nobody," Clint said.

"You never answered me, Ellred," Costello said. "Why haven't they quit? It's got to be because we have somethin they want. Would it be you? You and Durkin were friends—Would it be that he wants to cut himself in on your stake?"

"Who said we was friends?" Clint flared. "We done time together, is all." He stopped and faced Costello. "Look, Durkin knows why I done time—in the pen everybody knows why a man is there. Back there at the mine, I let him think what he wanted, and I let him know I would just as leave throw in with him."

"Would you have?"

"It crossed my mind—hell, I would have been shut of you. But I'll tell you what he said—he said he *knowed* that I was headed back to Chihuahua. And he said there wasn't nothin for them in Chihuahua but a rope or a firin squad and he was damned if he would set foot there again. He said they had what they wanted, right there at the mine, so I wasn't nothin to him but another mouth to feed."

"There's a friend for you, Ellred." They walked on and Costello shook his head. "But it purely baffles me. If he said that, then we've still got to ask ourselves—why in thunder haven't they quit? They don't need us, except for a little fun, and they sure as hell don't want to go to Chihuahua. Perrell was right. There is no sense to it."

They were at the Flyer then and Perrell was saying, "She's cooled down—we'll have to start her on gasoline again." And Hazard said, "Well, hurry, dammit."

"I'm *hungry,*" Buell said. "Bobby Joe, honey, if you're through feedin that chicken, you can start on me."

"Somebody crank her," Perrell said. Buell cranked and the engine rumbled to life. "Hear that?" Perrell said. "She's better, but the miss is still there. I'm afraid we'll have trouble when we get up into those switchbacks. It'll be too steep for her."

"No," Hazard said. "Don't forget, this is the Camino de Plata—it was cut for mules pulling *carretas* loaded with silver. It's a mule-power road. It can't get much steeper, or they could never have made it. That's why the switchbacks are there."

Snow swirled against the mountain in gusting clouds, and the crawling Flyer shuddered under its buffeting. The barranca was gray with blown snow, and above them the top of the cañon was lost in clouds. The turns into each switchback were so tight that Perrell had to back and fill to get the long Flyer around. He sat hunched over the wheel, fighting to hold her. His hands were wrapped in strips of sacking and he was bundled in tattered canvas. Buell and Clinton walked on ahead cutting trees, then pulling them back across the road when the Flyer rolled past.

"Make 'em worry," Clint said. "Make 'em sweat."

A rock loomed through the snow and blocked the road. Beyond, scattered over a thirty- or forty-yard stretch of the road, were a dozen or so trees, mostly encino, the sturdy little oak of the Sierra. Then there was an equal distance of open ground and a sharp turn that would carry the Flyer back directly above where she was now halted.

Perrell nosed the Flyer's steel-pipe bumper up to the rock and gave her throttle. The rear end chattered and slithered in the snow. The rock did not budge.

"Let's get chains on her," Perrell said. Digging down under the boxes and canvas in back, Hazard found the chains.

"Dark is comin on," Clint said. "This is a good place to double-shot 'em." He took cans from the rack. Perrell and Hazard were laying out the chains.

"You still don't think they will have quit?" Amanda asked. "This has been hard going."

"Not as hard for them as for us," Clint said. "Say we done twenty, twenty-five miles so far. Horses, even packhorses or mules will do you that much. I mean, we'd be better off with mules than with this machine. We wouldn't have to stop to cut trees." He nodded at Buell and Costello, who were cutting trees ahead on the road. "So, right here, we've got to make 'em hurt. I 'spect they know enough now to pull a tree out of the way with a rope when there is no way to ride around it. But that's work, see? Say they come to this mess of trees here, all in their way. All right, we give them a few trees that don't blow up. By then they are tired of the work, and that last tree is just a little old switch of a tree, anyway, and hardly in the way atall. That's where we'll rat-trap 'em."

"That's one. You said a double shot." She carried the cans for him as Clinton took a shovel and began to dig a hole in the place he had pointed out.

"Sure. Say they touch this first one off. The road is clear, beyond, see? They are happy to be through the trees. Now they can push on. So just yonder, out in the open—no trees there— we'll rat-trap 'em again. After that they ought to be too shaky to go on in the dark."

"Very nasty indeed, Mr. Clinton."

Perrell called to them that the chains were on. He nosed the Flyer against the rock. The brass throttle lever clicked under his fingers, and the muffled clash of tire chains in the snow sounded. Clinton and Hazard levered with poles. The rock skidded slowly, then toppled, crashing down and down.

Darkness fell as if the snow and wind had blown the last of the light from the sky. Then it was gray-dark and the Flyer was slanting through a murky fog of blown snow that carried with it the adobe smell of the dust of Mexico. Best not to show a light yet, Perrell thought. But, strangely, with the dusk and the turns he lost his sense of direction, for he no longer had the sun's light steadily at his back and the dark mass of the Sierra before him. The Flyer was simply chattering up an endless inclined plane as Perrell struggled to warp the monstrous machine over and around rocks and scrubby trees and yet cling to the crumbled remnant of the Camino de Plata.

In a gust of snow he lost sight of the road and overran a turn. As the left front wheel suddenly sagged down he thought for an instant that she was going over, and he was sick with the old ghastly dream fear of an endless fall into the void. He braked, then eased back and saw how the road swung up and around to his right. Shaken, he set the lever that dropped a steel pawl into rear-wheel cogs, to keep her from rolling back. "I can't tell where the road is. We've got to have light now."

Ellred Clinton swung down, plodded to the head lamp. Perrell reached down with his right hand and turned on the acetylene generator. Waiting for Clinton to strike the light, he strained to see through the shredding mist of snow.

Below them in the barranca, a white incandescent fireball erupted, followed moments later by the muffled *BLA-AM* of the explosion. The fireball danced behind his eyelids, orange, then green.

"My God, we're right over them," Costello said. "All those switchbacks . . ."

"Light it, man!" Perrell shouted. Startled, Clint struck the light and the head lamp snorted a long tongue of flame. He jerked his scorched hand back and closed the cover, then leaped for the running board. Perrell swung the wheel hard over and gunned the engine. The single head lamp slashed an arc against the mountain wall as the Flyer turned, then a lancing finger of light darted out along the road. A clear stretch. For once, there were no trees in the way.

*　　　　　*　　　　　*

Below, Red Durkin wiped muddy clots of snow off his face. His ears rang and he smelled scorched hair and hide. Gravel spilled from his hat brim. His exhausted horse bucked once under him, crow-hopped, then stood shuddering. Through the shouts and curses and whinnied screams of terrified horses, Durkin heard a man's lonely and outraged cry: *"Amigos . . . ayúdame-e-e . . ."* It came from far down in the barranca.

"Simmons," he shouted, "you and Avila—get some ropes and see who the hell was blowed over the side."

"Hey, look!" Simmons pointed up through the gloom of dusk and swirling snow. A beam of light swung against the mountain, then lanced out.

"By God, there they are!" Charlie Slotter cried. "We've got the bastards!" He drove his spurs into his horse's flanks and the animal lurched into a run. The road was clear. No trees. Slotter whooped. Other riders were with him, pounding through the snow.

Blue-white and brilliant, the second blast burst among them. Slotter, deafened and stunned, his mouth full of mud, found himself on his hands and knees among tangled, kicking horses. He was soberly considering what to do about all this when the iron-shod hoof lashed out and hit him just below the ribs.

Colored blobs of fire raged in Durkin's eyeballs. One of the first things he saw when they cooled down was Charlie Slotter, who was on his hands and knees pawing at the snow, Durkin thought, like a man who has lost something precious, but then he realized that Slotter was groveling in pain.

He remembered then that they were pursuing an old auto full of people who had stolen a seemingly endless supply of gasarene. He turned to call the men to action, then he saw that they had all dismounted, that they were unsaddling, that some were already gathering firewood. All the movements of making camp, but without orders. Fearing Vega's wrath, Durkin turned, looking for him. But Rodrigo Vega had dismounted also. He was sitting on a steaming saddle blanket in the snow, with his head in his hands.

# (28)

The storm appeared now to blow unchecked across the humped backbone of the Sierra. The barranca was gone, left behind, and the Flyer wound among wind-sculptured knobs and horns of stone, tawny red in the passing touch of the head lamp where they jutted up through the snow. Dry, frozen brush crackled under the wheels, and the canvas covering the Flyer's passengers popped in the wind, drowning the clash of wheel chains and the labored snarl of the engine. Then the Flyer plunged into a narrow *cajón,* a sheer-walled defile barely wide enough for the machine to scrape through, the walls themselves lofting into darkness above, the red rock slashed with snow-streaked ledges.

The *cajón* wound and twisted sharply, a half-mile or so, Perrell thought, then the Flyer emerged from the defile and slanted onto a downgrade, wanting to shake free and roll. A chasm opened darkly below them on the left, the mountain-side looming to the right, spiked with clumped pine and encino. Ahead, the road narrowed into a mere ledge under a great humped mass of red rock that jutted from the timbered slope.

Darkness suddenly yawned ahead under the beam of the head lamp and Perrell saw that the road was gone there, a piece of it broken away from the wall. He stamped on the brake and the Flyer skidded half around in the snow and stopped. He backed away from the edge.

Clint and Buell swung down from the car and walked forward with the hot light at their backs. They stopped next to a twisted, weathered tree stump and peered gingerly into the chasm, talking, shaking their heads and pointing. They came back huffing and swinging their arms. Buell opened the head-lamp cover and put his hands in close to the jet of flame. Clint pointed to the timbered slope.

"If we can cut some timber up above and snake it down, there's a chance we can bridge it. The gap is a few feet longer than the car."

Perrell hesitated, fearing to kill the engine. There was nothing else to do. He reached out and cut the ignition. Sudden quiet engulfed them.

"Hey, I see a big cave up there," Buell said. Light from the acetylene head lamp reflected off the snow and dimly illuminated a shelving cut into the red rock above and to the right of the Flyer. The overhanging stone was streaked with black from ancient fires, and a low wall of stone partly enclosed the space in front.

"Tarahumara," Tracy Hazard said. "Cave-dwelling people. Their caves are all over the Sierra, from here south. Yaquis or Mayos could have been here, too. Even Apaches. This would have been a perfect place to wait for a silver train to get into that defile back there." Costello suddenly remembered the old campaign map in Sheriff Newcomb's office, the penciled notation: *Gerónimo/Nana silver train '81.*

"The girls can build a fire there and get warm," Perrell said. "Even if we get this bridged, we won't dare try to cross until daylight."

"The rattraps done the job," Costello said, "or they would have caught up to us already."

"All right—say they stopped back there," Perrell said. "We've picked up an hour on them. Let's try to hold on to it."

He left the acetylene head lamp burning. He lighted the two small kerosene side lamps and unfastened them from their mounts. He gave one to Clint. "See what kind of timber is up there, will you?" The powder man grunted and Perrell watched the light bobbing away, around the great hump of rock and on up the slope, Buell and Costello following with axes and coils of rope, bulky and stiff in their wrappings of canvas and sacking. The women went back along the road looking for firewood.

Perrell played his kerosene lamp on the engine. Hazard was turning spark plugs out with a wrench. Perrell added oil to the engine, then poured kerosene into the makeshift fuel tank from cans in the cargo rack. "Is that the last of the fuel?" Hazard asked him.

"Almost. There's another can there, but it's the gasoline that I'm worried about." He took up a stick and rubbed it clean, then thrust the stick down into the gasoline tank. He pulled it out and held it to the light. The stick was barely damp on the end. He shook his head and tossed the stick away.

"What are the chances?" Hazard said.

"Bad. There may be enough to turn her over, but I don't think there's enough to get her hot enough to burn the coal oil." Perrell thought that Hazard, with his smeared glasses catching the light of the lamp, had a hurt, staring look. "But we've got to keep working anyway. Maybe . . . if we build a fire down here near the car and put a bed of coals under the engine, then hang tarps around like curtains, to keep the heat in, she would be warm enough to start easy and heat up quick."

"I'll do that," Hazard said quickly. "Leave her to me."

"She's tearing herself apart, too," Perrell said. "Something haywire in the ignition." He began to go over the wiring while Hazard finished cleaning the plugs. Holding the little kerosene lamp close, he took the head off the magneto, his chilled hands warming from the engine heat. A loose condenser wire could cause missing, he thought, but the Flyer had been pounding, knocking. The condenser wire was tight, though. He pulled out the rotor and scraped the brass contact blade clean with his knife. On an impulse he took it around to the bright light of the acetylene head lamp and examined it. He saw a tiny crack running across the Bakelite material of the rotor, away from the brass blade.

Holding the rotor, he turned and saw light flickering above, against the wall of the cave. Firewood, he thought. Tree gum. Suddenly feeling very tired and cold, he climbed toward the cave. His jaws were stiff and his tongue felt like a piece of harness leather. Amanda and Bobby Joe had a fire going under the scorched overhang. Amanda was kneeling before a broad, hollowed stone. The hollow was filled with grain and she was grinding it with a smaller, loaf-shaped rock. She laughed. "See? A *metate*. Probably the only thing they couldn't carry along."

He got down and examined the pieces of firewood until he found a pine knot and an oozed blister of gum. Seeing the question in her eyes, he said, "That knocking in the engine— in the States you wouldn't run her a city block, clanking like that. I was thinking what it would be—a broken ring, or a bent crankshaft, or a bad bearing. Something bad, see?" He held the cracked rotor in the light where she could see it.

"You mean that little crack would make it knock?"

"Like a sledge hammer. Here, the spark jumps and follows this little crack off to the side and fires some cylinder out of order, so that cylinder works against the others, like banging heads." He gouged away a chunk of gum and put the knife on a stone close to the fire where the gum would warm without burning.

She poured grain into the *metate* and pushed the rock over it, faintly smiling. "That sounds like our little group here. Some of us are firing away at contrary times. Banging heads."

He sat back, watching her grind the grain, liking the way she moved back and forth with the stone. At the same time his mind struggled with the dismal finality of the empty fuel tank. He could not accept it. He insisted to himself that there was enough gasoline left there to get them going again. No use talking of going it on foot, not with the snow. They would all be run down. He began to pack the softened gum into the crack, slicking it over with the heated blade. When it was solid, he went back down to the Flyer and clipped the rotor back into place.

Hazard had a fire going a few feet away from the Flyer. He had torn the top material loose from the bows and draped it around the front and sides of the car, with sticks to prop it up, and from time to time he skidded a shovelful of coals in under the engine. He had made himself a seat close to the fire with a little shelter of canvas, where he sat staring into the fire.

"There will be some chicken feed to eat soon," Perrell said. Hazard nodded. "That's a joke, isn't it?" he said, and Perrell said, "It's funny, all right, but it's supper."

Climbing back up to the cave, he heard voices on the slope above and saw the light of Clint's kerosene lamp. Amanda and

Bobby Joe were cooking cakes of *pinole* on stones at the edge of the fire. Amanda handed him a cake and he sat on the low stone wall, eating it and watching her. He heard voices and a moment later Clint, Buell and Costello came off the slope onto the ledge fronting the cave. They were blowing on their hands and stamping their feet.

"We got some trees down and trimmed," Clint said, "but it'll take all of us to snake 'em down the hill."

They ate first, quantities of *pinole,* gritty from the stone *metate.* "There's nothin like a good hot meal to lift a body's spirits," Buell said.

Bobby Joe lifted a corner of the grain sack, now almost empty. "By tomorrow, when there ain't no more, you'll remember it like it was birthday cake." When they had eaten, she took some down to Hazard.

Carrying lamps, they climbed up the slope above the rocky shoulder overhanging the cave and the road. With ropes and poles, they skidded logs down along a cleft in the rock that worked for them like a chute. One at a time, the logs were skidded butt-first onto the road, just in front of the car, then the upper ends were toppled across the chasm, belayed by ropes from above. On the near side, the twisted stump kept them from rolling over the edge. Buell let himself down on a rope on the far side and anchored the logs with rock and packed snow.

"If we bridge her over solid," Costello said, "they will just trot right across after us."

"That would take a month to build, too," Clint said.

Perrell found that the Flyer's track, the distance between her front tires, was just the length of a shovel. With the shovel as a measure, the bridge was laid out in two segments, each made of logs bound together with rope, the cracks between filled with branches. They packed branches and snow at the ends to make a ramp onto the logs.

In the light of the head lamp, they saw no bottom below the logs. Simply blackness. "She looks terrible rickety," Buell said. "I would as leave walk across."

"You can all walk across when it comes time," Perrell

said. "Then we'll try to knock it apart and roll the logs over the side. If the Flyer doesn't do it for us."

"They will have to find another way past here, anyway," Costello said. "There ain't a horse alive that would cross that thing, without you set fire to him."

"Men and horses don't have to stay with the road," Clint said. "They could skin out over the top, up past where we cut the logs, and find a way on through."

"Slow goin, I 'spect," Costello said. "But s'pose we blow up that notch back there? What are the chances of that?"

"That calls for dynamite. This carbide stuff is mostly bang, not much bite. Not in these little cans, anyway. We might leave them a rattrap, just for the noise . . . Now, if there was a place where we could dump a whole bucket full of the stuff, with plenty of water, and bottle it up tight, the way you pack a stick of powder into a drill hole . . ." His voice trailed off.

"Like when we blowed the powder house?"

"That's right." Clint found himself looking at the bony, twisted stump that anchored the near end of the log bridge. He climbed up on the gnarled roots, grasped a clawing branch and pulled himself up. It was an oak that had lived to a great age, then succumbed to lightning. The trunk was too big to reach around, the shattered top some seven or eight feet off the ground. He felt down inside—it was hollow.

"Daybreak is not too far off," Costello was saying. "We had best try to catch some shut-eye."

Perrell crossed the bridge alone and afoot, feeling the logs spring a little beneath him. He was too tired to feel more than a tremor of fear at the dark emptiness below the logs. Then he walked on along the road in the snow. It slanted steeply up. He walked seventy-odd paces before the road crested and started down. Whatever lay beyond the crest was lost in darkness, but it had stopped snowing and the wind had died down. No trees in the road. Too rocky.

He walked back. A shower of sparks swirled up near the Flyer—Tracy Hazard, tending his fire. Perrell saw the man's eyes following him, heard him clear his throat as if to speak, but Perrell thought that if he stopped walking he would fall flat on his face. He climbed on up to the cave.

They had raked the coals away from the back wall of the cave and put down pine branches covered with canvas to make a long bed against the wall over fire-warmed stone. The fire burned now against the low stone wall in the open face of the cave. A hand reached up and pulled at his coat. Amanda. He was between her and Costello, and he saw Bobby Joe's small head beyond her. He let himself sag down and she pulled the edge of her *cobija* across to cover them both. The bed was deep and soft and smelled richly of pine and wood smoke.

After a moment she whispered, "All the work of building that crazy bridge—and I heard you tell Tracy that you didn't think you could start the Flyer again. Why the bridge, then?"

"We have to try, that's all. And we only get one try. If it works, we need the bridge, too." He thought that he could say something that would sound better—he struggled to put it together, but his tongue and jaws would not function for him.

"As long as I could believe the Flyer would go, I could be halfway *brave.*" She turned toward him and moved quickly into his arms. "If you're going to tell me things like that, you'd better hold me. It's too much to be frightened to death and lonely, too." She laughed softly and her breath flowed warm against his throat. "There's something about six in a bed that's terribly respectable."

He felt himself slipping, down, down. Her voice came again, held him back. "Mm-m?" he mumbled.

"I said, couldn't you start it with the gas thing? Not gasoline—the other. The stuff you burn in the head lamps. Acetylene?"

He was gone. She did not call him back again.

# (29)

The *renegados* were awake an hour before dawn, eating strips
of broiled beef and coffee laced with mescal. Red Durkin uneasily told Rodrigo Vega that eight of the men had deserted
sometime in the night. Tracks indicated that they had gone
back down the trail to the west. Durkin was thinking that they
were left now with only fourteen men, some of whom were
injured or severely scorched.

Vega was curiously unmoved. *"Carcajos,* to do bad things
with pigs," he said. "They suppose they will go peacefully on
through Baroyeca? Eight of them? That the people will wave
and bring out their daughters?" He raised his voice so that the
other men would hear. "Twenty men would not be too many,
going back that way, to watch each other's backs."

The snow had stopped falling. A hint of gray brushed
across the sky, pale behind dark, fast-scudding clouds. Vega
sipped—his cup was stoutly fortified with Mrs. Sibley's brandy
—and studied the indistinct mass of the mountain. "The
horses have had grain? Good. You remember how we saw
their lights go—this way, then that?" He cut a sharp *Z* in the
snow with a stick. "Necessary for the machine, but not for us.
A quick climb, away from the road." He made a peculiar noise
into his cup which Durkin interpreted as a laugh, then he
reached out and poured the last few drops onto the fire. They
sputtered and flashed into flame.

Amanda Sibley woke him a little before dawn and gave
him a tin plate of hot *pinole.* He saw in the firelight that her
hair had fallen loose. It swung now in a loose twist of dark
auburn and for a moment she looked as young as Bobby Joe.
While he ate the *pinole,* spooning it with the little stick she
had used to stir it, he noticed that the others were gone.

"I let you sleep as long as I could, but we need you now.

I . . ." Even in the dim light, he could see that her face was pale and that her hands were shaking. He put the plate aside and came to his knees. She swayed toward him. He reached up and pulled her down to him, her face blurring close. A shout sounded in the distance. Clinton's voice. Another answered close by. Costello. She buried her face under his chin. "I'm thinking of all the time that goes by that you don't want and don't care about, and now—"

Another shout, the alarm clear and sharp in it. Then Perrell took her hand, pulled her up and ran with her. Outside, on the ledge fronting the cave, he heard Costello call out again. He looked up the slope and saw the detective clinging to a branch of encino high on the slope, looking back toward the defile. Costello let go and skidded down in a shower of snow, pointing along the road. Perrell saw Clinton running toward them, long, loose-loping strides, snow puffing underfoot. He was carrying one of the cans.

Perrell ran down to the Flyer. Hazard, Buell and Bobby Joe were pulling the canvas fire screen away from the car. A fire still burned, a few feet from the car, flickering red flaring across the snow in the dim gray light.

Clinton's footsteps thudded. He reached them, gasping. "Went to set . . . rattrap . . . No good place . . . Saw them . . . Horses . . ." He paused, took deep breaths. "They must have made a climb . . . cut across—"

"How far?"

"Three, four minutes."

Tracy Hazard turned to Perrell, his face white, agony in his eyes. "There's something I . . . have to tell you—"

"My God, not now! Get on the crank!"

Perrell jumped up behind the wheel, set spark and throttle. "Slow 'em up if you can," he flung back at Clint. He let Hazard pull the crank through once, to prime the cylinders, then turned on the ignition. "Crank her, man!"

Hazard heaved and the Flyer rocked. Again. The engine coughed, then caught with a roar. Perrell held it with the throttle and grinned down at Amanda Sibley. "Go on, take Bobby Joe and go on across." She gasped and shook her head.

"Hurry!" he said, waving her on. Buell caught her hand and started across, pulling her with him.

Clint jerked a black metal drum off the cargo rack and thrust it at Costello. "Take it up there by the cave."

He leaned in through the rear-door opening, tearing through coils of rope and chain and thick-folded tatters of canvas, clawing . . . *the stack gun.* He got his hands on it and snatched it out, ripping canvas with it. *Godamighty*—He stood as if clubbed, staring down at the softly gleaming bars of silver on the floor of the Flyer. Then he turned and ran with the heavy steel cylinder, his mind fuming with the vision of the silver.

He charged up the slope and on past the cave to where the ledge commanded the dark opening of the defile. He skidded on his knees in the snow next to Costello. With the stack gun, he hacked a trench in the snow and mud, bedded the cylinder with its butt hard against the rock. He laid his cheek on the icy steel and sighted along its stubby length. "What do you think? Lay her dead on?"

"Hell, I don't know. We're about twenty foot higher here. Hundred yards' range . . ."

Clint pulled a piece of fuse from his pocket, hacked off a very short length with his knife and pressed it into the touch-hole. Then he lifted the stack gun, stood it on end and poured coarse grains of black powder from the keg into the bore. The keg was almost empty. He up-ended it. "By God, they will think this is Gettysburg."

"What will you load it with?" Costello asked him. Clint wadded a rag in on the powder and tamped it with a stick, then reached into his sagging jacket pocket and pulled out a length of logging chain. "This." The chain was about six feet long and filled the bore of the gun clear to the muzzle when it was packed in on top of the wadding. He took a handful of snow and packed that in on the chain to keep it from slipping out.

"That's a terrible short fuse," Costello said.

"When we see 'em, it'll be 'most too late. Take the can and run. Go on, git. No, Jesus, *wait!* Give me a match."

Costello fished matches from his vest pocket, then ran

down in skidding leaps. The Flyer had not moved at all. They should have crossed already, he thought. Then he realized that the engine must have stopped. I'm too old for this, he was thinking as he ran.

The engine had run for thirty or forty seconds, clean and strong. The clattering knock was gone. Then it gasped and died and Perrell felt panic squirm through him. Hazard cranked again. The engine throbbed once. Died.

Across the chasm, Amanda Sibley heard the engine stop and turned. When it died again, she cried out and ran back toward the chasm and the Flyer. Bobby Joe caught her arm and tried to hold her. She threw the girl off and ran. She saw Perrell looking at her, his arm flung up, waving her back.

Buell caught her as she reached the logs and swung her around. "Lady, you stop right here or I swear I'll bust you one. You and Bobby Joe git back up the road and wait for us." He pushed her, not gently, then turned again and ran back across the rickety log bridge to the Flyer.

Perrell felt himself freeze when the engine died again, his mind and volition suddenly sapped. He knew he should move, but could not. The Flyer jiggled under him as Hazard went on cranking. Then Perrell heard Amanda Sibley cry out and saw her running and in that instant her words flashed through his mind: ... *start it with the gas thing? ... stuff you burn in the head lamps. Acetylene?* The words had simmered in his mind through his exhausted sleep, and now he suddenly saw the Flyer's acetylene starter system there in his mind, as clearly as a diagram. He thought, That rig is designed to crank her over once, then let the gasoline take over, but if I keep pumping acetylene into the cylinders, she will keep firing.

He flicked on the water control on the big brass acetylene generator, then turned on the valve on the dashboard that would allow the gas to flow to the engine, then he pumped the brass handle on the dash.

Hazard had collapsed against the radiator. Buell moved him aside. Perrell nodded and Buell swung the crank. Smooth, easy swing, his whole body uncoiling into the crank. The engine caught with a roar, a roar that quickly sagged. Perrell pumped again and the roar swelled, subsided. He pumped and she bellowed.

"I've got no throttle!" he shouted to Costello. "The pump is the only throttle . . . It's only supposed to kick her over once, see? It doesn't work through the throttle—"

Above them, Clint shouted.

"He sees the bastards!" Costello cried.

"Let her roll, then." Perrell eased in the clutch and pumped. The Flyer lurched ahead. Pumping, he steered to the logs in lunging bounds. Front wheels bucked onto the logs, stopped, then lurched ahead as he pumped. He was suddenly appalled at the vast, murky depth of chasm that opened beneath the now jouncing and swaying Flyer. The logs of the bridge seemed suddenly flimsy and limber. He pumped and the Flyer leaped, then the logs sagged sickeningly. He was in the middle of the span, pumping, surging, then sagging back, and he knew she could not make it. He swore fiercely. Seeing Amanda and Hazard staring helplessly at him, he clamped his jaws together. Still pumping, he eased off the clutch. Hazard crept out onto the bridge and clung to the head lamp.

"I'll try to keep her going," Perrell called. "Get her hot enough to turn on the kerosene . . ."

At the rear of the car, Buell and Costello gave up trying to push, and clung, gasping for breath. Shrill cries sounded over the engine noise. They looked back and saw horsemen appearing in the mouth of the defile. Above on the ledge, Clint left the stack gun in a great bound, then the gun belched red flame with a concussive *BLA-AM*. Shredding powder smoke whipped away. They saw horses down. One horse, on its knees, riderless, rolled and toppled off the edge of the road in a puffing cloud of snow.

Ellred Clinton reached the Flyer, teetering on the logs as he reached past Costello and tore at the carbide drum.

"Jesus, I thought you would be *acrost!*" he gasped.

"Well, dammit, so did I." Costello's feelings were hurt.

"Bring the canteen and canvas, quick!"

The powder man jumped up onto the gnarled roots of the stump with the drum under his arm and dumped carbide into the hollow. Lots of it, pouring away into the stump. "She's hollow plumb to the roots." He passed the drum down, took the canteen and emptied it. Fumes gushed up and he jerked his head back, snorting. He pulled a rattrap from a coat pocket, gently cocked it, then lowered it down and hung it by its wire hook, leaving slack in the trigger thread. He stuffed canvas into the opening, pulled snow from the limbs and packed it onto the canvas.

"I need bait." He held up the trigger thread. "Give me your coat. Hurry."

"Hell, no! I'll freeze without it." But Costello was skinning out of the coat, passing it up.

"No, I need the wallet, too."

"There ain't but two dollars. Durkin took the rest—a hundred and ten dollars, my own money."

Shots boomed from the defile. Clint hung the coat from the stump and stuck the wallet in the exposed pocket with ears of bank notes peeking out. A bullet thudded into the stump. He snapped a look. One horse was still bucking there, riderless, but others were breaking loose into the open, two or three riders, screeching like Apaches and firing. Costello yelled at him to hurry. He finished tying the thread to a buttonhole of the coat.

"A jumpy powder man is a friend to nobody," he said. Then he ran.

Perrell could feel the heat of the engine on his face. He turned the valve that fed kerosene to the carburetor. The engine's snarl deepened, blue smoke gushed beneath the Flyer. She backfired and then raced, answering the throttle. He slipped her into gear, felt the drive chains bite on their sprockets. She rolled, jouncing on the springy logs, chain-wrapped rear tires biting and chewing, slashing chunks of bark and spitting them back. Then the kid was pushing, and the powder man and Costello. The Flyer lifted her splendid snout. Ahead, Perrell saw Amanda Sibley, her eyes wide and staring, fixed on his wheels. If she screams, he thought, I'll know it's time to jump. Or maybe just too late. Below his right elbow, he saw dirt and rocks crumbling from the cliff wall, showering down and down.

Suddenly he saw her hand go to her mouth. He hit the throttle hard, hearing her cry faintly over the roar of the engine as the Flyer's driving wheels spun and spewed white wood. He felt the logs sag. The rear end slewed. *Going down* — A terrible pang stung him like a hot blade and for an instant he saw himself and the Flyer tumbling end over end for all eternity. Then Hazard was there, reaching out and pulling at bumper and fender, and Amanda and Bobby Joe, all straining as the Flyer rocked and bucked, rolled off the logs onto solid ground. The logs quivered, skidded a little, then hung there. Buell grabbed an ax and turned back.

*"Leave it!"* Clint said. Buell threw his weight against the Flyer. With six people bending their flesh and bone to the wood and steel of the Flyer, the great machine struggled toward the skyline, where the road crested against the flaring light of day.

Behind them, four riders pulled up their lathered horses on the spot where the Flyer had spent the night. They were all spattered with the blood of John Wesley Simmons, train and bank robber, alumnus of an Alabama chain gang, lately a horse soldier in Villa's Legion, whose whole life, unerringly as a flung javelin, had brought him to that instant in time and space when a length of whirling chain fired from a smoke-stack gun had sheared his meager intellect from his body.

The four riders, badly shaken by the cannon fire, stared across the chasm as the great machine churned the snow into mud forty yards away. They fired four or five futile pistol shots from the backs of their plunging horses. They saw that they could not get across the chasm on horseback. Two dismounted to run the logs on foot. They shouted and waved to the others to follow.

A chipmunk squirmed out of a tiny hole low on the twisted stump, skittered onto a coiled root and sat chattering and sneezing, its tiny button eyes bright, its tail flicking. One of the dismounted men—his name was Narciso Avila, and he was born in Doña Ana, New Mexico Territory, in 1889, to the profound regret of a future generation of law officers—saw the chipmunk scolding him. Then his eye fell on the black suit coat hanging there, and the gray-green ears of bank notes.

*"Híjuela!* What the *chingaos . . ."* He blinked and approached the stump. The chipmunk scuttled down and fled. Avila wrinkled his pocked nose at the biting odor, but he reached to shake the coat off the stump. He dimly sensed disaster, but he did not want to share the *dinero* with the wop Corsiglia, or the others. More riders galloped up, shouting. He pulled and the tree blew up. It blew to the extremities of its hollow, gas-filled roots and the many-chambered rodent dens and runs, and the fissures that riddled the rocks.

The Flyer was showered with mud and snow. Clint and Buell and Costello, pushing against the rear of the Flyer, and Amanda, who was looking back, all saw the blast, saw Narciso Avila flung through the air like a dirty rag, saw the slow sag of the shelf of earth where the Flyer had camped, and saw then the scrambling and wheeling of horses and riders pressing back for the feel of solid ground under them.

The shelf of earth slipped down into the cañon carrying three horses and two riders—Red Durkin flung himself from his own horse onto solid ground and missed the long plunge on the crumbling yellow island of dirt and rock.

The big wooden steering wheel shivered in Perrell's hands. With her drive chains chattering on their sprockets and her wheels biting and spinning, the Flyer gained the crest. He let her roll a few feet, then braked so that his exhausted crew could crawl aboard.

A long troughlike valley lay across their course, the road winding down among upflung masses of yellow rock patched with snow and bristly with clumps of pine and cedar and encino, cut by twisting streams.

Morning sun flared through gaps in the knobbed and turreted ridge across the valley and close above the Flyer, the sky was pocked with fiery red tufts of cloud, like bursts of cannon fire. Rumbling and snorting, rocking in and out of the ancient wheel-cut ruts, the Flyer crept into Chihuahua.

# (30)

The Sierra Madre Occidental sprawls like a vast, tawny, humpbacked, horn-cut, brush-scarred beast wallowing in the primordial mud of the continent. From its knobby spine, the hide of the brute is gashed and rent with barrancas falling steeply westward to the coastal plain and the Sea of Cortez. And on top, strangely, there are long, gently dished valleys caught between knobbed and bony ridges. There are stands of timber, pine, encino, cedarlike *tascate.* There is grass here and there, depending, and clumps of *lechuguilla,* the spiky maguey used by the *serranos* to brew their fiery pulque and mescal. And everywhere there are tawny, soft stone surfaces in sheets and slabs, smoothed by wind and water, seamed and scarred by hoof-cut trails.

The ancient Camino de Plata snaked a tortuous course between slabs and knobby outcrops, crossing stream beds and rising again to enter *cajones,* the narrow defiles and cañons that would carry them to valleys beyond. But unlike the barranca, where the road was not only the best but often the only trail, here in the high, open Sierra, close to the sky, horsemen were not bound to the writhing *camino.* It was possible from an elevation to look out and trace the course of the road by eye, then to strike out cross-country. That is what the *renegados* did.

After the explosion they made an exhausting climb afoot, leading their horses, up and around the mountain, entering the valley finally high above the *camino.* The downgrade was racking—fleshless, half-lame horses shambling, their bony withers hacking, a gait of merciless frictions and impacts. The horses splashed into a down-trickling stream where it pooled behind a broad, flat shelf of rock overlooking the valley. The riders let the animals sink their muzzles into the cold water. Red Durkin strained on squealing leather to ease his raw, slick flesh away from the hot, wet fabric that was fused to it. A greenish pallor glistened through the red stubble on his jaws. He turned a sickly countenance to Charlie Slotter.

"Jesus, Charlie, my butt is galded so bad I cain't hardly stand it." A wretched sigh shuddered from him.

Slotter picked at his thin nose—the red, cutting edge of his hatchet face—his pale, milky eyes shining and feverish. "We was ahead of the game yesterday mornin. We had a place to stay and plenty to eat. I'm tryin to figger out what's got into us."

"Forty thousand dollars is what. A man wants to better hisself, Charlie." He studied the silhouette, still elegant at forty yards or so, of Colonel Rodrigo Vega spurring his horse onto a snow-clotted promontory of tawny-red rock. "It's just way too much money to let dribble through our fingers. We can catch 'em—by God, we can."

Charlie finally gained, plucked from his nostril the treasure he had so diligently mined. "Shee-it," he sighed.

Rodrigo Vega turned his strangely luminous almond eyes upon them, his face serene and glowing with purpose. His slender gloved hand flung up, pointing. *"P'alla . . ."*

They looked and saw, perhaps two miles away, a thin feather of dust and snow crystals rise from the valley bed.

"Payroll, Charlie," Durkin said, "the only one there is, and by God, it's right there in sight. The way I look at it, them people *owe* us . . ."

Buell perched high up on the back of the rear seat, clutching the bare and clattering bows, watching the ridges behind them for some sign of the *renegados.* Perrell dared not take his eyes from the winding road. The Flyer's near-solid tires thudded from stone to sand, churned through patches of snow and brush, its course wavering from north back almost to south with little progress to the east apparent at all.

The road continued its insane swing. The Flyer was now headed almost west. Perrell was filled with dismay, thinking he had missed the road somehow—no, his wheels still cramped into the ancient ruts.

"No, go back!" Amanda Sibley cried out. Perrell saw horsemen over the bouncing head lamp of the Flyer and for a long sickening moment, the car actually began to close with the onrushing riders, who broke into a ragged gallop no more than a quarter of a mile distant.

"You're goin the wrong way!" Buell bellowed at him.

"No, it's the road!" Perrell shouted. Then the road bore sharply around again. He swung with it and the Flyer skidded through a horseshoe turn. The road steadied toward the east once again and the Flyer pulled away.

The sun climbed slowly, flashing through roily, broken clouds. Costello, in his wind-whipped shawl of sacking, was grateful for each burst of its warmth. The snow thinned, became patchy and disappeared then as the Flyer wound between towering, castled outcrops of red stone and let down into a deep-ribbed valley beyond. The Sierra Madre was gradually crumbling toward the high desert plateaus of Chihuahua.

Smoky-mouthed caves stared at them from the cliffs, and old corn patches scarred the hillsides—signs of people long gone, Perrell thought. Then he was startled by the drifting scent of wood smoke. A little later Amanda pointed and he saw one small child running, driving black and white goats back into timber. So the people were there, somewhere, hiding as the alien snarl of the Flyer's engine burst upon their world.

The road itself was less distinct, the deep-cut ruts in soft stone splaying out, then coming together again, like a meandering river seeking its true course, with burro paths branching away from it like tributaries. Perrell worked the Flyer around potholes, lurching across trenched ruts, around trees and splashing through streams. And kept going. That was the thing—the Flyer was making time. Eight miles an hour. Twelve miles an hour. Winding miles, sometimes steep. No time or place now to set rattraps. Scarcely possible even to talk over the engine noise and clash of tire chains, beyond a shouted word or two.

Nor possible to think clearly. Perrell fought the wheel and mumbled figures to himself. Fuel for three hundred miles, level ground. And Cusichic was what? Costello said seventy, but those were crow-flight miles—so how far, he wondered, would he have to drive to go seventy miles?

A downgrade opened before them. Steepened suddenly. Perrell braked, but the brake faded and she was already rolling too fast to shift down. *Ride it out.* The Flyer roared downhill, fish-tailing, drifting, shot over a hump in the road and was sickeningly airborne for a moment before she crunched back to earth with a solid clank of outraged springs.

Perrell heard Clint's startled rasp—"Godamighty, man!"—and sensed Amanda's white face turned to him in horror. The Flyer sped like a stung beast. Coming off the grade, he skidded broadside in the sand of a dry stream bed to stop her.

"Brakes—they're gone," he gasped. "We hardly needed brakes going uphill, but we need 'em now. Look what's ahead of us."

They stared down along the steepening, brush-choked road. The open high valleys and timbered heights were behind them. Ahead lay a barren tawny-red confusion of turreted cañons, the weather-worn walls falling back in spires, crenelated towers, obelisks—all like a grim and monstrous adobe ruin.

"What you need is a drag," Clint said. "Like a trap log."

"A Mormon brake," Costello said. "Mule skinners call it that." He swung down with Clint, took an ax. There was no standing timber nearby, but there were bleached snags scattered along the stream bed where they had been thrown by past floods. They chopped out a section of heavy log from one of the bony trunks. They bolted a length of chain around its middle, then fastened the other end of the chain to the rear cross-member of the Flyer's frame, beneath the body. Together they lifted the log onto the cargo rack and wedged it there with the blade of a shovel.

"You're the brakeman, kid," Clint said. "When he hollers, you pull the shovel out and kick the log off."

"How far would you figure we've come?" Costello said.

"Since daybreak?" Clint looked at the sun. "It must be getting close to noon—I'd say fifty or sixty miles, by the road. Maybe more."

"Those are crooked miles, though," Perrell said.

"And the horses have only had to do maybe half that," Costello said. He had long since thrown off the sacking, in the warmth of the sun and woodcutting. "There is no way on earth to know for sure, and I ain't sayin we're through the worst of it, but take what we done today, put it with yester-day—"

"Fifteen miles to go?" Perrell suggested.

Costello shrugged, but he looked pleased.

Thunder growled and rumbled, back toward the humped ridges of the Sierra. Thunderheads, heavy-bodied and glower-ing, were rising in a long line. From that distance, the rain was like a smoky, drifting fabric hanging from the black-bellied clouds, moving slowly north and east, almost indiscernibly angling toward them.

They drove out of the sand, on down the twisting road. Perrell shouted for the drag when the grade steepened. Buell kicked it off and it took hold, thumping and skidding behind. When the road slanted briefly up again, Perrell tried to drag the log. He felt a tremor through the pedal—the clutch was slipping. They had to stop then and take the drag log aboard until the next downgrade. Even so, he was thankful now for the log; if the clutch failed, too, there would be no stopping or even slowing her on a grade. Yet it was a nuisance. "We are like a tired swimmer who has found himself a log to hang on to," Perrell told Amanda. "He's afraid to let go and the sharks are closing in."

In an hour the squall line of thunderheads had drifted over the mountains and was skidding down upon them. Where they had passed, the hills were purple-dark under the rain. The road ran alongside a dry and sandy stream bed, following it into a broad open draw that was ribbed like a spread fan where it gathered rivulets to itself. A gentle descent—until those rivulets and dry washes came together and funneled sharply down between ribbed and turreted cañon walls. The Flyer broke through whipping brush and the road was sud-denly steep.

"The log, quick!" Perrell called. A moment later he felt the pull of it, then the chain spanged off the frame and the Flyer lunged ahead. He skidded her nose into sand and brush and stopped. Clint and Buell climbed out.

"You're too slow with the log, kid," Hazard scolded.

"I done it as soon as he told me," Buell said.

"You nearly wrecked us."

Clint was dragging the log back to the car. He let it thud into the sand and swung around furiously. "It ain't the kid and the goddamn log that's wreckin us!" He stepped to the car and caught Hazard's coat at the shoulder, lifting him half out of the seat. Hazard tried to wrench free, his face suddenly red. With his free hand he snatched off his glasses and threw them into Bobby Joe's lap. At the same time he got a foot under him and hurled himself over the side onto the powder man. They sprawled in the sand, Hazard pummeling awkwardly as Clint arched his back to throw him off. He shook a hand loose and drew it back to hit as Perrell and Costello ran to separate them.

"Hey!" Buell yelped. Yellow water was licking at his shoes. It swirled in the dry sand and ran on beneath the struggling men. In seconds the sand was covered, the water lapping against them. They broke apart and scrambled up.

Costello pointed. The black-bellied clouds were nearly over them, the rain curtain sweeping darkly close. Thunder grumbled, half lost in the mutter of the Flyer's exhaust, then an explosive clap burst, deafening, almost overhead.

"That water is makin up fast," Costello said. "We had better get some high ground under us before she—"

Light flashed against the dark cloud and his voice trailed off. There was light from bridle bit or rifle barrel as horsemen appeared against the sky at the head of the cañon, bright, sun-caught figures against the gloom. Buell snatched up the drag log.

"Leave it!" Perrell snapped. He sprang to the Flyer's seat and fed her throttle as they bent to push her in the wet sand. The Flyer sawed and swung, spewing sand and crackling brush. Shots sounded.

"Get in, man!" Costello gave Hazard a boost as the Flyer rolled faster. He heard shots again. Jets of water spurted and something chunked into the Flyer above his shoulder. He heard the *slap-slap* of torn flaps of rubber on the rear tires as he caught the doorframe and scrambled aboard, spitting sand.

# (31)

Lieutenant Hobart Tomlinson was lost and frightened. He had only two or three hundred feet of altitude and the Curtiss JN-2 would not give him any more, buffeting along the narrow, winding cañon. Indeed, the plane had barely managed to get off the ground at Guerrero. It was a running joke among the aviators of the Punitive Expedition that they should be designated a submarine service, for the aircraft had been proven on paper to have only four horsepower more than enough to keep them airborne at sea level, and in Chihuahua they were having to make takeoffs from fields seven and eight thousand feet up.

It was no joke now. The lieutenant's orders were to deliver to General Pershing at San Gerónimo an account of the battle for Ciudad Guerrero, which had been fought that morning between the 7th United States Cavalry and several hundred Villistas. Having twice failed to get the JN-2 into the thin air, the lieutenant had left behind his observer, who weighed one hundred and sixty-two pounds in his cavalry boots. Airborne at last, he did not feel well. A couple of weeks in Mexico had left his bowels decidedly unsettled; they were furiously restless now as he nursed the shuddering aircraft through the bumpy air. And his throat was dry from swallowing, trying not to gag. He had seen a great many bodies that morning—the first dead he had ever seen, except for a few funerals in New Jersey—and he had been shocked and frightened at the damage caused by rifle bullets and falls on stony ground beneath running horses.

The takeoff was made in bright sunshine from a dirt road between two rivers. He had followed Río Papigochic and the tracks of the Mexican Northwest Railroad north, in order to get around the mountains eastward to San Gerónimo. Within twenty minutes a thunderstorm was sweeping over the valley ahead of him. Mountains were close on his right hand. Swallowing hard, he veered slightly to the left, which he almost never did because the JN-2 had a sickening inclination to turn a left bank into a diving spin. In order to bank he had to lean his body into a shoulder harness from which wires went out to the ailerons.

He lost altitude in the turn. A few feet off the ground, and still turning, he saw a large body of horsemen ahead. He raised his hand into the slipstream to wave, but then he saw the big steeple-crowned hats, the raised rifles and the smoke puffs and realized that they were shooting at him. They were no doubt the force of Villistas that had escaped that morning. In fascination he watched two long ribbons of fabric peel back from his lower wing and stream fluttering over the trailing edge. He banked away from them to his right, following a river and heading west.

Then he was under the storm, rain pelting the fabric and blearing his motoring goggles, flying along a twisting mountain cañon a few feet above a brown torrent, mountains on either side of him rising high into the dark, flickering belly of the cloud. In the pocket of his coveralls he carried a blueprint of an old Mexican map, but he dared not take his eyes off the cañon to look at it. A glance at his compass showed him that the instrument was unwinding from his last turn. He knew from sad experience that he would have to fly a long way straight and level before it settled down.

Buildings flashed beneath him, a steeple, children waving, a fountain in a walled courtyard, burros—then a road slanting away like a chalky scar. Impulsively he swung with it, which he immediately regretted because the road snaked steeply down toward him from an imposing battlement of eroded red cliffs. The ground rose beneath him, and with the cliffs appearing to close in from either side, he dared not turn.

A moment later he was in a narrow cañon with pillared cliffs rising so steeply that there was scarcely room for his wings. Rain drummed.

He leaned out and peered ahead—incredibly, an automobile, a big old touring car, was churning across yellow water. People, a *woman,* their turned-up faces white in that moment. Then they were behind him, and a few hundred yards farther on where the cañon opened out before him, he saw horsemen, perhaps a dozen of them, with big Mexican hats, galloping downstream in shallow water in the direction of the touring car. The horses shied and reared as he swept over them, then he caught an updraft and gratefully rode with it. When he looked down again, he had lost them. With the storm clouds pressing hard on his right, he leaned into his shoulder harness and swung in a broad, gentle turn to his left. Streams, as he passed over them, appeared to be foaming torrents.

He saw the road again, well to his left. He kept it there until he passed over the village again, the wind behind him now as he saw a gash through the mountains. He was back in Guerrero in thirty minutes—in bright sunshine, trying to explain the thunderstorm to the hawk-beaked old cavalry colonel. When he mentioned the Villistas who had shot at him, the colonel stopped cussing and listened. Then Lieutenant Tomlinson told him about the big old touring car.

When the aircraft swept over the Flyer, Amanda glimpsed astounding great wings, blunt nose and sticks and wires, a young man's goggled face. Then it was gone as the car bucked out of the water and she was desperately hanging on to the seat. The rain, no more a drifting wisp, was a drenching thunder-blasted cloudburst. The tawny earth darkened with it, and turreted sandstone bled rivulets of red mud.

The road turned and ran down the left bank, barely above water. A few hundred yards ahead, the cañon narrowed suddenly between columns of red stone, and the road was lost in a choking tangle of brush where the cliff closed in from the left. *"Where is the damn road?"* Perrell shouted. There was no room for the road to get past the cliff. His eye fled to the far bank and he saw a pale streak bearing away from the gorge on rising ground at the foot of buttressed red pillars—the road. So there had to be a ford across the stream, somewhere in the tangle of brush.

Buell shouted. Amanda Sibley looked back. "Water! Flood water—it's coming down!"

Perrell gave himself an instant's glance back and saw the appalling brown flood. He drove on with no clear idea of how far away it was, knowing only that he could not stop or turn aside, that if they could not ford the stream in time to reach that shouldering high ground, they would be flushed like ants in a muddy ditch. Lightning flared and a ghostly ball of blue fire rolled along the cañon wall like a fiery tumbleweed. Thunder drowned the snarl of the Flyer's engine as Perrell's hand struck the throttle lever down.

Rain streamed into his eyes, and in the last blurred seconds he saw with sudden sick horror how the bank steepened and the water fell away below, brown and ropy, as the sharply narrowed V of the gorge slashed down where the road had to cross. *There was no ford.*

Then the brush was there, with the bony, twisted arms of a dead and fallen tree clawing up behind it. The Flyer struck the brush, sheared through the branches of the dead tree, shattered white branches spinning away as the great machine soared free of the shelving ramp of wet stone trailing a veil of muddy spray from her wheels, Perrell aware in that instant of empty space beneath her and brown water falling away in the gorge under splintered ends of long-gone bridge timbers.

The hurtling Flyer crunched down onto the far side, with a screeching impact that drove Perrell's nose against the rim of the steering wheel, the Flyer skidding on, plowing up onto a ridge of stone, a fender lifting like a broken wing, coming to rest then, her snout upthrust and hanging from the ridge. Perrell shook his head, his eyes stinging with rain and grit, and sharp burning tears from his smashed nose. Amanda Sibley slid against him, toppling, and he caught her shoulders as the thundering flood of brown water engulfed the narrow cañon. The road they had traveled was swallowed under it. A foaming surf rose around the Flyer's rear wheels and gushed over the side into the rear. With helpless horror on her face, Bobby Joe clutched the wounded bird and saw the water rise above her knees. The Flyer shivered, swung a little, then tilted with the flood.

"Stay with her," Perrell shouted. "Keep your weight on her or the water will get her." A sputtering cry sounded behind the Flyer. Buell. Clint wallowed around in the back seat, hung his leg over the side and reached down, then slowly drew up the kid's head and shoulders. Buell got his elbow over the top bows and kicked. Clint hauled him in, coughing and spitting.

A piercing, mournful cry sounded. Out in the torrent a man's head appeared, moving very fast. He went under, appeared again, then he saw them and raised his hand. An instant later he was swept past the remains of the dead tree. He clutched for it, but a branch snapped off in his hand and he went down the gorge with a last desperate wail of terror. Upstream, a horse floundered at the stream's edge, found footing and struggled ashore.

The car shifted and teetered for endless seconds, then grounded solidly. In moments, the crested waters of the flash flood had sunk gushing from the Flyer and the red-slabbed ramp of stone. Still stunned and shivering from the impact and the icy rain, they watched the ancient, shattered remnants of bridge timbers appear again, as brown water thundered in the narrow funnel below.

"Thirty, forty years that bridge must have been out," Perrell said. He was still thick-tongued from shock. He looked at Amanda. Thorny brush had stripped away part of her sleeve and left thin scratches on her skin. Her cheekbone was puffy and one eye was starting to close. He touched the cheek. "That is going to be a dandy eye. A crackerjack."

She dabbed at his lip with her scarf. "I hit my own knee, but here, you do look a mess. Your nose must be broken."

Costello tried to climb up out of the seat and fell back. Hazard groaned. Costello squirmed around and got a knee under him and peered back through the rain across the gorge.

"Where in hell are the damn rannygades?"

\*          \*          \*

The shock of seeing the aircraft pass directly over, almost low enough to touch, was unnerving to the *renegados,* who were strung out at the gallop, crossing the stream bed in a foot of water. They were fighting their terrified, squealing, pitching horses, deafened by thunder that blanketed the roar of the flood water until it was upon them. Those riders still in the stream bed were engulfed, rolled, tumbled and swept on down the gorge. Vega and Durkin and Charlie Slotter, with others, were able to wheel and flog their horses up the embankment.

From that high ground, exhorting and shouting, they watched their men crawl from the flood. In the end they counted three men missing. They saw one horse climb onto the far bank, downstream. Recovered from the torrent, they reined up onto a narrow, sloping bench and saw there shallow caves undercut in banks of red stone. They smelled sharp wood smoke from fires of cedar and brushy *granjeno* and saw tethered goats grazing sparse grass, jaws munching sideways. They saw the People, watching them from the shadowed caves, eyes like obsidian chips, their smoky dark hair streaming, skin deep copper against the stained, coarse, shirtlike *mantas.* Half a deer hung in one cave, dark with smoke.

Most of the beef from Dos Cabezas had been on the Ford. Lost in the barranca. Now, in the rain with the flood waters running high, the men exhausted, the horses standing spread-legged with heads down and ribs heaving like bellows, Vega was moved to do what all good cavalry officers do—take care of their men and animals.

"Unsaddle," he ordered. Then, nodding benignly toward the hanging deer meat, he said with a sigh, *"Un hombre debe comer"*—"a man must eat."

"They won't be able to get across till the water goes down," Costello said.

They crept down from the car very slowly and stood back shakily to look at the awesome wreck. The Flyer lay wallowing, with her long nose angled up. Her red lacquer was scarred and streaked, washed sadly bright in the rain. The right front fender was gone altogether and both head-lamp glasses were shattered, the lamps themselves dented and blindly cocked awry. The side-mounted kerosene tank was gone, its strap-iron braces bent out like antennae, the copper fuel line quivering gently. Perrell knelt and looked at the battered undercarriage.

"Her front axle is what anchored us. It hung up over the rock." He stood, slowly shaking his head. "But the kerosene tank is gone, too." Helplessly he kicked at a front tire. A chunk of rubber broke off and fell. The wheel quivered on loosened spokes.

Amanda's eyes glittered. She tried to smile, but her chin quivered. "I can't believe she's finished."

"So, it's shank's mare at last, is it?" Costello said.

Perrell nodded. "Let's get moving. And we'll take some water . . . what's left of the corn . . . an ax, maybe. Anything else?"

"Give me a little of the corn," Costello said. "I'll go catch that horse—the ladies can take turns on him."

"Hold on," Clint said. "Long as we have to leave, I 'spect you'll want to know what we'll leave behind us."

He looked fiercely at Tracy Hazard, who still sat hunched and gray-faced in the rear seat, his glasses streaked with rain. Clint reached through the open door and began to pull out wet and soggy canvas, sacking, coils of rope, wire, the dynamite box full of coiled fuse, rattraps and tape, the sack of corn, lengths of chain—all the debris of the voyage. On the bottom was another canvas, its edges tightly tucked under. Clint pulled the canvas loose and threw it back.

Softly gleaming, the bars lay in neat rows. The floor of the Flyer was paved with silver. Perrell sagged against the car. His eyes blurred. He tried to speak and couldn't. A pulse thudded under his jaw. His voice, when he found it, was a raw whisper. "You crazy bastard," he said to Hazard. "We hauled you and that damn stuff clear across the Sierra. Six hundred pounds. That's like . . . four more people. And you let us do it." He wagged his head helplessly.

Hazard's lips were pale, compressed. His breath hissed in

spasmodic shudders, his eyes staring. Fingers of one hand fluttered, picked at his jacket.

"You let us do it," Perrell repeated. "Goddammit, is that the price you put on us? Is it? No wonder they followed us—and all I could think was that the engine wasn't pulling."

"Couldn't help it," Hazard said weakly. "Tried to tell you, but . . . couldn't do that, either. Thought . . . just get a few miles, see? Toward the railroad. Hide the silver, then someday—"

"Someday," Perrell interrupted, his voice suddenly vicious. "Someday is now. It's all yours, mister. You can sit here and figure how you're going to spend it."

Hazard was slowly toppling forward. Amanda gasped. Perrell caught Hazard with a hand against his chest. A froth of red bubbled on the man's lips. Rain washed it down his chin in a pink stream.

Perrell and Costello scrambled up to the seat. There was a small hole in the back of Hazard's corduroy jacket, high up on the right side. Easing down the jacket, Perrell cut the shirt fabric with his pocket knife and tore it back from the wound. There was not much blood. A blue-rimmed puncture. Costello put his ear close to the wound and listened.

"Got him in the lung. Hear his wind suck in and out? Seven-millimeter Mauser, I expect—one of them short saddle guns. Steel-jacketed and a damn good thing." They eased him back against the cushion and pulled a piece of canvas over him. Costello found a folded bandanna in a hip pocket and tucked it under the wounded man's shirt. Hazard's voice, when he spoke, was very weak. "No good. You have to leave me."

They looked at one another uncomfortably. Then Costello said, "Kid, go ahead and take the sack of corn and catch that horse." Perrell had turned away, head down, restless.

Hazard shook his head. "I'd pass out . . . can't . . ."

"I was thinkin of a litter," Costello said. "A travois."

"Poles," Clint said. "No poles here."

"A stretcher then. Use the top bows from the car. Carry him ourselves."

"No." Perrell had climbed down. He stood back from the

car. Bending, hands on knees, he studied the Flyer. "No, we would just be too slow. As soon as the water is down, Vega will be across."

"But we would be leaving the silver for him," Amanda said.

"That might have been enough when we started, but not now."

"You can't be sure."

"*I'm* sure," Clint said. "It will be too easy to pass up. After what we done to Vega, he won't let us go. I wouldn't myself, by God."

"It will kill him to put him on the horse," Costello said.

Perrell walked back along the car, then he turned and faced them. "There's only one way we can make it. We've got to get the Flyer going again." He frowned and raised his hand at the babble of protest. "No, listen—"

"But the fuel tank is tore off," Costello said. "What will you burn?"

"Acetylene."

"That stuff nearly killed us this mornin," Buell said.

"I know. But that setup was only designed to kick her over for starting. If I take the old fuel line, I can pipe it straight to the carburetor."

Hazard fluttered a hand. "You'll just blow us up. Acetylene . . . damn dangerous stuff."

"So is gasoline!" Perrell flared. "Look, the water will stay high for a while. It gives us a little time."

"But not time to walk very far," Amanda said. "Tell us what to do, John Trouble."

# (32)

They lifted the top bows of the car and threw canvas over it to shelter the wounded man. His pulse was thready and light and his teeth were chattering. Amanda wrapped her *cobija* around him and covered that with canvas, also. He insisted on sitting up.

"Listen to me," he whispered to Perrell. "Crazy thing to do, yes. Don't know what got into me. Leave the stuff now . . . with me. Go on. Don't mess with acetylene. Damn stuff won't work. You'll kill everybody."

"Shut up now," Perrell said. "I watched a guy run an engine off a welding torch once."

"No, it's too explosive, see? Acetylene can . . . blow itself up."

"That's under high pressure, mixed with air." Perrell was taking tools from the dynamite box.

"Listen, you get the wrong mixture, you'll burn the metal . . . eat carbon right out of the steel. Melt like wax."

"You can burn an engine up with gasoline, too. Look, it doesn't have to work long. We figured sixty or seventy miles to—"

"Cusichic," Costello said. He looked at Clint, but the powder man looked away.

"Cusichic, right. Even if we have only been making two or three miles an hour, we must be close. Maybe ten or fifteen miles."

"A mile ain't a mile in the mountains," Clint said. "It's maybe straight up or straight down, or sideways. Sideways miles ain't miles."

Perrell glared stubbornly. "The first thing we have to do is haul the Flyer off that rock." Buell was back, leading the horse, a skinny, staggering, hammer-headed, spotted roan with splintered hoofs. It carried a worn Chihuahua saddle and an empty rifle scabbard. "You handsome devil," Amanda said, "let's see if you can pull."

Perrell tied a rope to the front end of the Flyer. Clint lifted Bobby Joe into the horse's saddle, tied off the rope to the massive horn. "Point him yonder, sis," he said. She clucked to the horse and the rope tightened. "He'll need help," she said. Levering, heaving, they strained, but the axle of the Flyer was well over the knob of rock.

"The wheel is bent way out of line, too," Buell said.

"Take the wheel off," Perrell said, "so it won't hang up on the rock. The tie rod is bent and that throws it out of line. When we get her down, you can take the tie rod loose and pound it straight."

Perrell set a jack under the side frame on the left side and cranked the Flyer up until the axle was free. Buell took the wheel off, chunks of rubber and pitch crumbling under his hands.

"Haul away now, sis," Perrell said. Bobby Joe clucked to the roan horse again. He pulled directly off to the side. The Flyer's nose swung, the jack toppled under her and she came down with a crash, level and free of the rock. In the back seat, Hazard moaned. Amanda climbed into the car, her feet on the bars of silver, and eased him around so that his weight was not on the wound. Bobby Joe tied the horse's reins to the cargo rack at the rear of the Flyer. When the rooster saw her, it flopped its bound wings and lunged at her with its beak open. She caught the bird and stroked its head as she watched Amanda feel for Hazard's pulse.

The rain had stopped. A brilliant beam of sunlight slanted into the cañon and ran swiftly across the decrepit Flyer and the flooded gorge, then winked out on the far bank.

"He looks terrible dry," Bobby Joe said. Amanda nodded. Hazard's lips looked feverish. His breathing was quick and shallow, his pulse thin. His eyelids fluttered. Amanda gave him the last trickle of water from the canteen. The water bags were both empty.

Bobby Joe looked at the muddy torrent in the ravine. "All that mud and no water."

"There ought to be clear water up high," Amanda said. "A pool or something. Stay with him and keep him warm." She took the canteen and the water bags and climbed down. Perrell had gotten tools from the dynamite box and was showing Buell and Costello how to take something loose at the front of the car. She began walking, the brush in the road plucking at her skirt and boots.

A small ravine, narrow and steep, led up away from the road between towering, erosion-fluted walls. She followed the ravine up, and up. In a few minutes she was high above the gorge, the sound of the torrent softened to a murmur. A big red hawk with a white-banded tail sailed past and cocked his head to look at her. She no longer heard the bright chink of tools on metal. There was only the wind's whisper and the crunch of her boots on wet red stone.

The ravine opened out onto a great worn brow, ridged and humped with twisting, wind-smoothed shapes and pocked with craterlike holes filled with rainwater that mirrored the sky. One crater was oval-shaped, broad and deep, with smooth sloping sides rising five or six feet above the water. It was easily large enough to have held the Flyer.

A thin wisp of smoke curled up from the far side of the cañon. Above the cliffs it was caught and torn by the wind. As her eye followed the smoke down, her breath quickened. The smoke came from the far side, above the gorge, a sloping bench of high ground. She saw horses grazing, figures. The smoke—cooking fire, probably. The stream itself was still running high. Watching the renegades from such a distance made them seem oddly remote, peaceful.

Turning, she saw the thin scar of the road disappear into a maze of malpais, barren, badland cañons still overhung by the storm and its drifting dark curtain of rain, then the curtain thinned, parted for a moment. She glimpsed sunlight beyond, a pale flash like whitewashed adobe, then the curtain covered it again. How far? Ten miles? Twelve? Or thirty. She was not good at distances. She blinked and rubbed her eyes, wincing because the left one was very swollen and painful. She climbed down into the pothole, a deep bowl in the red stone.

The water was clear. She knelt to fill the water bags, and the unruffled water mirrored her face against the sky. Shocked by what she saw, she touched her face, her matted hair. She looked around—the rim of the bowl was higher than her head. She was alone against the sky. Warm sun flooded the sheltered bowl. Quickly she filled the canteen and the two water bags, then she sat on the smooth stone and began to pull off her boots.

She hung her wet things over a twisted arm of brush that was precariously rooted in a cleft in the rock. The water was icy, but marvelous. It left her shivering. She lay back on the stone and let the sun dry her skin, feeling a little pang of guilt for staying so long. The sun was an orange blob through her closed eyelids. The shivering stopped and she was drowsing, the skin of her body hot, dry and tight—drowsing, floating, not feeling the stone beneath her, the terror gone in the clean rain-wash and the whispering wind.

Rodrigo Vega, possessed of his strange, withdrawn calm, picked delicately at his *comida*—exceedingly tough, strong, saltless deer meat made palatable with brandy. He spoke softly to one or the other of his men from time to time, always in French. Red Durkin, with one of the Legion's unpronounce-ables, a Serb, scouted down the cañon as far as he could get and reported that the automobile was on the other side, but that it appeared to be wrecked. The water was going to be too high to ford for some time. Vega murmured graciously, think-ing, If the pigs are going to be afoot, there is no need to hurry. His rest was a serene one. As always, he slept with his almond-shaped eyelids parted, showing a gleam of eyeball like a dog dreaming, and also like the dog, he twitched and mouthed small noises. The superstitious *soldados* disliked falling un-der his sightless gaze. Making various signs to ward off its baleful effects, they retreated to the shelter of the Indians' cave, where they sat scratching and drinking mescal under the shuttered, malevolent stares of the People.

The Serb and two others at length drifted idly from the cave. Not until it was time to saddle the horses again did

Durkin realize that they were not returning. There were now left, besides himself, Slotter and Vega, only six men of the Legion. And not the best by a damn sight, he thought disgustedly, yet enough to handle the people in the car—and barely enough to carry away the six hundred pounds of silver.

Amanda snapped alert. Listening, she now heard nothing. But the sun had moved, slanting down. She scrambled quickly, gathered her things, chill-damp but drying, cold to the skin. Hearing a muffled *clop-clop,* then, closer, the scuff of leather on stone, she whirled, lifting the leather skirt to cover herself as a man's face appeared over the rim of the bowl, craggy and scarred, the eyes filled with torment as he slid down the sloping dished stone and took her by the arms.

Later she would remember seeing the bone-white skin where Clint's tattered shirt was torn open—the muscle ridged and humped, without fat, the white glazed scars like splattered candle wax, but cratered, with drawn edges—would remember that he was immensely strong and that she had not cried out, not resisted. Not really resisted, that is. She was at least quite strangely and remarkably calm, crushed close in his arms, not moving, waiting, his breathing shaky in her ear. Then the arms went slack around her and his hands eased on her back. "I've watched you . . . lady. If you could know—" His voice was breath only, without fiber.

The hard hands skidded across the skin of her back. Clint stepped away with his hands still on her arms and looked down at her with frank, deliberate pleasure and infinite regret. He shivered and said again, "If you could only know," and his hand clumsily pushed the bundled skirt and cloth at her. She took them and turned away—not that it mattered now.

"They know you've gone?" she said, thinking, Inane thing to say.

"No. They was busy, messin with the auto. It don't matter none. I won't be goin back." The fretful *clop-clop* sounded again, a hoof pawing at stone. "Hear? The horse is tied yonder."

"He won't carry you far."

"Not me, no. Six bars of silver. A little stake."

Silence then. Rustle of cotton. She pulled on her scuffed boots. He sighed.

"Things go wrong, don't they?"

"What?" She was startled.

"I needed the canteen, that's all. And you had it. I never meant to do . . . for this to happen. Or maybe thought I didn't. Used to think about it, in the pen. What it would be like, see?" The words came painfully. "I promised myself I wouldn't pay for it, and I wouldn't—"

"Very sensitive of you, I'm sure."

"No, I mean it. A man makes hisself promises, thinkin about things, all that time."

"And things go wrong, do they?"

He saw that she was nettled. A trace of a grin touched his face. He helped her up. "No offense, lady." The grin widened. "A jumpy powder man is a friend to nobody." He seemed to think something was funny. Whatever it was, she did not understand it.

Then they were up out of the bowl. She saw the roan horse tied to a stunted manzanita at the head of the draw, the saddlebags behind the saddle sagging with their small but heavy burden. She could see the horse's heart thud against the ribs. A pathetic escape for the dynamiter. She was suddenly furious.

"Why did you leave? We were all in this together and we were *making* it."

"We caught the horse. That set me to thinkin—it would make one less to carry if I was to pull out now. It would give me a chance to shake Costello and I could leave with a little stake. Who would foller me for that?" He jerked a thumb at the saddlebags.

She shook her head irritably. "No one. But I heard you say you were paid up."

"Look, I was put away for ten years. I done the ten years and kept my mouth shut. Paid up? There wasn't one damn thing it could buy for me except to get out at the end of it and get back to Mexico—but not with Costello." The slow, rueful grin crinkled across his face again. "But it would almost be worth it to see the look on his face. The joke would be pretty near as rough on him as on me."

"Joke?" She was puzzled now. "Don't you *know* what you would be going back for? You were in on it, weren't you?"

"Oh, I was guilty, all right. And I never had nobody to blame but myself. I had a terrible mad on, see, settin in jail for tryin to bust a deputy's jaw."

He has never told a soul about this, she thought. The one thing I can do is listen. But his words were halting. "That's what you mean by the little things going wrong, isn't it?" she urged.

He nodded. "The whole deck was full of jokers, and I drawed every damn one of 'em, right from the beginning." He laughed sharply. "We blowed the mail car, all right, and headed south into Mexico, the three of us. And we pushed hard. Someone was certain to be after us."

"I thought the law couldn't follow you into Mexico."

"So did I, and they can't, but the Pinkertons can. They don't have no authority, is all. Sure enough, it was Costello who was after us, though we didn't know that yet. He was about a day's ride behind us."

"What could he do, without authority?"

Clint shook his head. "He had a gun. And a man like Costello would aim to get the local law to go along with him. I remember that Wiley, he turned to Ben and said there ain't but one thing could go wrong now—he said if I thought Pat Costello was after us I would be worried. Me, I didn't even know who Costello was until then. Well, that was terrible hard country, down along Río Aros where old Geronimo used to hide out. By the third day our horses was rode right into the ground. We got as far as a big ranch. A terrible grand place it was. Ben was for stealin some horses, but Wiley wouldn't hear of it. He said it would be certain to bring Mexican law down on us, too. Wiley, he told the rancher we was mining men and said we wanted to buy some horses. Right there is where things commenced to go haywire. The rancher looked us over and said we must have a meal with him, then we would talk horses."

"Couldn't you just refuse?"

"He wouldn't let us, and he had about twenty vaqueros around, all packin guns. When the meal was over, the vaqueros brought out some horses. The rancher said the price would be the amount of gold we had with us. Naturally his men had gone through everything. Part of the mail-car money was in gold and the rest was paper. He wouldn't take any paper atall —he was full of smiles and jokes about it. So we left with good horses under us, but what we didn't know was that he had sent a rider to turn us in to the *federales* for stealin his horses. Along about dark, we stopped at a little town to get something to eat. There was an inn, with tables set around a fountain in the patio . . ." His voice trailed off for a moment, his brow furrowed with the memory of it.

"And the soldiers caught you there?"

He nodded. "Ben was hit, almost the first thing. We pulled some tables together next to the fountain and forted up. Trouble was, Ben was hurt bad and our rifles and most of the ammunition was with our saddles, in the corrals. I went after 'em. Wiley was to cover me and try to draw their fire. I remember, the last thing I saw when I lit out for the corral—Wiley was shooting and he rolled over the rim of the fountain, right into the water. I thought he was hit, but the shootin went on, and later I figured—" He blinked and stopped himself, then after a moment, he said, "Anyway, I never got there. A long time later, I commenced to crawl away."

"And Wiley?"

"They was afraid to rush him. He saved one for himself, Costello told me. He got there at daybreak, but it was all over. Costello and the soldiers trailed me up into the hills. They found me, but without the money, see?" He laughed again. "I was pretty near dead and couldn't tell him nothin, even if I wanted to. The thing is, I didn't know myself where it had went to. Not then. It was a long time later before I could put it all together, and by then I was headed for the pen on a downhill pull. Telling the law would not have cut my time ten minutes, and I always figured that when I got out, I could come back down here. If I was right, it would be something like . . . wages."

"Well, then, what is the joke all about?"

His grin returned. "There was a catch to it. There wasn't but one place it could have been hid. I've told you too much already. It's as much as I knowed when Costello caught me and maybe more than he knowed, or he would have figured it out for himself and not waited ten years for me—"

Clint suddenly stiffened, staring over a smooth parapet of wind-carved stone into the gorge toward the streamer of smoke still rising there. "Vega and Durkin, they are fixin to move, down there." Amanda saw men leading horses down toward the stream. "The water is down some," Clint said. "They'll have to cross over to this side upstream, on the rocks. Then they'll work down the cañon afoot, leadin the horses. Perrell better have that machine runnin—and if you're goin with them, you better get back down there."

He leaned out, trying to look down on the Flyer. It was cut off from view by the stone, but he could see most of the gorge and a long narrow wedge of brushy ground along the bank just upstream from the Flyer. He slapped the stone with a big hand.

"By God, I see somethin I could—" His voice broke off.

"What?"

"No, things have went too far."

"Too far for you to go back?" she flared. "Because you've got your hands on the silver and don't want to give it up, is that it? You've thought of something that would help us, damn you, and I want to know what it is."

Staring down at the distant, moving figures, he growled, "It's always the little things goin haywire. Like bustin the deputy. Like catchin that miserable horse, like needin the damn canteen and findin you had took it." He looked ruefully at her. "Except for that, I was in the clear." He swung the canteen by its strap and smashed it so that it burst on the red stone. Water streamed down their faces. He let the canteen fall, shaking his head slowly, then he took the horse's reins and started back down toward the Flyer.

# (33)

Perrell tightened the fitting that fastened the copper acetylene fuel line into a carburetor vacuum tap. He looked up and saw Amanda Sibley and Ellred Clinton. The powder man was leading the horse and the two dripping water bags were hung over the saddle horn. Amanda lifted them off and walked directly to Perrell.

"How much longer will you be? We saw Vega's men looking for a place to cross upstream."

Perrell turned to look over his shoulder, but his view was restricted by the eroded red cliff, where it thrust out almost to the water's edge, a hundred yards upstream. The Flyer shook and a sharp clank sounded. "Hold 'er," Buell said, and struck again with the back of the ax. "A little more," Costello said. He was sitting in the mud, bracing the tie rod against a rock with hands and feet.

"We're about ready," Perrell said to her. "A few more minutes, if it works at all—it's a crazy rig." His face was drawn, intense.

"I told you," Hazard gasped from the back seat. "You should have gone on."

"Hush, Tracy." Amanda handed one of the bags to Bobby Joe, who sloshed some water into a tin cup for him. He sucked greedily at it, then fell back mumbling.

Costello crawled up out of the mud. Ellred Clinton thrust a drum of carbide into his arms and turned back to the car. He was rolling silver bars into folds of canvas.

"What the hell are you aimin to do with that stuff?" Costello said. There were rattraps in the powder man's pockets. Amanda held the horse's reins with one hand and a shovel with the other as Clinton grunted, swinging the pack of bars across the saddle, then reached back into the car for a coil of baling wire.

"Dump it where it will do us some good," Clinton said.

"If the silver buys us two minutes' time," Perrell said, "it'll be cheap." He bent over the carburetor again as the three of them hurried away, leading the plodding horse with its burden of silver. He heard Clinton's voice saying, "Dump the stuff where I show you, then take the horse back for the rest of it. I want a loop of baling wire around every one of them bars . . ." Then they were gone, walking upstream along the brushy bench of ground between the red cliff and the gorge. Buell's wrench clanked on the tie rod under the car.

Perrell went back over the fittings at the generator tank and carburetor. The storm was gone now. Late afternoon sunlight was warm on his back. He glanced once at the falling brown water, as a man will glance at his watch—the water was far down. He forced himself to concentrate on the pieces of the pressure regulator valve he had dismantled. Hazard moaned again and tried to sit up. He glared at Perrell. "Damn you, Perrell, you'll kill all of them. You don't have any way . . . to control the mixture and the throttle, both. If you change the throttle . . . it will change the mixture, too. Don't you see that?"

"Sure I see it. I—"

"Well, how in hell . . . can you drive? If you open the throttle, you'll thin out the mixture . . . burn up the engine." Hazard ended with an exhausted groan.

"Shut up before you kill yourself arguing," Perrell said. "The carburetor does all that with gasoline. We needed something to meter the acetylene. I took the pressure regulator apart and reversed the spring and diaphragm, see? That makes it a *demand* regulator now. I mean, it will deliver however much acetylene the throttle calls for, so the mixture will stay constant—" He stopped and looked down as the Flyer shook again. Buell was letting it down off the jack.

Ready to start, Perrell thought. He had the altered regulator back together now and he was setting the adjuster screw that would control the flow of acetylene. The setting was critical and he was having to guess at it. He remembered Hazard's words: "the wrong mixture . . ." That was it, the secret. Too much oxygen in the mixture would be like turning a welder's torch loose in the engine, leaching, melting, fusing. An engine could overheat and seize up in minutes. He grunted suddenly.

"What?" Buell said.

"One thing that will keep it from getting too lean is the altitude."

Buell looked blankly at him.

"We must be at seven or eight thousand feet up here, so it will be hard to feed it too much oxygen." Seeing the look on Buell's face, he stopped. "Let's wind her up, kid."

Perrell turned on the acetylene generator on the running board, then reached in to the brass quadrant on the steering wheel and set the throttle and spark. Ignition. He nodded and Buell cranked. Perrell saw water beading on the radiator hose. No tape left, he thought, and no time. The engine hissed and grunted, suddenly fired with a high nasal snarl, then quickly died. He opened the adjuster a little and Buell cranked again. It fired and died twice before he could hold it with the throttle, a high-pitched and somehow furious sound.

Listening, sniffing, he turned the adjuster on the valve that now fed the alien fuel into the monster's gullet, trying in his mind and intuition to penetrate the miracle of combustion that drove the plunging pistons. *All the storms of hell under a man's hand,* his dad had told him—he was fifteen years old and it was the first time he had ever seen a combustion engine.

He tried the throttle. A thin, ragged snarl. More fuel, a touch of spark, a little throttle again, and she wound up. Watch it! he thought. She's touchy, touchy . . .

Buell's voice at his elbow: "The son of a bitch looks like a stepped-on frog."

"You watch your nasty mouth, Buell Ashbaugh," Bobby Joe said tartly. Hazard's head was cushioned on her shoulder and the bandaged fighting cock was tethered to one of the roof bows at her elbow, a yellow eye blinking.

Perrell stepped back and looked at the maimed Flyer. Shorn of one fender, side tank and most of her cargo gone, folded-down top bows bare, her engine uncovered, she looked naked. And the cocked head lamps gave her a wild-eyed look.

The front wheels were clearly splayed and her nose sagged sadly toward the dirt; her frame was sprung from her great leap and her springs were coming unleafed. Frayed strips of rubber hung from the tires. Perrell poked at the wadded chicken wire inside one of the tires and crumbs of pitch dribbled into his hand. Wooden wheel spokes wobbled to his touch, the entire great, wounded machine jiggling in crippled rhythm. *But she was running*—and time was gone.

"Let's roll!" Perrell waved.

Amanda, Costello and the powder man were strung out along the brushy bench upstream, about seventy yards away, the roan horse tied at the foot of the cliff where it closed in toward the stream. Amanda ran for the Flyer. Clinton was kneeling over something, Costello shoveling furiously. Costello tossed the shovel aside and ran to the water's edge, then sprang out over the water on tumbled rocks and stopped, poised, looking upstream. Shots boomed and white feathers plumed in the water around him. Echoes faded raggedly. Costello turned and jumped back to solid ground, waving to Perrell to go on.

Amanda reached the Flyer and scrambled up, gasping. "They will catch you up ahead there, where the road goes out of sight by the cliff." Perrell saw Costello swing onto the roan horse and kick the scrawny brute into a gallop, heading back along the bench toward Clinton. Costello kicked loose a stirrup and yelled. Clinton half turned, caught the stirrup leather on the run and was swept along with the horse, his feet hitting the ground in great bounding strides.

Perrell saw that they were bearing toward the road ahead. He hit the throttle, forgetting in that instant the explosive touchiness of the acetylene. The engine's pitch rose screaming and the Flyer's drive wheels spun with a great clatter of chain, spitting twin arcs of red mud behind, the rear end slewing half around before he checked the throttle. She backfired sharply, found traction and plunged through the brush, shedding chunks of rubber from the tires. She headed into the red wall of stone and he wrenched at the wheel. He felt a grinding clunk through the steering as she came brokenly around.

Costello and the roan horse were quartering in on his right. He dimly heard more shots and saw the horse's head go down between its forelegs and then it was rolling, Costello on the fly. Clinton scrambled past the downed and kicking horse, caught the little detective by the arm and lifted him, hobbling.

Perrell hit the brakes and nothing happened. He swung the Flyer into a broadside skid to stop her and throttled back, the engine crackling with its strange new snarl. Putting a shoulder under Costello, Clint heaved him over the side into the Flyer, then leaped onto the running board as the engine crackled and the Flyer sawed away, a fan of red mud spewing behind. The stone pillar thrust against the gullied road, bullets chipping from it as the Flyer churned on.

A wild screech rose behind them. Amanda looked back at that instant and saw *renegados* hurling themselves from their saddles, running ahead, falling, *groveling* . . . then the Flyer was around the pillar of red stone.

The men of the Legion forded the stream on a ledge of stone. Leading their horses, they picked their way in single file among the rocks at the foot of the cliff. A projecting shoulder of the cliff prevented their seeing the wreck of the machine. Suddenly Slotter, who was in the lead, saw one of the fugitives spring out onto the rocks below the cliff only fifty or sixty yards away. "It's that goddamn Pinkerton dick!" he snarled and opened fire.

The *renegados* mounted and broke into a reckless gallop, still more or less in single file as they rounded the cliff. Instead of finding a wreck, they heard the sudden staccato snarl of an engine and saw the great touring car slithering away with mud spurting under the drive wheels. The Pinkerton dick was mounted on one of their own horses and galloping for the car. The *renegados* screeched wildly and began shooting. Durkin and Vega rounded the cliff and were stunned to see the men in the lead suddenly rein in and leap to the ground. They pulled in their own horses, cursing and shouting at them, furious, as the automobile rolled over a rise and disappeared. Something flashed brightly from the ground. Durkin saw Corsiglia pounce on it and hold it triumphantly aloft. Then he saw that the afternoon sun glinted from bar after bar of silver spaced along the open bench of ground before them. Two other men scooped up bars, whooping and laughing. Shouldering one another like boys, they rushed on and Durkin saw Corsiglia hurl himself onto another bar.

He opened his mouth to shout a warning and the ground blew up under Corsiglia, a white-centered blast of red mud. Too late, just beyond, another *renegado* tried to sheer away from a shining bar, but he was diving headlong—his sudden wail was smothered in the blast. His steepled hat spun, slowly drifting to earth. A horse galloped away, kicking.

Mud-splattered *renegados* fought to quiet their horses, then stood frozen, staring at the silver bars. Every one of the bars was now clearly seen to have a loop of wire around it. It slowly dawned on them as they stared that not all of the bars were mined, for the first four or five had not exploded.

*"How we goin to tell which ones is mined?"* Durkin said plaintively.

Vega raised the Smith & Wesson and fired. One of the bars jumped and the bullet droned away. The *renegados* excitedly lifted their weapons. At that moment the snarl of the Flyer's engine was clearly heard and the machine teetered into sight again, topping another rise less than a quarter of a mile away.

One *renegado* bent to pick up the bar at his feet. Vega screamed and leveled his pistol at the man. He jerked the muzzle toward the fleeing machine. *"Ahora!* This will wait!" The voice rising shrilly: "Now to sink the iron in them! *Adelante, hombres!"*

Mounting, spurring, they rode.

# (34)

The road was an outrage of eroded hillocks, water-filled sink-holes and brush that exploded like gunfire under the Flyer's pounding wheels.

Perrell fought to hold her warped frame running true, to keep her from plunging off into brush or rock. A touch of throttle sent her churning madly, a wheel-spinning surge with crackling exhaust—back off, her snarl died away to a gasp. Too lean, he thought. He slowed her to a crawl, heeling far over, and bent down to the generator tank on the running board. A half turn on the adjuster. Tried throttle. She leaped. Bobby Joe wailed behind him and he knew he was hurting the wounded man, but in his mind he saw steel soften, saw the mushroom head on a valve sheered off—*leave it there.*

Ahead, the road wound through a tortured maze of low sand hills. He saw the ragged trace appear, turn back upon itself, then coil away again, climbing toward a notched sky-line in the red hills. Cloud-patched sky beyond, and blue haze of distance. A band of wild burros galloped wildly across in front of the Flyer. The little stud brayed and lashed out with his hoofs as the car skidded on.

Amanda turned and looked back across the loops of road, shouted in his ear, "They're spread out and cutting across—closing on us."

A gray horse appeared at the far edge of his vision and hung there mocking him. *Vega.* The wheel shuddered in his hands. The hill steepened and the horse dropped back.

Perrell heard a heavy thudding. A black wing of rubber flailed from the right front tire, round and round, pounding, black chunks flying from it. Watching the tire, he could see that it was wobbling—either the split rims that held the tire on were going, or the wheel spokes themselves. They topped another rise and saw again the notched skyline and the valley beyond. A mile to the notch? Then downhill.

Amanda cupped a hand at his ear. "When I went for water . . . saw buildings, beyond."

"How far?"

"Don't know . . . miles."

The road slanted down, twisting away, then back. Red hills loomed. The horsemen pulled off the road, cutting across broken, gullied ground. A straight run for them. Damn the road. He dared another notch on the throttle quadrant. The Flyer surged, weaving. The flap of rubber flew off. The thudding wheel was pounding her spokes out. Now there was thrashing from rear wheels too.

"The chicken wire is comin loose!" Buell shouted.

One of the horses broke stride and went down rolling. The Flyer hit the bottom of the grade and splashed through shallow water, sprouting white wings of spume and gushing huge clouds of steam, then she thundered up the bank and sawed back onto a long rise toward the notch. The Flyer shot past an old mine, a crooked gallows of timber, and suddenly ahead there was a burro-drawn *carreta,* piled high with wood, an old man looking back in terror from his perch on top as Perrell yawed past, ripping out yards of brush with the left front fender.

Amanda cried out and pointed to the left. There, horsemen were even with them, only a hundred yards away—even and beginning to close. Shooting . . . distant muffled *pops.* The grade was steep. Perrell felt the Flyer falter under them, yet the engine's snarl wound higher. He cut back on the throttle and felt it take hold again, thinly. But the edge was off her momentum. He tried to give her throttle again. *The clutch won't hold.* A plume of white steam sprouted from the radiator hose and he smelled the sharp, acrid, biting stench of hot metal. The steam flared into a high-gushing rooster tail.

The notch opened ahead, bright sky beyond. Fifty yards. Forty. The gray horse galloped onto the road before them and wheeled. The radiator hose blew completely off, and through the white steam Perrell saw the horse rear. Vega fired. Fragments of hot metal stung his face.

Just rolling now. No clutch at all. Still he rammed the throttle lever to the bottom of the quadrant and heard the engine wind up, a mad screech of tortured metal—as he destroyed her. The Flyer skidded broadside toward the terrified horse. Her cylinder heads exploded like cannon. The gray horse reared away, screaming, and fell backward. Perrell fought the wheel over, hard. The Flyer straightened, momentum gone, slowing, short of the crest.

Perrell pulled at Amanda's hand, clapped it onto the steering wheel and leaped over the brass gearshift lever to the ground, shouting, *"Push! Keep her rolling!"* Then Buell and Clint were down, and Costello, hobbling, pushing the Flyer on her tatters of shredded tires. Another cylinder head blew off. Chunked metal flew, droning.

Perrell turned to get his back into the Flyer, his legs churning. He saw the gray horse, down on its side and kicking, Vega crawling, clutching for a pistol in the dirt.

Clint saw the alarm in Perrell's face. His lips peeled back in a wolfish snarl, the powder man uttered a grunting, wordless cry, tendons ropy in his throat, as he turned back from the Flyer, his legs driving him, furious, across thirty feet of endless space. Headlong, he flung himself at Vega.

Perrell heard the shot and saw Clint land sprawling, then the Flyer was rolling away under him. He started to let it go, but heard Amanda cry, *"I can't turn her!"*

He ran, clutching for a handhold before he lost her. Standing on the running board, he hauled at the wheel, wrenched it across, feeling grating metal through it. Looked back for an instant. He saw Red Durkin with a carbine at his shoulder aimed at Clint. The carbine swung toward the Flyer, then Durkin lowered it and watched the Flyer roll away as Buell and Costello threw themselves aboard.

Beyond Durkin, drawing near on stumbling horses, came the others—those of the Legion who were left. Three of them Perrell saw in that moment before his line of sight was occluded by the hill.

"Help me hold her!" Amanda cried. She struggled with the shuddering walnut-rimmed wheel, and the Flyer crabbed sickeningly. Amanda shot a desperate glance at Perrell. He forced the wheel back across and shouted, "Move over!," sliding into the seat as she moved.

The Flyer gathered speed in terrifying silence, the blasting roar of her engine gone, given way to wind rush and muffled rumbling, and chocking of disintegrating tires and wobbling wheels.

The winding grade steepened, the badlands melting chaotically toward the valley floor. The Flyer's speed was suddenly appalling. Perrell stood on the brake pedal—nothing. With clutch and brakes gone, the Flyer was running wild. Beside him, Amanda's long hair flowed in the wind stream like black smoke.

The road was a speed-blurred scar twisting down the withered shank of the Sierra. Through the still-gushing plume of steam and oil smoke, Perrell glimpsed distant scattered adobe buildings clinging to treeless red hillsides. The cañon mouthed out into scorched cornfields, mountains rising blue again beyond the glistening thread of river and the narrow valley.

Caught now in the wild wind rush, squinting through stinging eyes with the taste of fear sharp in his mouth, Perrell felt the inmost self of him looking down in strange and timeless calm, seeing with sharp and glittering clarity the Flyer pound herself to pieces, each wheel shedding chunks of chain and shredded rubber, long shards of wadded chicken wire and black pitch tearing away in front, spinning off, coils of steel cable lashing out from the rear wheel, and the wheel itself dropping with a clash onto the rim, and the rims, front and rear, going too then, the segmented wooden felloes shattering into splinters, spokes chewing down to stumps, the Flyer passing tawny adobe houses, a family caught in astonished frozen motion, staring as chickens scattered and goats plunged away to the ends of their tethers.

The road widened, became a broad and barren street sloping down toward the river, flanked by scattered adobe houses. And centered at its foot beneath a dusty-leafed encino tree, an ancient building squatted, blindly staring back over low adobe walls through shadowed, arched *portales.*

The Flyer threw solid chunks of pitch, wheel spokes and drive chain in a grinding broadside skid, a brown surf of dirt lifting, subsiding. The Flyer was stopped.

Hot metal ticked. Steam curled in wispy tendrils. Perrell's hands fell away from the wheel. He heard his pulse thudding. Saw people then, children running, and horsemen, a ragged column of them emerging from the river bottom.

# (35)

Perrell crawled from the Flyer. Smoke and steam drifted. He staggered against the car as the horsemen approached from the river bottom in a shambling trot, a column of twos. There were about twenty men, the horses' legs wet from fording the river, the men unshaven and dirty in army khaki and peak-crowned campaign hats. One carried a lance streaming a 7th Cav guidon. But the horses were lathered, stumbling, with heads sagging and ropy slime stringing from their jaws. A young officer with motoring goggles hanging around his neck reined up close. He looked down on the smoking Flyer in disbelief.

"We heard the gunfire. Villistas? How many?"

"It's Vega," Perrell said. "Rodrigo Vega and five or six men. But I'm going with you. We lost a man back there."

"No. I don't have a horse for you."

"By God, I'm going with you." Perrell moved stiffly toward the lieutenant, his fists knotted. He was weaving a little on his feet.

"Mister, we've come all the way from the fight at Guerrero, and yesterday we did fifty miles before that," the lieutenant protested, "and I just had to destroy two more horses. I can't—" He broke off, seeing the look on the battered, oil-streaked face before him, then reluctantly he turned and called a man from the rear of the column.

"What we need is a wagon," Costello said. "I saw Clinton go down when Vega fired."

"Find one!" Perrell shouted, running as the trooper reined up and kicked a stirrup loose. Perrell swung up behind him. The horse's hindquarters buckled.

"Hey, lieutenant!" the soldier complained. "This goddamn horse is too stoved up for this."

The lieutenant winced and jerked a thumb at the soldier who promptly threw his leg over the horse's neck and slid down, smiling thinly. "Have fun, pal," he said to Perrell.

Cusichic was a village of two dozen scattered adobe houses and an inn, or *posada,* which sat at the foot of the dirt street behind its low-walled patio, only a few feet from where the Flyer had come to rest.

The ancient walls of the inn were pitted with bullet holes. Fallen plaster exposed naked adobe. Carved lintels overhung weathered doors. Amanda Sibley stood inside at a window and looked out across the deep-shadowed veranda, through an archway into the patio. Flower beds were littered with drifted sand. The large circular pool of the fountain was bone-dry, littered with rubble. Bobby Joe sat on the rim of the fountain feeding the tethered chicken from her hand. The bird's wings hung down and it limped, but it pecked at her hand with vigor. She jerked her hand back, laughing, and slapped at the bird. It dodged her, staggering, then thrust the long, green-hackled neck back, seeking out her hand.

There were several scarred and weathered tables and chairs of heavy oak in the patio. At the far end, almost a hundred feet away, a heavy studded gate hung aslant on iron hinges in an arched gateway, and beyond that Amanda saw children playing on the hulk of the Flyer in the fading light.

"Amanda?" Tracy Hazard spoke in a husky whisper from the sagging brass-knobbed bed behind her. She went to him and held a cracked teacup of water to his lips. He nodded. "Where . . . the others?"

"After we got you in here, John Tr—Perrell went with the soldiers to see if they couldn't bring back . . . Ellred Clinton. Buell and Mr. Costello are out trying to find a wagon."

"He's hurt?"

"Yes. I mean, we don't know yet. Hush now, Tracy."

"Amanda, I've been thinking . . . about that ore we took out. No, listen. Damn good joke on Ev. We took out . . . three hundred tons, running close to a hundred and fifty dollars a ton." He coughed, shook his head when she touched a finger to his lips. "A hundred and fifty dollars a ton. Right where he didn't want me to dig. Pretty damn funny, Amanda. Maybe we got all the good stuff. Go back some day, find out. You tell Ev—"

Amanda shook her head. "I won't be seeing him again, Tracy. I'm going to stay with you here until you get on your feet, then you can write to him or go see him when we get you back to the States. It won't matter to me. You hush now and get some sleep."

She touched his cheek, then went into the next room, a lofty room where the señora was cooking over a small iron stove, the pipe of which went through a broken pane in a side window. Of all the rooms in the old inn, all but three were occupied by rodents, bats, swallows, chickens and a family of pigs. Those three were occupied by the aged *alcalde* of the village and his wife. This room was one of the three and it was immaculate, the cracked walls whitewashed and hung with chromolithographs of haloed figures. Candles flickered before a small painted plaster figure of the Virgin on an aged and blackened mahogany *cómoda* with one drawer missing. Seeing Amanda, the señora went to a cabinet and extracted a bottle and another teacup. She poured a splash of clear liquid into the cup and held it out.

"*Aquí, señora, un trago por el corazón*—a swallow, a drop, for the heart." She was tiny, her face shrouded in a black *rebozo*. Amanda took the cup and sipped, felt her tongue go furry with the heat of it. She started to speak when she heard footsteps, and Costello's voice. She put down the cup and ran outside onto the veranda. Costello and Buell and the old *alcalde* walked through the arched adobe gateway from the street and approached the fountain. Costello saw her and shook his head.

"There's an old wagon over yonder by the corrals"— he nodded toward decrepit adobe walls that lay sixty or seventy yards away, off to Amanda's left—"but there ain't a horse or a mule to be had. Pancho Villa's men have cleaned out the town." He hesitated. "It probably won't matter a whole lot. We'll just have to wait for Perrell and the soldiers."

"You can't be certain about him, can you?"

"About Ellred? I saw him jump and I heard the shot. He was hit, all right. And Durkin was right there too by then. I saw him shoot at him, too." Costello scraped the toe of his boot in the dust, then he lifted his face and looked toward the tumbled red hills. "The damn fool—Ellred, I mean. It's a funny thing, but I've got to say it. He was a first-class man."

Amanda sank down onto the dusty tiles of the fountain's rim. Her fingers picked at crumbling mortar. There was a burning in her nose and her eyes blurred. "He almost made it. While you were all busy working on the Flyer back there, he started to clear out. To leave. He had the horse and a few bars of silver. It would have made one less for the Flyer to carry, he told me, and he would have gotten free of you. But I stopped him, persuaded him to come back. That is just an unspeakably bitter thing to me now."

"Ellred always drew the bad cards. There is no accounting for that."

"At least he is free of you!" she said in sudden anger.

"To be strict about it, ma'am, I wasn't after *him*. I was after sixty thousand dollars that my company was under contract to recover. All he ever had to do to get free of me was to tell me where it was hid."

"I don't suppose you mean that to include the first time, when you caught him down here."

"No, naturally not then. But I 'spect he could have got off with only two or three years. He wouldn't talk, though."

"He told me he *couldn't* talk!" she flared.

Costello smiled, which she found infuriating. "Now, Mrs. Sibley—he had to know."

"He also said there was never a time since this all started when anything he said was taken for truth," she said accusingly.

"It's my job to find the truth, Mrs. Sibley, and I will smite 'em hip and thigh to get at it, as the book says, but truth is a mighty scarce commodity in this line of work. Pretty near as scarce as it is in politics or horse tradin.'"

"Please don't jolly me, Mr. Costello." She could not shake from her mind the soured memory of how virtuous she had felt a few hours earlier when she persuaded the powder man to come back to the Flyer with her. Or had she shamed him? That was worse, if anything. She knew she was being very sharp with Costello, but she could not help herself. She flared again. "He told me he couldn't talk after you found him because he didn't know, and I believe him."

Costello spread his hands. "You will have to ask yourself why he came back here, then, soon as he got out of the pen?"

"Because he figured it out, after he was patched up and shipped off to prison."

Costello frowned. "Come on now, Mrs. Sibley. Don't kid yourself." He tried to smile again, but she saw that he was annoyed. That pleased her.

"You decided that simply because he was with those two other men, he had to know where the money was hidden, and you refused to believe him when he said he didn't know."

Costello merely looked levelly at her, his jaw thrust out.

"But he wasn't *with* them when you found him," she said with heavy irony.

"No, he wasn't." Costello looked again toward the hills, the red darkened now almost to purple, then he pointed to the adobe-walled corrals. "He was shot over yonder by the corrals. He *crawled* up into the hills during the night, three, four miles maybe. Ellred had plenty of sand—nobody has to tell me that. But he made an easy trail to follow, you understand, the shape he was in. If he had hid the stuff, I would have found it. But he *was* with the other two until the soldiers jumped 'em right here. That money could have been any place, from the border on south to here. I always figured that stealin the horses was their bad move and that they must have seen they were bein followed. They didn't want to get caught with all that money on them, so they hid it."

"There you go again!" she flung at him. "They didn't steal the horses."

He laughed sharply. "I can't credit that, Mrs. Sibley. Stealin the horses is why they got caught. Aside from knowin that they blowed the mail car in the first place, stealin the horses is the one unvarnished piece of fact in the whole business. It was a damfool, jug-headed thing to do and it brought the *federales* down on 'em, but I'll tell you, lady, takin road agents as a class, brains is scarcer than truth, if that be possible."

Costello pulled irritably at his mustache. It was the first time she had seen him really ruffled, and although it made her feel a trifle childish to do so, she enjoyed it.

"Nevertheless, Mr. Costello, they did not steal the horses," she said loftily.

He frowned intently at her. "You seem awful sure of yourself. It appears to me that you know something I don't."

"I see you're getting angry with me," she said, the moment's pleasure already tasting flat to her. "I'm sorry I was— unpleasant, if that's the word."

He shook his head. "No, never mind that. Why did you say that they didn't steal the horses?"

"It's one of the things he told me, that's all." Across the fountain from her, she saw that Bobby Joe was leaning exhausted against Buell, half asleep. Fretfully, Amanda said, "What on earth is keeping them?"

"Tell me what he told you, Mrs. Sibley," Costello persisted. "Please. Try to tell me exactly what he said."

"I don't see what difference it could make, but—" She wanted desperately now to stretch out, to sleep, but she forced herself to concentrate, to tell Costello flatly and without color how Clinton and his outlaw partners had tried to buy horses from the rancher, and of the price they had paid. All the gold from the mail-car robbery. " . . . so they *bought* the horses, after all," she finished, "but the rancher turned them in anyway. *Federales* caught up with them here at Cusichic—"

"For *horse*-stealin!" Costello said. "So the rancher got his horses back and kept the gold too."

"How much did it amount to?" she said.

"There was twelve thousand in gold coin and about forty-eight thousand in paper."

"How come the man didn't just take all the money," Buell said, "and have his own men finish them off?"

"No, he was smart," Costello said. "It was foolproof. He had no way of knowin where the money came from or who might be after it, see? So this way, the trail of the money did not stop with him. It stopped with the *federales* and a horse-stealin charge."

"It could still kick back on him if they talked," Buell said.

"Not likely. Knowing that in Mexico horse thieves would get the same treatment as bandits or murderers, he knew they would not be alive long. Which is just what happened." Costello looked at Amanda. "This is a piece of information I never had before."

"You wouldn't have believed it if he had told you, would you?" she said acidly.

"Not at first. No, but I would have had it to work with and you see it makes a big difference in where the rest of the money is likely to be hid."

She was startled. "Why?"

"They would have figured they were clean, see? Shy of the gold all right, but clean. And they would have had the rest of the money, the bank notes, with 'em when they got here to Cusichic." He was silent for a moment. "What else did he tell you?"

She shook her head and smiled. "Naturally, he didn't tell me where it was, Mr. Costello. But he was certain that he knew where to look. If I hadn't talked him into staying with us—and getting himself killed," she added bitterly, "he would have come back and found it, and to be perfectly frank, I would have been delighted to see him get away with it." She glared at him. Tears flooded into her eyes, spilled over and trickled down. Costello soberly found his bandanna and handed it to her.

"Sentiment in a lady is not misplaced, I 'spect, but I would have follered Ellred to hell for it." He pulled his dented hat low over his eyes and abruptly turned away from her. He walked away from the fountain until he reached the arched gateway in the endwall, then he turned and looked back at them, and at the patio, the littered flower beds, the broken tiles, the weathered tables, the fountain, desolate in the dusk. Amanda saw that he was looking not so much at what lay before him now, but at what he remembered.

He walked back to the fountain and stood before her again. "I got here just after daybreak," he murmured. "The fight was over, but you could still smell the gunsmoke." He looked at one of the heavy oak tables nearby, then stepped over to it, and grasping the table edge, tipped it over. The heavy carved trestle base was braced with wrought iron shaped to look like vine tendrils. Amanda saw bullet marks in the planking. "They pulled these tables up against the fountain and forted up behind 'em," he said, pulling an end around to show her.

"Were they . . . *dead?*" Buell asked uneasily.

"Yes. But not long. Not Wiley, anyway. He had held out all night and then finished himself off." Costello tapped the ground next to the fountain with the toe of his boot. "Right here he was. Wet, too, from bullets splashing into the fountain."

"No," Amanda mused. "He told me—" She stopped, disconcerted as Costello turned intently to her.

"What? What did Ellred say about it?"

"Just that . . . he said *the last thing I saw when I lit out for the corral, Wiley was shooting and he rolled over the rim of the fountain right into the water.*"

Costello stared at the fountain, then he said to Buell, "Son, would you do me the goodness to rustle up a shovel or a grub hoe whilst I try to persuade Señor Cruz to let us dig up his fountain?"

Costello held the oil lamp as Buell picked at the ancient bricks with the point of a battered machete offered by the old man, who stood silently by, watching. The circular rim of the fountain was nearly two feet through, built of thin fired adobe brick and faced with tile. The bottom was littered with dirt and pieces of broken tile and brick. The pool was a dozen feet across and in the center was a tiled tower where water had once trickled down in a series of falls. Dark red tiles were bullet-broken or fallen in numerous places.

A grunt sounded from Buell. "These are loose," he said. He pried with the machete blade, low down inside the thick rim. A loosened brick tumbled out, then others quickly as Buell pulled at them.

"Watch it!" Costello said. Buell jerked his hand back from the foot-square hole and a scorpion scuttled away in the rubble. He reached in and pulled. Slowly a pair of saddlebags emerged, the leather blackened, stiff and hard as wood. He put the saddlebags on the tiled rim and Costello fumbled with brittle straps and green-black brass buckles. The straps broke away in his hands and leather crackled as he forced the cover flap back. Gently, Costello reached in and pulled out a handful of paper packets.

Dust and powdery flakes of paper sifted down. A corner of one packet crumbled away in his fingers. The edges were brittle, serrated by the gnawing of insects.

Fascinated, yet stung with small persistent pangs of regret, Amanda watched Costello raptly as he laid out the crumbled packets. Hearing the murmur of his voice counting and the rustling of the paper, she missed the distant muffled sounds of horses' hoofs and bit chains and squeaking leather. Then, startled, she turned, shielding her eyes from the lamp, and dimly saw the column slowly plodding toward them. As they came past the Flyer, the lieutenant spoke a low command and most of the men turned aside toward the corrals, about half of them on foot, leading their exhausted horses. But several continued on along the outside of the low adobe wall. With the light at her back and her eyes adjusting to darkness, she could see more clearly.

The lieutenant and another rider were first. They reined in abreast of the fountain, only a few feet away. Incredulous, she saw that the rider was Red Durkin. Behind them, a man led a horse. It was Perrell. She walked toward him. A mumbled growl stopped her. A dark hump on the horse's back stirred and she saw the slumped figure of a man. Lamplight flickered on the craggy face under a clumsy turban of bandages. Amanda's hand went to her mouth, her knees shook and she leaned against the wall. It was Ellred Clinton.

Behind her, Costello muttered a startled oath. Clint half fell from the saddle. Perrell caught him and helped him sit on the wall and swing his legs across. Clint glared fixedly at the fountain and the people gathered there around the stacked packets of paper. Grunting with pain, he got his feet under him and tottered to the fountain. He picked up a packet of money. Flakes crumbled away and spun down. The paper was coming apart in his fingers. Costello took it from him.

"A man would have a hard time passing this as money now, Ellred," Costello said in a choked voice, "but it will serve my purpose well enough. It's all here, except for the gold. Forty-eight bundles, a thousand each."

Clinton turned and stared fiercely at Amanda. She stepped close to him and put both hands on his chest, looked up into the cavernous eyes. "We thought you were . . . dead," she whispered. "It was my fault. I talked too much. If I had known, I would never on earth have . . ." She did not know what else to say.

He took hold of her hands and held them for a moment as if he would crush them, then he slowly seemed to sag. "It don't hardly matter none now." He looked past her at Costello. "Once I figured out where it was hid, I used to lie awake nights thinkin about it—about what water would do to it. And time." He slumped onto the rim of the pool, wagging his head.

"Do you remember the name of the rancher who skinned you out of the gold?" Costello said.

"I'll never forget it. It was Diéguez."

Costello turned to the old Mexican. *"Señor, conoce usted el hacendado Diéguez?"*

The old man's eyes gleamed in his saddle-colored face. "Don Plácido Diéguez," he said. His shoulders shook, an expression not simply of pleasure, but of appreciation for what he appeared to consider a very funny joke as well. *"Don Plácido ha pagado sus impuestas a Pancho Villa."*

"He says the man has paid his taxes to Pancho Villa," Costello said.

"In Mexico," Amanda said, "when people say that a rich man has paid his taxes to Pancho Villa, they mean that he is dead."

"So Pancho Villa is the only one who got anything out of this," Perrell said.

"I got the ten years," Clinton said.

Perrell saw Amanda looking at Red Durkin. "When we got there," he said, "Red Durkin had Clint patched up and he was waiting for us. He looked damn uneasy, I'll say that for him. He said that Slotter and the others took one look at Vega and turned back, hell-bent, to get the silver."

"But we saw—" Amanda started to say.

"I know. Clint tried to reach Vega. Durkin claims he shot Vega himself. I—think he did."

Costello thrust his jaw out and stalked toward Durkin. "Red, how come you never went with the others?"

Durkin chewed his lip uneasily, then at last he said, "No good would come of that. The game was up. I figured it was time I come back to my own kind."

"By God, I take that as no compliment," Costello said. He suddenly reached over the wall and caught Durkin by the front of his jacket. Durkin tried to pull away but his hands were tied to his saddle horn. Costello held him half out of the saddle and with his right hand reached in and snatched a leather wallet from an inside pocket. He let go his grip and Durkin nearly fell. Costello ripped some bills from the wallet, threw it down in disgust. "A hundred and ten dollars you lifted from me . . ."

For Amanda, the lamplight suddenly became a rushing yellow waterfall, with Costello's voice lost in the noise of the cascading water. As she puzzled over this, the light and the noise faded and became nothing.

*   *   *

Amanda awoke to the distant, dull thudding of horses' hoofs and the hum of voices. Sunlight splashed across the floor. A small bird chirped at her from the foot of the iron bedstead. When she stirred, it flew out the window. Memory rushed and in an instant she remembered everything that had happened out by the fountain, yet she did not remember coming to bed.

In a few minutes she came out on the veranda. Perrell and Costello were sitting at one of the heavy tables, talking.

"It goes against the grain to cooperate with the law," Perrell said, "but I'll do it."

Seeing her, they stood and made room for her. "A lady," she said, "does not join gentlemen saying 'Do what?' "

"When I get back to Tucson," Costello said, "I mean to see to it that a certain matter of record in police files is put straight. It will require statements from witnesses—" He spread his hands on the table—"most of said witnesses being present here."

"Otherwise?"

He shrugged. "It could go hard with Ellred Clinton, once the army is through with him." He saw her shocked expression and laughed. Then his laugh faded and he frowned darkly. "One thing about all this burns me up. Red Durkin. I would like to see him strung up by his heels and flogged, but the lieutenant, he tells me the army badly needs men who know the language and the country and the habits and practices of the enemy. It galls me to say it, but Durkin qualifies." Costello bit down hard on a wooden match.

"Durkin," Perrell said, "is a survivor. Anyway, we told the lieutenant that he had better take Ellred along to keep an eye on Durkin, or General Pershing's watch will wind up in Durkin's pocket."

"I'm still for the floggin," Costello said, "but that's where it stands unless we prefer charges on him. Ellred and Durkin are civilian scouts employed by the army."

The lieutenant, a gaunt young man in faded khakis and a mauled campaign hat, came along the veranda and stopped at the table. He touched his hat and said "Ma'am." He seemed nervously aware of a large rent in his trouser leg. "You will want to know, ma'am, that we recovered part of the silver. The renegades could only carry part of it. As it was, they tried to take too much and overburdened themselves. We found one of them." He was pale, his eyes bleak from what he had seen. "His horse, first, dead. Then the man, a little farther on. His head was—" The lieutenant clearly did not want to go on and said instead, "Tracks indicated that the renegades were followed by Indians, afoot."

"Señor Cruz tells us," Costello said, "that these Indians are Tarahumara. The way they hunt is to run the animal till it falls. They have been known to run for days. Then they . . . use rocks on 'em."

"The man Durkin said that Vega's men butchered some goats belonging to the Indians," the lieutenant said. He looked uneasily toward the mountains. "They are probably still running up there." With an effort he pulled his eyes away. "We will be pulling out of here in a few minutes." He touched his hat and said "Ma'am" again and walked away.

"I see that people are deferring to me in the matter of the silver," she said.

"You are the—" Costello started to say.

"No, I'm not—whatever you were going to say. But if you insist, I'll tell you what to do with it. First, I don't want to know how much of it was recovered. You must just get it to a bank in El Paso and see that the proceeds are divided equally among us all. Call it . . . travel expenses. Will you do that?"

Costello smiled. "I can't join you myself—the Pinkertons are touchy about such matters—but . . . yes, I will."

Iron wagon tires rumbled. Buell drove the wagon from the corral, turned along the adobe wall and stopped the team under the dusty-leafed encino tree. He leaned down and said something to Bobby Joe. She said, "Hush up, you Buell Ashbaugh from Jump-Off Joe." Over by the corrals, a noncom barked commands and troopers swung into saddles with a slap of stirrup leathers.

"Things are moving too fast, suddenly," Amanda said to Perrell. It was scant minutes later, minutes blurred with faces and hurried goodbyes. Costello was gone and she had not seen him go, and she was back at the table and Perrell was looking at her, his face grave suddenly, and uncertain. "Too fast," she said again, "and now I'm lonely already, even though everyone is still here."

Mounted troopers riding from the corrals, column of twos, looked curiously down on the desolate hulk of the Flyer as they passed.

"Foolish, yes, I know it's foolish," she went on, her head down, talking rapidly as if to hold back the rushing minutes, "loneliness like that. But I'm free of it now, do you understand—" Perrell's hand reached out and his fingers touched her cheek, then he, too, was gone. She looked up and saw his back moving away from her as he walked through the gate off the veranda and out to the wagon.

Curiously unmoved, she stood and smoothed her skirt with her hands. She walked out into the patio past the fountain. Beyond the low wall she saw the Flyer where it had come to rest on splintered spokes and shards of pitch and chicken wire.

The lieutenant nodded and the noncom sang out. The column of twos set off, leaders first, like an inchworm, then the others as there was room for them to step out, until the column was strung out and moving. Not looking at it, Amanda walked slowly out across the patio and through the gate, until she came to the Flyer. She stepped into it, settled herself on the dusty cushions and gently placed her hands on the steering wheel.

Costello sat with his legs dangling off the end of the wagon bed. The powder man sat next to him. Behind them was a wooden dynamite box containing bars of silver and the recovered packets of paper money. Behind that, Red Durkin sat cross-legged, picking at the frayed straw of his sombrero, looking nervously about. Seeing Perrell approach, he tried to grin, but his eyes skidded away and he gave it up and went back to raveling his hat brim.

"So you're comin with us, are you?" Ellred Clinton said to Perrell, his voice blunt, fibrous. "You only done ninety days when they put you away. By God, it wasn't time enough for you to learn nothin." He glared under the cotton bandages. Buell clucked to the team. The wagon was moving.

Perrell quickened his step. "No, I just wanted to tell you that ever since I saw you on the beach that morning, I've been trying to get shut of your company. And now, I've finally done it . . ." The wagon pulled away, rumbling. Laughing, he let it go.

When he turned away from watching it, a moment passed before he saw her on the seat of the Flyer. He began to walk toward her, the dust of Mexico puffing beneath his shoes.

## About the Author

WILL BRYANT is from a pioneer Arizona family. He spent his boyhood years on the move in the desert and mountain states. In all, he attended forty schools. He is a graduate of the University of Utah. He was a naval aviator in the Pacific during World War II. He has been an illustrator and designer. Most of his work has been concerned with the American frontier. He is the author of *The Big Lonesome*. He now lives with his wife, Nancy, and their four children near the village of Katonah, New York.